Readers love the Triquetra Trilogy by Marguerite Labbe

I0613993

Vol. 1

My Heart Is Within You

This book took me by storm.
—Literary Nymphs

A distinctive and passionate story.
—Romance Junkies

Vol. 2

Haunted By Your Soul

Beautiful and heartbreaking on many levels to read.
—Rainbow Reviews

A bright and talented author bringing light to
her characters and having them dance
off the page with every word.
—A Night Owl Reviews Top Pick

Our Sacred Balance

Marguerite Labbe

Dreamspinner Press

Published by
Dreamspinner Press
4760 Preston Road
Suite 244-149
Frisco, TX 75034
http://www.dreamspinnerpress.com/

Our Sacred Balance
Copyright © 2010 by Marguerite Labbe

Cover Art by Dan Skinner/Cerberus Inc.   cerberusinc@hotmail.com
Cover Design by Mara McKennen

ISBN: 978-1-935192-74-9

Printed in the United States of America
First Edition
January, 2010

eBook edition available
eBook ISBN: 978-1-935192-75-6

For Jamie Labbe, friend and sister, seek joy.

Chapter 1

SOFT whimpers of distress and the breeze from the fan blowing across my bare skin drew me out of sleep. I opened bleary eyes and glanced at the window. Pink and pearly gray stained the sky, bleaching the dark indigo away from the horizon. I groaned, burying my face in the pillow, and only another mumbled sound of fear had me biting back the vicious curse I'd almost let slip out.

Four months of waking up at the butt crack of dawn. It was enough to drive a man nuts. Morning and I had never been on the best of terms.

Kristair had stolen the covers again, leaving me buck-assed naked. He'd wrapped them around him like a cocoon and curled up in a tight ball in the middle of our bed, completely covered in blankets and sheets. He was either going to suffocate or roast. Still, I knew, Kristair would've burrowed even deeper if he could, anything to escape the morning sun and the dreams it brought.

We'd tried blackout curtains, and they'd worked like a charm until Kristair took them down again. He'd said he'd never adjust if we kept them up. And while he might have had a point, I argued he should give himself some time to become used to dreaming again, along with all the other abrupt changes of being mortal. But there was one thing I could say about my lover: he made stubbornness into an art form. Not that I could talk, to be honest.

Kristair struggled as I peeled away the covers, his hands fisting in a death grip in the folds. Still, he didn't wake up when I tugged them free. I'd never met anyone who could sleep as heavily as he did. I drew the blankets around us again, and when I pressed against his back, slipping my arm around his waist, he quieted some and nestled into me with a soft sigh. Closing my eyes, I nuzzled the nape of his neck, breathing in the scent of him.

It was still early; we could get a few more hours of sleep. I curled my body around his, closing my eyes, and then Kristair trembled, tossing his head restlessly, and I knew it was a hopeless cause.

If only I could have slipped into his mind. I'd have soothed away every fear he had, especially the ones he refused to name, pretending instead that they didn't exist. We might not have had our mental connection anymore, I might not have been able to hear his every thought, but no one knew Kristair like I did, not even himself. He was locking too much away, and one day it was all going to come bursting out. I just hoped to god I was there for him when it happened.

I kissed his shoulder and slid my hand down his warm hip. Four months and it was still a wonder to me to feel the heat in his skin when he didn't have to think about using blood he'd fed on to put it there. Or listening to his heartbeat and his steady breathing. He was my miracle. He had given up everything because he loved me, and that was a sacrifice I refused to take for granted.

Kristair murmured when I rolled him onto his back, limbs heavy with sleep, but he didn't stir, not even when I nudged his thighs apart and settled my weight over him. I wished the camera were near. I would have taken a dozen naughty photos of him and made my own shrine. His skin held a golden vitality in the early morning sun. His lashes curved and shadowed his deep-set eyes, and lord, he looked just fucking bitable.

I kissed along his jaw, rubbing my lips against the rough growth of his morning beard until they tingled. "Wake up, sleeping beauty. No more bad dreams, not this morning," I whispered.

His lips parted when I kissed their warm softness, and the tension began easing from his body as his subconscious began to switch from fear to pleasure. This was becoming my new favorite morning ritual. After all, if I was going to be up, I might as well be all the way up.

Kristair's cock stirred against my thigh, and I smiled, breaking the kiss, rubbing my lips against his own. "Come on, sleepy head. If I'm awake, you're damn well going to be awake too," I murmured, dragging my tongue down his throat and giving it a little bite. "I could cover you in marks and you wouldn't know it until you went to take a shower," I teased, imagining what he'd have to say about that.

I tugged the blankets away from us again, pulling back enough to look down at him. Damn, he was beautiful. I knew he always said that about me, but he needed to take a hard look in the mirror. Long, lean limbs with just the right amount of muscle, dark golden skin, his chest and arms covered in blue tattoos that matched mine. His brow had furrowed, making little lines and accenting the ruggedness of his features. His chin tapered to a point, and his nose was strong and prominent, and damned if he wasn't just perfect.

Kristair tried turning on his side, reaching for the covers, but I had him pinned, and as I pulled his hands away from his goal, another idea struck me. Leaning over to the nightstand, I grabbed the lube and a cream-colored silken scarf I kept intending on using. Kristair always distracted me away from the idea. Well, he wouldn't be able to do that now.

"Oh love, you're in so much trouble now." I snickered, rubbing my lips against his jaw. "You sure you don't want to wake up before I have my wicked way with you?"

Kristair muttered something intelligible and buried his face in my neck. I wished it were a sign he was waking and not that he was seeking comfort, but the distress in his tone told me he was still caught up in his nightmare. It made me ache inside to see this strong man with naked fear on his face, to feel him tremble.

I lashed his wrists to the headboard and took a moment to admire my handiwork. The cream silk emphasized his skin tone, and lord, there was something sexy about a strong man helpless. Making a mental note to remember to put the camera on the nightstand for the next time, I turned my full attention to my bound lover.

Dragging my mouth down his throat, I kissed the steady pulse there, remembering those days in the hotel when I'd woken up to find him cold and unresponsive. Now he sighed and arched his throat, turning his head to the side.

"Jacob," he murmured, the corners of his mouth lifting in a small smile, and his cock throbbed against my thigh.

He was almost awake, and I wanted to be inside him when he realized what was happening. I lubed my cock and slid my arm under his knee, spreading him wider as I began to push inside him, groaning from his welcoming heat. Long, pure black lashes opened, framing his dark eyes, revealing the lingering fear and growing desire.

Kristair's lips were so damn soft and inviting as they parted in confusion, and I kissed him, surging deeper into his body as he groaned, until his heat completely surrounded my cock. I stayed there, releasing his leg, tongue tangling lazily with my lover's.

I wanted to whisper in his mind as I made love to him, and since I couldn't, I broke the kiss and smiled down at him. "Good morning."

"Jacob… what…?" Kristair twisted his head back to look up at his bound hands, his knees rising up instinctively to cradle my hips, sleep still hazing his eyes. My lover had many sterling qualities and significant advantages over me in most things, but being quick to react upon first waking up wasn't one of them.

"If you have to ask, then I'm doing it wrong," I teased, circling my hips until his breath caught and a tremor rippled through him.

"I'm sorry I woke you." Kristair wrapped his hands around a slat on the bed and levered himself up to kiss me. "Untie me and I'll make it up to you," he promised.

I snickered and eased out of him before thrusting hard, savoring his gasp as his eyes darkened to midnight. "No way that's gonna happen. That would be reasonable and I'm not a reasonable man, especially at this time of the morning. Consider this my payback."

I leaned over him and gave his nipple a stinging bite. Kristair groaned, arching against me, his long legs coming up to wrap around my waist. Both of us sighed with pleasure as I surged into him deeper.

"And now that I have you tied up and helpless, the last thing on my mind is letting you go."

"You are a wicked man," Kristair replied, a smile tugging his lips.

"Yeah, but you love me." I winked at him as he laughed, all trace of fear gone from his expression now.

"That I do." Kristair's eyes glinted as he levered himself up again, his lips teasing my jaw and then down to my neck. He clenched around my cock, making me gasp, his tongue tracing around the pulse in my throat. "I love hearing you breathless even more."

Tied up my lover might have been, but he certainly wasn't helpless anymore. Fuck, he made me weak when he feasted on my throat like that, teeth scraping, mouth sucking, and the memory of how it had felt when he fed turning my bones to water.

Two could play at that game. I pulled back out of reach of his mouth, grinning as a small pout crossed his lips before he banished it. He'd have kicked my ass if I told him he'd pouted and would've denied it to his last breath. "Brat," he growled, clenching again.

"Is that the best you can do?" I teased, bracing my hands on either side of him, snapping my hips harder as his lean, dark body twisted and arched. I could have watched him like that all morning.

"Oh, there's plenty of other names I could call you." Kristair's eyes half-closed, his mouth going soft as desire played across his features. "If you'd give me a moment to gather my thoughts."

"Not a damn chance." I slid one hand under his ass, cupping the smooth cheek in my hand and squeezing it before lifting him higher. Now this was a morning ritual I could look forward to: listening to Kristair's needy sounds of pleasure and having him wrapped around me instead of what we had been dealing with.

I leaned low over him and kissed the hard plane of his stomach, dragged my tongue over the tattoo low on his ribs. Kristair moaned, and I smiled against his skin, looking up the length of his chest. Fuck, he was beautiful, and he was all mine.

"You're giving me that look again," Kristair murmured.

"Yeah, love, what look is that?" I kissed his stomach again and gave it a sharp nip, trying to hold onto the passion spiraling out of control within me.

"Like you're going to haul me off to your cave and keep me your prisoner there."

I grinned again. "Sounds like a wonderful idea. I might just do that, collar you and mark you at the same time." Kristair's dark eyes flashed—with want or pique, I didn't know—and before I asked, his legs tightened around me as he drove his hips up.

"If you don't get up and kiss me, I'm going to…."

"Nothing," I chuckled. "You'll do nothing."

"We'll just see about that," Kristair promised.

Laughing, I kissed him, tongues mating as our bodies twined and moved together. I lost myself in his clenching heat, the sweet softness of his lips, the scent and sounds of sex. Kristair's cock throbbed against my stomach, our skin now slick, and those needy, urgent moans of his drove me out of my mind.

"Untie me. I want to touch you," Kristair said, rubbing his jaw against my own.

Oh, the thought of those long-fingered hands on my skin was a temptation, but I shook my head, capturing his lips again. The long, languid thrusts became quicker, harder, as the lazy, just-woke-up feeling vanished under the mounting heat.

I broke the kiss, pulling back just enough so I could watch Kristair's unguarded expression. I loved the moments like this when he held nothing back and I could read him as easily as if we still had the mental connection. It was these moments when Kristair shared his wants and needs and vulnerabilities without walls.

He smiled, tongue tracing over my lips as he panted. "So close… just like that… don't stop." His moan had my stomach jumping and heart skipping a beat. I couldn't tear my eyes away from him as, with each rock of our hips, the pleasure rippled sharper and hotter over his face.

Then he arched, a soft cry falling from his lips, his body tensing under mine as he came. Enthralled, I paused, buried deep inside him, feeling every rippling contraction as his muscles went limp from his release. I shifted, the head of my cock nudging his spot, and he gasped, biting his lip against the overstimulation.

Kristair's eyes flew open and his gaze locked on me as I began circling my hips again once I regained my composure and my own impeding orgasm tapered off. "Oh damn," he whispered, and then he cried out as I drove into him hard enough to rock the bed against the wall.

Each shout from my lover, each writhe of his body, spurred me on. I attacked his throat, nipping and sucking until his flesh was hot against my lips. And all too soon, it was over. One rough moan from Kristair, the hard clenching and buck of his hips, and I was lost, my climax hitting me so fast that it was like lighting zipping through my body, there then gone, leaving me trembling in the aftermath.

"At least we didn't break the bed this time," Kristair said, after we'd recovered our breath and the tremors eased from his thighs.

I started laughing and lifted my head from where it had been resting on his shoulder, dropping a kiss onto his lips. "I blame you for that one."

Kristair turned his head, glancing at the alarm clock we never had to use, and his eyes widened when he saw the time. "Oh for... Jacob, It's not even six a.m."

"Nobody knows better than me what damn time it is."

Kristair attempted to tug his hands free again with no success. "I'm sorry if I woke you. Why don't you catch some more sleep and I'll make us breakfast in a little bit?"

"Nope, not gonna happen. One, because for some sick reason, I can't sleep if you're already up and about, and two, I'm already wide awake." I eased off of him and gave his flank a teasing slap as I rose from the bed. "I'm gonna grab a quick shower; then I thought we could go for a run."

"Don't you think you're forgetting something?" Kristair asked with a pointed tug of his bound wrists.

"Nope." I grinned and sauntered into the bathroom, ignoring his insistent call. Now this was the way to wake up. Pleased with myself, I lingered in the shower and ran through the different ways my lover would attempt to seek revenge on me before deciding I was safe. Kristair would forget all about it by the time he returned from work and I from the gym and meetings with the coaches.

When I came back out again, towel wrapped around my hips, I found Kristair sound asleep again. He'd somehow managed to get himself free and was curled up again under the covers, snoring away. Old habits died hard, I guess.

Another wicked idea struck me, and grinning, I grabbed a hold of all the blankets and yanked them off to the floor. Kristair sat up with a shout, reaching vainly to cover himself. And fuck, the look on his face was so priceless I doubled over laughing before I could say a word. "Kristair… oh my god, if you could've just seen your face, you…."

The growl was the only warning I got, and the next thing I knew, I was flat on my back on the floor and Kristair was leaning over me, his face twisted into a snarl. Desire surged all over again in my veins. "About that run…."

"Shut up, Jacob," Kristair snapped, pinning my hands above my head. "You're not going anywhere."

"I have no problem with that," I managed to say before Kristair kissed me, rough and insistent. Oh yeah, I'd gotten him good.

Chapter 2

I CROUCHED down in front of the refrigerator, studying its contents. Eating was still such a novelty. I'd never paid any attention at all to what humans consumed before, except to make sure those I cared for did eat. By the time Kayla came to me, she already knew how to cook enough to feed herself, and she'd always done her own shopping with the money I'd given her. Usually, by the time I'd woken up in the evenings, she'd already fed and put everything away.

I hadn't realized eating could be such a sensual experience. The tastes, textures and scents all mixed together in more varied ways than could be dreamt of. Discovering and exploring it all provided me with endless fascination. More than once, the things I put on the table made Jacob snicker, but my lover always ate it. Pursing my lips and consulting the handy book balanced on my knees, I started to draw out the ingredients for something called "eggplant parmesan." It sounded intriguing.

"What's that?" Jacob asked, coming into the kitchen and pouring himself a cup of coffee.

"Breakfast." I handed him the eggplant and rose, balancing the other ingredients I'd need on my book.

Jacob dangled the vegetable in front of his face, then shook his head, and stuck it back in the refrigerator. "Save the shiny, purple monstrosity for tonight. I can't handle anything called eggplant first thing in the morning."

"You eat eggs."

"There's a world of difference between eggs and eggplant." Jacob shook his head after another disbelieving glance at the refrigerator's contents. "Do you intend on trying everything in the produce section?"

"Why wouldn't you?" I glanced back down at my book and huffed. I supposed I could wait until evening, though it seemed absurd not to try it just because of the time of day. I began flipping through the pages, searching for another picture that caught my eye. "I like the produce section. I can see what I'm buying. Did you know that they get upset with you at the store if you try to look in the boxes to see if you're getting what is actually described?"

A sound suspiciously like a snort drew my attention, but when I glanced at Jacob, his expression was smooth. I narrowed my eyes. I hadn't paid him back sufficiently for his shenanigans this morning. Tying me up before the sun had even crested the horizon. As if Jacob could still read my mind, he smirked, his bright blue eyes vivid with mischief and that oh-so-knowing smug expression that turned my blood to liquid fire.

Brat. And I loved him for it.

My fingers itched to sink into his tousled hair to make it even more of a tumbled mess than it was. I suppressed the tinge of wistfulness, and before my mind could stray even more, I turned my attention back to my book. We could not spend the entire day in bed today, despite how I might wish it.

"Fine, then, I'll make this cheese and onion tart. And before you say anything, it has eggs in it. I still don't understand why some things are considered breakfast foods and others dinner. Food is food. It all goes to the same place."

"I didn't say anything. I was just gonna ask you if you wanted a cup of coffee." Jacob topped off his mug and flipped the television on.

I shook my head. I'd tried it several times when the aroma tantalized me, but I couldn't acclimate to the harsh taste of coffee. Our morning runs were usually enough to energize me, though this morning's activity had accomplished the same end. Waking up had also taken some time to get used to. It was unsettling, feeling the lethargy when I first opened my eyes. It reminded me too much of that time just before the Ascended took me, when it got harder and harder to rouse in the evenings. I pressed my lips together and suppressed a shudder at the memory.

"If you could heat up some water for tea, that would be appreciated."

"No problem, love." There was a nonchalance in Jacob's voice that had me tensing as I laid out what I would need to prepare the breakfast. Sure enough, after my lover had filled the kettle and set it on the stove, he came to lean against the counter next to me. "Do you want to talk about it?"

"There's nothing to talk about," I replied, tensing despite my best effort not to.

Jacob leaned closer, and I was unable to escape seeing the concern written on his face. "How about those nightmares you're still having? You're holding yourself aloof, the way you always do, setting up your walls. You don't think I can't see it? Did you ever think that if you talk about what you're afraid of that—"

"Afraid?" I stiffened, shooting him an indignant glare. "I am not afraid of anything, Jacob Corvin, least of all a phenomenon that has no power to hurt me anymore."

"Liar." Jacob smiled and touched my jaw in a tender gesture that robbed me of most of my pique. "Everybody's afraid of something and you're no different. I know everything's been turned upside on its head for you, but you don't have to tackle it alone. Just think about it."

How could he know so much? How could he see into my heart and mind so well when we no longer had our connection? It was unsettling to be so exposed when I thought I had presented another image, and at the same time, this was Jacob…. If there was anyone I'd want to see me vulnerable, it was my young lover.

To my relief, Jacob dropped the ridiculous conversation. I steeled myself, shaking my head. Afraid indeed. Where he got such ideas, I didn't understand. When I was asleep, I couldn't rationalize centuries old instincts away; they plagued me at a time when I couldn't rein them in. Eventually I would adapt, that was all.

I eyed him warily out of the corner of my vision as I cracked eggs into the bowl and whisked them with unnecessary force, but he didn't seem inclined to try to push the topic anymore as he watched the morning news. I would have let myself relax, only Jacob was not the kind of man to let an issue drop just because I didn't wish to discuss it. His tendency toward stubbornness bordered on the extreme.

He turned and caught me watching him as the teakettle began to whistle and grinned. "I know I'm good looking and all, but if you keep staring at me like that, I'm liable to get an ego."

I couldn't help but laugh, and the tension broke. "*Mo chroí*, you need no ego stroking. You're bad enough as it is." I leaned in and kissed him. "Go sit down, your hovering is likely to give me fits."

"Doesn't take much," Jacob teased as he danced out of swatting range and went to sit at the table.

I let the tea steep as I finished preparing breakfast and set it in the oven. The morning ritual and Jacob's presence were almost enough to banish my lingering unease. It irked me that I could let a mere dream affect me so.

I took my tea and sat down next to Jacob, turning my attention to the news. The weatherman predicted another humid day and expected thunderstorms later on in the afternoon, which was no different from the past few days.

"At least you don't have to worry about practice yet."

Jacob snorted. "When training camp starts nothing's gonna stop it, maybe not even lightning striking the field. You gonna drive out to Latrobe and watch?"

I grimaced, thinking of the car that awaited me in the driveway. The car that I hadn't driven once since Jacob had purchased it for me and insisted on a test drive. Now that was a memory for nightmares. "We'll see. I still have to get through these interviews intact."

"Give it up. You're never going to be happy with anyone other than Kayla in your office. Besides, now that you have day hours, do you really need someone to man your desk? It's not like she was there full time anyway."

"I don't understand why she felt the need to quit," I grumbled. It still rankled that she had left to go to Baltimore to start up that shelter for teenaged runaways with Steve, of all people. I tried not to feel betrayed—after all, she had a right to her own life, which was why I hadn't argued when she told me of her decision. "She could've funded her trust into any number of places here."

"Because if you and Steve didn't stop bitching at one another she was going to shoot the both of you." Jacob squeezed my hand. "And I might've helped her."

I dropped the issue before Jacob felt the need to defend Kayla and her so-called boyfriend any longer. He'd heard my complaint often enough. It was little comfort that I knew Steve disliked me just as much and, in all likelihood, had to hear Kayla defending me. After all, the bastard had still stolen her out of my life.

However, I thought I behaved myself rather well considering the circumstances. I had been scrupulously polite to him up until the day he started packing, fully intent on leaving with my daughter and her money. At least neither Jacob nor Kayla knew of that incident. If I could get away with going down to Baltimore to look in on her, I would.

How could I not have known the shelter was a dream of hers? Had I gotten so wrapped up in my own affairs that I'd lost touch with my daughter?

I'd brood on it later, when Jacob wasn't around to notice and worry over me. Instead, I busied myself by pouring a cup of tea and checking on breakfast. In the background, the newsman announced a breaking story, and Jacob cursed, turning up the sound. Frowning, I turned to see police and firemen swarming outside a downtown high rise in what had become an all too familiar scene.

"The police have still been unable to identify the accelerant used on the victims. Whatever chemical it is…" the reporter was saying with an expression of grave concern on her face.

My stomach twisted in a curious combination of horror and morbid curiosity. "They found another one?" Stupid question—I could see for myself that they had. The sixth victim in as many weeks, dragged out of their house at dawn, stabbed to death, and burned outside. "Poor bastard."

"The police still have no suspects." A number flashed across the scene. "Anyone with any information is urged to come forward and...."

"What kind of sick fucker does something like this?" Jacob seethed, glaring at the TV as the reporter bemoaned the lack of any evidence and the cops went about their grim business.

"One for whom killing is a pleasure, an art form in some respects." A soot-smudged cloth covered a pitifully small lump. I had seen some atrocities in my time and admittedly killed my share of people, but this display was sickening.

I pushed aside the useless reaction and took another sip of my tea, unable to tear my eyes from the screen. Six victims: three men, a woman, a teenaged girl, and whoever this person was. Six victims killed at the break of dawn, their bodies destroyed by fire. A chill raced through me as Jacob raged in the background.

"It takes a real fucking douche to stab somebody while they're sleeping and then set them on fire. That's one real piece of shit. Let them try that bull-fucking-shit here and we'll see what kind of a big man they are." His rant continued in crude terms I had thought he had been moving beyond.

Despite my best efforts, my dreams returned to me. The sun slipping over the horizon, rays eating into my flesh as I burst into flames, screaming. And Jacob reaching for me, fangs just visible between his lips as he caught fire as well and I was forced to watch him die.

"Kristair!"

Shuddering, I pulled myself out of the memory. It was just a dream, nothing more, and not even a very realistic one at that. "Yes?"

"Are you okay?"

I met Jacob's concerned eyes and smiled. "Of course." Disappointment and frustration flashed over his face, and immediately guilt twinged. I knew he thought I was pushing him away. I didn't know how to explain to him that I wasn't, that there was merely no point in rehashing issues that didn't matter. But for his sake, I had to try. "I shouldn't let it disturb me. After all, whoever it was was long dead before the flames touched them."

"Something like this disturbs anybody with a conscience."

I pulled the tart out of the oven, and despite the delectable scent, I'd lost any interest in sampling it. The sound of the reporter's voice winked out, replaced by Jacob's favorite XM country station. "I was thinking of calling those detectives I know to see if they'd drop us a hint or two. Only knowing them, they'd come up with a way to blame me, especially Kuykedal."

"He does seem to have it out for you, but he hasn't charged you with anything yet."

"Not for lack of trying."

I served the both of us, knowing Jacob would fret if I didn't eat after all my effort. "Besides, what would you do even if they gave you a lead, chase it down? I thought you wanted a nice, calm, normal life now. No more adventure."

"Call me paranoid, but it's been too quiet. I keep waiting for the bogeyman to come bursting out of the shadows shouting 'boo.' Given the fact that I now know vampires and magic are real, I wouldn't put it past the bogeyman to exist." Jacob poked at the tart with his fork and took a cautious sniff. "Looks pretty good."

I shook my head; he didn't have to sound so surprised at that. "I haven't poisoned you... yet."

He grinned at me. "Not for lack of trying," he said again. "There's still an eggplant in the fridge."

I dug my fork in, but the delicate cheeses and caramelized onions failed to lure me out of my thoughts. I couldn't shake the feeling of premonition hanging heavy over me. Maybe I was finally letting my dreams get to me, but I'd never put them to rest if I kept ignoring them as I had done. "Would you do me a favor? Call those detectives of yours. I just want to make sure that those victims were already dead before the fire."

Jacob looked as if he were about to argue but thought better of it. "I'll leave a message for Aderson. He's better about getting back to me without the hassle. I'll let you know as soon as I hear anything. You do realize he might not tell us jack."

"I'll keep that in mind." I covered his hand with my own. "Thank you. It's probably just the conspiracy theories of an old man, but it will soothe my restless curiosity knowing one way or another."

"Okay, gramps. I'd better get to the gym before I meet with the execs and my agent again." Jacob rose and placed his dish in the sink, then came over, and gave me a hard kiss. "Try to put it out of your head. It's just some whack job who's preying on people who've got nobody to look out for them. The police will get him, eventually."

"I'll be fine, I promise." I watched Jacob go from the screen door and cleaned the kitchen. And then it was time to go out and face the day. It was easier when I was with Jacob doing our morning runs because I didn't want him to see my apprehension. And it had gotten to the point where cloudy or rainy days barely made me twitch.

Sunlight flooded our yard, bright and glowing golden. The summer heat struck me as I stood on the porch, reminding me quite vividly of the burns I'd suffered when my office had been on fire. Intellectually, I knew I wouldn't burst into flame when I walked out into that light, but it was difficult to ignore two thousand years of instinct shrieking and clawing at me.

Taking a deep breath, I stepped off the porch and managed to keep from flinching at the same time. I'd passed the test another day. I refused to become a prisoner in my own home during the day. I would get used to my new existence through a sheer effort of will if nothing else.

By the time I arrived at my office in the Cathedral, I'd almost put worries of sunlight and murder victims out of my mind. I had chosen a different kind of life, one with peace and companionship in it with the love I'd always craved. There was no sense in seeking out the blood and battles that had occupied my time before. There was no sense in giving into my fears of change.

Then Jacob called.

Frowning, I set the phone back on the receiver and stared at it for a long time, unease slithering over my skin and my intuition jangling. According to Detective Aderson, the victims had been dead already, and each one had been found with a knife still lodged in their heart.

Killers didn't leave their murder weapons behind. Unless the knife wasn't a murder weapon and was merely used to keep its victim immobile so the sun could do its work. Was it paranoia, my own fears haunting me, or was it significant?

I checked my watch. It was almost time to pack up anyway and head home. I could leave a bit early, take a different bus, and swing by the crime scene beforehand. It wasn't that far from our house, and then....

And then what? Investigate? Get myself noticed by the police still doing their work? Bad enough I had Jacob call and get on their radar. My young lover would rightfully throw a fit if I involved myself, as I would if he had. I rose and pushed the idea out of my thoughts. The past was buried—best just to let it be.

Chap┼eı 3

I PEERED in on Kristair as I carried the dirty dinner dishes to the sink. He sat in his favorite chair with a book open in his lap, though I had yet to see him turn a page. It was only another sign of his distraction. He denied being lost in thought, but I hadn't been able to draw him into a conversation all evening, and he hadn't uttered a word of protest when I offered to load the dishwasher and clean the kitchen.

It proved my point, at least to me, but now I was stuck with the chore.

I glanced at him again as I went to scrub down the table, and it struck me how young he looked. Maybe a year or two older than me at the most. Sometimes I forgot he had been my age when he was turned into a vampire. When he gazed at me with his ancient eyes or spoke in that proper manner of his, his youthfulness faded.

The windows and back door to the kitchen were open, letting in the night breeze to soothe away the sultry heat of the day. It was almost getting to the point where we'd need to keep the AC on at night as well, but I kinda missed the liquid heat of Louisiana. I'd never had AC growing up, and I sure as hell appreciated it during the day, but sometimes it made me feel like I was living in a box with no outdoor sounds. Kristair never seemed to be bothered by the heat or cold—or he just hid it damn well.

I didn't hear a sound, no creak of the back porch, no sensation of eyes on me, so when the knock came on the screen door, I nearly jumped out of my skin. "The fuck!" I tossed the sponge into the sink, turned, and froze. Ghedi Ussier's dark face peered at me through the screen. For once, there was no trace of dimples, and his gray eyes were glacial.

"What do you want?" That came out far more belligerent than I intended, but good god, my heart was still pounding. Sneaky, soft-footed bastard.

"Good to see you, too, Mr. Corvin. Is the old man home? I need to speak with him."

"What about?" I made no move to open the door or to invite him in. Dammit, I'd never told him Kristair had returned, and I was pretty sure my lover hadn't either. Couldn't say I was too surprised he'd found out, though, but it was unsettling to think we might've been vampire gossip. If Ussier knew, how many others did? Did they know Kristair was human now? That he was vulnerable?

"Jacob," Kristair said from behind me.

I flinched inside. Kristair wouldn't chastise me in front of others, wouldn't even consider it, but boy, right now was one of those rare moments when I was glad we didn't share our mental connection. I could sense his disapproval for my manners even without glancing at him.

"Ancient One." Was it my imagination, or was there a note of almost welcome relief in Ussier's tone? I'd never heard anything like it in all the time I'd known him. Then, to my surprise, without a word of invitation from either of us, Ussier had the gall to open the door and walk right in. I thought there were rules against that.

"It doesn't work that way. You know that," Kristair said in an undertone as he strode forward and clasped Ussier's hand. "It's good to see you, old friend."

"I thought you couldn't read my mind anymore," I muttered under my breath, snagging a beer from the fridge.

"Your expression spoke volumes. I don't need to read minds to know what you're thinking."

"That's true, Corvin, you never did make an attempt to hide what you thought or felt about something."

I opened my mouth to tell Ussier that when I wanted his opinion I'd ask for it, but the tension around the vamp's eyes stopped my words. Something was wrong, seriously wrong. Kristair cast me a glance that was both a warning and a plea for patience, and I subsided with a mental grumble.

"Please, let's sit and you can tell me what brings you here." Kristair gestured to the kitchen table, and I cocked my head and studied my lover's face. It was as smooth and unreadable as ever, but something in the shade of his voice made me wonder if he already suspected the reason for Ussier's visit. He'd better not have been holding out on me.

Ussier pulled out a chair and leaned back with careless grace, as if this really wasn't anything more than a reunion between friends. Only the intensity of his gaze gave away his agitation, and that was more than I'd ever seen from him. Frowning, I sat down as well, admitting to myself that my curiosity had been raised.

"Is this about the serial killer?" Kristair asked, and to my double shock, Ussier nodded.

"Yes, whoever it is has been targeting vampires, striking them just at dawn when they're the weakest, then staking them outside to let the sun do its work for them."

"Wait a minute, they're vampires?" I asked Ussier and then turned to Kristair. "And you knew this?"

"No, I merely started suspecting it this morning." Kristair glanced at me, his expression inscrutable. I could have sworn he was trying to tell me something, something he didn't want to say aloud with Ussier here, so I bit my tongue. For the moment.

"What made you suspicious, old man?"

Kristair turned his attention to Ussier, a thoughtful frown furrowing between his brows. "The timing bothered me, for one. If the hunter was going for humans, then he ran the chance of running into them awake. For instance, this morning was a workday. So were most of the others, if I recall. Many of his victims would've been up and about if they were human. Two or three a.m. would have been a better time to strike."

It hit me then, what Kristair didn't want Ussier to know. His dreams. That must've given Kristair the first connection. But weren't they only nightmares brought on by his return to humanity and not prescience? After all, the dreams had started long before the murders.

"The fact that none of the victims had any family or friends searching for them was another clue, but there were no other similarities between them. They were of different ages, men and women, from various backgrounds. They only thing they had in common was that they were alone in the world. Still, that wasn't enough to satisfy me and make me jump to the conclusion that they were vampires."

"That's why you had me call Aderson. But I don't get it, if they were vampires, wouldn't autopsies show they were already dead before the fire? No matter how badly they were charred?" I scratched my head. Come to think of it, how did that work? How would a coroner find cause of death on a body that had ceased changing however many ages ago? "How does that make a difference one way or another?"

"The fact that the bodies were so badly destroyed by the fire was another clue. A human would have something left, no matter how bad the fire was. And all of these fires were reported rather quickly. I asked some more questions after you called and it seemed that whatever remains there were, none of them made it to the coroner's intact. The older a vampire is when they finally perish, the quicker they decay. Besides, only vampires burn so easily. No other creature, mortal or supernatural, immolates so fast, and your detective friend admitted they couldn't find traces of any accelerant."

"You have been giving it some thought, Ancient One," Ussier said, a pleased smile flickering across his lips. "How come I'm not surprised? Anything else you care to add to your theories?"

Kristair slipped his fingers into my own, giving my hand a squeeze. "Not really, there were other things that bothered me, but I didn't know for certain until you showed up. That's why you're here isn't it? You need someone to help you hunt down whoever's preying on the vampires."

"Oh, no way in hell." I glared at the both of them. "You're outta yer damn mind, Kristair."

Ussier's cold gaze zeroed in on me. Only lines of strain and worry around his mouth and eyes made him seem at all human. "Whoever's doing it is only attacking us at dawn, not at any damn time we can fight back. They certainly aren't vampire, that's for sure, and the majority of us don't have any defense against these kinds of attacks. I don't even know how the fuck they're finding out where their victims are sleeping."

"What about Lisabeth? Has she been able to divine any leads?"

"Nothing tangible, the only thing she's been able to tell me is that whoever's behind this has their soul divided. Whatever the fuck that means."

Kristair was staring, off, a finger tapping against his chin slowly. "Have there been any other attacks on your people other than the ones we've heard about on the news?"

That had to be a good sign—Kristair wasn't lumping himself in with his old friends—but I did wish Ussier would stop indulging his curiosity, even if I was a bit interested myself. It just couldn't be good that he showed up here tonight. To distract myself, I rose and finished loading the dishwasher as I listened in on their conversation.

"Not yet. At first we thought it might be a werecreature, given the gruesome way they were killed. Or an especially tenacious hunter. But Silverfeather insists it's not one of his people, and I doubt he'd be willing to break the truce we have at this time. And a random hunter popping up here doesn't make much sense either. There are more notorious vampire lairs than Pittsburgh."

"Whoa, now wait a goddamn minute." I turned around and glared at the both of them in exasperation. "Have I been living in a bubble all my life? How come I heard none of this until you popped up?" I pointed at my lover.

"Humans only believe what they want to believe. How often did you hear somebody claiming supernatural sightings and dismiss them as jokes, crackpots, or lunatics? Welcome to the real world kid," Ussier said with a hint of his old grin.

"I'm probably going to regret asking this, but what is considered a notorious vampire lair?"

"Mexico City comes to mind. Of course, with all the unrest in Kabul and Peshawar and other locations in the Mideast, more vampires are flocking over there. Unexplained bodies don't raise such a fuss in such places."

"These attacks could be personal," Kristair said softly.

"No shit they're personal. Someone wants to get our attention and make their damn point." Ussier scowled, his voice grim. "I get the feeling it's personal, only I don't have a damn clue who they're trying to get at. We all have enemies of one kind or another."

"Has anyone in your circle lost someone close to them?"

"The gentleman this morning got together with Artemise once a month, but the rest were on the fringes or just passing through."

Kristair's head shot up. "Bedwyr?"

"Yeah, I forgot, you would've known him too. Otherwise, there doesn't seem to be any real pattern to whose targeted, unless it's just opportunity. Except for Bedwyr, none of the victims were too old. They wouldn't have the safeguards the rest of us do. Though, whoever it is, Kristair, they're not leaving one damn trace for us."

"Have you considered that the assassin is using magic?" Kristair asked, and I studied his face, searching for any signs of grief for this Bedwyr person, but my lover seemed as inscrutable as always.

Ussier grimaced. "Yes, but if they are, it's not a form either Lisabeth or Artemise recognizes."

"They're the experts," Kristair said thoughtfully, his eyes far away. I recognized that expression, when his thoughts were moving so fast it was damn near impossible to decipher them. It used to give me a headache when he did that. Then he pinned his gaze on Ussier, for the moment every inch the ancient vampire he used to be. "You're here to call in old favors."

"It is the currency of the undead," Ussier said smoothly.

Kristair inclined his head toward him. "It would be my honor to help you in any way I can."

"Wait a minute—"

"It's not open for discussion, Jacob." The utter finality in Kristair's voice and the direct look he gave me brought me up short. He'd never spoken in that tone before.

"Fuck me," I cursed viciously, glaring at him and trying to penetrate that thick skull of his with some other choice words.

"I think it's time I leave you two lovebirds to discuss this." Ussier rose and shook Kristair's hand. "You know how to get a hold of me."

"Of course, my friend."

Ussier nodded to me. "See you around, Mr. Corvin."

Guilt made me writhe a little inside. For Christ's sake, it wasn't that I didn't sympathize with Ussier, and I knew I owed him, but someone here had to have a little common sense. I stared after him as he walked out the door and then let out a groan of frustration. "Wait, Ussier."

To my surprise, Kristair didn't try to follow me out, and Ussier paused, waiting for me on the porch. "Look, I know I owe you, I owe you big time," I said in a low voice. "But dammit, you can't ask him to do this. We're only human again. We're gonna get ourselves killed."

Ussier paused and grinned. "Only human? Somehow I doubt that. Besides, I'm not looking for you two to start a war. I'm more interested in using that old man's mind. He's been around longer than any of us. If anyone can put all the pieces together, it's him. You're pretty damn clever yourself. You two make a good team."

I considered that as I walked him out to his 4Runner, weighing the danger with everything the vampire had done for Kristair and me, and then sighed. "Okay, so you're just seeing if we can run down a new angle, not take whoever this is out."

"I'd be very put out if you did. Just see what you can dig up; then pass it on. I'd like to get my hands on them personally. And don't fuss so much. The old man hasn't been around this long without learning a thing or two about survival. Human or not, it's going to be hard to catch him unawares."

Ussier didn't know my lover the way I did. Kristair's intelligence and tenacity I didn't doubt for one bit, but I did worry about his state of mind. And damn him for being such a closed-mouth ass on that score.

Ussier clapped me on my shoulder, giving it a squeeze. "I really do appreciate this."

"Why did you help me after Kristair was gone? For all you knew, it was over and done with, you owed me nothing. Forgive me if I'm offending you, but you never struck me as a man who did anything without anticipating getting something in return. What did you think I could possibly offer you?"

Ussier laughed. "You're kidding right? Maybe you don't appreciate just how unusual you are. Not only did you capture the old man's devotion, but you bonded with him on a level I still don't understand. You were the only human ever to have a vampire's abilities without changing into one yourself, which meant you didn't have any of our weaknesses. I don't think you realize how much power you were sitting on."

"I knew. Even though I didn't want to know," I replied softly. Then I shook my head, banishing old memories. "When we've got your answers, are we done? All debts cleared?"

Ussier regarded me steadily, and for a moment I thought I might've pushed the vampire lord too far. "You really are hell-bent on protecting him aren't you? I can respect that. Yeah, you get me the answers I want and the table's clean between us."

"Somehow I doubt it's the last I'd hear from you though."

He laughed again and clapped me on the arm before unlocking his 4Runner, only reinforcing my opinion that Ghedi Ussier was not the kind of man who let anyone slip through his fingers that he could use to his benefit. "I do like you, kid. See you around."

Chapter 4

I LISTENED intently for Jacob's return, the stomp of his feet and the second slam of the screen door, only when he did come back, he did so quietly. I had my back turned to him, busying myself at the counter, but I sensed his return like a coming thunderstorm, somehow all the more ominous because he wasn't ranting.

"You're angry," I said, turning my head in his direction just enough so I could see him out of the corner of my eye, though I remained where I was.

"Doesn't take a genius to figure that one out," Jacob said, his voice deceptively soft. I knew that tone. He wasn't in one of his shouting, arm-waving fits—he had gone past spitting furious to obdurate reason. He wanted some concession from me and wasn't going to ease up until he got it. And the anger was still there, simmering under the surface, fueling his determination.

"I'm sorry I spoke to you the way I did. I didn't want to argue about it in front of him. It was…." I paused, searching for the right word as Jacob laid a hand on the counter on each side of me, caging me between his body and the counter. His closeness was electric and robbed me of my words. "Discourteous, especially after—"

"Oh, I know why you did it," Jacob interrupted, his breath fanning the back of my neck, causing a ripple of awareness to strum through me. "Our old mental speech would've been quite handy then. Don't you think?"

I shrugged a shoulder. "Having you rage in my head would've been distracting."

"You're doing it again."

My lover knew just how potent he was to my senses and used it shamelessly to his advantage. Right then we were so close I could feel the heat of his body, though he wasn't touching me. Between that and the force of his anger, which was warranted, I admitted to myself, I found it hard to gather my skittering arguments. "Doing what?"

"Every time I bring up our old connection you dismiss it or ignore it. Why's that, you think?"

I set down the pile of silverware I'd been sorting and tamped down my initial dismay. "I'm not going to waste my energy pining for something I cannot have."

"You know what I think?"

"I think you think too much," I said with exasperation.

But at this moment, I'd dearly have loved a peek into his mind, if only to discover the best way to soothe him without breaking my word to Ussier. That I couldn't was an open wound I tried my best to ignore. Trust Jacob to stir up things that were best left alone.

"I think you're hiding again, love."

I stiffened and glared over my shoulder at him. "Are you calling me a coward?"

"Don't be ridiculous. But you do guard your heart, Kristair, and you don't acknowledge anything that might hurt you. And you refuse to admit that you're afraid sometimes, when I know you are."

Jacob saw so much. Even without our connection, he understood, he knew me in ways that no one else had my entire long existence. Which made it doubly pointless to talk about, if he knew already there was nothing to say. "What would admitting it prove?"

"That's my point exactly."

"Then please enlighten me," I said through clenched teeth. "Because I'm failing to see it. And what does this have to do with your anger over Ussier's request?" I turned around to face him, which was a mistake. Jacob's eyes were a blazing, hot blue, and his face was set at its most stubborn. There was something about Jacob all fired up that got to me in the most primitive way possible.

"Everything, fucking everything. You've found yourself in a world you don't understand, you feel like you're powerless and lost, and instead of turning to me, you're shutting me out. And I really don't give a damn what the reasons are, but I want you to stop. What, you don't think I won't understand how it is to feel like that?"

I gaped at him, amazed at how close he came to the truth. How did he do that? Even with him knowing me, it was uncanny. "No, that's not it at all. I know you do." So many reasons flooded my mind, and I couldn't articulate even one.

When I didn't say anything else, the fire in his eyes ignited even more, and deep down, another thrill of anticipation rippled through me. Not that I wanted Jacob to be angry with me, but he made furious breathtaking.

"You refuse to acknowledge that we once had that connection. I bet you don't even think about it because it hurts too much."

"Mourning it is not going to bring it back, Jacob. I'd rather save my energies to adapting." Which was as close as I was going to get to admitting that he was right. I'd been human once before; I could be human again. At least this time I had Jacob's own experiences to help guide me. His memories had saved my pride on more than one occasion.

Some of the heat faded in Jacob's gaze, and he gave me a small smile. "Why can't we get it back? We didn't have that connection because you were a vampire, not really. It's something you learned to do by exercising that brain of yours and your people's spell helped reinforce it. You keep saying my mind and will is strong, what's to stop us from trying to develop the connection again?"

"You don't think I haven't thought of that?" I shook my head. "Yes, in theory it's possible, but part of the trick is believing it will work, training your mind until the thought becomes reality."

"Then there's no problem." Jacob grinned and pressed a quick, tingling kiss to my lips. "We know it will work. We just need some practice."

"No, we don't know. We don't know what the Ascended have done to us. If they reduced us somehow to keep this from happening at all. I'm sure they were prudent enough to set limits. I know I would've, if I had been in their position."

That shut him up for a second, but then Jacob's chin jutted out stubbornly. "Whatever, maybe they did, but that shouldn't stop us from trying it."

I sighed, struggling for patience. "Jacob, *mo chroí*, consider this. What happens if we do try and it works?"

"That would be rather fucking awesome." When I didn't immediately share his jubilation, Jacob's smile turned into a frown. "So please tell me why you don't think it's awesome."

"I'm concerned that it would give the Ascended an excuse to take me back. After all, I am supposed to be merely human now. And if they do take me back, I doubt they'd allow me to escape a second time."

"Fucking a!" Jacob crossed his arms and scowled. "Dammit, I didn't think of that. Okay, you've got a point," he snapped.

I tugged his hand free as his eyes narrowed and kissed his knuckles. "Let it go," I said softly, trying to appeal to my lover at his most stubborn. "Worrying at it won't solve anything."

He snorted and pulled his hand away, caging me between himself and the counter again. "You don't know me very well, then, and we're not even close to being finished."

"What is there left to argue about? I'm not changing my mind about helping Ussier. I owe him a huge debt." By all rights, Jacob should've been dead. If Ussier hadn't helped him after I'd been taken…. I didn't even like to think about what would've happened to him, because the best-case scenario was him being murdered outright. And the worst I couldn't bear thinking about.

"We both do, and my conscience won't let me ignore it either, as much as I bitched about it. And I'll probably bitch about it pretty much non-stop until it's over with. I'm going to help too."

I wanted to smile at Jacob's sour response but kept it hidden. Jacob's sense of loyalty and fairness wouldn't allow him to deny

Ussier. I should've remembered that. "I know you wanted a normal life, *mo chroí*, and I'm sorry that once again my past is intruding on it."

"Our past, and that's not what's pissing me the fuck off either," Jacob said with his teeth clenched.

"Then what is it?" I raised my voice, goaded past patience. "Please, tell me what it is so I know."

"I don't trust you," Jacob ground out, the words cutting deep. "Do you know how much it fucking infuriates me to admit that? As long as you keep things from me, as long as you keep all this bullshit locked up, I can't trust you."

"I have given you no reason at all to not trust me," I lashed out, anger and hurt bubbling up out of a deep well. How could he say such a thing?

"Haven't you? Think on it, Kristair, and when you do, get back to me." I stared, aghast, as he walked away, and a few minutes later, the furious sounds of one of his video games drifted in from the living room.

Seething, confused, and hurt, I put some water in the kettle and placed it on the stove to heat before moving to the doorway between the kitchen and living room. Jacob sat cross-legged on the ground, his game controller on his lap, cursing a vicious storm as his character was riddled with bullets. His concentration was shot. I'd seen him make this run through the deserted, ruined city flawlessly a dozen times.

My lover knew I was there. Jacob's shoulders had stiffened the moment I darkened the entryway, but he didn't turn around. I stood and watched him, trying to make sense of it all, until the kettle began to whistle.

Even the ritual of making tea didn't settle me down, and I took my steaming mug out onto the wraparound porch. Cool, soothing shadows enveloped me. A large maple stood in the yard, blocking most of the night sky. The moon was a bare sliver of silver and the stars distanced by the neighborhood streetlamps. The swing creaked as I sat down in it and stretched my legs onto the railing. Daylight was too harsh. This was the world I understood. A world that I reveled in.

Only it was no longer my world.

I could no longer penetrate the shadows and see as clearly as if it were day. I could no longer scent an approaching intruder as they neared, hear distinctive sounds amidst the motley background noise. If someone came at me, I had to rely on human strength, human reflexes. I couldn't keep Jacob safe in the manner that I wanted to keep him safe.

We no longer had our supernatural abilities, but we couldn't hide behind the safe ignorance of humans either. We were aware of the other world just as they were aware of us. A beautiful and terrible world. We couldn't ignore it and hope they'd ignore us in return. We had to find a way to embrace both sides to survive.

Becoming a vampire had been a far more terrifying change at the onset, but I would admit, this change back to being a human was harder to adjust to. And it irritated me all the more because I was having such difficulties reconciling what I had been with what I was now. I had never been one of those who had railed against being a vampire, who had thought it was a curse. Still, I believed the sacrifice was worth it.

I couldn't understand what else Jacob wanted from me. I was trying to adjust in the only way I knew how. Couldn't he see that?

I wasn't sure how long I sat out there, but my tea had grown cold by the time I heard the screen door open and Jacob stepped out onto the porch. The ache in my chest swelled up, and I closed my eyes. I hated quarreling with him. It left me shaken and uncertain, vulnerable in ways I'd never allowed myself to be before he came into my life.

He didn't say a word, but I knew he was looking at me the same way I had been studying him before I came out here. I finally turned my head and met his gaze. His face was cast in shadows, but I knew this man better than my own self in many ways, and he was aching just as much as I.

"Did you come out here to see whether or not I took your car and went out on my own?" The accusation came out before I could censor it. It was as if I had some perverse need to nettle him.

"The thought did come to mind."

"I wouldn't dare touch your baby." That car, a royal blue '79 Camaro Z28, had been Jacob's first purchase after he'd signed with the NFL. I'd helped him piece it together, following his tutelage, until it was fully restored. It now sat gleaming in the driveway, and I hadn't a clue of how to drive it. All I knew was that it was more complicated than my own. I could let Jacob's memories guide me as I did in other things, but I wasn't sure he had that good of a grasp on driving himself.

"You are too proud and stubborn, and I didn't come out here to fight with you again," Jacob said evenly.

"You are just as guilty as I am when it comes to being proud and stubborn, Jacob Allen Corvin."

"True." He crossed over to me and took my mug, setting it on the railing before kneeling on the swing and straddling my lap. "And I'm sorry for what I said."

Jacob apologizing first was a novelty, and it was enough to make me back down from my defensive stance. "If I admit that I'm afraid, will you tell me why you don't trust me?" That bothered me more than I could say, and Jacob's expression softened.

"That came out wrong." Once again, frustration crossed his face. "Fuck. I don't know how to explain it. But it comes down to this: It pisses me off that I can't figure out how you're going to respond to this investigation. Everything's changed for you and you haven't reacted at all. You've had your damn poker face on since you've returned. I keep feeling like you're shoving everything away and one day you're just going to explode when it gets to be too much. And I can't help but wonder if this is going to be the trigger or not."

"Jacob, may I point out that you're the hothead, not me. I don't explode."

"Oh really?" Jacob gave me a penetrating look. "Maybe you don't go off all half-cocked like I do, but once you consider someone an enemy you hunt them down without any mercy."

"That's the way it should be. Leaving an enemy around to hound you again is pure foolishness."

"Wait, I'm not done." Jacob fisted a hand in his hair. "Just because I run hot and you run cold when it comes to fighting doesn't mean the same things don't drive us, the same emotions." I had to concede Jacob's point there. Sometimes I forgot how well he understood how people worked. He had an innate wisdom when it came to others.

"And when you get caught up trying to protect someone, Kristair, you don't always think things through. I worry to death that you're gonna forget that you're not some badass vampire anymore now that your friends are threatened and that you're going to get yourself killed. Either because you haven't given yourself a chance to adapt yet or because you're trying to prove yourself."

Jacob watched me as I floundered for a reply. Sometimes he could show remarkable patience, and he did so now, waiting for me with at least a semblance of calm. This wasn't a random lashing out as I had thought. Jacob had very valid reasons for being upset, and for once, I didn't know how to reassure him. I was going against two thousand years of instinct, all of which said to chase down whoever was behind the murders and do whatever was necessary to destroy them.

"I will admit that I haven't thought of it from quite that perspective." Jacob breathed a sigh, and tension I hadn't realized he still carried flowed out of him. "You're right to worry and all I can say is that I'll try, I swear I'll try to be extra careful and diligent about what I can and cannot do."

Even admitting that much of my limitations stung.

"Well, that's a start, and I'm not going to push you for anything more now." Jacob leaned in and brushed his lips over mine. "Look, I know I hurt ya with what I said, and…."

"I didn't say that."

"You wouldn't." He ran his fingers over my scalp and rubbed his thumb along my jaw. I slid my hands up, cupping the back of his head. "But I know I did and I'm sorry."

"No apologies are necessary, *mo chroí*, not if you kiss me," I said, drawing his head down, anxious to taste him, to feel the physical connection again and know that everything was once again okay between us.

"I'm gonna do damn more than kiss you," Jacob said in a husky voice, and then our lips met, and I knew.

Chapter 5

THE air weighed down on us with the humid promise of scorching heat to come as Kristair and I jogged through the steely light of dawn. We had skipped our run the day before, and I was not about to do that twice, despite how much I hated rising at this hour. Still, it was the best time to jog. Later on, it would be brutal, and I couldn't let my conditioning slip, not when training camp was starting in a few weeks.

Kristair insisted on going with me every morning, pushing himself hard. I think he worried he was going to lose his edge or something. Or get fat and lazy now that he was human. My man had issues. Still, I wasn't about to argue. The company kept me from cheating, and I loved watching him run. He made it seem effortless with his fluid lope. I'd asked him about it one time and he'd told me his people hadn't used horses if they wanted to get somewhere—they had run or walked.

Knowing my lover, he'd do that instead of getting into a car any day. That probably would explain his aversion to anything with wheels too. In some ways, Kristair was just stuck in the past.

"Mind if we take a detour?" Kristair said, jogging in place as we waited by a light. I shook my head, and he took the lead as we crossed the street. Half a mile later, as we headed deeper into the heart of Pittsburgh, I wished I'd asked more questions. Where the hell did that bald-headed freak think he was going?

Then the reek of stale smoke assailed my nose, and I knew damn well where we were headed. The street had a hushed quality about it, as if the high-rises themselves were cowering back in fear. Of course, that could have been my own overworked imagination.

Still, a shiver of foreboding went through me as we neared the building where the vampire had been killed. The ground out in front was littered with bits of broken police tape, ground ash, and charred bits of something I didn't even want to think about. I groaned as I slowed to a walk to cool down. "What are we doing here, Kristair? Last fucking thing I want to see before breakfast is what's left of a dead body, or where a dead body has been. Or anything to do with murder and mutilation."

"I figured you'd rather look at it now, before others start crawling all over it again, than going last night in the dark or me going by myself." Kristair gave me a wry smile. "I'm trying to remember my promise."

"Sneaky bastard," I grumbled. I had no damn argument against that little bit of logic. Absently, I stretched as I stared at the destructive scene in front of us. "I have no idea where to even begin." We had to be out of our fucking minds to get involved in this, promise or no promise.

Kristair crouched down next to an oblong length of the ground that had been marked around with a string. I inched closer, the hair on the back of my neck stirring. "You think the dude was aware? I mean, if he'd had that knife in his heart, he was paralyzed, right? Wouldn't be able to scream or nothing."

"Oh no, there was screaming." Kristair crouched down and brushed his fingers over the scorched ground, his expression more enigmatic than usual. "The kind of screaming one does when sanity has snapped and one knows that there is no hope. It was beyond agony."

I grimaced and hunkered down next to him. "I thought you weren't psychic anymore."

"Everyone is sensitive in some manner or another. You mean you can't feel that? As if the earth itself is crying out?"

A finger of sensation brushed across my awareness, and I firmly shut it out. "No, and I'm damn glad I can't." The last thing I needed was to relive a bloodsucker's last moments in the sun. "I can imagine you're extra sensitive to it, given the circumstances."

"You mean my nightmares?" Kristair's glance was cool and unruffled. How much of it was an act? He'd known this dude for years at least, if not decades.

"Sorta, you think they're connected at all? Seems to me you'd have lots of things your subconscious could fuck with while you're asleep, lots of bad memories, but this has been the one thing bugging you since you came back."

"If it is, I can't figure out why." Kristair rose with a sigh, looking around at the scene again. "The police picked over it pretty well. I doubt we'll find anything they haven't bagged for evidence."

Frowning, I stood up too. "I suppose I could call Aderson and Kuykedal again. I don't know if they'd be willing to say anything two days in a row. Maybe if I give them some info in exchange. You think Ussier would mind?"

Kristair pursed his lips and tugged on his chin. "I trust your discretion. They already know about vampires. If you let them in on it being a vampire matter, they might be more forthcoming. I think we should also pay a visit to Alette Dupree. There had to have been a connection between all of the victims and she's just paranoid enough to see it all."

"Don't you think Ussier's done that already? She's a creepy bitch." As soon as the words left my mouth, I had the weird sensation we were being watched, and for one terrified instant, I thought she somehow had managed to hear me and had taken offense. But Kristair had spun around, too, staring intently at each window facing us from the high-rise.

To my horror, he took off at a dead run toward the building. "Kristair!" He didn't pause or glance back as he burst through the front doors. Son of a bitch! I took off after him, more intent on biting a piece out of him than finding whomever he was chasing.

I caught up with him in the lobby just as he was about to disappear into the fire escape and grabbed his arm. "What the fuck do you think you're doing?" I snarled.

"Don't be ridiculous. Someone is watching us. You felt it too; I saw it on your face."

"Doesn't mean we have to go barreling in there. What if they're armed? We don't have anything on us."

Kristair's brows snapped together in a ferocious glare. "You aren't suggesting that we walk away, are you?"

"No." I opened the stairwell door and slipped ahead of him. "Just let's move more quietly, okay?"

Kristair snorted and followed so silently that only my sense of him behind me told me he was there. Showoff. We paused at the first landing, and Kristair brushed his fingertips against the door. After my nod, he opened it cautiously. The hallway was empty, apartments stretching out to either side in silent rows.

"This is ridiculous," I muttered under my breath. "If it is somebody, they won't be in the hallway, they'd be in an apartment, and how are we going to tell which one? And even if we do, we cannot start busting in doors. We'll end up arrested ourselves. That would be a fine beginning to my career."

"I may not have ever personally visited Bedwyr's apartment, but trust me, we'll know which is his at a glance." Kristair made his way up another flight of stairs with the quick, silent grace of a predator. He peered through the door and then grunted in satisfaction. "There, see."

I glanced over his shoulder at the apartment door covered in police tape. Damn him for being so smart. At least he wasn't one to gloat about it. "Just wonderful," I muttered. "Now how are we supposed to get in?"

"I thought you knew how to pick locks."

"For crying out loud, Kristair, I don't carry tools for that shit in my jogging shorts." I stared at the door, another chill running through me. "This shit gives me the fucking heebie-jeebies."

"I thought you were going to work on your language."

"Fuck you." I glared at my lover, who had a slight smile on his lips and an avid glint in his eyes. "Ass. You're enjoying this."

"What's there not to enjoy? This is rather invigorating." The hallway was clear, and Kristair eased out. I grabbed his wrist just before he tried the door to the apartment.

"You have fingerprints now, babe." I took the hem of my shirt and tried the knob. To my surprised dismay, it twisted and opened without a hitch. Fuck, there was no stopping Kristair now. "Try not to touch anything."

"Calm down, Jacob. It's not like I'm in any police database."

"Let's keep it that way."

Kristair cocked his head, listening intently. "I think whoever was here is gone now." He drifted over to the window and glanced down right at the spot where we'd been standing moments before.

"Saw us coming and skedaddled." I started looking around the room. It seemed ordinary enough to me, cluttered with knickknacks and Playboy magazines. The kitchen was empty, the fridge unplugged. Yeah, this was a bloodsucker's den, alright.

"I don't like the sound of that at all. It implies that whoever this is may know us and know what we're about," Kristair said with a thoughtful frown.

"You just had to say it, didn't you." I stopped to glare at him. Ugh, I really hated feeling like I was being watched. My skin was still crawling.

"Say what?" Kristair poked his head into the bedroom, and his voice turned grim. "At least Bedwyr had a chance to put up a fight."

I followed him back into the bedroom, staring at the chaos. Sheets lay in a tangled puddle on the floor, the nightstand overturned, blackout curtain ripped off the wall, an ugly dark rust stain on the wall. "If our vamp got in a good hit, anyone with a fresh injury might be a good place to start."

Kristair made a noncommittal sound, studying the room intently, gaze methodically sweeping every inch. "I think this is pointing more and more to someone leaking information."

"I think you're paranoid. But if you're not, that's nice and convenient, all we have to do then is find out who the idiot is and let Ussier deal with him. His last moments are bound to be very, very uncomfortable." I nudged a boot out of my way with my toe and crouched down to glance under the bed. "Picking up any more psychic hoodoo?"

"Not a glimmer. Whoever was here is long gone now, and any traces below are locked in the spot where he died." Kristair peered into the bathroom; then he opened the closet door. "Doesn't even look like the killer looked in here at all. Maybe it was just an execution," he said as I walked back out into the hallway.

I glanced through the last door in the hall and let out a whistle. The room had once contained a computer and several bookshelves, but that had all been destroyed. "Kristair, you gotta see this."

The burned-out husk of the computer sat on the desk, monitor cracked from the intense heat. The shelves were covered in sooty ash, but not one burn mark scarred the wood surface of either the shelves or the desk. "What the hell could do that?" I demanded, pointing at the desk and the piles of ash around the room. Soot marred the wall, but again, not one burn past the books. The hard drive was smashed in and melted, little bits of plastic fused to the floor. There would be no data recovery from that mess.

Kristair examined the destruction, his lips pursed. "Well, it's definitely not the strange accelerant the media's been talking about. If I had to hazard a guess just from looking at this, given that we're dealing with a vampire hunter, I'd say magic of some kind has been used."

"Fucking figures," I swore. "What now?"

Kristair clasped my shoulder in a gentle rub. "Now we go home. I'll look through my library today to see if I can discover anything about such fires and you talk with your cop friends. Then tonight, we'll go by Alette's club and see what we can dig up there."

"Sounds like a game plan to me."

"THIS is the second time in as many days you've pestered me about this case. Don't you have a training camp to get ready for?" I followed Aderson back into the file room and shut the door as he continued talking. "Look, kid, my partner's got money riding on you this season. He'll throw you in lockup if you disappoint him."

That gave me pause, and I grinned. "Really. I thought ole Kuykedal would've bet against me."

"He was tempted, believe me, but he's too much of a diehard Steelers fan to do that." Aderson stuffed the file in a drawer and turned back to me, lowering his voice. "You don't want to get mixed up in this shit. Go play football, forget that this whole other world exists. You were lucky enough to escape it once, don't get dragged back in."

"It's too late for that." I sobered up and moved closer to him. "If I promise to share what I know, off the record, will you answer my questions?"

"Just tell me why you need to know first."

I ran my hand through my hair, trying to figure out the best way of saying it without giving too much up. "After my protector was gone, some guys helped me out, saved my ass. They called in the favor."

Aderson was quiet for a long moment. Then he pulled on his long nose. I noticed his hair was even more steely gray than the last time we had seen each other. "So all the victims are vampires."

I couldn't see any harm in admitting it. "Yeah, for right now that's the only connection we've got."

"What do you want to know?"

"Was there anything recovered from the latest victim's office? Books, flash drives, anything like that?"

"There was nothing left to recover. We bagged a laptop, but don't even think about asking to take a look at it, because you can't. It's not even open for discussion."

"Fine, I won't, then." Maybe Kristair would have some ideas getting around that. "Was it fried too?"

"To a crispy critter. Our best techs are looking to see if they can recover anything. I've suspected that whatever was behind these murders is paranormal, and you've confirmed it, so I doubt they'll find anything."

"You've got the wrong people working for you. What about with the other victims, same M.O.?"

Aderson glanced at the door and lowered his voice even more. "They were all killed in the same way. Some of them also had books and computers destroyed, but not all of them."

I gave him an assessing glance, trying to rectify the smooth, lawyer image with a man who understood there was so much more going on around us than the mundane world most lived in. The two images didn't mesh. "What happens to cases like this, ones that don't involve humans? Is there some special department for the weird?"

"You watch too much TV, kid. Eventually they get thrown in the cold case files and we move on. Most people don't even want to admit that there's anything like this going on. If you're smart, you keep it to yourself, or else you'll end up in a nuthouse."

"How'd you and Kuykedal find out about vamps?" I asked, knowing I should mind my own damned business, but curiosity compelled me.

Aderson's face went stony, and he drew himself up. "That's a story for a bottle of whisky. Anything else you want to tell me that you dug up?"

Now that only whetted my curiosity. "Nothing yet, going to meet with someone tonight who might be able to tell me about the victims, see if there was anything else they had in common other than being a vampire."

Aderson pushed his glasses up on his nose and shook his head. "I can't believe you're not dead yet, but you're really asking for it. Concentrate on football and leave it alone."

"I wish I could, man, I really do." I sighed and wondered what Kristair was doing at that moment. Probably sitting in his library. "Got anything else for me? Anything left behind at all the scenes or something?"

"Nothing other than the knives, and there is nothing remarkable about them. You can buy them at any Wal-Mart in the country."

I chewed on my knuckle, trying to decide whether or not to tell him about our unseen watcher, and then shook my head. The last thing Aderson needed to know was that I'd gone into a crime scene unasked again. "Okay, I'd better get to the gym. If I get anything else, I'll let you know, and you do the same, okay?"

"Kuykedal won't like it," Aderson grunted.

"I'm sure I'll hear all about it from him."

Chapter 6

THE lonesome cry of a saxophone spilled from the double doors out onto Carson Street. The row of old brick buildings between the Monongahela River and the railroad tracks had been renovated into pubs, restaurants, and trendy clubs, turning the south side of Pittsburgh into one of the top hang-out spots. Not that I'd ever been inclined to spend much time here.

Jacob grabbed a sports coat out of the trunk of his Camaro and slid it on despite the oppressive heat blanketing the city. I frowned at the leather holster now concealed at the small of Jacob's back. "Must you carry that thing?"

"I'm not walking into a vampire club unarmed. And until this shit is over and done with, I'm carrying." He gave me a speculative glance as we waited for a clear space to cross the street, and I shook my head against the suggestion I knew was coming.

"Don't."

"I really wish you'd let me teach you how to shoot," Jacob said, ignoring my request.

I suppressed a shudder of distaste at the thought. "For the last time, and I won't be saying this again, I have absolutely no interest in learning how to use such a graceless weapon."

"I never thought the day would come when you said you weren't interested in learning. You have to have something to defend yourself with. You can't go around with a war club or a sword for god's sake," Jacob snapped under his breath, grabbing my hand as we dashed across the street between the traffic.

"Trust me," I assured him.

"You're really pushing it, babe."

Alette's club stood on the east end of the row. A wrought iron trellis comprised of musical notes instead of the usual stylized swirls meant to represent leaves or vines supported a balcony. A few clubgoers stood up there, sipping drinks or smoking cigarettes with the windows wide open to catch the music. The name of the club, Midnight Whispers, was emblazoned in blue neon script over the establishment.

A couple of beautiful young men stood outside on the sidewalk, checking IDs and taking the cover charge. One of them with spiky dark hair and smoky eyes motioned us forward ahead of the other people waiting to come in. He was one of Alette's pets, no doubt about that, and not for the first time, I wished I'd been able to come up with a reason to keep Jacob away from her. Not that she'd have tried to interfere with another vampire's interest, at least not when she was lucid.

"Mr. Mercer, Mr. Corvin, we were told to let you right on in."

"Okay, that's creepy," Jacob muttered. "They keeping that close of an eye on us?"

"I don't think so, at least not yet. Ussier no doubt anticipated that we would want to talk with certain key individuals in the city and let them know to clear a way for us ahead of time."

Thunder rolled across the sky, for the moment drowning out the sound of the music and the traffic. Somewhere in the distance, a lonely train whistle blew. Ominous sounds, Jacob would have said, but he was more in tune with such things than I. Very sensitive and intuitive to his surroundings. Perhaps it was rubbing off on me.

"But tonight? You'd think they wouldn't be expecting us so soon."

"I'm sure Ussier doesn't expect us to waste any time. I have no doubt Madame Dupree gave her boys our description and told them we were a priority. It wouldn't matter when we came or if she was there. Until this is solved, they'll cater to us."

"If we solve it quick enough." Jacob sighed as we walked through the doors, and the sultry jazz number swelled into full life, smothering out the murmur of conversation. "I'm glad at least one of us is certain."

The club was small, with walls papered in royal blue, and framed records of artists such as Miles Davis, Johnny Coltrane, and Muddy Waters were highlighted in places of honor. Beveled Tiffany-style lamps provided dim lighting as a quartet played on the dark wood stage.

"Try not to cause a ruckus," I said in a low voice, scanning the small tables arranged in intimate circles for Alette Dupree. "This place is her pride and joy."

"I'll be on my best behavior," Jacob promised.

"Somehow that doesn't inspire me with confidence."

Jacob flashed me a grin that was pure imp. "Trust me."

I really did love the brat. I should've known it wouldn't take him long to throw my own words back at me.

"There she is, just in front of the stage, with two hot chicks."

I looked over to where Jacob indicated. Alette Dupree sat with all of her attention seemingly on the performance, though I knew she was aware of everything going on around her. Sure enough, she said something to the woman with alabaster skin and a short cap of jet-black hair who was sitting next to her. She rose and came toward us with a gracious smile. "That would be Celeste Roy," I said in an undertone to my lover. "One of Alette's protégés, she designed the balcony. She's a rather renowned artist, Alette likes to surround herself with artists and musicians of all kinds."

"Nice dress," Jacob said with a wicked grin.

I studied Celeste again, trying to see what Jacob saw. Her elegant black dress ended at mid-thigh, her waist cinched with links of beaten silver. The dress clung to her curves, and the neckline dipped low, but I didn't understand Jacob's fascination. "If you say so." I shrugged.

He laughed softly and squeezed my hand. "She's another bloodsucker, I take it?"

"You would be correct in that assumption."

"And the other chick?" Jacob whispered as we went forward to greet Celeste. I had to grin at the rather demure image Taylor Ussier made in her tailored suit. Most times she wore far more flamboyant clothes and dragged Celeste into her debauchery, but for some reason, she seemed to like Alette's presence and behaved for the most part while she was with her.

"That, Jacob, is Ussier's youngling, Taylor. She's also an artist, draws comic books and writes stories about vampires." I chuckled. "Some say she trapped Ussier into making her into a vampire and now he can't get rid of her."

"So this place is crawling with vamps? Just wonderful," Jacob said in an aside. Then he assumed a charming smile as Celeste approached. "Though they are damn hot."

"Kristair, it's so good to see you again," Celeste said, kissing me lightly on each cheek before turning to Jacob with frank interest in her eyes. "And who might this be?" Her rich, low laugh rippled free. "A personal friend of yours? You must be Jacob." She held out her hand to him and preened with delight when he gallantly kissed the back of it.

"Nice to meet you, Celeste."

"Aren't you just darling for saying so?" She slipped an arm through both of ours and started to lead us to Alette's table. "I hope you both have a chance to talk a bit after you're done with Alette. It's been a long time, and I'm sure there's all kinds of… stories." She smiled up at Jacob.

"We will see," I demurred.

Alette and Taylor looked up as we approached, and Ussier's youngling grinned. Taylor didn't look like a vampire. Her skin tended to have a healthy glow about it even if she hadn't just fed. Her electric eyes were a sea-green blue, and I had watched her use them to mesmerize a man more than once. And Taylor did love to play with both men and women. I started to have second thoughts about bringing Jacob. "Hey there, old man."

"Good evening, Taylor, Madame," I said, inclining my head to each one of them.

"Watch your manners," Alette said, gesturing for us to take a seat with a gracious, chilling smile. "Ancient One, Mr. Corvin, what may I do to help you?"

I pulled out a chair for Jacob and then sat down next to him. "I'm sure you know Ussier visited us last night." She nodded, and I continued, "I wanted to discuss the victims with you."

Celeste's lips formed into a pout. "Sounds depressing." She drew her finger down Jacob's chest. "Can we steal you away to entertain ourselves with?" Jacob grinned as Celeste glanced at me. "Or would that offend? I don't poach."

Before I could answer, Jacob rose from the table, much to my surprise. "That's a wonderful idea. Why don't you ladies take me over to the bar and we can talk."

Taylor bounced out of her seat, flipping her dark brown hair over her shoulder. "You know, Celeste is as good as she looks, I should know." She took Jacob's hand and pulled it over her shoulder to lead him away. "And I'm even better."

Jacob's eyes twinkled as he glanced at me and winked. "I'm all yours, ladies." Then he slipped his arm around Celeste's shoulders and sauntered off with the two of them toward where a mirrored bar with polished brass accents was doing a brisk business. What was that brat thinking?

"Probably for the better. I don't want to scare Celeste and Taylor, things are tense enough as it is," Alette said. "May I get you something?"

Reluctantly, I turned my attention back to the task at hand. Jacob could handle himself, I just had to remind myself of that fact. Though he had never stood toe-to-toe with the kind of trouble Celeste and Taylor could cause. "No, thank you, I am fine."

"So what was it you wanted to know that Ussier couldn't tell you?"

"We didn't get a chance to speak at length last night. He just asked us for our help and then left us to discuss it." Jacob had leaned back against the bar, beer in hand and a girl on either side of him. He looked to be in his element—young football player surrounded by pretty girls—though I'm sure this wasn't the club he would've chosen.

It irked me that he could divide my attention so easily.

"These victims," I continued, angling my body away from the bar. "Were they all from Pittsburgh?"

"Actually, only two of them were. Bedwyr and Cybil Haas." I closed my eyes for a moment in sorrow. I had hoped that Ussier had been wrong about Bedwyr. I knew I would've had to have known some of the victims, but these two I had considered to be somewhat more than acquaintances. We had researched together, shared knowledge in the past, Bedwyr especially, but then again, we were tied by more than our shared love of history. There were precious few who could remember Britain as I had.

I glanced toward Jacob without even realizing I did so and found him watching me, almost as if he knew. Oddly, it comforted me.

"And the other four?" I asked.

"The other woman we don't know. She could've been just traveling through our territory. Most have the courtesy to announce themselves and their intentions, but it doesn't always happen. The other three men did seek Ghedi out. The first victim, Simon DeSaur, had only planned to stay in town for a few nights. He told Ghedi that he was here to buy a rare book from a collector in town. We're not sure if that happened or not because he was killed the next dawn."

I frowned. I knew Simon as well, though only through correspondence. He rarely left Montreal, and then only under extreme duress. The right book might have just been enough to lure him out. It would've had to have been a very rare one indeed, and he would've needed proof it existed before leaving his sanctuary. He was rather paranoid.

The idea that he'd been lured out was disturbing to say the least.

"And the last two?"

"Gerard Manheim and Thomas Burris." A chill raced through me at those names. What were the chances that I knew them as well? Fellow researchers, historians, though Gerard's specialty was more in magic and ritual than journals and books. "Thomas was searching for his missing youngling and the trail had led him to Pittsburgh. Gerard never said why he was here, but he did visit Lisabeth and Artemise."

That made sense; still, I didn't like how the lines were connecting. Gerard had been to Pittsburgh more than once to visit with those two, and I'd consulted with him a number of times myself. Thomas came from even further away, and as far as I'd known, he'd never visited the United States before. There was a connection between them all, a connection I didn't want to consider, but it was staring right back at me.

Every single one of those individuals had helped me research what happened to the Ancients. We'd shared information, lore. They were considered experts as much as I. There were only so many vampires who put much effort into such studies; most were concerned with simply surviving, or they were enjoying their new state too much to think about a few thousand years into the future.

There were a few others, Mirella Brant, Lisabeth and Artemise, a fellow in Greece, and another in Egypt. Several of us had already disappeared, and I'd met them again as one of the Ascended. But what of the rest? What chances did they have of still being alive?

"Thank you, Madame. I know you often screen newcomers for Ussier. If anyone else comes into town and introduces themselves, would it be too much trouble for you to arrange a meeting between them and me?"

"I'll see what I can do. Will you be talking with Lisabeth and Artemise tonight?"

I rubbed the bridge of my nose, trying to decide how well the conversation would go. "With Artemise, and then I'll take it from there." He would be the most open-minded about the situation.

A slight smile crossed Alette's exquisite, inhuman face, as if she understood my hesitance. She probably did; I had never met anyone who didn't step softly around Lisabeth. "I'm afraid you'll most likely find them together. They have an"—she paused as if considering her words—"interest in each other."

That would complicate things, but if what I suspected were true, Lisabeth should be warned as well. If only I could leave Jacob behind when I went to go talk with them. I didn't like having certain vampires' gazes on him, but that wasn't even a possibility. "Where would I find them?"

"Tonight? Most likely at the conservatory in the park. They are rather fond of the place." Alette hesitated, an uneasy expression crossing her face before she smoothed it. "How can you stand it?" she whispered. "How can you stand being human again?" Her features twisted into disgust.

I looked at my lover, deep in conversation with Taylor and Celeste, and what I felt for him was a physical ache, it was so strong. "I admit there are aspects to my old life that I miss, but Jacob more than compensates for that loss."

"Love is illusory, Ancient One. I thought you would've learned that lesson by now."

"Perhaps for some, Madame, but I have touched the deepest part of him, and there is no illusion there."

Chapter 7

I NEVER thought I'd find myself caught between two vampire women and not be in the least bit afraid. That was kind of funny, because these two vixens probably had to be the most dangerous pair of vampires I'd ever met. At least to my immortal soul. I was sure they'd leave me alive, if only to have the opportunity to play again.

Taylor smiled at me, wearing wicked sensuality like a second skin, and if Kristair hadn't gotten his hooks into me first, I wouldn't have hesitated one moment to take advantage of what she was offering. Her or Celeste. Jesus only knew how many men and women they'd corrupted.

"You should come by my own club. It's not quite so stuffy as Alette's."

I flicked a glance at Taylor, who leaned against the bar, blue-green eyes twinkling. She had a certain scent about her, leather and roses, clad in a sexy pinstripe pantsuit and deadly stilettos. "You're getting me into enough trouble as it is without me making it worse by going to your club. Not that I'm not intrigued."

"Don't you know it, and she's just getting started," Celeste said on my other side, laying her hand on my chest. "We'd have a great time, and you can bring the rest of your teammates."

I laughed out loud and finished the rest of my beer, setting the empty bottle on the bar. "Ladies, if I did that, training camp would be a disaster. The two of you would do more damage than an opposing team."

"I like you, Jake," Taylor purred, tracing a nail down the shell of my ear. "You've got balls. If you change your mind, my club is called the Slap and Tickle. It's down by the railroads."

I'd heard of that club. It had a reputation for being a wild place where anything went and everything did. "How come I'm not surprised you two run a place like that?"

"I don't run the place," Celeste demurred with a modest smile that did nothing to belie the wicked laughter in her eyes. "I merely play."

Taylor gave me a quick electric kiss on my lips and glanced toward Kristair. "I think we're making him jealous. I don't know how you did it, but you certainly lit a fire in him. It's kind of sexy."

"There's quite a bit more to him than what you see." My lover stared right at me, one elegant brow arched in question. He had the same expression on his face that he'd had when I walked away earlier, a combination of so damn puzzled and a little bit hurt. It was kinda sweet.

I had wanted to kiss him hard when I left the table but didn't, not wanting to offend his sensibilities about what was proper in a place like this. I was going to have to change my mind. That would wipe that expression off of his face, even if it would exasperate him.

"I never thought I'd see the Ancient One besotted," Taylor murmured as Kristair excused himself from the table and came toward us. "See you around, Jake." Then she was gone, tugging Celeste along with her. The two of them had their arms around each other's waists, moving with impossible grace in those heels.

I stayed against the bar, sipping my beer and watching Kristair's progress. I didn't think he understood just how elegantly sexy he was with his perfectly pressed dress pants, gleaming white shirt, and black vest. He had that innate kind of smooth grace and dignity that just made me long to drag him off somewhere, muss him up, and reveal the passionate man I knew.

Kristair stopped in front of me and searched my face. "Everything okay?"

"Sure."

Kristair glanced back at the girls, his brows furrowing. "You miss being with women?" he asked stiffly. It was a measure of his unease that he'd even entertain such a question, and it was so ridiculous that I couldn't help rolling my eyes.

"There isn't anybody out there that has what we have." Even without our mental connection, our bond went far deeper than I had ever dreamed was possible. Yep, I was changing my mind. I wrapped my arms around his waist and tugged him flush up against me as his dark, long-lashed eyes widened, and before he could protest, I kissed him.

Much to my surprise, he let me, though his eyes snapped heat when I let him go. "You're trouble in more ways than one," he muttered. Then he closed his eyes and a smile tugged at his lips. When he opened his eyes again, the tension seemed to have left him. "And I wouldn't change you one bit."

"Good." I took his hand and led him back out of the club, grateful to be away from the lingering eyes of the Pittsburgh vampires. When we'd settled into the Z28, I turned toward him. "I'll admit I like women. I like how they smell, and I like how soft they are, and how they curve in all the right places. And I know I'm a flirt, I'll always be a flirt, but I don't miss that part of my life, not when I have you."

Kristair laughed, a strange little sound like he'd just had a revelation. "I said something very similar about you back in the club."

"Now you've got my curiosity up."

"Alette asked me if I'd missed being a vampire. There are things that I loved about it, but it doesn't matter that I don't have them anymore. I guess there's no sense in regrets when we have what we fought for."

"Glad you understand," I leaned in and kissed him again, my tongue sinking into his mouth as his hand slid into my hair. "Is there any other place we have to go tonight?" I had visions in my head of taking him home and slowly stripping those clothes off of him and showing him just how much he did excite me.

"Unfortunately, yes. I need you to take me to Schenley Park."

"That's a good necking spot." I trailed my lips along his jaw. I could work with Schenley Park.

"We need to talk to Lisabeth and Artemise."

A cold finger ran down my spine, and I pulled back. "Way to ruin the mood there, Kristair." Artemise, I didn't mind so much. He had a funky sense of humor, but if Alette scared me, Lisabeth terrified me out of my damn skin. You couldn't get more unnatural than her.

The Z28 roared to life. It never ceased to give me a little thrill of pride as I turned my baby toward the park. "So what did Alette have to say about the homicidal maniac hunting down bloodsuckers and staking them in the sun? She wasn't getting twitchy, was she?" That was the last thing we needed. "It worries me. If this drags out too long we're going to have a handful of pissed of vampires."

"You would know her mental state if you'd stayed. Why'd you run off like that?"

"Alette looks at me like she wants to add me to her harem." I suppressed a shudder of revulsion. "I figured we'd play to our strengths. You're good at dealing with Madame Creepy. Besides, I thought she might open up to you more if I wasn't there. I get the feeling she doesn't know what to make of me."

"Your instincts were probably right. She was rather calm tonight though. Taylor and Celeste were there and their presence tends to make Alette less...." Kristair paused, searching for a polite way of phrasing it.

"Bat shit insane?"

Kristair chuckled. "That's one way of putting it. Did the younglings have anything to offer, other than the obvious, of course?"

His prim tone made me want to snicker, but somehow I managed to keep it in as we drove over the Liberty Bridge. The lights of the city stretched out before us, revealing the skyline. Pittsburgh was damn beautiful at night. It got a bad rap sometimes, but I really loved the place. It had a whole different vibe from back home, one that suited me.

"They didn't drag me off to their lair and have their wicked way with me." I reached over and linked my hand with Kristair's. "According to them, the vampires are getting nervous, some of the more itinerant bunch have already moved on to other cities. There's some grumblings toward Ussier and his gang, though no one's really dared to say anything out loud against them."

I swore as a guy cut me off and swerved around him, hitting the gas. "Jacob… you want me to talk about what scares me," Kristair said, his voice a little breathless, and when I took my eyes off the road to glance at him, he was gripping the door handle with white knuckles. "Your driving scares me. Will you please stick to one lane?"

"Ha! You may be two thousand years old, but I know driving. Why don't you stick to telling me what you found out. So did she have a conspiracy theory about what connected all the victims?"

"You're not going to like it," Kristair warned.

"And you're just mentioning this now?" My stomach sank. "Don't tell me it's the Syndicate again."

"What? Oh no, they've been obliterated, at least enough that they won't be a threat for a long time. No youngling wants to be associated with them anymore, so it's going to be hard to get new recruits. No, the Syndicate has been laid to rest; you don't need to worry about them anymore."

"Kristair, don't make me yank answers outta you," I growled, glaring at him as the Z28 zipped through traffic. I fucking loved my baby. Damn, she responded to my every touch.

"I'm the connection."

Silence descended as I tried to absorb the shock of that statement. The ominous chill his words provoked in me seemed to be a rather fair indication he was probably right, but I wasn't ready to believe my intuition.

"What makes you think you're the connection?"

"I knew all the victims." How could he sound so calm and matter-of-fact with an announcement like that?

"That's pretty fucking slim evidence if you ask me. Kristair, you're older than Christ. I'm sure you know most people. I bet you even went to Jesus's bar mitzvah. Got anything else?"

"Only two of the victims actually resided in Pittsburgh, the others were lured in and murdered within twenty-four hours of arriving."

"I still don't see…."

"Let me finish. One of the victims I'm not sure of, because she hadn't let anyone know she was in Pittsburgh, so they don't have a name for her. However, every single one of the others helped me research what happened to Ancients when they went mad and disappeared."

"Son of a fucking bitch." My hands tightened on the wheel, and I had to force myself to slow down before I plowed into a jersey wall or another car. "Why?"

"If we knew that, Jacob, we'd know who the killer was. I need to warn Lisabeth and Artemise. They also provided some insight into my research. It's odd they haven't already been targeted, but I won't quibble over one good thing out of this whole mess. Alette did tell me that one of the victims had come to see them before he was killed."

"Kristair, has it occurred to you that we might be walking into a trap? Schenley Park is huge. There's a ton of places where we could be ambushed during the day and we're going in there at night?" I didn't like it, felt like I was being lead around by the damn nose.

"We certainly wouldn't be able to talk to either of them during the day."

I narrowed my eyes, Kristair's continuing calm irking me. "That's not the point. What if they're the bad guys?"

"You cannot be serious. Lisabeth and Artemise may be many things, and both can be quite ruthless, but staking vampires in the sun is not their style. If they wanted to take somebody out, they wouldn't hide. They wouldn't play games. Their target would just disappear. Jacob, they're powerful enough they wouldn't need to go about in that manner. Besides, whoever did this had to be able to walk in the sun, and despite their knowledge, that is a whole new kind of trick."

"It is possible though," I argued. "Think about it. You've said yourself that vampires are capable of learning anything, it's just a matter of mental conditioning and will, right? They strike me as having quite a bit of both."

"That is valid reasoning," Kristair said, and I preened under Kristair's praise even though I knew the "but" was coming. "However, just say that they did learn how to walk in the sun. That's not some simple trick, realizing that it is possible would have been quite profound. Jacob, it would almost certainly have to trigger the Ascended."

"Dammit, I hate it when you're right. You're always right."

"Hardly." Kristair pointed to the sign as we entered the park on the Boulevard of the Allies. "Head to the conservatory."

"It's closed now."

"Do you argue with everything out of some innate need to be bullheaded?"

I started laughing at the testy sound of his voice. At least something could break through his façade. "Probably, though in this case I think I'm arguing because I prefer the simple solution to the alternative." Lights along the road began to turn off as we drove, and I frowned. The park closed at eleven, but for some reason, I had thought they kept them on all night.

Despite the late hour, the conservatory was aglow with a golden light, and I dismissed the phenomenon. I guess it didn't make much sense to waste electricity on streetlamps after hours. Besides, the conservatory provided more than enough light. The curved panes of glass made the whole structure seem like a delicate fairyland. I parked the Z28 as close to the entrance as possible and turned toward Kristair.

"I don't like you being the connection. I'd rather have it be anybody but you. That makes this shit personal and I don't know if I can fucking handle that."

"I must admit, I don't like it either. There isn't much we can do about it though. We certainly cannot ignore the situation." I sighed, and Kristair smiled as he took my hand. "If they wanted my attention, they certainly have it. Come on, *mo chroí*, the quicker we're done here, the quicker we can go home."

Grumbling, I got out of the car. I hated to admit Kristair was right. I didn't have to like it, but even if Ussier hadn't come to us, it looked like we were going to end up involved in this mess one way or another. We must have been giant magnets for supernatural shit or something.

Kristair laughed, and there was a funny, thoughtful expression on his face.

"What do you find so damn funny?"

"I was just thinking about how hard I tried to keep you out of this. I was so determined when the Syndicate first showed up to shield you from this part of my life. To keep them from ever learning you existed. I thought it could keep you safe." His expression sobered. "Keep you innocent."

"Jesus, Kristair, I haven't been innocent since Lauren and I stole my Ma's truck and went parking."

Kristair rolled his eyes. I loved making him do that. "That's not what I meant."

"I know what you meant. You've said it before. I'm not a violent man, at least not normally, and those I've killed, well, they needed killing. I don't think my soul's tarnished for defending myself or those I love. So you can stop fussing about it. My conscience lets me sleep at night."

"I'll try to stop fussing. I make no promises though."

"It's funny, about that night in your office when Dominic and Claudia showed up. I was so damn frustrated because I wanted to be by your side, helping you. I thought I'd just get in the way, that I was useless." I grinned. "Now I am involved and everyone knows how much I mean to you and it looks like we were both wrong. You don't need to try to shelter me from the big bad world, and I do have something to offer this partnership of ours."

Kristair looked at me over the roof of the Z28, and a smile tugged his lips. "I think I have to say that I'm glad we were both wrong. I'd rather have you at my side than locked up out of sight any day."

"Let's go before I drag you into the back seat and teach you about necking."

"Necking? This is the second time you've mentioned that. What is this necking?"

I groaned. "Come on, Kristair, later. Conversation first, necking second. Jesus, I can't believe I said that."

Chapter 8

"SO HOW is it these two can get in after hours?" Jacob asked as I tried the side entrance Alette had told me about. Sure enough, it opened.

"Money. Between Alette and Artemise, they've spent quite a bit on beautifying the city over the years. She got rich on the steel industry and I think she's been trying to make a few reparations since then. Regardless, she's behind many such things in the city, and Artemise, well, he has his own interests."

One of them, probably Artemise, had turned on the lights in most of the rooms. The conservatory was serene and beautiful, exotic plants spilling color and scent. "Let's try the Orchid Room first. I'm told that is considered to be a romantic setting."

"You mean they're here on a date?"

"I doubt they'd term it that way. In fact, I wouldn't say it to them if I were you. Artemise might find it amusing. I doubt she will."

"That's just gross, Kristair, she looks twelve." Jacob sounded utterly appalled.

"She's not twelve. I don't believe she has ever been twelve." I cut off Jacob's protest with a squeeze of his hand. "Would it help you to know that she'd already had a child of her own before she was created as a vampire?"

"Now you're just fucking with me." Jacob looked at me, his eyes searching. "No, you're not. Damn."

"Rules were different hundreds of years ago and life expectancy wasn't that long. Besides, she was a slave. It's not as if she had any say in the matter. She was expected to breed other slaves."

"I can't imagine anyone with the balls or idiocy enough to try that with her. I bet she was still creepy as a human."

"No doubt. I'm sure they lived to regret the decision. I believe the Orchid Room is this way. I haven't visited in quite awhile." We wandered around, hand in hand, half looking for Artemise and Lisabeth and half enjoying the sights on our own. The conservatory had a hushed atmosphere, quiet and soft, and the night sky through the multitude of windows was very dark. The air was layered with scents from sweet to spicy, earthy and damp.

"Oh wow," Jacob said as we entered the Victoria Room. "I never got to really appreciate this place last time I was here. I was being chased."

I frowned, turning toward him. He hadn't told me about that. "It's not when the Syndicate was hounding you last fall, was it?"

"Oh no, nothing like that. I'd come here with Steve and Tony during Halloween for their haunted house. The year before I met you."

I paused along the walkway to look around me. The glassed-in room featured a delicate gazebo in the center and a large pool with a fountain. The greenery was lush, as in all the other rooms, and the occasional splash of colors from the flowers made for a dramatic effect. It seemed to me that Jacob and I had not had many quiet moments like this where we could just be. Intimate moments.

It was a strange thought. It had been a very long time since I'd considered romance. Jacob and I had not had the luxury to pursue such things, and he deserved them. I would have to make it a priority when this investigation was done.

"You know, I've been thinking," Jacob said casually, messing with the controls of the interactive fountain, changing the lights and the way the water flowed. "That we should get married."

I stared at my lover in surprise. For the life of me, I couldn't figure out where this notion had come from. "I seem to recall us already being bonded. The night the...."

"Don't you dare, like I'd forget that night." Jacob turned around to face me, taking my other hand also, his bright blue eyes intent. For some reason, my stomach started doing weird flips. "I know we were bonded, and for me that's just as permanent, but there are some real reasons for getting married too."

My mouth went dry. He looked so serious. How long had he been considering this? I searched for my voice, which he seemed to have stolen. "Please, enlighten me."

"Okay, first we'll go into all the legal ones before I get into the personal ones. For instance...."

I shook my head. "I understand the legal ones. I'd never thought of it before, but I can see the validity of your concerns. Go on with the personal ones." That was where I was sure the crux of his argument lay.

My brain spun, not that I had any personal objections to getting married. To be honest, the thought had never entered my mind, not since I had become human. I just couldn't understand why Jacob didn't believe that the bond we'd created was enough. It was intense, personal, and intimate. The thought of parading around in one of the ceremonies I'd seen on TV was... distasteful.

"Well, for starters, my Ma isn't going to fall for me telling her we already did the deed in a private ceremony between the two of us months ago. I'd like her to know that you're the one I've chosen to be my mate for the rest of my life. She would want to be there when I get married. I bet Kayla would like to see that too."

"Invoking my daughter is very sneaky, Jacob."

"I know my man." Jacob grinned, and then he drew in a breath. "There's another reason. Something I've been thinking about since Rome."

I raised my brow. "That's quite a bit of time to have something on your mind. Is it something we've discussed?"

"No." Jacob hesitated. "I was never sure how you'd take it and we've been a little busy, plus I kinda needed the time to let the idea sink in myself."

Now my curiosity raged. I resisted the temptation to peek into his memories of that night to discover what he was talking about. Something this important to him, I'd rather have him tell me in his own words. Besides, he was nervous, a condition he was rarely afflicted with. So I waited him out.

Finally, Jacob let out an explosive breath, glaring at me. "Okay, so I want kids. I want a family with you and it would be a hell of a lot easier to adopt if we were married." He paused, a disgruntled expression crossing his face. "You know, that's a very bad habit you have, looking at me all enigmatic like that so I don't know what you're thinking. It's just wrong."

I barely heard him as I sank down onto one of the ledges around a flowerbed, my thoughts whirling even faster, something akin to panic gripping my insides. How could one man get me as flustered as Jacob seemed to do all the time? I looked up at him, latching onto his most absurd idea. "Whatever gave you the idea that I'd be a good father?"

Genuine surprise flashed across his face. "You're kidding me, right? Have you already forgotten Kayla?"

"I didn't adopt her, she adopted me. It was entirely her idea, and she didn't give me much choice in the matter." I grimaced. "I still think she was out of her mind to choose me." When she had been under my care, I'd constantly worried whether or not I was hurting her more than I was helping her.

Jacob's eyes softened as he looked down at me, and he touched his fingertips to the back of my scalp. "I think you doubt yourself too much when it comes to her, Kristair. In every way that matters, Kayla is your daughter. You may not have been there for her like you wanted to, but she's alive and strong because of you. And the fact that you felt inadequate and wanted to do more tells me you'd make a kickass father."

I shrugged, uncomfortable with Jacob's praise. Not that the brat seemed to care one way or another. By the dancing in his eyes, I'd have said he'd regained his equilibrium and was taking satisfaction in seeing me so off balance.

"So what do you say, Kristair? Will you marry me, or are you going to make me get down on my knee and embarrass us both?" He looked too roguish and charming at that moment for my own good, with that wicked smile on his sensuous lips.

"I should make you, springing this on me the way you did." My glare had no effect on him because he just grinned even more. "Yes, I'll marry you, *mo chroí*." My stomach flipped over at that, but Jacob's answering smile blazed through me. "I swear, though, I don't want anything fancy or a whole lot of people attending. I don't want that. Nice and simple, promise me."

"That's okay, I was thinking of it just being us, my Ma, and Kayla and Steve."

"You have given this some thought," I said, shaking my head in amazement.

Jacob took my hands and tugged me up again, wrapping his arms around my waist. "I have. I love you, Kristair." He kissed me, long and lingering, with a sweetness that made me ache inside. When we broke apart, my heart was racing.

If we hadn't had an agenda for being there, I'd've stripped him of his clothes on the spot and made love to him on the bench. If there wasn't a danger of Lisabeth and Artemise walking in on us, I'd've been tempted to do it regardless of our investigation. "I love you, too. Now come on, this is not a moment I want others to interrupt."

"Wait, you still haven't said anything about kids. Seriously, what do you think about adopting?"

"Don't push it. That's something I need to ponder some before I answer. I'm still adjusting to the idea of being an engaged man. I've had quite a bit of turmoil in my life this last year." A smile tugged my lips. "I blame you," I teased.

Sure enough, Jacob's eyes blazed. "Start running now, Kristair, and I may be nice when I finally catch you."

I laughed. Served Jacob right. "Maybe I'm not interested in you playing nice."

My lover growled and pushed the door open into the Sunken Garden. "Just you wait until we're done here, Kristair, just you fucking wait."

Jacob's threats had a way of making my blood sing in anticipation. The Sunken Garden was a long, low walkway with the plants growing high on either side like a half-buried grotto. The gentle gurgle of the stream was a quiet background song as the two people we came to meet entered through the door across on the other side.

Artemise smiled in pleasure and came forward, cane in hand. Lisabeth held back, black eyes assessing, before she joined him. "Kristair, Jacob, it is good to see you again," Artemise greeted and shook both of our hands. "I'd heard you were doing well, my old friend, but I never thought our paths would cross again."

"Shit has a way of happening," Jacob said, and Artemise chuckled.

"Succinctly put, young man." His eyes darkened as he gestured us to a bench and held out a hand for Lisabeth before finally sitting himself. "I take it that this visit has everything to do with the rather unpleasant individual who's taken to haunting our fair city."

"You'd be correct." Once again, I wished that Artemise had been alone. "For the moment, I'd like to keep this conversation between the four of us until we've had a chance to track down our leads and see if they really have merit or not."

Lisabeth's gaze sharpened, but she didn't say anything, and Artemise nodded. "Of course, my friend, proceed."

Jacob's presence beside me was solid and reassuring as I told the two vampire elders everything I knew. It was such an odd feeling of role reversal, almost unsettling. The last time I had talked with these two, I had been far more powerful than they. Now I seemed almost diminished, aware of my own frailty as I hadn't been in a long time. Still, I was far older, and at least to these two, my years counted for something.

And Jacob had worried I'd forget what I had become, that I was now merely human. I'd have to tell him later that his fears were groundless. A predator understood where he sat on the food chain. So did prey, for that matter.

"Very interesting," Lisabeth said when I was done, her expression inscrutable. "Gerard had come to speak to us, as Alette told you. He'd been troubled over the last couple months from some visions he'd been having. He wanted to talk with us about them. Afterward, he left."

"What were his visions about?" Jacob asked, not scoffing at the idea as he might have once done.

"A war in the heavens. Worlds being ripped apart. Nothing clear, you understand, Jacob, that's the way his visions always worked. It's up to the person to interpret them as they will. Though sometimes I've wondered if Gerard wasn't influenced by events in the media. He could be gullible, all of the recent theories about 2012 could've affected him," Artemise said thoughtfully, chafing the head of his cane. "Still, we live in monumental times, my friends."

"Just wonderful, I'd prefer quieter times myself." Jacob looked at me. "Anything else you wanted to add?"

"I'd like to reiterate that if my theory is correct, you two are the most at risk. I'm only going on what I know so far, but tomorrow I'll start tracking down some old contacts. If any more of them have been assassinated, then we'll know that it has to do with my research and we can figure out where to go from there."

"I'd be very surprised to find out you're wrong. I trust your instincts, Kristair." Artemise's brow furrowed. "Under normal circumstances, I'd never ask, but perhaps it might be better if we knew what happened between your disappearance in the warehouse and when you came back as a human."

"I cannot," I replied as Jacob stiffened beside me. I echoed his reaction. "Even if I wanted to tell you, it wouldn't be permitted. I have no doubt I'd be eliminated before I said three words. Some things, Artemise, must be found out on their own."

"Somehow, I thought that would be the case. Don't worry, my old friend, I won't ask again."

"If there is a connection, we'll figure it out." Jacob rose and held out his hand to me. "Are you ready? There isn't much point in rehashing this. Tell Ussier to watch out for any new arrivals to the city. They'd almost have to be targets."

"If so, we'll pass it on to you." Artemise said. "I'll stop by in a few nights if I haven't heard from you to see if you've learned anything new."

"Fair enough." I shook his hand again and nodded to Lisabeth, who watched us with her cool, unreadable eyes. "Enjoy the rest of your evening."

Both Jacob and I were quiet as we walked back out to the Camaro. Thunder still rumbled and heat lightning lit up the clouds, but the storm didn't seem any closer to breaking than before. Jacob slid behind the wheel and took off deeper into the park. "I think that went pretty good. What do you think?"

I rubbed my finger along my temple, weighing the conversation. "It went about as suspected. Artemise is an ally and Lisabeth is an unknown." I smiled as Jacob grumbled. As much as he complained about this whole other world that he sometimes was forced to interact with, he was uniquely suited to it. "However, I do believe we're not in any danger from her. We're too valuable."

"I don't know if that's any better, and right now I don't give a crap." Much to my confusion, Jacob turned onto Panther Hollow Road and pulled over when we reached the lake. The environs were very dark around us except for the Cathedral of Learning rising up behind the trees, lighting the sky like a beacon.

"You know, I used to think of you as the lord of the tower, all arrogant and alone," Jacob said, clambering into the back seat.

I twisted around to face him, cocking my head in question. "What are you doing?"

"Our work's done for the night and we're now engaged." Jacob crooked his finger at me. "Come 'ere, love, it's long since past time that I taught you about necking."

"Here?" I had no idea what Jacob meant about this necking, but it had to be something sexual, considering his wicked expression. The back of his Camaro, with the rear window sloping low, didn't seem the place for such activities. My pulse started to race though, despite my best efforts.

Jacob smiled, a knowing sort of smile. "Yes, here, that's a part of it. Now get in the back seat with me, Kristair, or I'll drag you back here."

"You will, will you?" I said, amused at the thought.

He nodded. "I would, and then I'd have to punish you."

"You wouldn't dare." As soon as the words left my mouth, I rethought them. He would dare and more. Before Jacob could reply, I climbed awkwardly into the back seat to join him. "You're incorrigible."

Chapter 9

I TURNED to face Kristair and slid my hand around the nape of my lover's neck, fingers pressing into his warm skin. His expression was so wary it was almost comical. "You fuss too much, Kristair." I leaned in until I was just a hair's breadth away from his lips. "Now shut up and kiss me."

"Jacob, somebody might come by and see us."

I'd never realized what a streak of prudery Kristair had. When he had been an Ascended and had been sent back to me as a shade, he'd walked around buck-assed naked, though now I would bet he never would've done that if there had been a chance anyone other than me could see him.

"So what, let them look." I laughed softly and rubbed my tongue lightly over his upper lip. "This is what it's all about. I've got a sexy bitch of a car, a hot man in my arms, and all the time in the world. Now kiss me."

Kristair ceased his protests, and his lips were firm as he kissed me. When they parted, my tongue swept into his mouth. Surrender never tasted sweeter on anybody than it did on him. I could have just held him and kissed him forever, savoring the slow burn. His breath came quicker against my cheek, and oh, how I loved that sensation. His breath, his warmth, all signs of what he had given up for me. To stay with me.

"Fuck, I love you," I murmured against his mouth as the kiss broke.

I felt his smile as his fingers came up to lightly circle my throat. "You know, when you first mentioned necking, it made me think of biting you."

I shivered. "I miss that, not enough for you to become a vamp again, but I do miss it." I tipped my head back as his mouth slid down my neck, and then his tongue was tracing along the vein just as he used to before sinking his fangs into me.

"I miss it too. I loved your scent when you knew I was going to bite you, so sharp with anticipation, and the way you tasted, fiery and passionate. I could've gotten drunk off of you." Kristair nipped the tender skin of my throat, and I caught my breath.

"Jesus, Kristair." I unbuttoned his vest, tugged his dress shirt free from his waistband, and slid my hands under it. His stomach tightened under my touch. "You make me crazy."

"We must be crazy to be doing this in a public place."

I stifled a laugh and kissed him again, determined to make him forget all about where we were and think only of the pleasure of kissing and touching. Slow heat simmered as our tongues tangled lazily. My fingers stroked his stomach, slid around to his hip, and he made an impatient sound as he tried to press closer to me.

Kristair's hand slid down my back, under my sports coat, and then he stiffened, pulling back. "Jacob, get rid of the gun."

"Whatever you say, it would only get in the way for what I intend." I tugged off the holster, left the gun inside, and put it all in the front seat.

"And just what do you intend?"

"You'll see," I whispered, and I reached for him again. This time, he didn't protest at all. The stubble growing in on his jaw teased my lips as I kissed along there, and his hand sank into my hair as I nipped and sucked.

"I think I'm in trouble," Kristair murmured.

I grinned against his throat and nipped again. "Very much." Once again, I slipped my hands under his shirt, tugging him over me until he straddled my lap, his head tucked to keep from banging into the rear window. "Mmmm, free rein." Our lips met, and as we kissed I squeezed his ass. Lord, he had a fine one, more than a handful, and all thoughts about keeping this tame fled. I wanted to see him with his pants around his thighs, on his hands and knees in the backseat as I fucked him.

My cock throbbed to life, and Kristair tore his mouth free with a soft gasp. "Why don't we go home, *mo chroí,* and we can finish this there."

"Oh hell, no, I'm having too much fun to stop now." I unbuttoned his shirt enough to find one flat nipple and caught it between my teeth as his breath hissed through his teeth.

"Jacob."

I smiled at the sound of his voice when he said my name. I'd be hearing that for the rest of my life, when I woke up and when I went to sleep. On our wedding day. I grinned at the thought. My lover, my soon-to-be husband, my damned miracle.

I cupped his cock in my hand, feeling the heat through his pants. I rubbed the hard length of him and thrust my tongue into his mouth, swallowing his low, urgent groan. Kristair fisted both his hands in my hair, tugging my head back, and bit my throat. Fuck. Not enough to break the skin, but god, it felt fucking good.

"So would you let me do anything I want?" Good intentions were overrated, and I ditched them now with a wicked chuckle as I impatiently fought with the rest of the buttons on his shirt.

"Don't you anyway?" Kristair groaned.

"True enough." I grabbed one of his hands and brought it down to my aching cock, groaning as he squeezed. "I want your mouth, and then I want you to ask me to fuck you."

Kristair shivered and bit my throat again. Then his hands were undoing the zipper, and I moaned as he slid his hand inside my pants and began stroking me through my boxers. "You want all that? What if I don't?"

"Then I'm just going to have to fuck with you until you do," I said, breathless as desire raced through me.

He laughed softly as a cold slither of awareness touched my mind. My hands tightened on his biceps, and I turned my head to stare out the window. It was dark, so damned dark outside, and suddenly I felt very exposed.

"What is it?" Kristair straightened, pulling his hand free of my jeans.

"Something's coming, can't ya feel that?"

Kristair tensed, his head cocking to the side as if listening to something only he could hear. "Yes, get your gun."

The rear windshield shattered, showering us with glass. To my horror, something wet struck the back of my neck, and then a head dropped onto the seat next to us. I recoiled with a shout, bile rising into my throat. "Holy fucking shit!"

Dead, colorless eyes stared back at me from an ashen face, dark hair matted with blood and worse stuck to its cheek.

"Stamatis." Kristair snarled, and then his warmth was gone from my lap as he scrambled out of the back of the car and took off.

"Shit." Cursing, I struggled to get my jeans back together and get out of the car at the same time. "Don't you dare; wait for me." I slammed the door shut in time to see Kristair disappear into the trees.

I was going to fucking kill him.

I took enough time to grab my gun from the front seat, and, keeping my eyes away from the damage to my car, I took off after Kristair. As much as I wanted to shout for him, I forced myself to keep quiet. There was no damn way of knowing how many of them there were, and there was no sense in announcing where the hell I was.

Several yards into the trees, I lost track of them as utter darkness consumed me. Even if there hadn't been a new moon or clouds, I wouldn't have been able to penetrate the closely woven branches.

Setting my jaw, I pressed forward. I stretched out one hand to keep from getting struck in the face and kept the other one clasped around my gun. Twigs caught my clothing, slapped against my palm, and the underbrush crackled despite my efforts to be quiet.

There were hundreds of acres in this park. That was it. Kristair was going to start carrying a cell phone whether he like it or not. The fact that I wouldn't have dared call him right now didn't matter. It was the fucking principle of the matter. Since we didn't have our connection anymore, I had to have a way to get a hold of him in situations such as this when we were being stalked by crazy motherfuckers.

Fury built up with each yard. Hadn't we just fucking talked about this the night before? Hadn't Kristair promised me he would think before he went all gung-ho super predator mode? He'd sworn he'd remember that he was human now and use extra caution. He'd given me his word.

It was as dark as Satan's asshole underneath the trees, and every sound was magnified by the knowledge that there was a very sick individual somewhere out there with us. Every crack of a dry twig, every goddamn cricket's keening song leapt out on me from all sides.

The bastard had thrown a head through my windshield. And not just any head, but the head of a vampire. And if he had been friends with Kristair, he had to have been old on top of it, so we weren't talking about some youngling, powerless bloodsucker either. And my lover hadn't taken a moment to think before chasing after him, weaponless. Like he was still some badass himself with super powers.

It took several minutes before the awareness that I was being herded broke through my seething thoughts. Sweat broke out on my brow, and my hand tightened on the gun. There were parts of this park that probably didn't see people for days, and that was where I was being driven, further away from the car, the roads. Why hadn't we paid more attention to all the lights going out in the park before? I had no doubt that whoever was behind this had been waiting for their chance.

And now they were behind me. How the hell had that happened?

With ice trickling down my spine, I began circling back toward the car, trying to get a glimpse of my pursuer in the process. I walked as fast as I could and while still remaining quiet. I had never been so grateful for all those years I'd spent trekking through the swamps with my friends. Growing up near a bayou had taught me a few tricks and about sneaking around outdoors. *Come on, Kristair, where are you?*

The trees opened up into a little clearing, and a rush of relief swept through me as I saw my lover emerge out into it, a few feet off to the side. Inwardly, I cursed my own stupidity. I'd spent this entire time running from Kristair instead of toward him. I might as well stamp "idiot" on my forehead.

I stepped forward to call out to Kristair, and the words died on my lips as he turned toward me, looking all around him intently. I couldn't say what it was about him that chilled me so, what was so very wrong, but I shrank back further into the shadows and froze.

His eyes passed over me. The faint light that managed to make its way through the trees gleamed on his bald head. He turned and loped into the trees away from me with the terrifying speed of an alligator that had zeroed in on its prey. I listened, still frozen, until the sound of his passing had disappeared and the normal song of the woods returned.

"Fuck." I let out an explosive breath. What the hell had I been thinking about? Kristair had been right there and I'd let him walk away! Snarling at myself, I stalked after him, but he was long since gone, as if he'd never been there. Where could he be?

Weariness and a sick sensation in my stomach plagued me. I leaned my palm against a tree trunk, drinking in the feeling of the rough bark, the scent of earth and greenery. Real things in this hellish dark. It was almost as if I'd fallen into a waking nightmare.

There had to be a way of finding Kristair that didn't involve me running around the park like a clueless jackass. Kristair and I were still connected. I didn't care what he or anyone else said, we were. I might not hear every thought, I might not feel him so intensely, but it was still there, dammit.

Leaning against the tree, I closed my eyes and pictured Kristair. The way his dark eyes lit up with enthusiasm when a new idea came to him or how they softened when he looked at me. The way his lips would tug into a smile or frown in thoughtfulness, his disapproving expressions and quiet laughter. I had once felt his heartbeat inside of me every time he wished it, and now it seemed, in that silent moment, I could sense an echo of that.

Following the instinct that tugged at me, I pushed away from my tree and started tracking him. I must've walked half a mile before the trees began to thin out again on a hill that sloped downward. The pull was stronger now, and I paused at the tree line, straining to see in the dark.

A very familiar snarl drifted up through the night. "Kristair." I raced headlong down the hill, bracing myself to keep from tripping and falling the rest of the way. Someone laughed, low and throaty, shadows writhed, and I came close enough to make out Kristair grappling with a tall, slight figure on the ground.

The other person kicked him off, and Kristair went flying back, landing hard before rolling up into a crouch. Blood trickled from the corner of his lip, and he touched his tongue to it, a slow smile breaking out over his face that about took my breath away, it was so feral.

His opponent laughed again, and shock jolted through me. It was a woman I'd heard. She jumped to her own feet and pushed a tangle of hair back from her face. It looked inhuman, like a blank mask on top of skin, her features blurred and indistinct.

I frowned, coming closer up behind her, and pulled my gun. I raised it and pointed it toward the back of her head. There was something familiar about the woman, but I couldn't quite put my finger on it.

"What do you want? Why are you hunting vampires?" Kristair straightened, his eyes flicking to me as I came within several feet of them, keeping my gun trained on her.

"You really have no idea what's going on around you." She shook her head, her voice laced with mock pity. "But you will, before it's all done and over with, you'll know, and you'll weep alone for centuries."

"Just say the word, Kristair," I said, bristling at the threat to him and cocking the gun.

The woman turned her head, glancing at me over her shoulder. "I'm not afraid of your weapon. But maybe you're not smart enough to figure that out. I ripped off a vampire's head with my bare hands, what does that tell you?" She smiled as Kristair snarled and took a threatening step toward her. "Call off your pretty boy or he's dead right now."

"I don't think so," Kristair said, his voice icy. "You kill him now and it ruins your game, doesn't it? That's all this is, isn't it? A game. You wanted my attention and now that you've got it you want to try to confuse me."

"Close, but not quite."

She was bluffing, or at least I hoped to hell she was bluffing. One thing was for certain, with her odd face and those white creepy eyes blazing through her tangled hair, she wasn't an ordinary human. There went the hope that we were just dealing with a vampire hunter.

"Why are you killing vampires?" Kristair demanded again. "One way or another, I'll drag the answers from you."

"You two? I hardly think so. You'd better hurry and figure it out, Kristair. You're running out of allies. Do you know why Nerissa turned you into a vampire Kris? Because you never stopped fighting. Even when you were dying, your lifeblood spilling on the ground, you wouldn't stop. That should make this game all the more interesting."

I sensed Kristair's sudden tension, the coiling strength of his body just before he attacked, but then the woman was gone, scampering off into the shadows quicker than a blink. Just fucking gone like she'd never been there at all.

Kristair snarled and leapt forward again like he was about to go after her, and I grabbed his arm. His vest was torn and the white shirt was splattered with blood, but from what I could tell, it wasn't his. Must've been that guy, Stamatis, he'd called him. "Just where do you think you're going?" I snapped, furious all over again that he'd gone running off once already. "She's fucking with us. We're never going to be able to find her in those trees unless she wants us to find her. She has all the advantage."

Kristair quivered, seething. I could practically taste his need to hunt her down. He shook it off and glared at me, struggling to get himself under control. I studied the trees again, getting the feeling we were alone again.

"You and I are going to have words, Kristair, just sayin'." The man managed to rack up some rather unusual enemies, and I couldn't figure out how he did it. He wasn't an ass, he didn't flaunt himself or try to screw people over. He was content with his books and his quiet life. But damn, people just wanted to fuck with that.

He didn't say anything, and when I looked at him, he was glaring at the spot where she had disappeared, his jaw set. I touched his hand. "Stamatis, he was one of those you used to trade information with?"

He nodded.

Thunder rumbled overhead, the air heavy with the promise of a storm that just wouldn't come. I slid the safety on the gun, tucked it into my waistband, and took his hand. "Come on, let's go home."

Chapter 10

IT WOULD take several days for Jacob to recover from the double insult of having his beloved car vandalized and me forgetting to show caution so soon after I'd promised to do so. I was torn between wanting to placate him and just letting the storm ride out. Jacob didn't stay mad long, even in situations like this, and he was easier to reason with once his fury was spent.

I'd messed up. I knew I had.

It seemed instinct ran far deeper than I'd expected. When our interlude in the park had been interrupted and I'd been confronted yet again by another fallen colleague, it had been enough to set my blood on fire. Just knowing that my enemy was close at hand threatening the both of us was enough for me to taste blood in my mouth. I craved the thrill of the hunt, the savage triumph of destroying my enemy.

Jacob probably wouldn't be reassured, but I was gratified to learn I hadn't completely lost my predator's edge by becoming human. I might have been slower and weaker than I had been, but I'd caught the woman. Next time I wouldn't let myself be distracted and I'd drag her before Ussier.

My phone made a funny little bleeping sound, and I warily stared at where it sat on the table in my library. Jacob had insisted on giving it to me this morning when he'd dropped by soon after I'd gotten to the library. Wanting peace between us, I'd agreed, though I hated the idea of being tied to a phone. I didn't mind Jacob being able to reach me at any time, but the thought of being available to anybody who called was irksome.

Making calls on it wasn't difficult, and Jacob had thoughtfully added in the phone numbers for his own phone and Kayla's, not that I remembered how to access the contacts. I just dialed direct, much to his disgust when he caught me doing it.

The only problem was I knew that bleeping sound meant my lover had sent me another text message, and for the life of me, I still had no idea how to recover them. I picked it up and flipped it over. Sure enough, on the screen, there was a little envelope mocking me.

This was the fifth or sixth message he'd sent in the last hour or so. Whatever it said couldn't be that important, or he'd have followed it up with a call when I hadn't answered. But I itched to know regardless.

I carefully dialed Kayla's phone number. She'd help me without too much teasing, but when I heard my daughter's voice as she answered, all thoughts of text messages left my mind. Kayla sounded tired and drained, and my hackles raised. "What's wrong?"

"Kris?" Her voice brightened, though it seemed forced to me. "Where are you calling from? I don't recognize this number."

"Jacob insisted that I have a cell phone. He went out first thing this morning and bought me one."

She snickered. "Father, you may be two thousand years old, but if you're going to keep up with Jake you've *got* to join the twenty-first century."

Kayla wouldn't be able to foist me off that easily. "So are you going to tell me what's bothering you? You sound tired."

"That's because I am tired. There's so much to do to set up the clinic and it's frustrating because I want it to be done now and at the same time, I want it to be done right. It seems like I'm there night and day."

"How is Steve doing?" I could be polite, as much as I wanted to demand to know why he wasn't taking better care of her. Kayla seemed stressed enough without me adding to it.

"He's even more wiped out than I am. And before you say something, he is taking care of me. There's just more details involved in starting up a place like this than I had ever imagined. But that's not why you called. What's new with you?"

I thought about Jacob's proposal, however, that was something I'd rather reveal in person. And I wasn't about to mention the mission Jacob and I were involved in either. She would only worry, and she clearly had enough on her mind. "You mean I can't call just to check in on you?"

"You usually don't. You know it would just irk me. So what gives?"

"Don't laugh. I need to know how to retrieve text messages from a cell phone." I paused as she stifled a snicker, but she managed to contain herself. "Jacob has sent me several in the last hour or so and I want to know what he's up to. He's causing trouble, I just know it, or he would have called instead."

"I have no doubt you're right," Kayla said, sounding both fond and amused. "Okay, it's not that difficult." I took careful notes as she ran through the process. We talked for a few minutes more about the progress she and Steve had made on her clinic before she hung up. She sounded much better by that point, and I felt free to let my concentration return to Jacob's messages.

I followed Kayla's instructions to retrieve them, my curiosity firing anew at his first one.

Jake: *Just left the gym. Heading home for a shower cause I love ya like that.*

I scratched my head, trying to figure out the need for that bit of information, not that I minded the image of Jacob in the shower at all. It was rather nice. But it seemed odd he would go out of his way to tell me. And the tone of the message was almost playful, very much at odds with the attitude I'd expected given our evening.

The next message had arrived only twenty minutes later.

Jake: *At home now, grabbing lunch. Thinking of you and that library.*

I didn't need any more clarification to know what he was thinking. Jacob had some very vivid fantasies of me and my library. Some of which were locked in my head, thanks to the ritual that had given me all of his memories. I was sure he'd come up with more since then. I couldn't begin to imagine what he found so appealing about the combination.

Jake: *Squeaky clean. Still thinking of the library. Dirty thoughts.*

A tingle of awareness went through me. I knew without looking at the other messages that Jacob was on his way over here intent on whatever fantasy he was entertaining at the moment. This was his way of trying to say he had warned me while knowing I shouldn't have been able to get the messages at all.

He wanted the control.

The tingle turned into a shiver.

Jake: *On my way, you have 30 mins to call me back before I bend you over your table.*

My heart quickened at that image as I scrolled down to the next message.

Jake: *20 mins, your ass is mine.*

Jake: *10 mins, oh the look that is going to be on your face.*

What the hell did the brat think he was doing, texting while driving? At that moment, my phone chimed again. My heart skipped a beat and my body stirred as I looked at the final message.

Jake: *Took me too long to find a parking space. Hope I didn't leave you waiting.*

My thoughts churned as I shut the phone and sat it down on the table, staring at it over my steepled fingers. That Jacob would do what he set out to do I had no doubt, but that didn't mean I had to make it easy for him.

Jacob had his wicked way all too often as of late. As much as it made my knees weak, this time I wouldn't give in so quickly, if at all. A little challenge would be good for him. Glancing at my watch, I realized Jacob was in all likelihood already in the building. I rose, flicked off the lights to the stacks, and disappeared along the dark rows of my books.

Moments later, the door opened and awareness of my lover flooded through me. The hunt was on. My cell phone trilled, Jacob cursed, and I smiled. Oh no, *mo chroí*, you're not going to get me that easily.

"I take it you got my messages," Jacob said conversationally, walking down the aisle between the stacks. Then he paused and turned into them. Listening to the sound of his voice, I began circling around to come up behind him. "I guess you realized that talking wouldn't work, since you never called back, so that means I own your ass."

Jacob was still furious about the events of the previous night. I had hoped the thorough, detailed cleaning we'd done of his car late into the night and getting the new rear windshield installed would cool him down. He had yet to address how I'd taken off into the woods or how I'd confronted that woman on my own. And I was tired of waiting for the explosion.

A good wrestling match for domination would heat up our blood and get the unspoken out in the open. I slipped into another row, conscious of how Jacob was closing in on me as if he somehow had a direct link to me. Maybe somehow he did, after all, he'd managed to find me in the vastness of Schenley Park.

I eased around the corner into another aisle and ran on light feet, hoping to catch him unawares before he realized my change of direction. "I bet you're thinking that if you just stay quiet, I'll think you're not really in here and just go away. Come on, Kristair, you afraid a little sex is going to sully your precious books?"

I came around the corner, right behind him. He stiffened, and I caught him as he began to spin around. "I've got you now, *mo chroí*. I think your ass is mine, not the other way around." I nipped the back of his neck. "I hope you remembered to bring some lube with you."

Jacob wrapped his hand around my scalp and twisted to kiss me hard and possessive. He bit my lip hard, and I tasted my own blood as I kissed him back. We both growled, and I began walking him toward the table. To my surprise, he didn't fight me at all. His fingers twined with mine against his stomach, and the strength in him took my breath away. How had I not appreciated that before?

"You aren't gonna win, Kristair, not today," Jacob said against my lips. "You don't wanna win, but that don't gotta mean you have ta stop fighting me. It's turning me the fuck on."

With that, he pulled free of my embrace and spun around me. He was quick too; I had to give him that much. His hands gripped my shoulder and wrist, propelling me forward to the table. Adrenaline pumping, I flipped him over my shoulder onto the table and grinned as the air whooshed from his lungs. "I don't intend to, Jacob." I fisted my hand in his hair, tugged his head to the side, and bit his throat.

"Fuck," Jacob cursed, digging his fingers into my scalp and shuddering. "Fucking cheater. You know what that does to me." I sucked hard, nipping and teasing until his skin felt hot against my lips. I pulled back and ran my thumb over the livid mark on his neck.

"Just as you know how you get to me, so I say we're even."

"Yeah, I know just how to get to you." Jacob's lips curved dangerously. Then I heard the clatter of books and a cell phone falling to the floor.

"You are such a brat." I pushed away from the table and bent over to scoop up my precious books. I knew Jacob did it to get the upper hand, yet I could no more leave them lying on the floor than I could destroy one of them.

Jacob slid off the table and grabbed me around the waist even as I set the books safely on a chair. My breath came faster as we wrestled, my body coming alive. I twisted around behind him again and pushed him against the edge of the table. "Is this what you wanted, Jacob? Is your blood on fire yet?" I nipped the shell of his ear and popped open the button, tugging down the zipper as I ground against his ass.

"Just getting started." Jacob shoved back against me and swept his leg out, knocking me to the ground. Then he was on top of me and we were rolling around on the floor. The mood was both playful and dangerous. My cock surged as I slid my hands down the back of his jeans, squeezing his ass.

"This position's just as good," I groaned as he bit my collarbone.

"Yeah, flat on your back." Jacob snickered, grabbing a hold of my shirt and ripping it open.

"Jacob Corvin! How am I supposed—"

My lover silenced the complaint with a kiss, and I promptly dismissed my torn shirt. I was being consumed by the heat of his mouth, rough and possessive. Shoving his jeans down around his thighs, I sank a finger inside him, pushing past that tight ring of muscle, groaning in triumph.

Jacob moaned into my mouth and clenched around my finger. "Fuck, that feels good. I'll have to indulge you another day, but not this one."

I ignored that statement and thrust my finger again as the hard length of his cock throbbed against my own. Why was I still wearing my pants? Jacob needed to fix that. "You still seem to be laboring under the impression that you're winning."

I dragged his T-shirt off of him as he knelt up, and just looking at Jacob made me go all hot and liquid inside. The torc gleamed against his throat, the patch of hair between his pecs a golden brown that matched the sparser hair between his thighs. I rolled his balls between my fingers and then stroked his cock, long tugs that had him leaping hot and alive in my palm.

"Fuck… you've got magic hands," Jacob panted as I squeezed his length and rubbed my thumb over the head, smearing the pre-come. His eyes went hot on my face. "Lick it, Kristair."

I shivered, automatically responding to the command in his voice. "Like this?" I teased, bringing my thumb to my lips, never taking my eyes from his face as I laved it with my tongue.

He groaned, leaning back down to kiss me hard, and then shoved away long enough to yank off my shoes and pants. "Stop fighting me, Kristair." He jumped to his feet and held out a hand to me.

I hesitated, a part of me relishing the battle between us, but I couldn't deny the way surrendering to my lover made me feel. I gave

Jacob my hand, and he smiled, helping me up off of the floor. He slid his arms around me and walked me back to my table.

The next thing I knew, I was lying back on it and Jacob was stepping between my spread thighs as my breath quickened with anticipation. I wrapped my legs around his waist and drew him even closer as he fumbled for something in his jeans pocket before kicking them the rest of the way off.

Heart pounding, I slid my hand around the nape of his neck and tugged him down as I felt his hand fumble between us. I bit his chest and turned my head, his nipple dragging across my cheek until I tugged it into my mouth by his nipple ring.

"God damn it, Kristair. Yer making it a little hard to concentrate here," Jacob cursed.

Then he was gripping my hips, pulling me closer to the edge of the table, his lubed cock pushing into me. The burning ache turned me inside out. Only Jacob did this to me. Made me crave and want so much that I couldn't think past the pleasure of him penetrating me. His hands slid down the backs of my thighs, hooking my knees over his shoulders, and he bent my legs back against my chest as he leaned over me and sank in deeper.

"Jacob." My fingers pressed into his shoulders and the back of his neck as he began to move with hard, fast thrusts. I shuddered as the pleasure whipped through me and slid one hand between my thighs, tugging on my balls before I began stroking my cock.

"Fuck, baby, that's a beautiful sight."

"I thought you might like that." The scent of old books and leather, sex, and my lover combined in a heady fragrance. It was far more potent that I would've thought. And the fierce expression of lust and love on Jacob's face told me that the experience of fucking me in my own library was everything he'd fantasized it would be. "You like seeing me in this manner, don't you?"

"You mean without the oh-so-proper façade? Fuck yeah. Seeing you without that cloak of control, your oh-so-dignified air, with your eyes so hot and your expression needy. I love seeing all that wild emotion you carry written so clear on your face."

"Makes you crazy." And knowing that made my flashes of vulnerability worth every moment of them.

My thighs ached, and the table was hard and cold against my back, but the aching desire was incredible. Jacob's thrusts became harder and quicker. Then he groaned, and I clenched around him so I could feel every throb of his cock inside of me as he came.

I gasped as he abruptly left my body. Jacob knocked my hands aside, and his hot mouth sank over my cock. I dug my hands into his hair, on fire with need. His fingers wrapped in a hard ring around the base, and my heart pounded.

"Jacob, Jacob, Jacob...." I chanted his name, cursed him and begged in turn, and my lover didn't let me go until I was aware of nothing else but him, until my pleas echoed off the chamber walls.

Chapter 11

I LEANED back on my elbows and watched Kristair crawl around on the ground as he searched for the buttons to his shirt. I didn't know what he planned on doing with them when he found them. Unless he had a sewing kit stashed around here someplace. If anybody did, it would have been my lover. Always prepared. Wasn't that a motto or something? Suited Kristair perfectly.

Lord, he had a really fine, fuckable ass, round, with just the right amount of jiggle when we fucked. It was the kind of ass you definitely noticed as it went by, and right now it was in the air, his fine work pants clinging to every sweet inch. It was a crime that he was crawling around partially clothed. He should have been naked.

Kristair turned his face toward me, his expression unreadable—no surprise there. Then it softened into a slight smile. "I hope this encounter in the library was everything you'd fantasized it to be. But whatever it is you're contemplating, don't."

"I was thinking about how damn tempting you look on your hands and knees. And I'm working on summoning up the energy to go over and take advantage of it." I snickered as Kristair stood up and tossed me my jeans. He was so damn predictable.

"Get dressed, we need to talk."

"Hey, that's normally my line." I tugged my jeans on and scooped my T-shirt off the floor as Kristair dumped half a dozen buttons on the table. In my personal opinion, Kristair should have gone shirtless more often. I could have stared at his long, lean muscles, his dark, olive-golden, tattooed skin, and the thin trail of black hair down his chest and stomach for a very long time. Even if it was distracting.

"So what do you want to talk about? My foul attitude since last night?" At that moment, I was fine, unless I thought about all the bullshit too much. Then my blood started to heat again.

"No." Kristair turned to gave me, his expression grave. "First off, I want to apologize. You were right, my old instincts are too strong. I shouldn't have run off without you last night. You have a right to be furious. You only want to keep me safe, the way I want to keep you safe. Sometimes, I forget that."

I scrubbed a hand through my hair, fisting it tight. "Don't say you're sorry, 'cause you're just gonna do it again next time. I figure you've survived for two thousand years. I need to trust in your survival instincts. Otherwise, I'll go fucking nuts."

"Well, my survival instincts tell me that you were right. I do need a weapon. Whatever that woman is, she's fast and strong and has proven herself to be utterly ruthless."

"You're gonna let me teach you how to shoot?" As much as I wanted to, I just couldn't picture my lover with a gun in his hand. It just seemed wrong, even if it might keep him alive.

"No." Kristair walked over to a well-lit glass case and unlocked it. Inside were a number of relics he'd collected over the centuries. Kristair counted most of his worth in the books he owned, but a museum would have killed to get its hands on half of his other stuff.

Kristair drew out a rod of dark wood incised all over with strange symbols. It was about a foot long and half as thick as my wrist. "I'll use this," Kristair said, hefting the rod in his hand.

"What are you gonna do? Clunk them over the head?" I snickered. "Be serious, Kristair."

Kristair shot me a withering glance. "Don't be ridiculous." His brow furrowed in concentration, his dark gaze becoming intent. The next thing I knew, the rod had extended into a staff taller than Kristair.

"Whoa, how'd you do that?" I reached for the staff, and Kristair shook his head.

"Wait." Kristair concentrated again. The staff shortened, and a broad, long, wicked-looking spearhead appeared at the end.

I brushed my thumb over the keen edge and managed to cut myself in the process. I'd never seen anything so sharp. "What the hell is that and how did you get it?"

"I found it in my wanderings after I left Rome. I never knew what it was capable of until I became one of the Ascended. I'd forgotten all about it until I glanced in the case this morning." Kristair traced his fingers along the symbols that now decorated the wood just under the spearhead. "These tell you how to unlock its power; then it's a matter of concentration and will."

"What does it say? What else can it do?" I took the spear as Kristair handed it to me and hefted it. I found the weapon to be perfectly balanced, fitting nicely in my hand.

"It can be whatever I need it to be, but I suspect it will work far better with weapons that I am already familiar with." Kristair took the spear back, and it was merely a rod again. "I'll make a sheath for it so I can carry it with me without causing much comment."

I scrubbed a hand through my hair and shook my head. "Well, okay, then. I guess that problem is solved. Have you figured out who the next target is?"

"I believe it's either going to be Lisabeth, Artemise, or Basim Farooq Raza, a scholar I know in Egypt. And now they've all been warned. I'm almost positive now that the unidentified woman who was killed was Mirella Brant. From what I've been able to gather, she left her haven in San Francisco and hasn't been seen since."

Kristair set the rod carefully on the table and began going through his neat, precise notes. "I think this whole mess has something to do with the Ascended, but the why escapes me. Even if the Syndicate had the manpower and wanted to destroy all of these older vampires, they wouldn't destroy the information they'd gathered as well, and that's clearly what happened at the apartment we explored."

"What if it was those fanatics that Tony had sided with? You know, Claudia's bunch."

Kristair frowned, rubbing his finger alongside his nose. "No, even if they were behind it, they'd have to rely on a third party to do the actual killings. Someone who can withstand the sunlight and kill and older vampires. Even half-asleep because of the dawn, it wouldn't be an easy task."

"Okay then, you said you think this goes back to the Ascended. Could they be behind it somehow? This shit is personal and it's aimed at you. Maybe they're pissed at the way you left."

"Not in all likelihood. I said it might have something to do with the Ascended, not that they were behind it. They have a very strict rule about interfering. As long as I'm not down here giving away secrets or bringing attention to myself or them, I think they're content with leaving me be."

"Yeah, and they'd have the mojo to just blast you away without playing stupid-assed games like this."

"Even so." Kristair drew on his shirt, making a grimace at the way it gaped. He touched his collarbone where a livid hickey stood out. "You left a mark."

"So says the man who tattooed my entire torso." I took his hand. "Come on, I'm sure you have a spare shirt in the rooms behind your office, just in case you get an ink spot or something on the one you're wearing."

Kristair stuffed the rod in his pocket as we walked down the short hallway to his office. "I have noticed a few new curious things the last several days."

"Other than the world has gone crazy? I'm telling you this much, Kristair, it had all better be done and over with by the time training camp starts. I'm not going to be an hour away when shit starts going down here." The thought of Kristair being in trouble and me being unable to get to him made my blood turn to ice.

"I think things will be escalating rapidly. This woman has my attention now. The remaining players who are still alive have all been warned. We're going to need everything we can to defeat her. Which brings me to what I've noticed about you, *mo chroí*."

I squirmed a bit, thinking about how hard I'd been concentrating on renewing our link since the night before. I didn't think I'd made that much progress, but he must've noticed somehow. I couldn't stop myself, though. I didn't want to be apart from him and not know what the fuck was going on unless he chose to tell me.

"You managed to find me last night. I could've been anywhere in the park. Yet you came right to me." Kristair pulled a clean, pressed shirt out of his small closet, and I had to smile at the sight of two others neatly hanging up. He liked to be prepared, that was certain. If one plan didn't work, he smoothly went onto the next. It was somewhat reassuring. "At first I attributed it to coincidence, but then another oddity cropped up."

Kristair was too damned observant. At least he didn't seem irritated or worried about me stretching my mental abilities. There was none of the icy precision to his voice that he got when he was furious. When I didn't respond, my lover continued.

"Did you know I haven't had one nightmare since you woke me up the other morning?" He stripped off his buttonless shirt and donned the new one, his concentration seemingly on the row of buttons on his cuffs, but I knew it was really on me.

I straightened, startled out of my musings. "You haven't?"

Kristair shook his head and leaned in closer to me, his dark eyes both intent and warm before he stole a kiss. "Every time the dream starts, someone comes into my mind and smothers it or changes it into a distinctly erotic dream. Even if I didn't recognize your mental touch, only you would dare give me such images."

"Seriously?" Kristair nodded and turned his attention back to his buttons. "I didn't do it on purpose. I mean, I've been wanting to help you. I hated that you were being tormented like that, but I didn't know what to do."

"You have always been very strong-minded, Jacob. I'm not surprised you did it subconsciously. You have a knack for getting exactly what you want through sheer stubbornness and will." A slight smile played about his lips as he glanced at me.

"It wasn't all by accident," I admitted.

"I didn't think so. You were tracking me in the library. Not as easily as when we still had our connection, but the instinct was still very strong."

I shrugged, crossing my arms and leaning against the wall. "I had to find you. We were out there in the woods with god knew what hunting us down, and after I lost you the second time, I was just so damn frustrated. I know you worry that if you start using all those abilities the Ascended might come and get you again. The thing is, we both know how the Ascended have learned to do what they do, but we're not exploiting it or even trying to. That connection of ours came into existence before you were taken by them, so I don't see the harm in trying to use it. It's a personal thing, not some über-powerful ability that can change the world."

Kristair was quiet for a long time, his brows drawn together as he folded the ripped shirt and found a small bag for its buttons. When he finally spoke, his voice was subdued. "It is so very tempting, and that's what frightens me."

The tone of his voice had me pushing away from the wall. I stepped behind him and slid my arms around his waist, resting my cheek on his shoulder. "You're going to have to run that by me again."

"If I open that door, if *we* open that door. It'll be easier to open others as well. It'll become more tempting to cross that line. When we need something or it's an emergency and we tell ourselves it's okay just this one time, but it's never just one time."

"You have more discipline than anyone else I've ever met."

"And I also haven't lived as a human for long at all. It isn't natural for me. All the discipline in the world won't help me resist my inclinations if I start messing with my abilities." Kristair laid his hand over mine and twisted his head to kiss my brow. "And what about you? You don't like limiting yourself either. What if you start developing your physical abilities again? That could threaten your football career. You'd consider that cheating, and you have too much pride to cheat."

I hadn't thought of it in quite that way, and I could see Kristair's point. "I guess this means that there's no easy answer."

"There never is."

There was a long silence as we stood there holding each other, and I realized that the frustration of the last several days had vanished. Kristair was good at soothing me without even seeming to try. "Who was that lady?" I asked finally. "She seemed to know a whole lotta shit about you, very personal stuff." There was something familiar about her, something that tugged at my heart and instincts.

"I wish I knew."

"Was she right? About why Nerissa turned you into a vampire?"

"Perhaps." Kristair broke away from my embrace and turned to face me with a thoughtful frown on his face. "It sounds like a reason my Mistress would have, though I don't know for sure why. I never asked her why she chose me."

The memory of the attack on Kristair came back to me, the terror and desperate struggle of that dark night. I'd always wanted to know how a vampire was created, but I'd never delved that far into Kristair's memories. It seemed too much like a personal invasion. He was remembering it now; I could see the stark memory written on his face.

I took his hand in mine and curled my fingers around it. "What happens?" I asked gently, morbid curiosity gone under the sense that this was something Kristair had never spoken of and it was time that he did.

"Technically, a vampire drains a human of their blood and, when they're on the cusp of dying, replaces it with some of their own."

"I take it that 'technically' doesn't even begin to cover it."

If anything, Kristair's eyes became even bleaker. "It is a madness that descends on you. It's not just pain, it's as if every nerve in your body has gone haywire and is lying on the outside of your skin, as if every cell has been scraped raw and bleeding, and there is acid in your veins. And you're so cold. It takes months for that chill sensation to leave your mind and you become accustomed to it. And the hunger...." Kristair paused and shook his head. "You have some idea what it felt like, similar to when I had been burned, but without the discipline and control I'd developed since then."

I shuddered, recalling all too clearly Kristair's savage hunger. Both he and Tony had gone through that when they'd been turned. "How long does it take?"

"Forever, it seems at the time. The hunger assuages once you've fed, but you have to wait until either you can walk to go find it or until your creator feeds you. The pain lingers until the next night. By then, if you haven't gone mad and been destroyed by your creator, well, then you realize what you are and have to come to terms with that. All in all, it's not an easy change; it's not for the weak." He squeezed my hand and brought it to his lips. "Don't look so serious, *mo chroí*. It was very long ago and once the shock of it passed I rather enjoyed being a vampire."

"Don't I know it." I snorted and tugged him closer for a kiss. "It's crazy, I've always wondered what happened, especially when I thought about Tony. I was so fucking pissed at him, you know, and he'd been through all that. God only knows what his state of mind was those last two days when everything went to shit."

Kristair hesitated and then gave me a sad smile. "You don't have much say in anything when you first change. Your creator has complete control. They have to, because if their youngling goes on a rampage, then they take the blame by their peers. The mind is very susceptible those first few days. All she had to do was tell Tony that you were in danger, and he would've believed it with everything in him."

"Yeah, I know he didn't really betray me." I shrugged, grateful that I had already come to that conclusion before Tony had been murdered by the Syndicate. "How do you think he's doing now that he's a big, bad Ascended?"

"I know for a fact that he's enjoying himself immensely."

Chapter 12

THE dream had caught me in its snare. It wasn't the same nightmare that had been haunting me for months. Instead of being outside, waiting in terror for dawn to approach, I was trapped in the middle of nothingness. I couldn't see or speak or hear, but I could sense the disturbed minds around me. I stirred uneasily, aware on some level that I was tossing on my bed, but my mind was caught within the lucid dream. Or was it real? Was it a warning of some kind?

Emotions swirled, mistrust building into a seething morass of recrimination and anger. An explosion was coming, and I struggled to get out of the dream and back to the safe haven of my room before it erupted.

Abruptly the dream changed as someone else seized my mind, wrenching me awake and holding me prisoner. I stared up at the ceiling, my mouth working, though no sound came out.

Tired, so tired. Hands grabbing, shaking. *"Lemme alone."* Fury stirred, but it didn't push back the lethargy enough to be able to put up a fight. My heart pounded. Dawn was coming. Terror froze into a desperate scream. *"Help! Alette, Alette, Maman. She's going to kill me! Alette! Tabitha! Oh Maman, help me!"*

A grim determination laced through the other emotions, confusing me until I realized there were two distinct minds brushing against my own. Or maybe even more than two.

With a wrenching effort of will, I broke free and sat up with a gasp. Blankets tangled around me, strangling me, and hard hands shook my shoulders. I fought them in the dark, growling in warning as I kicked free of the sheets and tried to shove away my attacker. They weren't taking me into the dawn too. I hissed, baring my teeth, hands stiffening, ready to rake with my nails.

"Kristair! For god's sake, calm the fuck down. It's me," Jacob snapped, shaking me hard again. "What's going on, what's wrong? That wasn't like the other dreams. What the fuck is happening?"

I stilled and drew in a shuddering breath, twisting around to glance out the window. A sliver of light stained the horizon, just a bit, but enough to send another jolt of terror through me. There wasn't enough time.

"There's another attack happening right now." I knew it with absolute certainty, even as I jumped up from the bed and grabbed a pair of jeans from the dresser.

"What? Where? Are you sure?" Jacob flipped on the bedside lamp and glanced at me in worry, though he started to get dressed as well.

"I'm positive. You said that I was being tormented by these dreams. I think you're right. I think they might've been sent to me deliberately, or at least some of them. And I'm inclined to think it's the killer doing it." I shrugged into a shirt and grabbed Jacob's keys off the nightstand, tossing them to him. He caught them out of the air and finished dressing, shrugging on the holster for his gun. "I heard someone screaming for help… I thought it was just the dream, but it's real." Distantly, I was still aware of the struggle going on.

Jacob followed me out into the hallway. "We don't have much time. How are we going to find them?"

I grabbed the sheath I'd made for the rod and tugged it through my belt loops as we ran outside. "I don't know, right now I'm going by instinct. Whoever's doing this wants us to know. I'm still connected to them somehow. I think it might be enough to lead us to them."

"Then it could be a trap."

"Of course it's a trap, but we have to go anyway." My heart pounded as Jacob spun out of our driveway. Something big was coming, big and ugly, and if we weren't careful, we were going to end up being the flotsam and jetsam tossed about in the waves after a storm.

Jacob cursed a vicious stream under his breath as I guided him through the light traffic of the city and out toward Oakmont. Every second, the sky became a smidgeon lighter, and Jacob drove faster, his car roaring as it hugged the curves. For once his driving failed to me make apprehensive, urgency was thrumming so hard within me.

"Turn here! Here!" I stabbed a finger at a small hidden road off to the side, and Jacob slammed on the breaks, turning and almost skidding past it before he managed to sling the Camaro around and down the drive. A moment later he slammed on the brakes again as the trees parted and a large, wrought-iron gate came into view.

The door to the small gatehouse stood open, and a guard sprawled unmoving across the threshold. A chill went through me. This was Alette's haven. Though she'd never told me where she rested, I knew this was the place in my bones. I was pretty sure Artemise also rested here.

"Now what?" Jacob asked, frowning in thought. "I can climb the gate, but it's going to take some time."

"Ram it."

"Are you out of your goddamn fucking mind? I just got her fixed." Jacob's head whipped around, and I glared right back at him, pointing at the sky, which had lightened into a steely, cloudy dawn.

"This car is solid metal. We'll be able to fix whatever damage is inflicted, but trust me, if we don't save the woman being attacked, it will be hell tonight. Ram the damned gates, Jacob."

He snarled, turning his car into a screaming reverse before revving the engine. The car roared back into life, and with a hard thud and a squeal of twisting metal, we broke through the barrier, Jacob cursing the entire time. I'd have to make it up to him later.

I held onto the handle strap, staring grimly at the Tudor mansion that came into view as the driveway curved around out of the screening trees. At first everything appeared peaceful: no smoke marred the horizon, a breeze stirred the ivy clinging to the elegant façade, and the shutters were tightly closed over windows.

Then I saw another body sprawled grotesquely on the manicured lawn, and the front door had been torn off its hinges. "I think we're too late," Jacob said, slamming on the brakes in front of the mansion. "We should call the cops, leave a tip, and get the fuck out of here."

"We have to be sure. This is Alette's place; we have to be absolutely sure we have done everything in our power to help, or else she'll be able to read the lie in our minds tonight." Even then, that might not stop her from seeking retribution. Who knew what a madwoman would do.

I hopped out of the car, scanning the grounds, listening intently for any disturbance. Several more bodies littered the ground, leading around the side of the house, the Kevlar-clad bodies of fighting men, dead with their weapons still in their hands. Every single one of Alette's personal guards had been slaughtered.

"Wait, if it's her place and she kicks it, how is she going to come asking questions?" Jacob ran up the steps to the front door and glanced inside. "More dead dudes. Jesus, we're in over our heads. Does she have a fucking garrison here? Who are all of them?"

"Her guards and familiars. I doubt she is the target. Though now she will be far more dangerous running around raging for vengeance."

"No, we'd just have Ussier and Hugh after our asses if she's killed. That's not pleasant either."

"Not her, it's not her... Artemise had to have been the original target, but I don't think that's who they got." Frantic now, I ran around the side of the house. "Someone close to her, a youngling, perhaps Bethany or Tabitha...."

The screaming started again in my mind, shrieks strident with overwhelming agony and animalistic fear. I bolted toward the backyard and heard the pounding of Jacob's footfalls behind me. We rounded the corner and came upon the woman with the blank face as she fought with a guard. As we appeared, she snarled and ripped out his throat. His hands flew to his throat as he crumpled, his scream breaking off with rasping gurgle.

She shoved him off to the side and moved to stand over the bodies of two women, one with long blonde hair and an air of childlike fragility. Bethany. The other woman had a short brunette bob. I knew Tabitha better, for all that she was newly created. She had been a librarian as well before Alette had turned her. Both women lay lifeless on the ground, knives sticking out of their chests and wisps of smoke rising up from darkened spots on their exposed flesh.

Their assailant turned toward us, a grim smile on her lips, and I tasted the hot rush of battle. I roared, rushing toward her, my fingers stiffened into talons. "God dammit, Kristair, you've got a weapon!" Jacob shouted behind me.

The woman and I went down in a tangle of clawing limbs, hissing and biting, tasting blood as I went for her jugular. Fingers burned into my chest, ten points of searing heat. I shoved her away from me with a shout, kicking free, and rolled toward the first woman on the ground. Shots rang out, and then a woman's shout of pain as I yanked the knife out of Bethany's chest. She immediately began shrieking, sitting up and cowering into me, desperately scrabbling away from the sun as more spots appeared on her face, the smoke thickening. Even her nightgown was starting to burn.

Every second made the damage worse.

"Jacob! Get her inside!" I shoved Bethany toward him, trying to free myself of her clinging hands. Maddened with pain, sobbing with fear, and drugged by the sun, she didn't have the wherewithal to aid us.

Jacob smothered the flames on her nightgown and swung Bethany up in his arms. I jumped in front of the killer as she tried to grab for him, grappling with her and shoving her back. Tabitha smoldered, her face blackened now, and I counted time with each heavy thud of my heart. The killer snarled, her eyes narrowed and glittering white in fury. "You're too late," she spat, kicking my knee.

It buckled, pain flaring through my leg, and I sank down, startled by the sensation. That shouldn't have hurt the way it did. Being human had its distinct disadvantages. I shoved her away and lurched after her, intent on throttling her into submission, when Tabitha burst into flames.

"No, no, no!" In horror, I spun around, almost stumbling as my knee buckled again. As I leaned down to grab the knife paralyzing Tabitha, a weight jumped on my back from behind. The screams inside my mind sharpened in intensity, and the woman behind me snarled.

"She's gonna burn, burn into a pile of greasy ash, Kris. Alette is going to destroy everything you love for failing here."

Arms locked around my throat, cutting off my air. I grabbed for them, trying to pry them loose as she laughed and tightened her hold. The stench of burning flesh filled the air, and the screams in my mind began to dwindle. The woman's arms were like bands of steel, and my lungs burned. Her legs tightened around my waist, digging into my ribs, applying pressure until I worried they'd snap.

My fingers scrambled for the rod at my waist, and I ripped it from its sheath. Dark spots appeared before my eyes as my legs trembled. I concentrated, and then the weight and the heft of the object in my hand shifted. I fell to the ground, dropping back, and the arms around my neck loosened as her air whooshed out and she cursed hoarsely.

We rolled, and I stabbed into her side with the long-bladed knife I'd willed into being. I felt the shock of the thrust ripple through her, and then her hands grabbed mine, pushing the knife in deeper, twisting the blade as she screamed. "Finish the job, Kristair," she snarled, spittle forming on her lips.

Then Jacob was there again, ripping us apart, his blue eyes blazing and his face pale. The woman curled into a ball, hands pressed to her side, groaning in pain as her lifeblood spilled from between her fingers.

I turned toward Tabitha. "Help me, Jacob. It might not be too late." I couldn't hear her screams anymore, but she was of Alette's bloodline, and she was tougher than most. Tougher by far than Bethany, for all that Tabitha was younger. She had to survive.

The fire singed the hair off my hands, and searing pain scored my palm as I yanked the knife free and tossed it aside. White foam covered us in a hissing spray, dousing the flames as I tried to block the sun from

Tabitha as much as I could with my body. I glanced up at Jacob, seeing that he'd grabbed both a fire extinguisher and a blanket.

"You think ahead."

"Somebody's got to," Jacob snapped, switching off the device as the flames were smothered.

The woman appeared behind Jacob hands raised to attack. "Watch out," I shouted, jumping to my feet. Jacob spun around and threw the fire extinguisher at her head, but she dodged with preternatural speed. She must've healed at least some of the damage from the knife, because she moved without any hindrance at all.

My thoughts raced as I wrapped the blanket around Tabitha. We needed some time to get her under shelter. The killer might still be hurt, but we needed to find a way to contain her, hold her immobile. How much could she heal in one day?

Jacob shot at the woman, who laughed tauntingly. The bullets glowed in the air and fell harmless to the ground. She scampered to the side with another snicker, chanting under her breath in a sing-song manner. She was just playing with him in a mad kind of caper. She was dangerous enough without being insane on top of it.

I thrust Tabitha at Jacob, and he cursed, almost dropping her and the gun. "Warn me next time." He shifted Tabitha in his arms, tightening his grip on the gun.

"Get her inside. Go now!"

"But—" He scowled at me fiercely even as he turned toward the house.

"I'll keep her occupied." I had no idea how it worked, but it seemed somehow the woman was weaker when she faced me. I shouldn't have been able to stab her as easily as I'd had. Not with the nimbleness she had shown, though the damage I'd done hardly seemed to matter now.

I could figure the mystery out later. Right now, I'd take any advantage I could get.

I concentrated, and the knife shimmered and expanded into a quarterstaff. The woman danced back with her strangely blank features, her hair whipping about her face. "You want to fight? You've got to catch me first." She turned and bolted toward the back of Alette's property.

Letting her go wasn't an option. Not when Alette would be thirsting for blood when she awoke. We had to have something to tell her or someone to give her.

Trusting that Jacob would be able to find me wherever I went, I chased after her.

Chapter 13

THE house was goddamned creepy with its darkened windows and the quiet, empty stillness of the rooms and echoing hallways. The dead dudes scattered around the entryway and up the stairs didn't help either. I carried the woman into the inner room I'd found, one without any windows. The other woman was still there, curled up on the table, unmoving. At least she'd stopped screaming almost as soon as I'd laid her down.

I'd never met a hysterical vampire before, and I never wanted to again.

I laid my other burden down beside her. This bloodsucker didn't stir or make a sound, and the stench coming from the blanket was sickening. I didn't dare pull the edge of the blanket back. I didn't want to see what she looked like. If she was dead, there was nothing I could do to help. And if by some miracle she wasn't, I had no damned intention of offering myself as her first snack so she could heal herself.

Didn't matter. I had to get back to Kristair before he went toe-to-toe with that creepy-assed vampire hunter again.

The sound of footsteps in the hallway drew my attention. "Jacob?" I breathed a sigh of relief at the sound of my lover's voice.

"In here," I called back, searching the drawers of the cabinet along the wall. Just as I hoped, there was a tablecloth, and I caught a glimpse of Kristair's silhouette in the doorway as I shook it out.

"What are you doing?" he asked as I covered the blonde chick with it. Burns had made gaping holes in her nightgown, and she looked so damned vulnerable, vampire or not.

"I can't just leave her here naked. It's indecent," I said with exasperation. "What happened with freaky chick? Did you knock her ass out?" I shook the tablecloth over the both of them and tucked the sides in, feeling a little silly about the whole thing.

"What are we supposed to do now?" I continued when Kristair didn't answer. "We can't call the cops, they'll be crawling all over this place. If you say this house belongs to Alette, then sure enough they'll find her, and I don't think it'll improve her mood to wake up on a morgue slab with a toe tag. We can't leave the house unguarded either, not with the door hanging off its hinges and the front gate destroyed." Not that I wanted to stay and do the job. It was the last damn thing I needed.

The sound of a gun clip sliding into place had me spinning around only to find Kristair pointing a small fucking cannon at my chest. I'd never appreciated the size of a Desert Eagle until one was aimed at me.

"What the hell is wrong with you? Now's not the time to decide to take target lessons, Kristair. Put it away before someone gets hurt."

Our gazes clashed, and a chill went through me. This wasn't Kristair. He looked exactly like my lover, down to the long lashes and sensuous curve of his lips. He moved like him, the flowing grace of a born warrior. But even if the clothes weren't different, I would have known. I should've realized it the other night. The man just screamed wrongness. I'd been too distracted to notice when he'd come in. Just as he'd seemed so unnatural the other night—only then I hadn't realized it wasn't Kristair.

"What the fuck are you?" I breathed, ice slithering through me.

His lips twisted into a parody of a smile. "What's wrong, *mo chroí*? Don't like what you see?"

Rage flashed, burning away the ice, and I took a step forward, my hand curling into a fist, ready to pummel the asshole. "Shut yer fucking mouth, ya ain't got the right to call me that."

The creature bounded across the room, the barrel glinted, and I braced myself for a grapple. Pain exploded across my cheek, and the next thing I realized, I was on my knees with blood filling my mouth. I jabbed my tongue at my teeth, making sure they were all there, and worked my jaw, my head swimming. Motherfucker had pistol-whipped me.

The sound of the gun cocking drew me up straighter, and I glared up at the creature who looked so like Kristair as he pressed the cold muzzle against my forehead. "Kiss my pucker. You don't want me dead, or I'd be dead already," I rasped, glaring at him, spitting out blood on his shoes. "So what the fuck do you want?"

It was too unsettling for words. He looked just like my lover, not one facial flaw different. He had Kristair's smooth, rich voice. But it was the eyes that gave him away. They burned with a cruelty I'd never seen in Kristair's face, not even when he was looking at his most hated enemy or when he was at his most dangerous. When I'd watched him kill Claudia and Dominic, as furious as he'd been, as much as he'd felt I had been threatened, there had only been implacable resolve in his gaze.

It was easier to face this copy of him if I just concentrated on his eyes.

How this had happened? I couldn't begin to figure it out, but Kristair would have ideas when I talked with him. Knowing he was outside fighting that über-bitch only increased my urgency.

"That's a loaded question. There's so much I want from you, that I want to do to you, and lucky for us, we have a little time." His hand went down to his zipper. Cold horror stole through my stomach, and the ice returned, trickling down my spine.

"You may be pretty and all," I snapped, "but some bitch wearing Kristair's face doesn't really do much for me. You'll have to catch me again some other day." My muscles quivered as I forced myself to stay still when all I wanted was to jump to my feet and pound the guy's face in. The muzzle imprinting itself into my forehead convinced me that a bullet would move much faster than I could.

"All the more satisfying for me if you're not into it. Let's see what else you can do with that mouth other than hurl abuse," the creature purred.

"You put your dick anywhere near my mouth and I'll bite the fucking thing off," I promised through clenched teeth.

The bastard just smirked, his hand sliding into his pressed black dress pants. Just the kind of clothes Kristair normally picked out for himself. My stomach clenching, I closed my eyes, gathered my desperation, and stretched my mind out. Something warm and velvety brushed against my lips even as I sensed the creature, his mind so similar to Kristair's, but so fucking twisted that it was unmistakably not him.

Snarling, I stabbed out with my thoughts, and he stumbled back, hands coming up to his head and confusion clouding his gaze as he shook his head violently. He tried to brush away my mental attack as I stabbed at him again, but the attempt was clumsy. I knocked his hand as it started to come down, and the gun went skittering across the floor.

He recovered quicker than I hoped he would. Before I could grab my gun or summon up the energy for another mental attack, he was on me. Hard hands dug into my hair, wrenching me up to my feet, and a knee drove into my stomach.

Gasping, I bent over double, struggling to drag air into lungs that refused to work. I grabbed his pants, pulled them down around his knees, and then jerked backward on the fabric, yanking his legs out from under him. He went down with a shout of surprise and anger. I hauled back and kicked him in his gut, only to hesitate, doubt hitting me as he doubled over, clutching his stomach. He just looked so damn much like him.

The hesitation cost me, as he uncoiled and grabbed my leg, wrenching my knee hard and jerking me down onto the ground with him. Adrenaline rushed through my veins as we struggled. He rolled so that he was on top of me, pinning me under him. "This will do as well as the other," he rasped, and then he kissed me.

I froze in shock. God help me, he even tasted like Kristair. I found my body responding to that heated kiss whether I willed it or not, and my stomach churned.

"Don't." I drew in a ragged breath as he finally lifted his head. "Just fucking stop it."

"Don't," he mocked, lips twisted in a cruel smile. "Bitch, please, don't even try to deny that you're hot for it."

The flash of rage banished my confusion, and his crude language ruined the illusion he was trying to create. I talked like that, not Kristair. Snarling, I headbutted him and heard the satisfying crunch of bone. He fell back with a bellow of pain as I wrenched my gun out of its holster and pointed it at him, trembling deep inside. Somehow, it was even more horrific to have the gun on him instead of having something that looked like Kristair pointing it at me.

He stared at me, dark eyes glittering, blood pouring from his nose. "You won't pull the trigger," he said softly.

"Don't be so fucking sure of that." I gestured with my gun and rose, taking a step away from him so he couldn't grab my leg again. "Pull up your damn pants for god's sake." Now that the fight was over, doubt filled my head, and my thoughts raced. What the hell was going on? Who was this fucker?

The creature slowly rose to his feet, still moving with the easy grace of a predator. I watched closely as he righted his clothes and tried not to let how much he looked like Kristair affect me. I could still taste him on my lips, and god help me, it fucked with me hardcore.

"We both know you're not going to shoot me." He smirked and took a step toward me, grinning wider as I stepped back again. "Stop fighting me, Jacob. We belong together."

What the hell was I gonna do? What if it was Kristair and he was possessed or something? I'd left him just outside. Maybe I was wrong about the T-shirt he'd tossed on this morning. It had been so crazy. Maybe it had been blue instead of gray. Maybe he hadn't worn jeans; he rarely did.

I wet my lips, trying to think as he closed the distance between us again, and my hand tightened on the gun. "What do you want from me?"

"I just want what's mine, and you're mine, have been from the moment I saw you." He reached out to take the gun from my hand, and I gathered my will, reaching out for Kristair's mind in a desperate mental stab. If he was my lover, then he was in there somewhere.

A dark wall stood between us. I shoved the creature back, shaking my head in warning as I struggled to get a sense of him, and realization dawned that wherever Kristair was, it was far away from Alette's house. He was no longer on the property.

The wall shivered, and I sensed the cascade of Kristair's emotions as he chased down the woman. They were following railroad tracks. My gun was wrenched out of my hand, and the creature was on top of me again, driving me back toward the table. The stench of burnt flesh strengthened, and I almost gagged.

"You're not Kristair," I snarled.

"Prove it!"

"I don't have to." Far away, I sensed Kristair's sudden concern, the way it dimmed the urgency of the chase, and I sent him a wave of reassurance. The connection was weak, nothing like it used to be, but it was there.

I held onto the connection as hard as I could, using it to banish my doubts as I punched the creature in the face. As he reeled back, I followed up with other punch, then a roundhouse kick to his jaw. I didn't hold back either, hitting him as hard as I could and sending him flying back into the wall.

He straightened, baring his fangs, and came at me, hissing in fury. "You're slipping. Kristair isn't a vamp anymore." How the fuck this guy was running around during the day as one I didn't know, but that would just be one more question I asked my lover when I finally got a hold of him. At least he didn't have Kristair's former strength and agility.

His hand dug into my hair, wrenching my head back as he lowered his mouth to my neck. His breath brushed my throat, and I cried out as his tongue lightly traced the vein the way Kristair used to always do. He might not be intending to kill me, but if he bit me, he'd be able to weaken me enough that he could do any sick thing he wanted to me, and I wouldn't be able to stop him.

That thought gave me the strength to shove him off of me. My hand scrabbled for something on the table to use as a weapon and closed around a heavy, ungainly object. I swung it at the creature's temple as he grabbed me again, and the crystal vase hit his temple with a solid, sickening thunk. It was an awkward hit, but I hoped it would be enough to stun him.

He sagged with a groan, and I grabbed a hold of his shirt and hit him with the vase again for good measure. That did the trick, and I let him fall to the ground. The sense of evil I got from him was still there, which helped, because seeing him look so damned innocent unconscious fucked with me.

There wasn't much time. I needed to get to Kristair. I sure as hell wasn't about to let him take on that bitch by himself again. But I couldn't leave this bastard behind either. I grabbed my gun and tore the room apart, looking for anything I could use to bind him. I found cords tying back the heavy draperies in another room. Perfect.

I tied his hands behind his back, making the knots as tight as I could, and then bound his feet to his hands. He didn't make a sound as I dragged him outside and threw him in the passenger seat of my car. With any luck, he'd be out for a couple of hours.

The sun had fully risen, and the sense that we were running out of time dogged me as I peeled out of the driveway and followed my sense of Kristair. It pointed unerringly to the east. We had to get the woman too. The bastard next to me might have something to do with it, but she was the one behind it all. I just knew it. We had to have something to give Alette when she woke up.

The road intersected with the railroad and, wincing, I turned my baby off the road and onto the ties, hitting the gas. God help me. If a train came by, we were so fucked. There was a groan from beside me as the car bucked and jerked. We were getting closer though. Kristair wasn't too far ahead.

I kept checking the rearview mirror, my heart pounding, stomach lurching. A tunnel appeared ahead, curving into the mountain, and I jerked the car off the rails, trying to ignore the scraping of the Z28's undercarriage, and slammed on the breaks.

"Kristair!" I shouted, jumping out of the car and bolting into the tunnel. I tripped and almost went sprawling as my eyes tried to adjust to the darkness. It couldn't be far now; they couldn't be far. I heard twin sets of pounding footfalls echoing hollowly down the concrete walls.

A woman cried out in pain, and Kristair snarled. I breathed a sigh of relief as they came into view, struggling. I sensed the cold, implacable fury in Kristair as he dragged her up off the ground by her throat and raised his blade. "Kristair, wait! Don't!"

I ran up to them and grabbed Kristair's arm to stop him from killing her. I tried to put the words directly into his mind, to penetrate his predator instinct, but our link wasn't that strong yet. "Listen to me," I said again, aloud. "We need her alive for now."

Kristair lowered his arm holding the blade and turned his head to glare at me. The woman kicked out at him, legs flailing, nails digging into his hand to try to claw it away from her throat. His fingers whitened as he tightened his grip. There was a dare in her eyes that was downright eerie, as if she wanted him to finish her off.

"Kristair."

He snarled again, punched her in the jaw, and then caught her as she collapsed. "Are you satisfied now?" he snapped, slinging her over his shoulder.

I grinned and leaned in to steal a kiss from his lips. "Very. It's over. We'll toss her in the car with the other asshole and deliver them both to Ussier tonight. And then we don't ever have to deal with this shit again." The relief was almost overwhelming.

"Who else are you talking about?" Kristair asked, a frown furrowing his brow. "There's been no indication that she had a partner."

"You'll never believe it, Kristair, not in a million years." I still had a hard time wrapping my head around what had happened.

"Try me. I've seen any number of inexplicable things over my lifetime."

The Z28 came into view; the passenger door was flung wide open, the seat empty except for the shredded remains of the drapery cords. I froze, staring at it in horror. "No, no! Fuck me!" Behind me, Kristair shouted my name as I ran toward it, looking up the railroad track and scanning the underbrush for any sign of him, but the creature was gone.

Chapter 14

I STILL had trouble giving credence to what Jacob had told me, though he certainly wouldn't lie about it and he wasn't the kind of man prone to making up hysterical tales either. The idea of a copy of me running around Pittsburgh with homicidal intent was unsettling at best. What bothered me the most was I knew that Jacob hadn't told me the entire story of his encounter with the doppelganger.

I studied him out of the corner of my eye as we sat on the trunk of his car outside of Alette's house. The frustration ate at me.

Something more than a fight had transpired between the two. I was certain of it. His fury that the man had escaped masked deeper emotions that I couldn't decipher, not with so much else going on around us. It bothered me enough that I tried to reach out to him mentally as I'd sensed him do earlier, only I got the same blank wall that had stood between us since I awoke as a human.

"They're here," Jacob announced, hopping down. We'd tossed the woman in the trunk after we'd made sure she was bound and unconscious, but Jacob wasn't taking any chances on a second escape, not that I could blame him. From what he'd said, that doppelganger should've been unconscious far longer than he had been.

"I'm still not so sure about this plan of yours," I said, eying the unmarked police car as it turned into the circle. I got down more slowly, trying not to let the pain of my own wounds show. My chest burned with dots of fiery pain, and my hand throbbed.

"You're the one who insisted on not leaving this place unguarded, Kristair. Everyone else we know who we could bring in on this is dead until sundown. I'm not hanging around the whole day with all these corpses lying about, twiddling my damned thumbs. 'Sides, we've got to get *chica* hidden away."

I couldn't argue with his logic, though it didn't mean I had to like it. I'd fixed Alette's door, hanging it as best I could in the frame, but she and everyone else inside would be vulnerable to another attack. Especially if that creature was still running around, causing havoc; we still needed to hunt him down. And I couldn't in good conscious leave Alette and her younglings without protection.

I studied the detectives as they got out of the car. I'd seen them once, when I'd been stuck riding around in Jacob's mind. Detective Kuykedal had been driving. He was a wiry African man with the paler skin of mixed heritage, shrewd, hard eyes, and a scraggly goatee. He glared at Jacob, which, according to my lover, was his favorite expression.

Detective Aderson was tall and slim, body swathed in an expensive trench coat. He was at least a decade older than his partner, with a sharp widow's peak and hair going gray. There was an easy, competent air about him. He glanced around at the bodies on the lawn with no change of expression on his face. Dangerous men.

"Mr. Corvin, didn't I tell you at one time that you were in over your head?" Detective Aderson stopped in front of my lover, his dark gray eyes flicking to me, assessing.

"I'm still alive, aren't I?" Jacob couldn't help sassing them. I wasn't sure if it was them personally or the fact that they were cops that brought this out in him.

"Smart ass," Kuykedal muttered. "And who the fuck are you?"

I raised a brow and then inclined my head in a slight nod. "Kristair."

They exchanged glances, surprise evident in the minute widening of their eyes and the cant of their mouths. So Jacob's instincts had been right; they did have contacts among the vampires. Someone in Pittsburgh was using them as eyes and ears.

"Thought you couldn't go out in the day without turning into a crispy critter," Kuykedal said.

"I'm very talented."

Jacob cast me a quelling glance, and my lips quirked at the thought of him telling me to behave myself. "Look," he began, "I think it's time we all came clean here and helped each other out."

"I think you need quite a bit more than our help. From the look of things you want a get out of jail free card and I'm all out of those," Detective Aderson said. He glanced at me, and I grinned, showing my teeth as he cleared his throat. "But since you're involved, Kristair, I think we can spare a few moments."

"How kind of you."

Jacob was staring at the two of them like they'd grown second heads. Then he grinned in delight. "Wow, Detectives, you've never been so ready to listen to what I had to say without giving me a lot of shit. I should've had you around before, love."

I almost felt sorry for Aderson and Kuykedal. With the slim bit of deference they'd shown me, they'd lost any leverage they'd had with Jacob. "I thought you said your protector was dead," Aderson said.

"I was mistaken. Weird shit happens. I'm sure you know that."

Kuykedal aimed a narrow-eyed glare at Jacob. "Stop pussyfooting around. Damn, boy, what the fuck did you do? What part of 'stay out of it' did you not understand? You're supposed to be concentrating on football; I've got a shit ton of money riding on you."

"And I'll strive to satisfy when the season starts. Before I say any more, answer me this. Do you know Ghedi Ussier?"

"We may have run into him a time or two. We have a mutual understanding," Aderson replied.

I gave him a tight smile. "No, this is what happened. Sometime in the past, you did something and incurred a favor from him, and he's had you by the balls since then."

Kuykedal grimaced. "What of it? This isn't a damn Pollyanna world we live in. Ussier owns anybody he wants to own. We help each other out on occasion."

"What if I tell you that I can put you in a position so he owes you a favor this time," Jacob said.

"That would indeed be a feat," Aderson murmured. "We're listening."

"Remember our conversation about the serial killer and how he was really targeting vampires?"

"Yeah, you promised me you'd keep me in the loop."

"Well, listen a minute and I'll give you the update." I studied Jacob out of the corner of my eye as he talked, and it struck me how much he'd grown up in the year or so since I'd met him. His boyish cockiness had been replaced with the innate confidence of a man who knew exactly what he wanted out of life. I smiled inwardly, warmed by the thought. "There was another attack this morning. Does the name Alette Dupree mean anything to you?"

Detective Kuykedal began cursing under his breath in a manner that I knew Jacob would appreciate. "She was targeted this morning?" he demanded.

"I don't believe she was the actual target, but the killer did manage to drag out her younglings," I replied, and both men paled. "I see you grasp the significance of that act."

"She's going to destroy the city looking for whoever did it." Detective Aderson began examining the ground. "Where did it happen? Did they perish?"

"It was around back. We got them inside, though I don't know if one made it or not." Jacob gave me an uncertain glance, and I pondered it.

"Most likely Tabitha did not make it, but I hold out hope. We won't know 'til nightfall; if she is still alive then, she'll survive with care." I nodded toward Alette's mansion. "We'll face that problem at sunset. For the moment, my concern is securing her place until nightfall. Neither Jacob nor I are in a position to do so. Naturally, given your history with him, he thought of you."

Detective Kuykedal glowered at Jacob. "Thanks a lot."

"No problem," Jacob said with a smirk. "We'll leave a message for Ussier that Kristair assures me he'll get the moment he wakes up. He can get here before Alette goes berserk."

Again I nodded as all three pairs of eyes turned toward me for confirmation. "He's got ways, and Alette has other people who stay with her who will see to her when the sun sets. They'll be able to control her until he arrives." I was fairly certain either Artemise or Hugh stayed with her. "I just cannot leave them defenseless during the day when one of the culprits remains free."

"How did you get involved?" Detective Aderson asked.

"Ussier called in a favor," Jacob replied, his lips twisting into a grimace of disgust. "He needed someone he could trust who could operate during the day. He wanted us to find out who was behind it. With any luck it'll be over with tonight. The vamps will be satisfied, I'm sure with Ussier's help you guys could cook up something to explain away the serial killer to your superiors and get the kudos for solving that case. Everyone's happy."

"What's in it for you?" Detective Kuykedal thrust his chin out toward me. "Everyone seems to have a stake in this but you. You in it for shits and giggles?"

"That is an interesting way of putting it, and I'll admit that it has provided a distraction, but no, I'm not invested because of the entertainment value as you so crudely put it. As a matter of fact, I don't see how my motives are any concern of yours, Detective Kuykedal. After all, you don't intend on threatening me with arrest as you have Jacob on many an occasion, are you?"

"Of course not," Detective Aderson assured me, clearing his throat. I smiled at their discomfort until Jacob jabbed an elbow into my ribs.

I smoothed my expression, studying the detectives as Jacob finished his conversation with them. I didn't like leaving Alette's household in the hands of unknown humans, but I had little choice in the matter. We needed to secure the one culprit we had and find the other before nightfall.

Once again, necessity dictated my actions. And Aderson and Kuykedal were connected to Ussier. It didn't mean they were entirely trustworthy, but they seemed intelligent enough to know that failure or betrayal would end in a painful death for them, whereas doing this would ensure them rewards beyond what they dared to dream about.

We could not stay. I didn't want Jacob anywhere near this place when Alette awoke. If I could manage it, I'd take him out of the city. I didn't think my lover grasped the danger that the detectives were in— or we ourselves were in, for that matter. Jacob had had a taste of what it was like to be confronted by a maddened vampire after I'd been hurt, but his mind had been clouded by the unwavering certainty that I loved him and it would be enough to keep him safe.

Judging from the grim expressions on the detectives' faces, they knew exactly what they were up against, and that soothed my conscience somewhat. Aderson's gaze slid from Jacob to me and then back again. "You're sure Ussier will get the message the moment he wakes up?"

"I am, but it would be a wise idea to leave the area as dusk starts to descend. Even if they stir early, they won't be in a position to leave, but anyone wishing to try to finish the job won't risk trying it." If they did, well, that would solve one problem for us.

"We'll do it on one condition," Detective Kuykedal said.

"And that is?" Jacob asked.

"How much clout does your boy have with Ussier?"

I raised a brow. I could not remember the last time anyone had ever referred to me as a boy, Jacob's or otherwise. "I have known Ussier for over a hundred years. I'm not part of his inner circle because I prefer to keep myself apart, but I assure you Ussier will listen to my words if I vouch for you."

"Why? You don't know either one of us," Aderson pointed out.

"Jacob spoke for you and that is enough for me. Besides, if I feel it necessary either he or I could read your minds to verify your trustworthiness. It's not a pleasant experience, but it can be done."

They had no way of calling my bluff, and given the way I'd sensed Jacob earlier, I wouldn't have been surprised if he could do it, though I doubted he would. He had more scruples than I did.

"But mostly, I trust in your fear of Ussier if you falter."

I touched my hand to the small of Jacob's back. It was well into the morning, and we had quite a bit left to do. Mostly, I wanted him alone so I could uncover what had happened to him. There was an ugly bruise forming on his cheek and new shadows in his eyes that I railed against. When I found that creature, I'd rip his limbs from his body.

"Are you ready, Jacob?"

"Yeah, I guess that about covers it. If you need anything, if something new happens, give us a call." He shook Aderson's hand, nodded at Kuykedal, and twined his fingers with my own. "Let's go."

I waited until we were back on the highway and Alette's place was far behind us. Jacob gripped the wheel with both hands, his knuckles white and jaw set. "What happened, *mo chroí?*"

"Like I said, she wasn't working alone. She's got some dude working with her. I'd seen him before, that night in the woods, but at the time I thought I was you. And when I lost sight of him…." He shrugged. "I just dismissed it at the time."

I nodded slowly, searching Jacob's face, trying to figure out what he wasn't telling me. "And he attacked you in the house?"

"Yeah." He paused. "I think he was trying to make sure the job was done. Get rid of me and bring Tabitha and Bethany back outside while you were distracted with chick."

"And that's where you got this." Jacob tensed as I gently touched the bruise on his cheekbone. Neither one of us had escaped unscathed from the morning's battles. "What aren't you telling me?"

There was another long pause, and then Jacob glanced at me, his blue eyes dark and angry. "This guy… Kristair, he looked like you. I don't think you get that. He could've been your fucking twin. He even smelled like you, and—" The rest of what he was going to say was bitten off as Jacob pressed his lips together.

I could well imagine how that screwed with Jacob, to have to fight someone that looked like me. "And what?"

Jacob flexed his hands on the wheel. "He drew a gun on me. I'm telling ya, he gave me the heebie-jeebies. Even if he hadn't been packing I would've known it wasn't you. He felt...." He paused as if searching for the right words. "Wrong... unnatural. When I saw him in the woods the other night I thought he was you and I almost called out to him, but some instinct stopped me. Then he was gone, and I thought I lost my chance to find you."

Two attackers... one focused on me, the other on Jacob. What did it mean? More questions flooded through my mind. A copy of me. There were any number of ways a doppelganger of me could have been created. Cloning, though that didn't make much sense if it was full grown. Magic, even a combination of science and the arcane. But I thought whoever had done it would've had to have known me personally.

I'd never caught even a glimpse of this man, and my instincts told me Jacob was his sole target. I frowned. It all didn't add up in my head. "Was he trying to kill you?"

"He had a damn small cannon pointed at my head. What the fuck do you think?"

"I'm thinking that it makes little sense, even if this thing had counted on you not recognizing it wasn't really me. Did it think it would make it easier to kill you? Why use my face at all? For an upper hand?" I reached over and laid my hand on Jacob's arm. There was such tension in his body, and I mourned it. "What aren't you telling me?"

"Nothing!" Jacob exploded. "Will ya just fucking drop it?"

Troubled, I fell silent, and the rest of the trip remained that way as I tried to figure out what could have been behind Jacob's rage and silence other than frustration at having his attacker get away. It wasn't like him to push me away like this.

Chapter 15

THE silence bugged me, but I was too damned keyed up to cajole Kristair out of worrying. I couldn't tell Kristair what had happened because I knew he'd blame himself. It would eat at him, and at that moment, we didn't need the distraction. Besides, as bothered as I was by the encounter with that creature and its escape, the thought of trying to sneak a body into our house without being seen by our neighbors seemed to be a more pressing problem.

Not to mention how the hell we were going to keep her quiet until we could hand her over to Ussier. Or how we were going to find her partner in the meantime. When this whole mess was over with, then I'd talk to Kristair about what happened, if he still wanted to know, but not until then.

I turned the Z28 into our driveway, grateful for the trees that provided at least some partial screening. I parked my baby and drew in a deep breath. At least it was the middle of the workday. That made it less likely that our neighbors were at home. Still, I couldn't escape the sensation of eyes on me. All it would take was one person calling 911.

"Jesus, Kristair, what if somebody sees us dragging in a body?"

"So?" Kristair said, turning amused dark eyes on me. "What will they do about it?"

"Need I remind you that you're human again? There's no mental hoodoo that you can conjure up that will convince a neighbor or the police to mind their own damn business if we're caught. Just sayin'."

We got out of the car and walked around to the trunk. "Jacob, you must trust me. People will see what they want to see. We'll be fine." I popped open the trunk to reveal a squirming blanket, muffled cries coming from underneath it. Great, just great. She would be awake. My heart was about to jump out of my throat and do a fucking jig.

Kristair leaned in and slugged our captive somewhere in the vicinity of her head, and she went limp again. He picked up the blanket-clad body and slung her over his shoulder. "See? Not a problem."

I grumbled, unable to help casting a look around to see if anybody was watching from windows or peeking over the fence, even though it had to make me look as guilty as fuck. "One of these days, Kristair, you're going to be spectacularly wrong, and I hope I'm there to see it."

I moved ahead, unlocking the kitchen door, and breathed a sigh of relief as we got inside without one surprised shout. I tugged the blinds closed and cursed the lack of a basement. "Where do we stash her? And how are we going to look for that doppelwhosawhatsit thing? After the way he managed to escape, I don't want to take my eyes off of her for one minute, and we can't carry her around in the trunk all day."

"A doppelganger," Kristair corrected, and then he frowned, glancing toward our bedroom. "It would probably be easiest to tie her to our bed, but I don't want her anywhere near there."

I hid a grin. Kristair got prickly over the oddest things. "How about we tie her to a chair in the kitchen? We can set her in the middle of the floor, and it will be easy to keep an eye on her."

Kristair nodded and dragged a chair out, dumping his burden on it. "I'll get some more rope from the utility room. I'd prefer if we could manage to keep her knocked out for the day."

"That last punch should do the damn trick, at least for awhile." I unwrapped the blanket from around her, keeping her from slumping off the chair as I checked her bonds. I found it hard to believe that I had a woman tied up in my kitchen. Life had certainly taken on a surreal quality. Now, with her tangled, sweaty hair obscuring her face, it seemed hard to think of her as a stone-cold killer.

I brushed back her hair, wanting to fix those blank, unnatural features in my mind to remind myself what she was, and froze in horror at the sight of Kayla's face. "HOLY SHIT!"

"What is it?" Kristair came bounding back into the kitchen looking around for an attacker, and I stared up at him in dismay as his expression became stricken. "No!" he cried out, falling to his knees next to his daughter, gently tipping up her bruised face and brushing back her hair. "What have I done?"

Fingers fumbling, I scrambled to undo the knots binding her wrists so tightly together. "You didn't do anything, babe. Someone's screwing with us. First that creature that looks like you and now dragging Kayla into it. Somehow, the killer must've escaped, switched or something. They're a pair of tricksome bitches."

"No, I don't think so." I flinched at the haunted tone to his voice. Kristair lifted the bloody hem of her shirt, revealing a jagged, red scar on her side. Kristair let out a despairing soft moan and dropped the shirt to ease it back from her throat instead. There were mottled bruises there as well, and I remembered Kristair's hands around her throat, throttling her as I ran up to him in the tunnel.

"She wanted me to kill her," Kristair breathed. "Oh little one. I thought it odd at the time… I did this to her." He swept Kayla up in his arms as the ropes fell free. "Get some hot water and clean cloths," he demanded over his shoulder, carrying her back to our room.

Shaking from delayed reaction, I turned the hot water on and scrambled for a bowl and the first aid kit. My mind spun as I dumped some peroxide in the bowl and added hot water, grabbing a bottle of aspirin too. It didn't make any sense. Kayla was supposed to be in Baltimore with Steve. Where the hell had he been when all this happened? Fuck, did that mean the creature was somehow Steve made to look like Kristair, while Kayla was also made to look different?

I set the bowl down as my hands trembled even more and my stomach churned. Fuck, I could've killed him. I couldn't take having another friend's death on my hands. I just couldn't. Drawing in a deep breath, I forced myself to continue moving.

Kristair had laid Kayla out in the middle of our rumpled bed and removed her shirt. His face was grim as he took the bowl from me and began to wash the blood from her stomach and side, leaning over to examine the wound intently. "We should bandage it, just in case," I said, and he nodded.

The scar was puckered and raw, as if newly healed. As if she'd only healed herself enough to keep going, to keep fighting. I shuddered, rose to grab her a clean T-shirt, and then watched, helpless, as Kristair cleaned and bandaged the stab wound before moving onto each bite mark, his jaw set.

"You couldn't have known," I said, sitting down beside him once again on the bed, touching his shoulder.

"Don't." Kristair shook his head sharply. "Don't try to excuse me. I should've known. She's my daughter. There should've been some instinct, something." He eased the T-shirt over her. "You said yourself when I was mad with the need for blood that I wouldn't hurt you because I loved you, that I would sense it and stop myself. I didn't then, and I hadn't recognized it now either."

I ran a hand through my hair and fisted it. Damn, he was the most stubborn man I'd ever met in my fucking life. I made a note to knock some sense into him later. "What do we do now, Kristair? Ussier is going to be looking for an explanation come sunset, and we'd better have a damn good one for him."

Kristair drew a blanket around Kayla, tucking her in as if she were a baby, and a lump lodged in my throat. He'd never see it, but he made an amazing father, and I could all too easily picture him tucking our son or daughter in for the night. Then my lover turned toward me, his expression stark.

"You will take Kayla and go. I want you as far away from here as you can possibly drive by sunset. Go to the bank, take out as much cash as you can. I'll stay here and pack for you."

"Like hell I will!" I grabbed Kristair's arm. "I'm not leaving you to face that rabid bitch Alette by yourself. What if Ussier can't keep her in check? What if he's too pissed to listen to reason? I'm staying."

"Jacob, we don't have time to argue this." Kristair rose and pulled me up with him, and the next thing I knew, he was propelling me toward the door. "We can't have her anywhere near Pittsburgh tonight, you know that. Someone has to stay and talk with Ussier, and it's far better if it's me. You cannot argue the logic of that."

"Yes, I can." I pulled myself free and grabbed Kristair by the shoulders, giving him a hard shake. "If you think I'm going to let you sacrifice yourself because you think you've failed us in some way, you're out of your damned mind. I'll knock you out and take your crazy ass with us."

"Don't be ridiculous, I'm not sacrificing myself. Ussier won't kill me and he deserves the courtesy of an explanation in person. As soon as I've talked with him, I'll join you. But he cannot even suspect Kayla's involvement. As long as we don't know what is going on with her she is a danger to everyone. Do not expect any kind of compassion from him. Make no mistake, he runs the city as well as he does by being ruthless. I'm not taking any chances until I've had a chance to talk to him and feel out which way he will go. But even if he doesn't call out a hunt on Kayla, you can be sure there will be other vampires trying."

"What about Alette? What will keep her from ripping out your throat if you don't have a victim to give her?" I snapped right back.

"Any number of things. Alette is first and foremost a creature who believes in self-preservation first, then vengeance. She's not entirely sure what I'm still capable of and that will keep her at bay long enough for me to talk to Ussier. There are a few people in this city who are capable of controlling her, and they're all highly intelligent and not about to let anger and bloodlust rule their minds. It's what makes them more dangerous in the long run."

"I'm not even gonna argue with you about this, Kristair. It's crazy. I'm not going." He couldn't make me. It wasn't just the fact that he'd be in danger that made me balk. I knew how much he was hurting inside. I couldn't leave him alone with his guilt and pain.

"Jacob, *mo chroí*, please, do this for me. I'm trusting her with you. I'm trusting you to keep her and yourself safe when I want nothing more than to see to it myself." Oh, that was just not fucking fair. I glared at Kristair as he cupped my face in his hands. "You're the only one who can do this."

There was Steve, I wanted to argue, but I knew Kristair would never agree to that either, and we still didn't know if he was involved or not. Damn him, he had me. I glanced over at Kayla, so fucking pale, the bruises livid against her skin. She couldn't stay. By nightfall, all the vampires would be whipped into a frenzy, some eager to kill anything that had any kind of a connection to the slayings.

I glared at him, clenching my teeth hard enough that my jaw ached. "You give me your solemn word that you'll join me tomorrow. Because I swear if you don't, if you're delayed for a fucking minute or if I have any inkling that you're in trouble, I'm coming after you."

Kristair smiled, relief lightning the icy starkness in his dark eyes. "Thank you and I do give you my word. I'll leave as soon as I've talked with Ussier. I'll take the time to make sure no one's following me and I'll join you. After everything we've been through to be together, do you honestly think I'd let a pack of vampires get in between us?"

I glared at him and gave him a hard kiss. "I know someone who's got a cabin in Bellows Falls, Vermont." He was always trying to get me to go hunting, and I'd never taken him up on it. "I'm sure he'll let me use it for a getaway for a few days. If anybody's looking for us, they'd probably expect us to go Louisiana first."

"Is this place out of the way? Secluded?"

"Isn't everything in Vermont?" I checked to make sure my wallet was in my back pocket. "I shouldn't be gone more than forty minutes. Be fucking careful. That bitch who looks like you is still loose."

Kristair's face drew into a worried frown. "Do you think he can track you? You seem to be his target."

I shook my head. "Nah, he would've had me in the woods the first time I saw him if that was the case. Besides, I know it's not you the moment I get a good look at him, and now that we're onto him he loses his biggest advantage."

"Good." Kristair breathed a sigh of relief. "You'll be safe, then. I'll have everything ready by the time you get back."

I nodded shortly, not trusting myself to speak. I hated the whole stinking, stupid idea, even if it was necessary. I peeled out of the driveway, anxious to be back as quick as I could. At least I could alleviate one worry. Heart pounding, I grabbed my cell and called Steve.

"Hey man, what's—"

"This is really important Steve, so just answer my fucking question. Where are you?"

There was a startled pause. "Baltimore… it's in Maryland, just in case you lost what brains you had."

"Where's Kayla?" I swear to god if he said she was there with him, I was turning around and dragging Kristair with me whether he liked it or not.

"What? She's at the shelter. What's going on?"

"Are you sure, Steve, are you absolutely fucking certain she's there?"

"Yeah, I'm sure, she usually goes in early so she can help make breakfast. She should be home in another hour, for god's sake, cut the caffeine."

I worried my lip, considering that. "Go check." I cut off his argument as he started. "Just check for me and call me back, don't talk to anyone else. I'll explain it then. Just fucking go. Okay?"

"Jesus, fine, Christ you're a pain in the ass, Jake. It won't take long, it's just down the street, and then I want some answers."

"You'll get them."

Heart racing even more, I hung up. There were too many unanswered questions. Every new revelation only led to more questions and no fucking answers. I hoped Kristair had the sense to tie Kayla up again. Just because she was herself now didn't mean she wouldn't go all Mr. Hyde on us when we weren't watching. I didn't want him to be put into a position where he would have to hurt her again just to get her under control.

And it sure as hell didn't explain the creature that looked like Kristair. What had he called it? A doppelganger? Why? Something niggled at the back of my brain, but I couldn't lock onto it. Oh well, I had a long drive ahead of me to ponder the whys and hows of it all.

The bank transaction didn't take long, and I was walking out as my phone rang. I snatched it up, tensing as I saw Steve's number. "Well?"

"You'd better fucking start talking, Jake or I'm pulling your ass out through your face. Where is she?"

I drew in a deep breath, not sure whether to be relieved or not. "Okay, here's what I need you to do. Pack a bag for you and Kayla, enough for a few days, but don't weigh yourself down. Grab some cash; you can't use your cards. I need you to buy three train tickets. One heading south, New Orleans is good, another to Chicago, and the last for Vermont."

"That's not explaining shit, asshole."

"Shut the fuck up. I need you to meet Kayla and me in Bellows Falls, Vermont. Got it? And you can't tell a fucking soul. Get the third ticket for a few stops past Bellows Falls, but get off there. Don't tell anyone. There's something really bad out there, and it's trying to kill me, Kayla, and Kristair. And if you see anybody who looks like Kristair or Kayla make sure you're not seen. There's a good chance it's not them."

"Jake."

"Just fucking do it. And don't call me again. I'll find you at the station. Should be easy. You'll probably be the only black dude there."

Chapter 16

I FELT a little guilty for manipulating Jacob the way I had. Ussier was ruthless, true, but I didn't really think he would kill Kayla as long as there were unanswered questions. In his own way, he was rather fond of my daughter. However, there were plenty in this city who would, and they wouldn't care who they hurt in order to get at her. I had some immunity given my age and the fact that only a select few knew I was human now.

Jacob and Kayla did not share that immunity.

I didn't want Jacob or Kayla anywhere near this city when the sun went down. If I could arrange it, they wouldn't return until the whole nightmarish debacle was resolved. Sending them off to Vermont was the first step.

The house was too quiet after Jacob left. Kayla hadn't awoken yet, though Jacob assured me her breathing and heart sounded normal. I had been tempted to admit her into the hospital, but that would've left her vulnerable to attack. So I watched them drive off, my heart like a dead weight in my chest and unease stalking me. The best way to protect them was to stay behind—at least, that was what I kept telling myself.

And I had to keep reminding myself that Jacob could take care of himself. As a matter of fact, he'd done rather well against the Syndicate when I couldn't aid him. But still, he was being stalked by a creature wearing my face, and that had to eat at my lover.

I couldn't get the vision of Kayla's face, the wounds that I had caused, out of my mind. Nor that strange expression in Jacob's eyes after he'd encountered the doppelganger. Sleep was impossible.

I spent the day making the calls I needed to make, tidying up our home so that when we came back to it, it would be welcoming, and replaying events over and over in my mind. I went over every encounter again, searching for any clue, no matter how small, that might lead me to whoever was behind this.

It was an exercise in frustration, and for once, I dreaded sunset. Ussier was a very astute man. I did not know the range of his abilities as a vampire. Though he kept his abilities private, I was sure they were extensive. He wouldn't have risen to the power he had if they weren't.

It had been a very long time since I'd faced a vampire more powerful than I, and the knowledge that he could crush me easily was unsettling. Not that I thought he would, but it would take awhile to adjust to the truth that though I was still the oldest, I was no longer the most powerful.

As evening dwindled toward night, I put my bags in the trunk of the car Jacob had given me and double-checked to make sure the house was locked up tight. I eyed the car warily. Jacob had assured me it was safe and reliable.

I'd always prided myself on learning new things, but for some reason, certain skills continued to elude me. Using the computer, operating a cell phone... and driving a car. It wasn't just the mechanical part that was intimidating, but the fact that I just didn't trust others in the cars around me to behave themselves and obey the rules.

It was far past time that I got over it. I had a very long journey ahead of me this night. I figured that by the time I got to Bellows Falls, I would be an expert at driving. Millions of people had their license— how hard could it be? At least, that was what I kept telling myself. In truth, I didn't have much faith in the intelligence and skills of the mass of humanity.

The car dinged as I got behind the wheel, and I took a moment to orient myself with the various controls and sticks jutting out from the wheel. It shouldn't be too hard; Jacob's aborted lesson and his memories told me that D meant drive, and I dutifully pulled on the stick until it was pointing there. Nothing happened.

I scowled at the offending stick. Jacob swore to me that an automatic was easier than his Camaro, whatever that meant. I just took it as another sign he didn't want me to touch his beloved car.

I drummed my nails on the steering wheel, grateful that Jacob wasn't around to see my dilemma. The brat would have been snickering, no doubt. I could almost hear him despite the distance between us. I sighed as I realized I was being stubborn and stalling for no good reason other than pride. How often had I chided Jacob for not using my memories to guide him? It was no different for me.

Casting my thoughts back, I touched upon that familiar jumble in my mind that was my lover's memories. It wasn't the same as having our connection, not even close, but oh, it was sweet in its own way. The sense of his presence was enough that I could almost smell him in the car next to me.

Using Jacob's memories, I found myself turning the key in the ignition and backing slowly out of the driveway. Feeling more confident about the excursion, I turned the car toward Pooh Corner. At least this attempt was a welcome distraction from my worries.

Another car tried to pull out in front of me, and I pointed an imperious finger at him. "You will stop, right now." Much to my surprise, he did. Perhaps I could teach Jacob that trick, ordering instead of cursing other drivers. Hands clasped to the wheel, leaning far forward so I could see everything around me, I managed to make it to Deke's bar without any other close calls.

The sun hadn't quite set when I reached the old converted church. Parking in a straight box in the cramped lot proved to be a futile and impossible task, so I gave up and left the car where it was, slightly crooked along the curb next to Deke's. How Jacob did it with such casual ease, I didn't know.

Despite this little snag, I was more confident about driving to Vermont. As long as nothing complicated occurred on my drive up to Jacob, I was sure I would have no further problems.

I slid gloves on to hide the burns on my hand and strode into the bar, making my way toward Ussier's back room. "I'm expected," I said to the bartender, and then I slipped into the back, not even waiting for her nod.

I had maybe an hour at most before Ussier arrived, and it made me restless to wait. I would rather have been doing something, anything, than sitting there not knowing whether Alette's youngling would survive or whether Jacob and Kayla had made it to their destination safely. I forced myself to sit at the table and compose myself for the conversation to come. But driving what haunted me from my mind didn't happen.

A sound alerted me, and I rose from my seat as Ghedi Ussier strode into the back room. "Ussier. Did Tabitha survive?"

"Yes, barely, but a thread does remain." The cold sensation inside of me eased a trifle. Still, I didn't want to have Kayla anywhere near Pittsburgh for the next dozen years. Not with Alette around, not with the chance that she might find out the part my daughter had unwittingly played.

Ussier's smooth brown face was impassive, a granite slate as his gray eyes fell upon me. I noted with slight unease that he made no attempt at a salutation. "Ancient One, what happened at Alette's home?"

I sat back down again. I'd have one chance to explain events to Ussier's satisfaction, and I cast my mind about, trying to figure out what to say first. I'd gone over events and clues again and again the whole day. "It would be best if I began where I believe this all started. When I returned as a human."

I waited for Ussier's terse nod and then drew in a deep breath, sitting back and steepling my fingers together. "I've been plagued with dreams at dawn, of burning helpless with the sunrise. And for months, I took it to be merely dreams, until the murders came to light and we discovered that the victims were vampires. Now, I think the dreams were imposed by whoever is behind this as a promise of what is to come or a warning."

Ussier face remained expressionless. It was a rather irksome tactic, though Jacob accused me of doing it myself often enough. Now I understood why that bothered him so much.

"When Jacob and I started investigating, I quickly came to the realization that the one connection all the victims had in common was myself."

"Or more specifically, your research about what happens with ancient vampires when they disappear." Ussier's slate façade cracked slightly, allowing a knowing grin.

I couldn't say I was entirely surprised that either Lisabeth or Artemise had said something to the vampire lord. Perhaps, in a way, I had been counting on it. Above anyone else, I trusted Ussier's discretion and his ability to ferret out the smallest detail.

"Lisabeth?"

"No, Artemise." Yes, that did make sense. Artemise viewed himself as a teacher and everybody else about him as lads and lasses that should be instructed, no matter how old they were. He was an incurable mentor dedicated to Ussier.

"Everyone in the city who had helped me to look into this particular mystery has perished with the exception of Lisabeth and Artemise. I suspect that all the victims have been killed because of the connection to me more so than because they knew too much. I cannot be the only vampire who has researched this." Though I wasn't going to discount the possibility entirely. "I think the killer believed that these particular victims would catch my attention faster.

"I also believe that the attack at Alette's was to target Artemise and when they couldn't get to him, they went after the rest of the household." I frowned, lost in thought, idly tapping my fingers together. "Another dream alerted me. I could hear Bethany or Tabitha screaming." I remembered how I'd also sensed Bedwyr's screaming outside of his apartment building. "Somehow, I was able to follow the screams to Alette's place. As much as I hate to admit it, I think we were lured in. They wanted us to confront them, to be helpless to save Bethany and Tabitha."

"So you know the assassin's identity? Or am I assuming too much?"

"I do not know yet who is behind it all. Jacob captured one, but he escaped as we confronted another. His captive was out cold and hog-tied and still managed to escape in the few minutes Jacob had his back turned." I sighed and rubbed my temple. My head never used to ache when I was a vampire.

"First, I'll tell you what I know, and then I'll tell you what I suspect. Whoever is doing this is going at me in two ways. They have used a form of possession that is quite distinctive. Whoever's possessed has their features… erased, as if their face was made of clay and anything distinctive had been blurred and distorted. It's very noticeable. Secondly, they have created a doppelganger of me. That's whom Jacob captured. I don't know if they've created others or not. My instincts say not, but I'd rather err on the side of caution than assume that it is possible they have or will do so."

Ussier's hands slid into his pockets, and he pursed his lips slightly as he stared at the floor, absorbing my words. Without looking up, he spoke. "Where are Corvin and this doppelganger now? I need answers and this shape shifter may have some." Ussier glanced up, peering into my eyes intently.

"I don't know where the doppelganger is at the moment. It is my belief that it has targeted Jacob specifically, so I've sent him away. Even if the creature doesn't search for him, I don't want Jacob in the city when Alette is unbalanced and searching for blood."

Ussier's eyes narrowed. "Ancient One, someone… something is going through a shitload of trouble to bait you. This is obviously personal, unfortunately it's spilled over into my domain. Vampires have been destroyed; someone in my inner circle has had their home invaded. I really don't have to answer to anyone, but I hold myself accountable to my people, so I need concrete answers. Bring me Corvin. He may have seen or experienced something in his encounter that could give us a lead."

It was a demand from someone I'd given my loyalty to decades ago when Ussier had taken control of the city, and as such, it was hard to ignore. My protective instincts railed against the demand and

Ussier's tone, even as I knew he had the right. I almost refused outright, but I couldn't afford to alienate Ussier at this point.

"I'll admit I have made my share of enemies over the last two thousand years, most recently the Syndicate, which you have assured me is no longer a threat. Not that it matters. They would not have had the capabilities to do what has been done." I leaned closer across the table. "I'll have Jacob call you. Maybe he'll be able to shed some light on the events, but I doubt it. I think that once I figure out why I've been targeted, I'll know who is behind it. And make no mistake, I'll see that they are destroyed or handed over to you."

"Ancient One...." Ussier's features softened, and his brow furrowed. "Kristair...." His soft baritone dropped to almost a whisper. "A phone call will not suffice. We need the psychic impressions the doppelganger would have left on Corvin. For that, I need Jacob. You know this. From what you've told me, this is the best course of action at this point. It is what the others will demand."

Ussier's gaze swept over me, studying my reactions, both visible and imperceptible. He was the best in the city at finding out the truth, what was said and unsaid. "Of course, that may prove inconvenient for whatever secret you're keeping from me. You need to give me options, old man."

I studied Ussier, reassured by the vampire lord's use of my name. "I understand. We're both merely trying to protect our own, my friend." I hesitated, weighing my options. I needed answers, and Ussier could do what I no longer could: delve into another's mind, follow the psychic trail, and maybe he could also make sure that Kayla was no longer in a position to be possessed. It was a gamble, and all I had to go with were my instincts. "Who do you have in mind to read Jacob?" My lover was going to be absolutely livid with me, but I could see no help for it.

"Lisabeth."

I hesitated. The voodoo child was an undefined element. She was perfectly capable of going her own way for reasons known only to her, but as far as I knew, she was utterly loyal to Ussier, and she had no fondness for Alette Dupree. "This is not to get back to Alette." I waited for Ussier's nod. "The person possessed, at least in this morning's case, was Kayla. Whoever controlled her was doing their damndest to get me to kill her."

The furrow that had begun to chip its way into the stone visage of Ussier's brow became deeper. "I can understand your reluctance to share this with me. Ancient One, I… I thank you for trusting me with this. I won't betray your trust."

A surge of relief went through me as Ussier relaxed and shook his head. "Kayla—fuck. We need to move on this. I'll go with you to Jacob. I know Lisabeth creeps Corvin out, so I'll be there to hold his hand."

"Ghedi, not to be blunt, but Lisabeth creeps you out." Ussier grinned, flashing his dimples, acknowledging that truth. I checked the time on my watch. At this rate it would be well after sunrise before I got back to my lover and daughter. "I'm sure you have several things to take care of before you leave on a jaunt." I quickly ran through the entire encounter that morning as Ussier listened intently, and then I filled him in on where we were staying.

"Hugh's with Alette now. I think I'll take Deke, Artemise, and a couple others with me and follow the trail from her backyard to that tunnel. We'll see what we pick up."

"That will give me time to get to Jacob and prepare him and Kayla for your arrival. Tomorrow night won't be too late, I trust?"

"We'll be there." Ussier's features turned to stone again, and when he shook my hand, his grip was hard. "Be careful, old man. Someone's gunning for you hardcore. I'll be pissed if I get to Vermont and find out that it's burned to the ground and you with it."

"You won't be the only one. I'm sure I'd hear Jacob complain about it for the rest of eternity in our graves."

Chapter 17

I COULD sense Kristair's every mile as he came closer to me, though in my impatience his approach felt like a damn crawl. My head ached; my brain felt bloated with my constant effort to reach him, to keep that tenuous link open between us. I thought I'd go mad if I felt it snap one more time. And the waiting, the wondering, was making me a downright churlish bastard.

It was a beautiful morning. The sun shone down on gently rolling green hills, stretching up into tree-covered mountains. The town lay not too far southeast of the cabin, the creepiest place I'd been in a long time. There was something very old world about the ambiance, like the inhabitants were locked in another time or place. And everyone seemed to look at me sideways, suspicion written on their stony faces and evident in their New England twang. Of course, that could have been my own paranoia talking.

Even now, with the sun shining and the trees dappling the yard with gentle shadows and the fresh breeze, there was an air of menace. Of course, I was being hunted, most likely by friends now as well as enemies. That would have given anyone a complex.

I had thought we'd fit in better. After all, the town I'd grown up in wasn't much bigger than this, and I was sure this place had its share of outsiders, with the train station and tourists eager to see the leaves change color. I needed to force myself to stop dwelling on the town and its aura, or else the feeling of eyes watching me would get to be too much.

I topped off my coffee and snagged another apple cider donut. They were amazing. We'd found this little place just outside of town that sold them when we'd gone exploring after we picked up Steve. The cabin was still quiet. Kayla and Steve were probably still asleep, and who could blame them? It wasn't even seven yet. Kristair wasn't here yet, and still he fucked with my schedule. I took my coffee and donut out onto the porch so I wouldn't disturb them.

Poor Kayla had woken up an hour into our trip north, disoriented and hurting. She hadn't remembered a damn thing, but after I explained everything that had happened, she had insisted on keeping the handcuffs on. Lord, she'd looked so damned pitiful. It seemed wrong to see her like this, so wan with dark circles under her eyes, her face drawn in worry. But when she started teasing me about having matching bruises on our cheeks, I knew she'd be okay.

Steve had been so furious when he'd seen her, though. Enough so that I wondered if I'd made the right decision bringing him into this, but damn, he loved Kayla. I knew that. And if I were in his position, I would have wanted to be with the one I loved too. He'd have killed me if I hadn't told him. There was no way we could have kept it from him, and he would've freaked when she didn't return home. I couldn't do that to him.

I reached my mind out to Kristair, pain lancing through my temples. He was still a couple hours away, and I could sense a bone-deep exhaustion, never-ending whirling fear, and a quiet sorrow that tore at me. Yet I still couldn't soothe him. I didn't even know if what I was sensing was entirely real or if I was getting the impression just because I knew the man so well. The moment I had a chance, I was going to drag Kristair back to our room and make him get some sleep. I would have bet he hadn't slept at all after we left.

"I thought you were done with the whole enjoying nature thing, Jake."

I coughed down a swallow of hot coffee at the sound of the strangely choral voice and spun around to see Tony sitting on the porch railing, grinning at me. "Holy fuck," I breathed, a laugh bubbling up and chasing away some of the brutality of the last week. "What brings your ugly face here?"

"I thought I'd check in on you. It's been awhile, been busy. 'Sides, I didn't think they'd notice me sneaking here at this point."

"Oh shit, yeah, aren't there rules against that? You're not gonna get in trouble, are you?" I strode forward and caught him in a hug. "Hold on before you get yanked away." I ran over and stuck my head in the front door. "Steve!" I hollered.

I almost snickered when his head popped out of his bedroom, glaring darkly at me. "What the fuck's your problem, Corvin?" he hissed. "Kayla's still sleeping."

"Come here for a minute." I gestured to him and opened the front door wider.

"It can wait. I don't want to—"

"Don't be such a fuckrag. Come on, you've got to see who's here."

Steve's face darkened even more, and he shot me a murderous look as he came out of the bedroom and eased the door shut. "This had better be good, Jake, or I'm going to kick your ass right out of the state."

"Just shut up and trust me." When Steve approached, I grabbed his arm and hauled him out onto the porch, ignoring his furious, low-voiced protests, which cut off as soon as he saw Tony.

"Tony! Hot damn," Steve crowed, pulling free and going forward to hug Tony hard. "I swear you're the fucking Energizer Bunny. Damn, bro. Nothing keeps you down."

For a few minutes, it was just chaos of confused conversation, all three of us trying to talk over each other until Steve waved us to silence. "I can't hear myself think. You go first, Tony. I already know what this tool has been up to." He thwapped me in the back of my head, chuckling as I shoved him back.

"It's been interesting," Tony said, hopping back up on the railing. Damn, he looked good. The haunted expression had faded from his eyes. There was a confidence about him, an air of vital power and a knowing, ancient look in his gaze. "I was just getting ready to fill Jacob in. What are you two doing in Vermont?"

"Dude, your voice is fucked up," Steve said. "What the fuck you do? Swallow a radio or something?"

"Don't you know anything?" I gave Steve another little shove. "Tony's one of the almighty Ascended now, connected to the cosmos and all that shit."

"Oh yeah, sorry, Tony, I still haven't accepted that you were a vampire; it'll take me another decade at least to swallow that you're a god."

"A god?" Tony almost seemed to choke on the word. "Hardly, I can just kick your ass across the cosmos now. So come on, what are you doing here?"

"Later." I waved my hand. There would be time enough to talk of murder and being on the run. "What trouble have you stirred up now?"

"Me? I'll have you know that I'm just an innocent bystander in everything I'm about to tell you."

Steve and I exchanged glances and grinned. "I call bullshit on that one," Steve said.

"Ha, seriously. This one is your old man's fault," Tony said, teasing, and suddenly everything sharpened inside my mind.

I straightened, pinning Tony with an intent look. "What do you mean? Are the Ascended pissed because of what he did?" Oh man, that might explain so much, but if they were behind the attacks, how did we stand a chance at fighting them?

"Pissed? Nah." Tony tugged on an earlobe in reflection. "I'd say more befuddled that anyone would give up what he gave up. I think they were rather glad he was gone to be honest. He was fucking up their mojo with his connection to you and constant attempts at an escape. I think they might've even let him go without him having to trick them, but Nerissa wasn't willing to let it go."

"You're killing me, Tony, I swear to god, out with it man." It was good to have confirmation that the Ascended weren't gunning for my lover, though it still left the question: who? I wondered if I could wheedle the answer out of Tony. I was sure there were rules against it, but there was no harm in asking, right? Having him take a sip of the all-knowing Kool-Aid for our sake.

"Well, there's this sort of split between the Ascended now. Those that liked things the way they were and those who are interested in a little more interaction. Kristair's choice had made some of them see that there could be more than just meandering through the cosmos observing and studying. How much more could we learn if we got involved too? I'm not saying trying to shape things, but like right now, talking with you two instead of just checking in on you."

"You check in on us?" Steve asked.

"Hell yeah, though I have to be discreet about it. The hardliners get all offended if we peek into our old lives instead of moving on. It's not that I'm pining, I'm just curious, you know? I haven't done it in a while though, I've been trying to lay low and divert attention away from me."

My lips twitched in amusement. Tony had been Ascended less than a year and already he had blundered into trouble. "Hey wait, this isn't 'cause you helped Kristair, is it? They gunning for you because of that?"

Tony looked pleased. "You picked up on that? I thought you might, or I guess Kristair could've told you. I didn't really get into trouble for it. They weren't happy, but what's done is done, and I think some had issue with his memory being suppressed anyway. No, I've been ducking those among the Ascended who seem to want to make me the ringleader for their new faction."

"Oh sweet baby Jesus," Steve muttered. "How do you get yourself involved in these things?"

"It's a talent." Tony grinned. "But I really don't want the job. All I'm interested in is doing my own thing and staying out of trouble. If they want to be all revolutionary and usher in a new era for the Ascended, I'm not going to stand in their way, but I have no damn intention of being their flag bearer either. Kristair's lucky, if he was still with us, they'd probably try to shove him into the position. I can't believe we've been the only ones to ever buck the system in millennia."

"Yeah, but I can't imagine that it's easy to defy a group mind," I said. "Especially if you're the only voice calling for it."

"Well, there's quite a few more now, and it's keeping the old-schoolers busy trying to rein the rest of us in. So what have you two been up to besides getting down and dirty with Kayla and Kristair?"

Steve scowled, I fisted a hand in my hair, and Tony looked between us, sitting up straighter. "What's going on?" he asked, his strange voice ringing.

"You mean you don't know, Mr. All-Knowing Ascended?"

"Be nice, Steve, he's been busy gallivanting the universe and ducking trouble. Even he can't be everywhere at once."

"Stop fucking around and tell me," Tony insisted.

"You mean you can't read our minds?" I couldn't help but rag on him despite the seriousness of the situation.

"Do you really want me to?" Tony gave me a direct look. "I didn't want to intrude. I'm sure there are things in your head you'd rather I didn't see."

"Good point. Okay then, it's a long story, but here's the gist: Somebody's been possessing people and using them to kill vampires."

"They've been using Kayla," Steve interrupted.

"What?"

"Will you let me get this all out?" I glared at both Steve and Tony. "Save the interruptions and questions for later. Yes, they were using Kayla for at least one of the killings, but we haven't been able to figure out if she was used for them all. She doesn't remember doing it. Given that she's been in Baltimore and the murders were in Pittsburgh, I doubt it. Steve would've noticed if she was missing for hours on end often."

"Actually, I might not have," Steve said with a troubled frown. "She's been putting so many long hours into the shelter, and I've been running around trying to drum up grants and getting local business involved. She's been quiet and withdrawn lately, and I thought she was just pushing it too much, you know? But every time I tried to get her to step back and take it easy, it became a fight."

Well, so much for easing Kristair's worries with the possibility that it wasn't Kayla the entire time. "That's not all, Tony. The vamps in Pittsburgh are all stirred up and looking for blood. Kristair sent us away to lay low for a bit until we come up with some answers for them."

"How the hell did you get involved in the first place?" Tony asked.

"Yeah, I'd like to know that too," Steve said. "I thought you said you left all the supernatural shit behind when Kristair returned."

"Ussier called in a favor." I shrugged. "He needed somebody who could move around in the day, since at the time, we thought it was simply a vampire hunter. And then we thought that it might have something to do with Kristair's research before he became an Ascended. But the last two victims yesterday morning had nothing to do with that, as far as I know. Oh, and before I forget, we also have a clone of Kristair running about who wants to make me his pet bitch."

Silence met that statement, and Tony's eyes went wide. "Well, okay then. Clearly, I was right when I came back to visit you. You need a keeper."

"Jake...." A troubled expression crossed Steve's face. "What makes you think it's a clone? Maybe Kristair's just lost his fucking mind. Look at what he did to Kayla. I mean I know you love him and all, but he's old as shit, he's got to have a few kinks and bents. He's been a killer for a long time and...."

"You have no fucking idea what you're talking about." I glared at my friend, seething, and he glared right back. "He didn't know it was Kayla. I didn't know it was Kayla. You can't call him crazy without calling me nuts too. I took a shot at her."

"You stopped him from killing her."

"Only so I could give her to Ussier. You think she would've been any less fucking dead if that happened? Get real." Steve just didn't get it. I still had a bit of Kristair's soul in me, and he had some of mine in his. Though I couldn't read him as deeply as I used to, I knew he wasn't insane. And he didn't kill for sport or for the enjoyment of the hunt. Warrior, yes; sociopath, no.

"Don't start griping at each other." Tony hopped down and got between the both of us. "Jake, he doesn't understand, and Steve, I'm impartial in this, and trust me, Kristair isn't a wacko. If he'd known who was possessed, he wouldn't have touched her." Tony stared off, lost in thought and frowning.

"So you have any idea who could be behind it?" I asked, giving Tony a hopeful look. "Couldn't you at least drop us a hint? You wouldn't get into trouble for that, would you?"

"No, I can't," Tony said shortly, and my stomach dropped. "Because I don't have a damned clue, and I don't like that. I should be able to see something. Let me see what I can dig up."

I grabbed his arm before he could pull a disappearing act. "Don't get yourself into a lot of shit over it, okay?"

"I've learned how to be discreet." Tony punched me lightly on the shoulder. "Let me see Kayla. There is one thing I can do before I go. I'll make sure she can't be possessed again, so at least you won't have to worry about that anymore."

"I'll go get her." Steve snatched open the door as I caught Tony in a one-armed hug.

"Thanks, man."

"Not a problem. At least I can do something. Maybe Steve will calm down now and not try to bite Kristair's head off when he arrives."

"We can always hope." Somehow, though, I doubted it. Those two just rubbed each other the wrong way, and Steve wasn't going to ignore what had happened just because the situation had changed. I wished I could warn my lover before he arrived, but he'd flip if I broke his no-cell-phone policy.

Chapter 18

JACOB was waiting for me on the porch when I arrived, and the sight of him eased some of my exhaustion and anxiety. He smiled and came down off of the steps, meeting me as I parked. "Never thought I'd see you behind a wheel again," he teased, tugging me into his arms.

"Necessity breeds all kinds of changes." I returned his kiss, allowing myself a brief moment to relax in his arms before I pulled back. I tried to read his expression, confused by the change in him. The ugly bruise had mysteriously disappeared from his cheek, and his eyes were filled with a renewed sparkle. Not that I wasn't grateful for a good omen. "How's Kayla?"

"All better." Jacob beamed, and once again, my eyes flicked to his unmarred cheek as a breath of hope filled me. But when I tried to move around Jacob to check on her myself, he blocked me from heading inside.

"What is going on?" My eyes narrowed in suspicion, and I frowned, too tired to play games. "I'd like to see Kayla."

"Wait. Before you go in, I have two things to tell you first." Jacob laid his hands on my shoulders and glanced behind him at the cabin. "Tony popped in first thing this morning and made it so Kayla couldn't be possessed again."

I stared at him, incredulous. "He did? But…." That was wonderful. I shook off Jacob's grip and sidestepped him, determined to see with my own eyes. There were sure to be consequences from Tony's actions, but I wasn't going to argue about the gift. Tony knew what he was doing. "I take it he healed the both of you in the process."

Was it selfish of me to be grateful that I wouldn't have to see the wounds I'd caused again?

"How'd you know that? Wait, Kristair." Jacob grabbed my arm, halting me again. "There's something else I have to tell you." From the urgency in his voice, I gathered it was important and that it wasn't something I'd be pleased to hear. Before I could ask, though, the front door banged open and Steve strode out onto the porch.

I stared at him in shock, guilt hitting me all over again. "What is he doing here?" I snarled under my breath.

"He has a right to be here," Jacob replied quietly. "Kayla's in love with him, and as much as you might not want to admit it, he loves her too."

"I have a few things to say to you," Steve snapped, jabbing his finger toward me.

I nudged Jacob aside when he would've gotten in between us and met Steve's livid gaze. "There's nothing you could say that I haven't already said to myself."

I made no move to stop him as Steve grabbed the front of my shirt. "I hope you got a real damn good look at what you did to her, you bastard."

"I'll never forget it as long as I live." It would haunt me, and from the way Jacob touched my shoulder, I knew he understood that.

"Steve, stop it, man, he didn't mean it. How many times do I have to tell you he didn't know?"

"What, it's supposed to be okay because he didn't mean to?" Steve snapped right back, still glaring at me, seething. "Since he's shown up, you and her have been hurt again and again. We lost Tony. Fuck, all of us would've been better off if we'd never met him at all."

"Stop it, just fucking stop it!" Steve turned his eyes off of me as Jacob spoke and grabbed his forearm.

"Stay out of it, Jake," Steve snapped.

"No, this concerns me, too, in case ya forgot. Look, I know you're pissed at Kristair, but this is fucking bullshit. You can't speak for me and ya can't speak for her either. Why don't you ask Kayla what her life was like before she met him? You're so damn thickheaded. You only see what you want to see. And the truth is you both are so fucking alike it's not even funny."

Steve looked at Jacob like he had lost his damned mind, and for once, I couldn't say I disagreed with him. "Don't be ridiculous," I said, stiffly offended. "We have nothing in common."

"Jake, he's an over possessive control freak who doesn't know when to let go and back the fuck off," Steve said, turning his glare back on me.

I grabbed Steve's wrists, forcing him to let go of my shirt, though I released him once he had. "And you are arrogant beyond words, always so damned sure you're right," I snapped right back.

Jacob's lips twitched. "Yeah, like I said, just alike." He held up his hands as we both turned toward him. "Hey, I'm just pointing out the obvious. Steve's a chocolate-covered you, and you're a caramelish Steve."

Before I could reply to that ridiculous statement, the front door banged open again, interrupting Steve's scoffing reply. My heart leapt as Kayla bounded down the steps and hurtled toward me. I caught her and held her close as she threw her arms around me. "Kayla, little one...." My throat tightened. "I'm so sorry."

She shook her head hard, and I felt a tremble go through her. "Me too."

"You don't have anything to apologize for."

"Yeah, well, neither do you, Father, but as long as you continue this self-flagellation, so am I." My daughter pulled back and framed my face in her hands. "You look like shit, Kris. When did you get scruffy?"

I drank in the sight of her, checking her over for any sign of a bruise or other injury. Kayla's eyes were older, less innocent, and I mourned the loss, but she would be okay. Something inside me eased with that realization. My daughter had a core of resiliency in her that I often overlooked. I smiled and touched her cheek. "I was a little busy yesterday to bother with shaving."

"I think it's rather sexy," Jacob said, giving me a wink.

"You would." I tucked a tress of her hair back, embarrassed by the audience. "I've missed you." I glanced at Steve's impassive face and sighed. The upstart really did care for her, I couldn't deny that, as much as it rankled me to admit it.

"Me too." Kayla dropped her hands and laced her fingers with Steve's. "How did Uncle Ghedi take your explanation?"

"Reasonably, but he insists on being involved." I frowned, glancing at Jacob, steeling myself for the explosion. "He and Lisabeth are meeting us here tonight."

"What? Are you nuts? I thought the whole reason I had to leave Pittsburgh was because you wanted us to hide out from him."

"Mostly, I wanted you away from Alette and anyone else likely to try to take matters into their own hands, and I wasn't entirely sure about Ussier before I talked with him. You're going to have to trust me, *mo chroí*. I wouldn't have said anything to him if I thought for once second he would've come after you or Kayla." I was too worn down for an argument, and the day wasn't over with yet. They would be here before we knew it, and we had to be ready.

Jacob must've sensed it, because after a moment he nodded and gave me a gentle push toward the cabin. "I'm stealing you for the rest of the day. I'll make us something quick to eat while you shower, and then we're all sleeping. I doubt we'll get any tonight."

I raised my brow at his decisiveness but didn't argue. The thought of being clean and having food in my stomach was too seductive. Besides, the night was going to be long, and I needed to prepare him for what was going to happen. So I grabbed my pack and trudged up the steps, leaving the three of them murmuring to each other.

The room Jacob had chosen for us was simple, with a large bed and wide windows that looked out over the mountainside. It smelled of Jacob and pine and clean, crisp air. It was soothing.

I eyed the bed, tempted to just lie down for a few moments, but I shook off the temptation. Despite Jacob's insistence on sleep, we didn't have much time for resting. A shower and lunch would have to suffice. I shucked off my clothes and stepped into the small adjoining bathroom. By the time I'd emerged, I was revived somewhat, and Jacob was waiting on the bed with a plate of sandwiches and a cup of herbal tea.

"Thank you," I said, adjusting the towel around my hips and taking the plate and mug as he wordlessly handed them to me. I sat down next to him and related my conversation with Ussier to him as I ate, but his attention seemed to be somewhere else.

"What is wrong, Jacob?" I asked when I had finished with only a comment or two from him.

"Nothing, I'm okay. If reading me will help them find the doppelganger I'm cool with that. I'd rather hunt him than be hunted." Jacob took the empty mug and plate from me and set it on the dresser as all the energy seemed to drain out of me.

"I'm going to let Lisabeth read me as well." I was reluctant to do so. The thought of anyone invading my privacy in that manner was unsettling, but I couldn't ask Jacob to do something I was unwilling to do myself. Ussier could've insisted that I submit to it too; that he hadn't had been another factor in my decision to trust him. To me, it showed that the respect I'd earned from him was still there. Neither he nor Lisabeth would presume to ask an Ancient to open their mind to them.

"You don't have to do that."

"They'll limit it to our encounter with Kayla and the doppelganger at Alette's. They won't see anything they're not supposed to see. Besides, as you said, if it helps us capture them, it'll be worth the small loss of our privacy."

I took a deep breath and forced myself to rise to get dressed again. Jacob caught my wrist and tugged me back down again. I looked at him in surprise. "What is it?"

"Have you taken care of these at all?" Jacob asked, picking up my hand and turning my palm over. There were a few blisters from where the knife had seared my palm, but they were small and not as bad as I first thought. Jacob's eyes drifted to the ten deeper burns on my chest and bruises from where she'd bitten me in return.

"Kayla would be appalled if she could see you now, and Steve would shut his fucking trap," Jacob said, his eyes darkening as he lightly touched my chest. "Why didn't you tell me?"

"One thing happened after another. I'm fine, Jacob, they barely hurt."

"Liar. You stay right here. I'm grabbing the first aid kit and you're going to let me tend to you." Jacob rose and stalked out of the room. I didn't try to stop him. He wouldn't let me go until he was satisfied.

He returned a few minutes later with a box, a new mug of tea, and two little pills. "What are these?" I asked, poking them as Jacob set the box down and began going through it, pulling out ointment and gauze.

"Just take them. It'll take the edge off the pain so you can sleep."

I didn't bother telling Jacob that I wouldn't be sleeping, but there didn't seem any harm in the pills themselves, so I swallowed them down with a sip of the tea and watched curiously as Jacob tended to me. "Where did you learn this skill?"

"I was a very active boy, always getting banged up in one way or another."

Jacob studied my hand and put a little ointment on the blisters. "These aren't too bad." Then he tended to each of the smaller burns in the same manner, and I found his care a much better balm to me than his ointment. It struck me that until Jacob had come along, no one had tended to me in a very long time.

"Thank you," I murmured when he was done, and I sat up to brush my lips over his. In the short time that I had laid back, the deep weariness that I'd been holding off started to creep in again. It was time to get moving before I succumbed.

"You're not getting back up again until I say you're getting back up." Jacob slid his hand around the nape of my neck and tugged me down for another kiss. "I didn't sleep very well last night and you didn't sleep at all. Be reasonable, love. You won't be any good tonight if you don't get some rest."

I let myself get pulled down next to him with a soft sigh. "Jacob, I may be tired, but I'm never going to be able to sleep. My mind is going too fast."

"Then allow me to distract you."

"Now?" I glanced at the door. It was the middle of the day. Kayla and Steve were about, maybe even in the next room. "Be serious. What if they hear?"

Jacob chuckled, a low, wicked sound. "What if they do? What if we hear them? Who cares?" He nibbled my lower lip and rubbed his chin along the stubble on my cheek. "You are fucking sexy with the scruff, babe. I vote you keep it."

He kissed me again, and my lips parted as I sank into the embrace. I couldn't resist him on a good day, and at this moment, I had no defense against him at all. It had been chaotic and confusing and frightening since I became human, and it had only escalated after we started investigating the murders. The last twenty-four hours had been hell, yet in Jacob's arms I felt safe.

"Were you trying to reach me?" I whispered, holding him close to me. "I swear after you left there were times when I thought I sensed you." It had been like a ghost of a touch, but each time it came, it reassured me he was still safe.

Jacob nodded, rubbing his lips against mine. "Yeah, we're going to get that connection back; you just have to stop fighting me and let me in."

"It's not that simple."

"For once, it is." Jacob's hand tugged away the towel around my waist, leaving me completely bare to him. "I have it on very good authority that the Ascended don't give a rat's ass about what we do as long as we don't go around trying to change the nature of things or give away all their secrets."

"Oh, you do, do you?" His hand slid over my side and splayed on my stomach, and I closed my eyes, savoring the simple touch. I wanted to believe him, I really did, but I just didn't know if what he wanted was possible.

"Yeah." Jacob's teeth lightly scored my throat, and anticipation made my breath catch. "Let me in, love." He slid his arms around me, pulling me closer. "You're worn out, afraid and still hurting over what happened. I know. Let me in."

My eyelids were so heavy. I had never felt this kind of bone-deep exhaustion before, the kind that came from both lack of sleep and emotional turmoil. I wanted to surrender, but deep inside, I was still struggling. I slid my hands under Jacob's shirt and up over the contours of his back. He was warm and solid, and I clung to that.

Jacob pulled back long enough to let me tug off his shirt, and I heard twin thuds as he kicked off his shoes onto the floor. Then his warmth was over me again, his hands soothing as we kissed, tongues stroking, pain receding in the haven of his arms. I could still almost hear him whispering to let him in.

I shivered, a small, desperate sound locking in my throat. No one could batter down my defenses as Jacob did. He made it impossible to put up any kind of a fight. Not when all I wanted to do was give in. It seemed to me that we'd done this before. I knew I was safe with him... was he right? Was it me who'd kept us from being able to sense each other?

"Where do you get your faith, *mo chroí?*"

"From having you."

I opened my eyes to the sunlight pouring into the cabin and Jacob's tender smile. I smiled back and rubbed my thumb over his jaw, ran my fingers through his tumbled hair. His eyes were brilliant, such an amazing blue, and they saw right through me. "I love you."

Another smile flickered over his lips, and Jacob leaned down, touching his forehead to mine. I half-closed my eyes again and breathed in his scent, his nearness. "I know you do." He pressed a kiss to the corner of my mouth, and then another. "Let me in."

His mouth slid lower, tongue stroking my nipple into a tight, aching bud before he caught it lightly between his teeth. I stifled a groan and tugged on Jacob's nipple ring in turn. "I don't know how," I said, feeling a stab of frustration at that admission.

Jacob turned me over onto my stomach, and then I groaned again as I felt the hot trail of his tongue sliding up my spine. Desire clenched in my stomach, and I turned my head as I felt the bed shift so I could watch my lover get undressed.

Jacob was breathtaking. I could look at him naked for hours, touch him, taste him, and it didn't get old. I craved him even more now than the night we had first come together. I loved him more today than I had when I first returned. I thought that if it were possible to fall in love again, I was doing so in that moment.

He leaned over me again, kissing the nape of my neck, nuzzling there until I felt every inch of my skin react to his nearness. "Let me show ya, Kristair."

I shivered again and slid my hand back so I could touch him. "Yes, please."

Chapter 19

I SMILED at the softly whispered plea and kissed the back of Kristair's scalp. "With pleasure, love." I sat back on my heels and reached for the lotion on the bedside stand. Kristair's eyes were closed as he pillowed his cheek on his arm, his lashes dark and thick, shadowing the circles under his eyes.

I warmed the lotion between my palms, and Kristair's lashes fluttered open again as I brought my hands to his back and began to massage the long, lean muscles. "What are you doing?"

"Making you relax." Despite how tired I knew Kristair was, I could feel the tension in every line of his body. He was too keyed up to sleep and far too wound up to let me in even if he wanted to.

Kristair groaned as I slid my hands to his shoulders, kneading out the knots. "You're going to put me to sleep," he complained.

"Well then, I'll just have to wake you up again when I get to the fun part."

"You're taking gross advantage of the fact I've been up all night," Kristair mumbled, and I smiled as he yawned and closed his eyes again. I took some more lotion and massaged it down his spine, along his sides, feeling the tension melt away with each stroke of my hands.

"I know," I chuckled. "And when I've gotten you to the point where you can't move, I'm going to take even more advantage of your helplessness."

"Evil brat," Kristair muttered, and I chuckled again.

"Don't you forget it." I sat back on my heels again and nudged Kristair's thighs wider apart so I could kneel between them. Hot damn, he was sexy, his golden olive skin appearing darker against the crisp white sheets, the primitive tattoos following the flow of his muscles. His ass was just about perfect, high and round, his thighs parted just right so that I got a sweet glimpse of his balls. A hot punch of lust hit me, and Kristair stirred, looking back at me.

"Are you thinking indecent thoughts?"

I grinned at him and trailed my finger along the shadowed cleft of his ass as Kristair's breath hitched. "What makes you think I'd do a thing like that?"

"Experience." Kristair's dark eyes were hazy with desire, his lips parted, and I couldn't resist leaning over him to steal a heated kiss. He made a soft sound of surrender, half-twisting around and deepening the kiss. I stroked my fingers over the small of his back, down between his thighs, and I knew I could get all kinds of pleas from him, any amount of shameless begging that never failed to drive me wild.

No one saw Kristair like this. No one but me.

I used that fierce exhilaration to strengthen the ripple of thought I sent out to him. I sensed the jolt of surprise, then nothing as his mental shields came back up again. I didn't even think he realized how instinctively he protected himself. I smiled against his lips and broke the kiss, drawing his lower lip between my teeth and giving it a gentle bite. It was going to take lots of time and patience, and at that moment, I had both in abundance.

"You have got to be the most determined man on Earth, Jacob Corvin." Kristair turned around so that he could look up at me without craning his neck. He slid his foot along my leg, hooking his thigh on my hip, and dug his fingers into my hair. "Stop playing games and kiss me."

"Have I ever told you that you're damn sexy when you're demanding?"

Kristair gave me a little sexy growl and dragged my head down, kissing me hard. I admired his tactic, but I wasn't about to let him distract me from my goal so easily. There was something deeper here than just worrying that the Ascended would take exception to us dabbling with our old abilities.

Knowing Kristair the way I did, it probably came down to pride. He needed to present the façade that he had everything under control, especially when he didn't. He'd spent centuries developing his mystique, his aura of infallibility, his ruthlessness when needed. It had allowed him to survive for a very long time when so few of his kind did.

Now that everything had been turned upside-down, he clung even harder to the image he'd created. I could understand that need, the comfort of the familiar, the security it provided.

I broke the kiss and flashed Kristair a smile, sliding slowly down his body, kissing his stomach and then the bruises on his chest. "You're going to let me in, Kristair." His dark eyes flashed, but he didn't deny it. "Because you want to let me in."

"You're the only one I trust like that," Kristair said, fingertips dancing over my shoulders. "I know I'm safe with you. That's not the problem."

"Hush. Stop stressing about it. Just lay back and put yourself in my hands."

"Don't I always?"

Kristair subsided, laying back down, his eyes intent on me as I trailed my lips over his hip. I wrapped my fingers around his cock, tugging on it with long, slow strokes. He rocked his hips up into my hand, a soft sigh of pleasure escaping him. Such a damn gorgeous sound.

"Are you going to beg for me, love?"

Kristair smiled, his eyes going hot as he spread his legs wider. "You want me to?"

"Silly question." I circled my thumb over the silken slick head of his cock. Damn, I could smell his arousal, heady and musky. "I'm going to drive you so crazy, Kristair." So damn crazy that he couldn't even think about putting up a fight.

I kissed the flushed head, groaning as I slid my lips around him. "You already are," Kristair rasped, tunneling his fingers in my hair.

I cupped his balls in my hand, rolling them gently as I sank my mouth over him. I loved the way he tasted, how hot and vital he felt in my mouth. Our gazes were locked together, and there was such power in it as my tongue lashed his cock. Maybe I was trying too hard to get back what would come naturally. We'd always had a connection, even if it wasn't tangible.

I wanted Kristair to give it to me, not to take it from him by wearing down his walls, not to coerce and wheedle until I got my way. A little frown appeared on his face, pinching his nose, and Kristair reached down, pulling me up into his arms. "What is it, *mo chroí?*"

"Is it so hard to open up to me?" I slid my fingers over his scalp, touched them lightly to his temple as I watched the struggle on his face.

"Yes and no," Kristair sighed. "It's not you, it's just that it is foreign to me. I don't like showing my weaknesses, even to you."

"You think I'll think any less of you?"

Kristair shook his head. "No, you wouldn't do that. It makes me feel vulnerable and exposed, like the ground is shaking beneath my feet and I cannot regain balance. But I am keeping no secrets from you. And you know how I feel even without me telling you, and I take comfort in having you beside me."

I smiled at that and nuzzled his lips before kissing him slowly. "I like the sound of that."

"I know." Kristair looked at me as if he were having some kind of an internal argument. "I fight myself more than I fight you. If it were just a matter of letting you in, I would in a heartbeat. If it were a matter of just will and not instinct. I'm sorry."

"What are you trying to tell me?" I asked him, stroking my fingers down the curve of his neck.

"That I'm not against you trying to reopen the link between us. And I won't consider it a violation of my privacy if you succeed. I know I resisted the idea at the beginning, but I have no secrets from you. I may not be able to express myself very well with words, but I do not have a problem sharing myself with you in every way when our minds are linked." A slow smile crossed his lips. "If anyone could reopen it, it would be you."

"So you're saying that my plan of taking advantage of your exhaustion and seducing you with my mad skills so I could punch through your mental shields was a good one," I said with a grin and a little nip to his jaw.

The smile turned into a low laugh. "Mad skills? You certainly have a unique way of phrasing things."

"I try." I leaned over and dug a bottle of lube out of the overnight bag on the floor. "It's been a shitty twenty-four hours and I don't have the mental mojo for it right now. I just want to make love to you."

"I need you," Kristair whispered, catching me around the waist and rolling me under him.

"I'm all yours." I groaned as he nudged apart my thighs and settled against me, our cocks grinding against each other. I watched, enthralled, as the pleasure flickered over Kristair's face while he circled his hips. "Does this mean I don't get to finish going down on you? I was enjoying myself."

"That wouldn't be a good idea, Jacob. I just might pass out when you are through with me."

"All part of my wicked plan; then I could violate that pretty ass of yours in all kinds of lewd ways."

"You're incorrigible."

I was laughing when Kristair kissed me. He rocked his hips, and heat washed through me. I loved every damn sexy inch of his hard, lean body against my own. "God, Kristair."

I slid my fingers over his scalp and teased the back of his neck. A shiver rippled through him, and he groaned against my mouth. "I know each spot on you that makes you do that," I whispered and skated my hands down his spine to that sexy dip in his lower back. Kristair shivered again and kissed the bare spot on my neck between the ends of the torc.

"I know such things too." My lover lowered his head and caught my nipple ring between his teeth, giving it a gentle tug.

"Oh fuck." I gasped and arched up, grinding my hips into Kristair's. I didn't even want to move from this position right now; the friction felt too damn good. Kristair's tongue flicked and soothed the ache in my nipple before he gave it a gentle bite and brought it to an aching peak again. "You're such a damn tease. You know what that does to me."

Kristair flashed me a grin. "That I do."

Anticipation gripped me as he moved to my other nipple, driving me just as crazy with that one until I was in a fever of need. I palmed his muscled ass, teasing my fingertip against his entrance, scoring my teeth against his shoulder as he quivered. "You gonna fuck me, Kristair? 'Cause if you're not going to get on with it, I've got what I want right here." With that, I pushed my finger into his tight, grasping heat.

Kristair moaned, his body relaxing as he rocked back, seeking a deeper penetration. I couldn't get enough of the way he looked and tasted when he surrendered, and an idea struck me. I removed my finger and gave him a quick kiss on soft lips. "Grab the vibrator from my bag."

"I didn't pack that. Where did you get toys?" Kristair asked, incredulous, and I gave him a gentle push.

"I didn't know how long we'd be out here. I saw a little shop when I was checking out the town after Steve arrived." I ogled his ass as he moved to lean over the side of the bed, laughing as he shot an exasperated look at me over his shoulder. "Are you sure you're not reading my mind?"

"I have no need to read minds to know what's going through yours." Kristair returned to my side and handed me the slim toy, his expression one of wary curiosity. "Just what do you intend to do with that?"

I would have bet that in the entire history of Kristair's long life, no one had dared go after his ass with anything other than their finger. I couldn't understand that, even though I knew the air of reserve he carried about him could be a bit intimidating on its own. Add in the fact that he had been a vampire, and a powerful one at that, and most would have been too awed to give Kristair what he craved deep inside. But I dared, and the thought of the whimpers of submission I would get from him when I used the toy on him made me almost dizzy.

"Why don't you just go back to what you were doing and let me worry about the vibrator," I said, crooking my finger at him and spreading my legs so he could settle between them. "Don't you keep telling me you trust me?"

Kristair muttered an oath, and then he was there, his hard body over mine, kissing me breathless. I fumbled for the lube, and he groaned against my mouth as I slicked it over his cock. "Inside me," I mumbled against his lips, desperate for the feel of him. Then he was pushing inside of me, filling me with a burning sting.

God, Kristair made it hard to think.

I groped for the vibrator and lube as he sank into me, and I cradled his hips with my knees. Kristair whispered my name, his eyes dark and hooded, and a tremble went through him as I flipped on the vibrator, filling the air with a soft buzz. "Is this what you're waiting for, love?"

"I swear, Jacob, you could make me want for just about anything."

I took that as a yes and switched off the toy again long enough to slick it with the lube, a task made more difficult by my own trembling fingers. The sensation of Kristair inside of me, stretching me, sparking hot tingles, made me anxious to get on with it. My hips longed to rock, to arch up into him, and it took effort to remain still.

Our gazes locked together as I slowly pushed the vibrator into him. Kristair's lips parted on a soft, sexy sound. Heat flared in his eyes as I twisted it, almost eliciting a whimper as I turned it back on. I could barely breathe, he was so goddamned sexy. I loved every tremble, every quick intake of breath, the dignity and pride he showed in his submission. I didn't know how he did it, but it was addicting.

I kissed him, knowing the reaction that I was about to get and knowing he wouldn't want anyone else to hear. Kristair cried out into my mouth as I thrust the vibrator into him, and then he was moving, rocking into me with each stroke.

My lover burrowed his arms under me, and my cock throbbed against his stomach. We were so close, not an inch separating us, and it felt so damn good. Kristair broke his mouth away and buried his face against my throat. He quivered with each hard thrust of the vibrator, whispering my name over and over between soft pleading moans.

I rested my forehead on his shoulder, panting against his skin, fingers curling into his strong back. When neither of us were trying, I sensed him. The elusive swirl of his emotions, the love, the desire and need, the security he got in my arms. And I ceased worrying that he would do something reckless in order to prove himself. Kristair might not have talked about his fears with me face to face, but in his own way, he gave them to me every time we were in bed together. He gave them to me, and I helped ease the tension from him without even knowing I was.

Kristair gave them to me when he submitted and begged for release. When he showed his vulnerable side and let me take control and took comfort from that act. That was his way of getting rid of all the bottled-up feelings he kept hidden at other times. It was his gift, his way of coping, and I realized it was enough.

Kristair's orgasm was coming quick. I knew it with each hard snap of his hips, each muffled, desperate sound. "Not yet, love, not yet," I said, flipping the vibrator to a higher setting as he writhed on top of me.

"Jacob... Jacob, please," Kristair begged under his breath, his lips close to my ear. I could have lived off of the sound of his voice at those moments.

"Not yet, beautiful." I ground my cock against him, sweat and pre-come making his stomach slick. "You're not there yet."

But I was, and when I came, marking Kristair's clean skin with my scent, he went wild over me, nipping my shoulder and throat urgently. I wrapped my legs around his thighs, trapping him against me, the feel of him buried inside of me so hot and hard, throbbing with each heartbeat. I slid my arm around his shoulders, holding him down as he rocked his hips as best as he could, and worked the toy ruthlessly in him.

"Jacob… please… let me go."

"You don't want me to," I replied, twisting the vibrator, feeling him jolt as I found his spot. I smiled as he nodded, his fingertips digging hard into my back.

"I do… I do, Jacob, please… I can't take it…."

"You want to take it." I kissed him hard, tasting each whimper and sharp cry. I kept kissing and tormenting him until I felt his resistance fade, his mouth going pliant as he submitted. God, I loved him.

I slid my hand up to his scalp and broke the kiss, staring up into his dark eyes. Everything was there, all laid out and naked, and it made my heart ache. "Who's got you, Kristair?"

"You, *mo chroí*." A shudder rippled down Kristair's spine, and I nipped his lower lip hard.

"Come for me, my beautiful man," I said, kissing him again as he cried out into my mouth and his cock throbbed sharply in me. I held on tight as his orgasm ripped through him and stroked my hands over him, caressing until each ripple subsided. I never wanted to let go of him again.

Chapter 20

THE sun had long since set by the time I stirred. Jacob's side of the bed was empty and cool, but I could sense him in the other room. I wasn't sure if it was because he had made a breakthrough to me or if I had finally opened my mind to the possibility. The connection wasn't very strong, but it was enough that I could find him if I needed to, and that alone was vastly reassuring.

I lay in bed for a few minutes, trying to orient myself. I suspected that those pills Jacob had given me weren't just painkillers. I'd slept heavily after I'd fallen asleep so fast in Jacob's arms and was finding it hard now to shake off the lethargy. I didn't even remember him cleaning me up when clearly he must have. I frowned. I'd have to have words with my lover about that.

There was a soft knock on the bedroom door as I sat up, and Kayla spoke. "You decent in there?"

"Give me a moment." I dragged on a pair of jeans and a Steelers T-shirt Jacob had left over the back of the chair. "What time is it?"

"Almost ten." Kayla smiled at me as I opened the door and handed me a steaming mug. "Jake tells me you've gotten fond of tea."

"Yes, thank you." I took a sip and flipped on the lights so I could examine her face once again and reassure myself that there were no lingering injuries. "How is your side?"

Kayla rubbed the spot where I had stabbed her. It would be a very long time before I could think of our battle the previous morning and not feel that rush of grief and guilt. "There's not even a scar." She glanced past me into the bedroom. "May I come in for a moment?"

"Of course." I stepped out of her way and cleaned off a chair for her. "What are Jacob and your boyfriend doing?"

"Taking a walk around the cabin and making sure everything is secure before Uncle Ghedi gets here." She tapped my nose before she sat down. "Steve has a name, you know, it wouldn't kill you to use it every now and then."

I frowned, but I couldn't fault their initiative to make sure the perimeter was safe. "What did you want to talk about?

"Can't a girl want to talk to her father?"

"I seem to remember that particular argument."

A quicksilver smile crossed her face before she turned serious. "How bad are you hurt? I saw Jake with the first aid kit earlier."

"I heal quickly, I assure you. It is nothing serious, see?" I held up my hand so Kayla could take a look. "And you didn't do it to me, either, so there's no sense in causing yourself grief."

Kayla looked at me as if she didn't quite believe me, and she shrugged. "How are you otherwise?"

"Me?" I glanced at her in surprise, and it was on my lips to say I was fine when I thought of my lover. I smiled faintly and shook my head. "I don't know. I'm taking each moment as it comes, but I promise, I'm not falling apart."

"Somehow I just can't picture you falling apart. It would be like Ayers Rock crumbling to dust."

"Not quite." Silence fell as I examined her face. It had been a few months since I'd seen her last, and after my return, things had been chaotic. I hadn't got to spend as much time with her as I wished before she moved. Maybe that was why I hadn't noticed the new maturity in her face. "About Steve, I am sorry...."

"Don't." Kayla waved her hand. "He's promised not to antagonize you, and if you promise to do the same, I'm not going to say a thing. You two are going to have to work it out amongst yourselves."

I leaned over and took her hand. "We will, I swear."

"So Jake tells me you two are engaged." My mouth dropped open as I straightened, and she grinned. "Hey, we had a long drive, and talking about murder and possessions the entire time would've been damned depressing."

"Jacob is old-fashioned and he wishes to start a family. He believes that getting married will facilitate that."

"Oooohh, he didn't tell me that part." Kayla cocked her head, an impish light coming into her eyes. "You seem a bit unsure. Wedding day jitters already, Kris?"

"No, nothing like that. I have not one doubt inside me that he is the one. I just never considered I would ever get married." It occurred to me then how much I was looking forward to that day. I smiled. Perhaps I should to tell Jacob that.

"What about you and Steve?"

"It's a bit early for that." Kayla paused and cocked her head, eyeing and assessing me. "Would it bother you to know we are serious, though?"

"I gathered that. You did move away and start a dream with him, after all." As much as Steve irked me, I couldn't deny that he was a true friend to Jacob or that he'd been good to my daughter. "No, you have my blessing."

"Words I thought I'd never hear you say," Kayla bantered, still hiding darker feelings.

"What did you really want to talk about, little one?" I said gently.

Kayla's face crumpled. "I remember bits, not much, like fragments of a nightmare. Why me? Why did they pick me to possess? These people, some of them were your friends. They were Uncle Ghedi's people... what am I going to say to him?"

I went over to her and touched her hair. "I have faith you'll think of something. You'll face Ussier the same way you have faced every other challenge in your life, Kayla Mercer, with your head held high and with courage."

She gave me a wan little smile. "You would say something like that."

"Because it's the truth. As for why." I sobered, looking down at my hands as I sat down again. I could remember the sensation of the knife going into her with sickening clarity. The sight of Kayla battered and pale from my hands was burned into my mind. "Whoever is behind this wants to break me. So they are striking out at the ones I love the most. They are taking the city that has been a sanctuary for me for over a century and making me unwelcome there. I believe their goal is to hound me until I've lost everything, until I'm destroyed, and then when their fun is over and they are satisfied, I suspect their plan is to just kill me."

"How can you say that so matter of fact?" Kayla said, her expression appalled. "You can't let them."

"I didn't say I was going to let them get away with it, child." My interlude with Jacob and the chance to sleep had let me deal with the shock and grief, dulling its sharp bite. Now a cold fury fueled me, but I kept it in its place. I couldn't allow it to cloud my thinking.

"Who hates you that much?"

I frowned and finished off the last of my tea. "I don't know," I admitted. I wasn't in the habit of leaving enemies alive to come at me again. And I couldn't think of any others that I might have angered who could've discovered that I was more vulnerable. Unless, of course, it was the spirit of a fallen enemy. Stranger things had happened, and that was a possibility I could discuss with Ussier and Lisabeth when they arrived.

Abruptly, the sense of Jacob's mind went dark. The mug shattered on the floor as I leapt to my feet. "Jacob."

"What is it? What's wrong?" Kayla demanded as I grabbed the rod off of the dresser.

"Stay inside and stay quiet," I growled.

"Kris, wait!"

"This isn't open to an argument," I snapped, yanking the bedroom door open and glaring at her. Kayla pressed her lips together but nodded. Satisfied that she would stay put in the dubious safety of the cabin, I leaned down in a crouch and headed for the back door.

Steve's shout rang out as I emerged into the night. I followed the echo of the sound around the corner of the cabin. They sky was clear, the moon and stars providing a faint illumination through the trees. The underbrush rustled as somebody moved among the trees, twigs snapped, and Steve shouted again.

"Drop him, motherfucker, or I swear to god I'll cap your ass in the back of that bald head of yours."

I bit back an oath and followed after Steve on silent feet. The sharp crack of a gunshot cut through the air, and I abandoned stealth, bolting for the sound. Steve whirled around as I came up behind him, and I blocked his gun arm before he could train it on me. Bewilderment crossed his face, followed by relief, then suspicion. "Kristair?" He stepped back, his face hardening as he lifted the gun again and pointed it at me. "How do I know this is you?"

"Kayla is holed up in the cabin. If you fail to protect her, I'll tear you limb from limb myself," I snapped.

"That would do it." Steve looked over his shoulder toward the cabin, his expression anxious and torn.

"I'll go after Jacob. I'll be able to track him easily."

"Jake wasn't joking; he looks exactly like you," Steve said. "I think I winged him, though."

"That'll make it easier. If I don't get back before Ussier arrives, let him know everything that has happened. He'll be able to follow us." With that, I turned into the trees, searching for signs of the doppelganger. He made no attempt to hide his trail, the evidence of his progress plain through the woods. It wasn't long before I found dark drops on a leaf. Steve had indeed gotten a hit in.

It was harder to sense Jacob now that he was unconscious. I hadn't put forth the same effort he had to re-establish our link, a decision I now regretted in light of his conversation with Tony. Perhaps they were right and the Ascended gave us no more thought than they would have given any other insignificant curiosity.

Concern for Jacob now hampered my efforts, and I concentrated on the skills I still did have to track this creature. He was slowing down. Jacob wouldn't be easy to carry as a dead weight, especially since the creature was losing blood, and soon I could hear them crashing through the underbrush. I smiled, crouching down, the rod in my hand lengthening into a short, broad-bladed spear.

Then the sounds quieted, and I moved slower, placing each foot carefully as I advanced. There were deeper shadows ahead in the profound gloom under the trees. A grunt was followed by the sound of a body being set down hard. A profile of a man emerged from the dark, his face a pale blur, but enough that I recognized him as the creature Jacob had named.

He cursed under his breath, glancing back the way he'd come, gaze searching the trees for pursuit, and I eased another foot closer. Then came the sound of cloth ripping and more cursing as he started to tie a length of cloth around his leg. I'd have to praise Steve on his excellent aim.

I searched the shadows around the base of the trees and spied Jacob sprawled against a trunk, unconscious. I pushed a thought out toward him. *"Jacob, you need to wake."*

Silence.

Frustrated, I began to circle, hoping to get closer to Jacob before revealing myself. I didn't know if I'd inadvertently made a sound or whether he sensed eyes on him with murderous intent, but the doppelganger's head snapped up. He snarled and dove for Jacob as I leapt at him.

I made another desperate attempt to penetrate Jacob's mind, urging him to wake as my doppelganger went tumbling down. He rolled to the side, away from Jacob, to dodge the stab of my spear.

"You," he snarled in hatred, leaping to his feet as I crouched low between him and Jacob. Then, to my surprise, he turned and fled.

My fingers tightened on the spear, and I resisted the urge to throw it after him in the hopes of a lucky hit as Jacob stirred with a groan. I knelt down next to him, hands cradling his head as I searched out his injury. There was a good-sized lump behind his ear, but it didn't seem as if the skin had been broken.

Jacob awoke with a gasp, trying to jerk back from me. He landed a punch on my jaw that would've stunned me if there had been more force behind it. "Get the fuck off me," Jacob rasped, shoving my hands away, sounding dazed.

"Jacob, it's me," I soothed, reaching for him again. "He's gone."

Jacob lurched to his feet, clutching his head, and he fought my hands with a desperate snarl as I attempted to reach out and steady him. "Jacob, you'll hurt yourself, please let me help you, *mo chroí.*"

Jacob stiffened, his eyes blazing. "Don't call me that," he roared. Then his mind lashed out at my own, ripping through the barriers I'd unconsciously built as if they were paper.

I gasped, falling to my knees, overwhelmed by the unexpected attack. Jacob raged in my head, revulsion and fear dominating his mind until he realized his mistake and a wholly different kind of horror took its place.

I clutched at his legs but made no attempt to free myself. Instead, I embraced the link, opening my mind fully to him, laying myself bare. "Kristair?" Jacob said, and then again in my mind, with wonder, *"Kristair."*

A headache pulsed at my temples, but I didn't care. The connection was back as strong as ever, pulsing with vitality, and the Ascended had done nothing to stop it from happening. Unable to speak, I wrapped my arms around Jacob as he helped me up. *"Are you okay?"* he asked, his mental voice gentle as he attempted to ease some of the ache away.

"I should be asking you that." I held him tight, savoring the touch of his mind, clinging to him as if it would be snatched away again. "What happened to you?"

"Fucking bastard got the drop on me. He must've found some way of blocking my initial impression of him. The last two times when I saw him, I knew immediately there was something just wrong about him, but not this time. By the time I realized my mistake, he was on me, must've hit me or something." Jacob touched the back of his head and grimaced.

"I shouldn't have shoved myself into your head like that. I didn't know. I had to know if it was him or not." Jacob was grim, and I didn't quite understand the tone or the flintiness in his mind as he spoke.

"I'm not about to quibble over the results," I murmured. "Come on, let us get back to the cabin so I can take a look at that hard head of yours."

Surprise flashed through Jacob, followed by relief. He was hiding something from me. I'd suspected it earlier, and I knew it for sure now. Something about him and the doppelganger. As much as I hated dropping the matter, this wasn't the moment to press my lover. "How'd you know I was in trouble?" Jacob asked as we began to make our way through the trees back toward the cabin.

"All of your efforts to renew our link have left an impression on me. I had a vague sense of you when I awoke, enough to know when you'd been struck unconscious." I let him feel my pleasure at having our connection fully restored and felt his joy in return.

"Well, I suppose I can be grateful to that bastard for one thing. If I hadn't had to know so damn bad, it probably would've taken us a lot longer to reach this point." Jacob reached out and linked my hand with his. "Are you sure I didn't bruise your brain or anything?"

I chuckled and raised his hand to my lips. "I'll recover, and you ceased your attack once my walls were down. They weren't too sturdy to begin with, not when it comes to you."

"Good to know."

We fell silent, as there was really no more need for conversation. There was nothing quite like the intimacy of sharing my mind and soul with Jacob. We walked on in silence, lost in each other.

Chapter 21

THE cabin was ablaze with light when we emerged from the trees, and I almost moaned in relief. I was dying for some aspirin and a beer. The effort to block Kristair from some of my thoughts had drained me completely. Not that he was trying to get to them. All I sensed from him was patience, which only made me feel guilty, especially after all my talk about not wanting him to keep things from me. But this was different. I'd tell him everything that happened between me and the doppelganger after this whole mystery was solved, not before. I didn't want him putting more blame on himself.

"It's Jacob and I," Kristair announced from the porch. A curtain twitched to the side, and after a moment, the front door opened.

"I was beginning to get really worried," Steve said, ushering us in.

"Ussier isn't here yet?" Kristair asked, frowning as he glanced around the cabin.

"Nope."

"Sit down," Kayla said, looking at me and pointing to the couch. "The last thing you needed was to have your brains jostled again."

I smirked at her and gave her a wink. "Why don't you come sit on my lap and give me a little TLC?"

Kayla laughed and sat down on the couch next to me. "Do you do that to irk Kris or Steve?" she asked in a low voice.

"It's a bonus if I manage both." I flashed her a grin and then winced as she probed the lump on my skull, but I could tell it wasn't that bad. I'd knocked myself harder playing football.

"I think you'll live," Kayla said, kissing the top of my head.

"What about evil Kristair? Did you kill him?" Steve asked.

"Don't sound so eager." Kristair shot Steve an irritated glance. "He got away, but you did manage to injure him. He'll be moving slower now."

"Rock on."

I sensed Kristair's impatience as he glanced at his watch, his thoughts racing. "What are you planning?"

"I don't want to give the doppelganger too much of a head start. We have a chance of apprehending him if I...." Kristair hesitated and looked at me. "If we go after him quickly."

"Did Ussier say when he'd be here?" I asked.

"It should be soon. I got the impression he would leave as soon as the sun set. He was going to catch a flight."

"None of you are going anywhere," Kayla announced, giving each one of us a hard look in turn. "If Uncle Ghedi says he's going to be here, then he will. It makes no sense for you all to go haring off without backup."

"I always knew there was something I liked about you, girl." I jumped up at the sound of Ussier's voice and gasped as he stepped out of the shadows near the stairs to the loft. He held out his hand and Lisabeth emerged, followed by Artemise.

"What the fuck." Steve scowled and threw up his hands. "If you could do that, why the hell weren't you here earlier?"

"Mr. Teasia." Ussier nodded and clasped Kristair's hand, ignoring the question. "Corvin." He grinned at me, showing me his wolf's dimples, and held out his arms to Kayla.

Steve's expression tightened further as she ran to him and he enveloped her in a rib-crushing hug, picking her up. "You look damn good, girl. I thought you were hurt."

I sensed Kristair's sudden tension. Damn, I'd forgotten that Ussier and company didn't know about the Ascended, and they weren't supposed to know either. It seemed weird to have me, Kayla, and Steve in on something the vampire lord didn't know.

"I think one of the lingering effects of being possessed was quick healing. I couldn't really fight vampires and kill them if I didn't have some edge." Kayla clutched Ussier's shoulders. "I'm so sorry, Ghedi, believe me, I didn't know what was going on or I would've said something to Kristair."

"I know you would've. We'll to the bottom of this farce tonight." Ussier's face hardened. "I'll take care of the problem permanently."

"What happened to taking a flight?" Kristair asked.

"This was faster. I like having multiple travel options. Keeps people guessing. This isn't my favorite way of doing things, but it works well when I'm in a hurry."

"And the night isn't getting any younger," Lisabeth said. "And we have quite a bit of work to do. Have there been any other incidents since yesterday morning? Any strange thoughts, fugue states? To your knowledge, has the perpetrator tried to possess you again?"

"Not even a twitch," I said. "We kept her tied up for awhile. And then this morning we just figured we'd take them off and keep an eye on her, though she protested us letting her go. With Steve here we could take turns."

Ussier studied me, his gray eyes cold, his brown face rock-hard expressionless. I got the impression he knew very well that we were keeping things from him. But even if we could tell him about the Ascended, I didn't see how it would change the circumstances one bit.

I glanced at Kristair, whose expression was just as enigmatic. No doubt his damn way of telling Ussier he wasn't giving up any more info. I didn't like it. Uneasiness stirred as Lisabeth beckoned Kayla over to the couch with an imperious wave of her hand.

Steve started forward, and I caught his arm and shook my head. "But—"

"It might tell us something about who's behind it," I said in an undertone. "She's gonna take a poke at me too."

"What about him?" Steve asked with a pointed glance at Kristair.

"I will submit to Lisabeth as well," Kristair replied, his voice even, and the ice in Ussier's gaze softened some.

He inclined his head ever so slightly at Kristair, and a ghost of a smile touched his lips. "You humble me, old man."

"I sincerely doubt that," Kristair said in return.

Kayla stretched out on the couch, doing a damn good job of looking nonchalant as Lisabeth sat down next to her. When the vampire child closed her eyes, her expression smoothing, she looked almost innocent. Fucking creepy.

Lisabeth murmured to herself, her fingertips grazing Kayla's temples. I was reminded of the time I had had to delve into Angie's mind to heal the damage I'd done. I reached out to Kristair for reassurance and felt the soothing warmth of his mind. *"What if she finds out about Tony and the other Ascended?"*

"She won't. Tony is far more powerful than Lisabeth. He's smart enough not to have left a trace of his presence."

"What about us? She can find out about them when she reads our minds."

"Don't worry about it so much, mo chroí. If you can block me from certain things you don't want me to know, then you can block her as well. She'd have to force it out of you," Kristair said in exasperation, and then his voice gentled. *"She won't pry. She's only interested in your encounter with the doppelganger."*

Wonderful, just fucking wonderful. Even as guilt squirmed inside me, I fisted a hand in my hair, trying to figure out how to let Lisabeth, but not Kristair, see my fight with that creature. I sensed him stiffen and withdraw so that only the thread of our link remained.

"Don't." I reached out for him again. *"I'm sorry."*

"I do not understand, Jacob." Kristair tried to mask his hurt, but I still sensed it. *"Do you fear my reaction that much? Don't you trust me not to do something reckless? What happened that you feel you have to hide from me?"*

It wasn't that I was afraid Kristair would go stalking off to avenge my honor or anything like that, though I had no doubt he'd destroy this creature anyway if he could get his hands on it. No, I just didn't want him hurting, and god, it would hurt him when he found out.

Before I could tell him that, though, Lisabeth cried out in pain and crumpled to the floor, unconscious.

Before I could blink, both Ussier and Artemise were across the room at her side, and Kayla was scrambling to sit up. "What the hell? Is she okay?" I moved closer to the couch as Kayla rose and they laid Lisabeth's tiny body on it. Oh shit, this couldn't be good.

A worried frown marred Artemise's brow, and Ussier looked positively murderous, his mouth set in a hard, unforgiving line. Kristair drew Kayla to him, stepping in front of her. "Was it a trap?" he asked.

Artemise laid Lisabeth's hand down gently and sat back on his heels. "She will be fine in a few hours. Someone did lay a trap in Kayla's mind, and Lisabeth received a very nasty stinger."

"The fact that someone could catch Lisabeth like that speaks to their power," Kristair said, his eyes lost in thought. I brushed up against his mind to find it churning, running through possibilities and matching it up against people he knew. It still amazed me how fast he could think, even if it wasn't as freakish as it used to be.

"That is a damn good point," Ussier said, still at Lisabeth's side.

"Are you sure she's going to be okay?" Kayla asked, her expression stark. "I'm so sorry, I didn't have any idea that somebody was still in my head."

"Of course not, how could you?" Artemise gave her a kind smile. "It seems we're going to have to step very carefully." He looked at me, his blue eyes penetrating. "You, young man, do you have any reason to believe that there might be a similar trap in your mind?"

"I'm pretty sure there's not. Kristair's puttering around in there, and if there was a trap like that, I'm sure he'd either know or have sprung it himself."

Artemise glanced at Kristair, who nodded. "I concur. The bond is deep between us. I would've noticed if there was something different in his mind. You should be able to see the events with the doppelganger without interference."

I was grateful that it would be Artemise who saw the encounter and not Lisabeth. Just thinking of her poking around in my brain and seeing that made me ill. As I sat down on a chair, I sensed Kristair withdraw and felt a pang of renewed guilt. I'd make it up to him later, when this was all over with.

As I sat down, I concentrated on inane things, trying not to squirm. I didn't want anybody else in my head other than Kristair, even if it was Artemise. I rubbed my palms on my jeans and watched Steve lead Kayla over to the window, talking to her quietly. They really did make a good couple. When I saw them together, I felt a surge of rightness.

Artemise pulled up another chair next to my own, and my gaze darted to Kristair. To my relief, he hadn't turned away. Instead, he was looking at me, his dark eyes intent, and he gave me a small, encouraging smile. Man, I didn't know what I had done to deserve him, but I wasn't going to squander it either.

I almost reached out with my mind to grab a hold of him and tell him everything right there, but then Artemise was in my mind too, and that just seemed wrong to have him listening in on something so private. Damn, I was building it up to be a bigger deal than it was. Nothing had actually happened. So fucking what?

"Don't be so nervous.," Artemise's mental voice was just as rich as his other one. *"I assure you, the experience will be painless."*

Before I could argue, I was back in Alette's house, and the doppelganger was pointing the gun at my head. My heart pounded faster, my stomach churned as I rolled my eyes toward Kristair. Immediately, he was beside me, touching my shoulder in a soothing gesture.

Impulsively, I grabbed a hold of Kristair's mind and drew him into the memory with Artemise and me. I sensed Kristair's love and reassurance on a very intimate level, just between the two of us, where Artemise could not go. There was an acknowledged exchange between Kristair and the ancient vampire, and the memories unfurled, stark and ugly.

It was so real that once again I tasted the horror of the fight, the sharp bitterness of it in the back of my throat, the fear that the creature would succeed in his intent to rape me, and the worry over how Kristair would react if he did. He'd stop at nothing to hunt the doppelganger down. Nothing would stop him, not even self-preservation, just as he'd reacted other times when either Kayla or I had been hurt.

Once again I could feel the creature's hands on me, smell him on my skin, the aura of his mind dark and slimy, like something that grew diseased underground. I was furious all over again for letting it affect me so strongly, and I sensed Kristair burrowing himself even deeper into my being until, like a few other times, we were as one.

"Are you mad I didn't tell ya before?" I asked very softly on an aside that Artemise couldn't hear.

Mental fingers brushed gently over my heart. *"I understand why you felt you couldn't tell me at the time. Both the reasons said and unsaid. Thank you for letting me in now."*

I sensed Artemise withdraw from my memories as the ancient vampire sat back. The tension in the room seemed to ease some now that he'd contacted my mind and remained unscathed. "The doppelganger does have a rather strong, unwholesome fixation on our young friend here. It's almost as if a geas has been laid on him. As long as it's still in effect, he won't be able to stop himself from coming after Corvin. The only way to stop the creature would be to destroy it."

"So it should be close, then," Ussier replied.

"Oh, it's here already." Artemise rose. "I suppose we should've given them a chance to talk more before we jumped right into things. There has already been an attack this night on the boy."

"Um, I'm still here, you guys don't have to talk over my head."
Boy. Sweet Jesus, I didn't care how old they were, I wasn't no damned
boy.

"The attack took place just outside the cabin. Steve managed to
wound the creature and make it bleed." Kristair squeezed my shoulder
in acknowledgement of my irritation.

"Good job," Ussier said, glancing at Steve with a faint smile. He
looked at each one of us in turn, lastly at Lisabeth, who still lay
unresponsive, and his expression darkened. "I'll go put her in a place
where she will be safe until we get back. I don't want to waste any
more time this night."

"What is he going to do?" I asked Kristair as Ussier gently
picked up Lisabeth and strode out of the cabin with her. I'd never seen
him look at anyone like he did Lisabeth, and I wondered how long
they'd known each other.

*"I suspect he'll place her in the ground, similar to how I used to
hide myself in the walls of the cathedral. She'll be safe there. Even if
someone knew where she was, they'd never be able to dig her up."*

"So she'll be safe?"

*"As safe as any of us can be considering we don't know who's
still behind this."*

Ussier returned in about ten minutes, his face set. "Okay,
everyone is going with us. I'm not leaving you behind, Kayla. Until
this is resolved, I want you where I can see you."

"Understandable," Kayla said. "Besides, I want a piece of this
guy myself."

"Which means you, Mr. Teasia, are going to go as well, and
you're sticking by her side."

"You wouldn't be able to keep me away."

"Good to know. Does everybody have a weapon?" Ussier asked,
and when we all nodded, he flourished his hand to the door. "Okay,
gang, let's roll."

Chapter 22

THE doppelganger's trail emerged from the woods and disappeared on the road stretching back to town. "He must've stashed a vehicle here," Ussier said, examining the tracks on the shoulder.

"Great, now what?" Steve asked. "He could be anywhere."

"It won't be a problem, he's not far," Artemise said thoughtfully. "In fact, Mr. Corvin should be able to lead us right to him even faster than I could."

I glanced at Jacob, who grimaced and tugged on his earlobe. *"He's right, you know,"* I said softly in his thoughts, sensing his vast reluctance.

"I've touched his mind." The reluctance changed to a shudder of revulsion. *"I've been exposed to some really heinous shit, but that thing's mind is something else altogether. Besides, what if he can sense me? He'd know we're coming for him."*

"I doubt the creature can do that, or he would've sensed you in Schenley Park." I could only be grateful that it hadn't.

"Then how did it find me in Bellows Falls so damn fast?"

That was a very good question, and one I didn't have an answer for. I hoped that all of our questions would be answered by the end of the night.

"Jake?" Kayla asked, looking at him, her eyes searching. "Are you okay?"

"Yeah, I'm fine," Jacob said shortly. "Let's start with the town. It's not big, between you and I we should figure out pretty quick if he's there or not."

"Agreed." Ussier rose from his crouch. "Corvin, your car keys." Jacob cursed under his breath and fished his keys out of his pocket. Ussier caught them with a grin. "I'll be right back." With a blur of motion, he was gone.

"I swear, if there's one scratch...." Jacob growled.

"Do we have any idea of what the hell we're doing?" Steve asked after a moment.

"We're hunting down a dangerous creature that has been at least partially responsible for a number of deaths in the last couple months," Artemise replied.

"And then what?" I couldn't blame Steve for the wariness in his voice.

"We have a conversation with him," Artemise said genially.

Steve raised a brow, and the silent question hung in the air.

"Then we kill him," I said as all eyes turned toward me, and Artemise nodded.

"Avenging my honor?" Jacob asked with a slightly cynical twist to his lips.

"Let us be honest," I said to them all. "We will feel far more comfortable once this creature is no longer a threat."

"And it will give the other vampires in Pittsburgh a certain amount of satisfaction to know that it has been destroyed," Artemise added in. "It'll give us some breathing room to track down the other entity, if there is one. Perhaps the doppelganger and the person possessing you, my dear, are the one and same."

"You know, I never thought of that. We never saw them at the same time." Headlights appeared at the end of the road with the roar of an engine as the Camaro slung around the corner. Jacob stepped out into the street to wave the car down. "I swear, if he puts one scratch on my baby…."

"You keep saying that like you'll do something," Steve said.

"Just watch me."

The Camaro came to a stop in front of us with a low purr. I smiled as Jacob immediately went around to the driver's side and opened the door, jerking his thumb at Ussier. My lover could be such a possessive man. "It's going to be a tight fit in the back, but I'm driving."

Ussier uncoiled himself from the car with deadly grace. "That's okay. I'll run and meet you in town. It'll give me a chance to scope things out before you arrive."

"Maybe I'll beat you there," Jacob said. Ussier laughed, and then he was gone, leaving behind only a faint wind to indicate his passage. "I swear he does shit like that just to fuck with me," Jacob said.

I indicated for Artemise to take the front seat next to Jacob and then climbed in the back behind him with Kayla squeezed in between Steve and I. "Do you really think it might be the same person?" she asked.

"We'll find out soon enough." Jacob hit the gas once we were all settled, and I grabbed the handle and closed my eyes. "That asshole is going to tell us every last thing he knows."

The trip into town was silent, and I pondered the possibility. I didn't really think they could be the same. For one, I had been chasing Kayla when Jacob was fighting the creature. My instincts said that the doppelganger had been created for a very specific purpose. Most likely to destroy Jacob in slow degrees by torturing him with the face of someone he loved. I'd been considering all this time that whoever was behind all the madness was singling me out specifically, but now that thought altered. What if they were targeting us? That changed things.

I'd had two thousand years to acquire enemies, Jacob far less. And if it was someone targeting us both, then it would have to be someone we've enraged in the last year and a half. *That still leaves a whole shit ton of people,"* Jacob said. *"Everyone from leftover Syndicate members, to possibly dead ones, Angie or her pissed off brother....*" He trailed off as he considered that angle. *"No, I got the impression that they just wanted to stay the fuck out of it after we left them."*

"You are probably right."

The lights of Bellows Falls appeared as we emerged from another winding bend of the road. "Still think that it's in this direction?" Jacob asked with a glance at Artemise.

"I'm sure of it, young man. Let's check the north side of town first."

"How is Ussier going to find us?" Steve asked.

"I think we're probably going to find him already there," Kayla said. "It's not a big town, Uncle Ghedi should be able to smell the creature out."

"He's almost enough to make the rest of us feel useless," Steve said under his breath.

"Ussier is formidable," I agreed. "It's far better to have him on your side than not."

After wandering down a few streets and conferring with each other in low voices, Jacob and Artemise led us to a street enveloped in shadows. Several of the streetlamps were out, and trees obscured the houses set back and crouched in the darkness. Jacob parked his car at the end of the street near one of the burned-out lights and took a deep breath. "He's in one of these houses. I'll get a better sense when we're closer."

"It's the end one," Artemise replied. "I'm sure of it."

Fingers rapped on Steve's window, and he jumped, letting out a startled yelp. Ussier leaned down and grinned, beckoning us out. Steve muttered curses under his breath, and Kayla muffled a chuckle. We were all wound tightly, and I'd rather Kayla and Steve not be involved in the ugliness to come, but I had no hope of keeping them out of it either. I knew better than to even consider trying to leave Jacob behind.

"Here's the plan," Ussier whispered when we gathered about. "Corvin and I will go in the back; the two old men will take the front.

Girl, you and Steve are the lookouts. Stay in the car, you see anyone skulking about, call my cell and Kristair's. You do have a cell now, don't you, Kristair?"

"Of course."

"Put it on vibrate. You, too, girl." I pulled out my phone and looked at it quizzically, trying to figure out what he meant by "vibrate." "I'll send you a text if I want you to come in, Kayla, but if I call, get the fuck out of here and head back to the cabin. We'll find you." Jacob took the phone from my hands, fiddled with it for a moment, and handed it back to me with a wink.

"You're good to go."

"Thank you for saving my dignity," I replied, stuffing the phone back into my pocket.

"Anytime, Kristair."

Ussier handed Steve a pair of handcuffs he dug out of his pocket. "If Kayla's head starts spinning around or she starts talking in tongues, restrain her. If that happens and I find out you got all pussy on me and let her get away, I'll break your damn legs."

"Threats aren't necessary," Kayla said. "Steve knows what to do."

"Just making sure." Ussier glanced around at the quiet street. "It's still early, quiet and quick, you hear me?" He started walking away, just another shadow in the street. "You coming or not, Corvin?"

I gave Jacob a mental kiss as he cursed, tossed Steve the keys, and stalked after Ussier. I'd know anything that happened to him the moment it occurred, but I still didn't like being separated. Even if it made sense to have us on different teams with our mental link.

I waited until Steve and Kayla were settled in the Camaro with the doors locked and then gestured to Artemise. "Shall we go knock on the front door?"

"By all means, my friend."

We crossed the street and headed up the sidewalk. I sensed Jacob winding around the trees and bushes behind the houses, keeping up an acid running commentary in his head about the entire situation. The homes on this street were old, and some were in a state of disrepair. Most looked as if they had been converted into small apartments. Glass on the sidewalk crunched, giving evidence to what had happened to the streetlights, though whether it was a normal state for the street or the doppelganger had done it to hide his comings and goings I didn't know.

Artemise and I made it to the small path leading to the house we sought without seeing anyone, and no one appeared in the windows of the houses we'd passed to notice our passage. All in all, the street seemed far too quiet for so early in the night, as if an aura of evil hung over the row, suppressing the spark of vitality.

"We're here," Jacob said in my thoughts. *"Looks like the place has been divided into two apartments. There's an outside stair in the back for the upper apartment. That's where the thing is."*

I studied the building as we neared. It was painted a light color; the shutters and porch needed quite a few repairs. The lower level was quite dark and still, and light gleamed underneath a single window shade on the upper floor. I let Artemise take the lead as we stepped onto the porch, and he moved to the door on the right, testing the knob.

"Give me but a moment," he whispered.

Disgust flared in Jacob's mind. *"Ugh, what's that smell?"*

"Hurry, I think they're inside," I said.

"Almost there." With a click, the door opened, revealing an inner staircase, boarded up against the rest of the lower level. As we started up, the stench of death and blood flowed down to us. The rushing sound of feet and a startled cry came from above, and without a word, Artemise and I ran up the remaining stairs and burst into the kitchen.

I heard a scuffle coming from the room off to the right of the hallway, the room overlooking the street, and I sensed Jacob in there too. *"Are you okay?"* I demanded in Jacob's head.

"Yeah, Ussier's got him trussed up like a fucking Thanksgiving Day turkey, but the bastard's still trying to wiggle free. He gives me the fucking creeps."

I touched Artemise's sleeve. "Let us check out the rest of the place before we join them. Ussier's got our quarry bound." Artemise nodded, and we went down the hallway to the left. Artemise opened one door into a rumpled bedroom, and I peered into another one that was the bathroom. The scent of blood strengthened, and I flipped on the light.

The bodies of a man, woman, and child were piled in the bathtub, a clear plastic shower curtain draped over them. A leg draped obscenely out of the tub, and dried blood made swirls and smears on the tiles.

"Kristair?" Jacob must've sensed my disquiet at the scene, and I sent him a wave of reassurance. He didn't need to see this.

"I'll be right there in a moment, mo chroí. *We're just making sure there are no more surprises in the rest of the apartment."*

"Kristair, you might want to take a look at this," Artemise said softly. I flipped off the light again, shut the bathroom door firmly, and went to the doorway of the second bedroom. Children's furniture had been broken and piled into a jumble, half falling out of the closet. Poster-sized pictures of Jacob had been plastered on the walls haphazardly. Pictures of him taken when he was unawares. An icy chill seized me.

A nest of pillows and blankets took up the center of the room, surrounded by unlit candles. A ring had been driven into the floor with manacles attached; a ball gag had been set to the side along with implements of pain. A rushing, choking fury filled me as I remembered how much the thought of this creature filled Jacob with horror and revulsion.

I heard Jacob shout in my mind, but I was already racing down the hall into the room where my lover was with that thing. The doppelganger's eyes widened as I burst through the entryway and leveled my gaze on him. "You," he gasped, trying to shrink back as I hauled him up from the floor, lifting him up into the air. I yearned to hurl him through the window and let him fall to his death below. "What are you?" the doppelganger cried, struggling fiercely to get free, but his bound hands and feet hampered his efforts.

"I am your worst fucking nightmare," I snarled, jerking him closer, my hands tightening on him to keep myself from strangling him.

"I am the real Kristair, and you are nothing but a poor copy, an ill-created shadow. You'll never have him because he already belongs to me. Do you hear me? You will never touch him. You'll never know him as I do."

I sensed Jacob step closer to me, to that creature, and I snarled at him in warning. He ignored me and laid his hand on my arm. *"He can't hurt me, love, he never could get to me the way he wanted to. We need to ask him some questions. Set him down before you break him."*

"Jacob." The doppelganger cast anxious eyes at my lover. "Get away from him. He's dangerous."

Jacob ignored him as well, tightening his hand on my arm. *"I know you saw some real bad shit, Kristair, but you can't kill him just yet."*

"Ancient One, perhaps it's best if you wait in the other room," Ussier said.

"I'm staying," I snapped, forcing myself to set the creature aside with perhaps more force than was necessary. He landed in a crumpled heap several feet away, his ankle twisting under him with a nasty crack.

"Nothing like starting off a good interrogation with a broken bone or two," Ussier said, picking the doppelganger back up and shoving him onto a chair as he groaned in pain. "Now you're going to tell me everything I want to know or else I'm going to let my homicidal friend loose on you. I gather from his expression that there are any number of unpleasant things that he would love to do to you."

"Jacob won't let you," the doppelganger growled. It was incredibly eerie how much he did look like me, mannerisms, the tone of his voice, the way he looked at my lover.

"Don't count on it," Jacob said grimly. "I might just help him."

A stricken expression crossed the creature's face as Jacob took my hand, and I got the impression that simple gesture hurt him far more than his broken ankle or the gunshot wound in his leg. "You don't mean that, *mo chroí.*"

Before Jacob could erupt with the rage that was rumbling inside of him, I squeezed his hand. *"Wait, I have an idea."*

Chapter 23

I WAS almost afraid to ask Kristair what he meant. It was so damned surreal to be staring at that creature, see it looking back at me with hurt and madness in his eyes. Eyes that were so like my lover's. The sense of wrongness coming from it was even stronger now, diseased and twisted.

"What, you think if I sweet talk him a little he'll tell us everything he knows?" I asked in disgust at the very thought, and Kristair nodded, squeezing my hand again.

"Yes, I think it'll be easier on you in the long run than having Ussier interrogate him. His methods are... direct."

"Just come out and say it. He's going to torture him." I didn't know what to think about that, and Kristair's thumb brushed the back of my hand as the creature watched, his eyes darkening even more.

Ussier pulled out his cell phone, rapidly typed something in, and then he nodded at Artemise. "Meet the girl and her overgrown protector. Keep them in the kitchen for now. I'd like to see his reaction to her in a bit, but not right away."

I stared back at the creature, trying to pinpoint what was different about him. The first time I'd seen him in the woods he'd seemed calm and in control, with that innate dangerous smoothness Kristair had. Then, when he attacked me at Alette's again, it seemed as if he had control of himself, like he knew exactly what he wanted and he was going to get it at all costs. The only sense of him that I got earlier in the evening was one of desperation. He had come at me so fast that I barely had time to register his presence before I was unconscious.

Now, though, the creature seemed as if he was unraveling. He was unshaven, the same as Kristair, as if he were in some way mirroring my lover. Did Kristair's shock and horror yesterday morning start this? Did something else?

Ussier stopped in front of the doppelganger, but it paid him no mind, his eyes still locked on me. "That looks like it hurts," Ussier said conversationally, looking down at the bloody tourniquet around his thigh. I tensed, waiting for Ussier to punch it in the leg or dig his fingers into the wound.

"I have nothing to say to you, Ghedi Ussier," the creature replied, his eyes flicking away from me as he drew himself up, arrogance erasing the pain on its face.

"Come on, we know you're not working alone. We even know you're not the mastermind. You're just the puppet dancing along on your Master's strings. What did he tell you? Did he say you could have Corvin there if you played nice?"

"Jacob *is* mine," the doppelganger insisted. "He has been since the moment I laid eyes on him at his football game."

Kristair's hand clutched convulsively around mine, and I glanced at him with a small shake of my head. *"Keep your possessive instincts under control."*

"You're not one to talk, Jacob."

I fisted my hand in my hair, watching the flickers of distressed emotion cross the creature's face. At Alette's, he'd been hell-bent on just abusing me, seeing me degraded. He hadn't tried seduction or loving words except when he wanted to confuse me or get past my guard. I had no doubt at the time that the creature knew exactly what it was, a copy of Kristair sent to hunt me down. Now it seemed as if the creature believed its own hype. As if it really thought it was Kristair, and in its own twisted and confused way, it loved me.

I shuddered. Like things weren't bad enough as it was. *"I don't know if I can do it, Kristair. Play with it like that."* Have it beg me with Kristair's eyes and then walk away so it could be killed. It was somehow even more obscene than the thought of it trying to rape me.

Ussier punched the creature in the face. Bone crunched, and blood gushed from his nose. The vampire lord smashed a hand over its mouth as it howled in pain. "Look at me when I'm talking to you, not Corvin."

I couldn't watch, not when it was staring at me with my lover's eyes, staring at me like I was betraying him. "I think I'm going to just be a distraction in here. I'll go wait with Kayla and Steve."

Kristair nodded and lifted my hand to his lips, never taking his eyes off of the doppelganger. "Stay in the kitchen," he murmured.

"No, wait, Jacob, don't go." The creature's eyes widened, and his voice became desperate as I turned away. "Jacob, please, don't leave me with them."

I hardened my heart against how much the creature sounded like my lover and clung to the renewed link in my mind, letting it drown out the pleas as I left the room. I didn't want to know what they were going to do to him. I didn't want to see that thing with Kristair's face looking all bruised and bloody.

Artemise wasn't back with Kayla and Steve yet. I poked through the kitchen, trying to ignore the low murmur of voices in the next room, the sick thud of fists striking flesh, the muffled sounds of pain. It turned my stomach even as I sensed how Kristair blocked the worst of it from my mind.

Kristair had moved so damned fast when he'd confronted the doppelganger. He'd lifted the creature like his weight had meant nothing, tossed him like a rag doll. It proved he could still use at least some of his supernatural abilities, and the Ascended hadn't jumped in. Which meant that I still had the speed and strength, the ability to heal if I wanted.

That was the trick question, right? Did we want it? I certainly hadn't before, though I'd used the abilities when I had to.

Restless, I turned down the hallway, peering in the other rooms. My stomach churned when I looked upon the scene in the bathroom, and Kristair's mind sharpened. *"I thought I said to stay in the kitchen."*

"I didn't agree." I forced myself to look at the savaged and naked bodies of the family, the abject horror on their faces. Let it harden me against the creature. It had done this, and if we didn't stop him, he'd continue doing such things. It helped to put things in perspective.

I grabbed a sheet from the linen closet and draped it over the bodies. Some part of my mind shrieked about fingerprints and leaving traces of ourselves behind. When the cops found this scene, they'd start hounding us. Eventually it just might come back to catch up with us, but I couldn't bring myself to care.

I glanced in the other rooms, tensing myself against finding more bodies, but to my intense relief, there were none. Who the fuck knew what was downstairs in the other apartment. If there were any sense of right or wrong in the world, it would be unoccupied. I wouldn't have put it past the creature to have killed the entire block.

The scene in the last bedroom failed to move me at all. I hoped to god the family died quick and never knew what kind of fucking monster they had been confronted with. I kicked aside a candle on my way to the closet, and it bounced off the wall with a heavy thud.

A picture frame stuck out from underneath a dresser drawer that had half-fallen out of the closet. I leaned down and tugged it free, turning it over in my hands. A happy-looking couple with a laughing little girl stared back at me. I stared at it for a long time, then pulled the picture free from the frame, and stuffed it in my back pocket. Some things just shouldn't be forgotten.

When I returned to the kitchen, Kayla and Steve were there. Kayla stared at the ground, tapping her foot, seemingly lost in thought, and Steve's dark face was uneasy. "Where's Artemise?" I asked.

Steve jerked his chin toward the living room. The sounds of fists had stopped, though I could hear muffled crying. At least it wasn't calling my name anymore. My hands shook in reaction, and I wanted to go in there and throttle it myself. It had killed that entire family like they'd meant nothing.

"He's talking with the other two," Steve replied. "What do you think they're doing to that guy in there?"

"You don't want to know," Kayla said, touching his hand. "Trust me, you don't."

The crying changed to screams. Sudden, shocking, piercing screams that ripped through the apartment and made us all jump. "What the fuck are they thinking?" Steve swore. "They're going to have the cops down on our asses."

"I'm pretty sure Artemise took steps to make sure no sounds escape the building," Kayla assured him, though she also was now casting uncertain glances toward the living room. "Or they'll simply enthrall anybody who does coming asking questions."

"I don't get the feeling that the neighbors here ask that many questions anyway." The town had a vibe about it that was unnatural, this part of town even more so, though maybe it was just because the creature was here, infecting the entire area. I'd have to ask Kristair about that later. Or maybe the town was a bloodsucker den. It figured I'd pick a place like that. It was like I was some kind of supernatural freak magnet.

"Jacob! Jacob! What have you done with him? Jacob!"

I cringed, stuffing my hands in my pockets and feeling the picture there. Fuck. It didn't sound like they were getting anywhere. I touched Kristair's mind, sensed the implacable anger, the ruthless will, and I knew he wouldn't stop until he had the answers he sought. *"Any luck?"*

"The creature is remarkably stubborn and loyal. It will take time to break down its will."

"Do we have that time?"

I sensed his mental shrug. *"We'll make the time if need be."*

I suppressed another wince as the screaming started again. Fuck, I wished it would stop calling out to me. I'd been tortured twice, and it was just as horrifying on the other end of it. The hair on the nape of my neck stood on end. Steve's jaw tightened, and he laid his hands on Kayla's shoulders, rubbing them gently. "You sure you don't want to wait outside?"

"I'm a big girl. I can take it," she replied with remarkable calm and flashed me a sympathetic smile. "Though Jake's turning green."

"Hardly." There had to be an easier way. The creature believed it was Kristair, which meant in some sick, twisted kind of way, it loved me. Maybe Kristair was right—maybe I could reason with it in a way they couldn't. "I'll be right back."

"Jake, get your ass back here," Steve snapped, but I ignored him and went into the other room anyway.

I froze inside the doorway and stared at the scene in front of me. The doppelganger's eyes were almost swollen completely shut, his face almost unrecognizable, misshapen and covered with bruises and claw marks. His shirt had been ripped off of him, more claw marks tearing open his body, destroying the tattoos and, god, the blood, it was everywhere. His wrists had been tied to the chair, and some of his fingers were swollen and twisted, and his pants for air came out as a kind of terrible, wheezing whistle.

Ussier was staring at the creature grimly, his eyes the coldest I'd ever seen them. His hands were stiffened into brutal-looking claws that dripped even more blood onto the floor. But the creature's gaze was fixed in terror not on Ussier, but on Kristair, who was standing back, watching impassively.

"Jacob, you don't want to be here," Kristair said softly, taking his eyes off the doppelganger for brief moment. His gaze seemed even more ancient than usual.

The creature's eyes darted toward me, and his jaw worked as a wholly different kind of pain crossed his features. He was totally insane now, lost within whatever world he had created in his head. "Jacob," he rasped, struggling to stand up, not even seeming to realize how his bonds and injuries hampered him. "Run, they've all gone mad. Run, dammit. I'll find you. I'll always find you."

"There has to be another way. Why don't you just get the answers right out of his mind? You've all done that before," I demanded.

Artemise shook his head. "After what happened to Lisabeth, I'll only risk it when we need to. For the moment, this is wearing him down."

Somehow, I just knew they'd never be able to get answers from him by torturing him either. We could spend days, and the doppelganger wouldn't give up. In that way, too, the creature was like my lover. I touched the picture in my back pocket. Where it counted though, they were nothing alike.

I forced down the loathing I felt for the creature and held up my hand to Ussier to keep him from striking again as I stepped closer. I sensed Kristair's sudden tension, as if he wanted to snatch me away from the doppelganger, but he didn't try to interfere.

"Jacob?" the creature whispered. "Jacob, help me."

"It's okay." I steeled myself, moving over to him and cradling his face gently in my hands. "I'm here."

Tears glittered in its eyes, and the air in the room seemed strung taut with the threat of imminent violence. "Don't let them hurt me anymore, please."

I searched its face, trying to decide if it was playing games or if it was genuinely asking for help. "I can stop them, but you have to tell them what they want to know. It's important; can ya do that for me?"

"I can't." Its voice caught on a note of despair. "I can't, please don't make me."

"What's wrong? Are you afraid? After all the people you've killed, the horrible things you've done, are you trying to tell me that you're fucking afraid?" I couldn't hide the disgust and revulsion, and I lashed out at the creature, furious with its games.

It jerked back away from me, chest heaving as it stared wildly around the room. I yanked the picture out of my pocket and shoved it in his face. "Listen to me, you are not Kristair. The man I love wouldn't do what you fucking did to those people in the bathroom. Look at it." I grabbed his chin as he tried to twist his head away. "Fucking look at it, you bastard."

"Jacob." Kristair stepped up behind me and laid his hand on my shoulder.

"No, old man, let him," Ussier said.

The doppelganger snarled, once again trying to rise from his chair. His eyes fixated on Kristair, almost seeming to glow from within in madness. Like a rabid animal. "Get your filthy hands off of him."

Footsteps sounded, and Kristair stiffened even more in my mind, indignant and protective. "Kayla, turn around and go right back into the kitchen."

"Don't be ridiculous, Kris. I have just as much invested in this as you do."

The creature made a soft pitying sound, lowering its gaze in an odd gesture of submission. "Mistress." I felt him quiver under my hand as shock tore through me and Kristair.

"What did you say?" Kristair demanded, pushing me to the side and stepping in front of Kayla. He grabbed the doppelganger by his throat, shoving him back until the chair slammed into the wall. "What did you call her?"

As much as the creature twisted and bucked, it couldn't escape Kristair's hand. After several long moments, Kristair eased his grip, and the creature sagged down, gasping for air.

"Mistress, help me. Jacob?" He looked between Kayla and me, eyes pleading. Though the way he looked at her, with a kind of terrified subservient adoration, was rather sickening to see. Even worse than the way he looked at me.

"Oh sweet Jesus," I said as Kayla, Kristair and I stared at each other. "You don't really think it's her, do you?"

Chapter 24

I STUDIED my doppelganger in the wake of Jacob's question, my mind whirling. It couldn't be true. I didn't want to believe that Nerissa might be behind the madness, but I forced myself to consider the possibility. As disturbing as it might have been. At this point, I couldn't dismiss anything.

"Who?" Ussier demanded in a hard voice.

"The woman who made me a vampire," I replied, my heart twisting in my chest. The creature cried out, struggling to stand up again.

"No, she made me! Not you."

I tightened my hand around his throat again in warning, and he sagged back down again. He seemed to fear me the most, though Ussier had done the majority of the damage to him. He really believed me to be the unnatural copy, not himself.

"How can that be?" Artemise asked. "From what you've told me, she was an Ancient herself when she turned you. I thought she had long since disappeared. Didn't you try to use her journals to track down your own symptoms?"

"I can tell you that she is not dead. I discovered that when I disappeared myself." If it was her, then it raised many disturbing questions. I looked at Artemise and Ussier. "There are many things that I have been keeping from you because I wasn't at liberty to discuss them, but if this is true, it changes matters." I sensed Jacob's deep worry, and it echoed my own. "I need to know for absolute certain if he is telling the truth."

I removed my hand from the creature's throat and stepped back. "Artemise, do you think you can risk delving into its mind?"

"Wait, no! Mistress, I've done everything you asked me to. You said he was mine." The doppelganger thrashed in the chair, his burning gaze on Kayla's face. "Mistress, you can't let them! He's mine," the doppelganger raged.

He howled as Artemise laid his hand like a net over his scalp, fingers pressing into his temples. "I'll be fine," he assured us. "I don't throw my heart into things as much as Lisabeth does. At least I hope that's the case."

Jacob took an involuntary step forward as the creature jerked spasmodically, and I took his hand. He was torn between pity and revulsion, abhorring it for the things it had done, yet drawn to it because of the similarities we did share and the connection it seemed to feel with him. *What the fuck happened to it? Do you think Nerissa really did this shit?"*

"I don't want to believe it." The betrayal cut too deep. *"But it would explain a great many things."*

"Get me a bowl of water," Artemise ordered in a curt voice. "Preferably a metal one, if they have it."

Steve left the room as Artemise stepped away from the creature, his cultured features pinched in distaste. The doppelganger sagged, whimpering in his bonds, head lolling to the side. "There isn't much there to work with. His mind is too fractured as it is and worsening by the minute," Artemise said, wiping his hand on a handkerchief.

"Were you able to confirm anything?" Ussier asked.

"That this Mistress did create him for the sole purpose of dealing with Mr. Corvin. I gather that along with the Ancient One's appearance, he did have some of Kristair's knowledge and memories, but they have deteriorated as well. The only thing he has left is his want of you, my young friend, and he'll do anything to get you. He cannot stop himself."

Steve returned carrying a metal mixing bowl filled to the brim with water. "What do you want me to do with it?"

"Ah, perfect, Mr. Teasia. Set it down on that coffee table. I was able to extract an image of this Mistress from the creature's thoughts. I trust, my friend, that you'll be able to tell us if it is the woman you suspect."

Artemise sat on the edge of the couch and waited for the water to still. He stiffened one finger into a claw and sliced open his palm, allowing the blood to drip and cloud the water. The surface quivered, and Kayla's face appeared.

"No, dammit," Steve said harshly, stepping forward in front of Kayla. "I don't believe it."

"Patience," Artemise said smoothly, concentrating on the water as the image changed subtly, Kayla's eyes darkening, her face maturing until it was Nerissa's face that stared back at me. "This is the true appearance of the woman he dealt with. Does it mean anything to you?"

My heart sank, becoming leaden in my chest, and my throat tightened. I felt eyes on me from all sides as the silence stretched out, broken only by the creature's harsh, whistling pants for air and small animal sounds of pain. "It is Nerissa," I said through numb lips. "There is no other I can think of who would know of her appearance and who would make such personal attacks against me."

I tore my eyes away, hardening my heart, pushing the ache away. "And it means we have a very big problem on our hands."

"We'll discuss it later back at the cabin. You all go," Ussier said. "I'll take care of this place so there will be no evidence left behind that we were here."

Jacob hesitated as Steve wrapped his arm around Kayla's shoulders and led her out with Artemise following. *"Come on,* mo chroí, *let us leave Ussier to his business. He's very good at it."*

"He's going to kill him, isn't he?"

I paused, struck by the starkness in Jacob's mental tone. *"At this point it would be a mercy. He's only going to get more confused, lost, and increasingly dangerous with each passing day. I'm not sure what Nerissa did to create him, but I suspect she broke the laws of nature, and he is paying the price as we speak. Some things are just not meant to be."*

"I'm not saying it shouldn't be done. I'm just saying that it shouldn't be Ussier that kills him." I sensed Jacob's resolve harden, and I shook my head, knowing what his decision would cost him.

"Let it be, Jacob. It doesn't matter who does the deed. If it will make you feel better, I'll take care of it."

"It matters to me!"

I bit back further arguments as much as I wanted to voice them. "As you wish," I said softly, squeezing his hand. "I'll wait for you below." I brushed a mental kiss to his lips and gestured for Ussier, my heart breaking for my lover.

"Are you sure? I can knock him for you." Ussier said in an undertone, joining me at the doorway. We both looked back where Jacob was studying the doppelganger, who stared back at him with pleading, broken eyes.

"He is sure." I twined myself deeper into Jacob's thoughts and turned blindly toward the stairs. I wouldn't interfere, but Jacob needed me, whether he would admit that need or not.

"Jacob, please," the creature said behind us. "Don't leave, too, please."

"Hush now, I'm here. I've got you."

Aching for Jacob, I opened the door and gestured for Ussier to go on ahead. "I'll be right behind you."

"Will you go with me?" the doppelganger asked.

I slipped through the door after Ussier and shut it, missing Jacob's low murmur in reply. Whatever ability Ussier or Artemise used to make the apartment soundproof kept us from hearing the gunshot, but I felt the shock of it ripple through Jacob. "It is done," I said.

The vampire lord glanced back up the doorway, his expression reflective. "You have a good man there, Ancient One."

"The best," I agreed.

Jacob came out a few minutes later. The stairs creaked as he came down them, and I longed to pull him into a fierce hug, but I resisted, giving him the space he needed. He glanced at Ussier and took my hand. "Ready?"

"Of course."

"If it's any consolation, Mr. Corvin, if you hadn't felt any qualms about this, I would've lost all respect for you," Ussier said. "You went ahead and did what you felt you had to do. Not because that thing looked like Kristair, but because you felt pity for what you saw beneath the glamour. That's why you can be what I never can. You're a man and I'm a monster. I'd've shot that motherfucker in the face without blinking even as it begged for mercy." He inclined his head in respect and then disappeared up the stairs.

Jacob let out an explosive breath as Ussier disappeared. "He fucking scares the shit out of me."

"He has his moments." I brushed my fingers across his cheek. "Are you okay, *mo chroí*?"

"I'll be just fine." Jacob slipped his hand around the nape of my neck and touched his lips to mine. "I should ask the same of you. You've taken quite a blow."

"I don't know what to make of it, Jacob." I closed my eyes and leaned into him, taking comfort in his nearness and giving it back to him. "Things may have been contentious between Nerissa and I often, but in our own way, you could say we loved each other. We were family, even if it was unsaid. I cannot imagine what would've made her turn against me like this."

"You don't think denying her gift and choosing to become a human might've set her off? Because I'm pretty sure she considered you becoming an Ascended a gift."

"I do not doubt that it angered her. She would've thought I was wasting my potential and she never did like it when I defied her, but

Jacob, this is an extreme reaction. The things she did... not that she couldn't be ruthless, I agree that she could, but there was a bond there. And making that creature, that is just madness. She's not a god. What could she be thinking?"

Jacob rubbed his hand on my back. "Come on. The others are going to start worrying about us if we keep lingering here. We can discuss it between ourselves on the way back to the cabin."

We emerged back out into the quiet night. A breeze stirred, bringing with it the scent of growing things and dispelling the miasma of blood. Kayla and the other two were already waiting in Jacob's car, and they remained silent as we got in and Jacob drove off.

Kayla laid her head on Steve's shoulder. "What are we going to do, Kris? If it is Nerissa, how the hell are we going to stop her? I think Tony rocks and all, but she's got a lot of years on him and she's an über-bitch. He's too damned nice to go up against her."

I glanced at Artemise, who was staring out the window, but I knew he was listening intently to every word. I reached over and clasped Kayla's hand. "We will think of something, little one. If there is one thing I've learned in the last year, it's that nothing is impossible."

"She's got a good point," Jacob said in my mind. *"Nerissa handled us like we were babies before and that's when we still had at least a little supernatural mojo of our own. She's just fucking toying with us. She could've killed us any damn time she wanted with a snap of her fingers."*

"That is true. Perhaps she's not seeking our deaths but punishing us. Punishing me. Death might not be her goal."

"Which brings us back to asking ourselves what is her goal? Seems to me like she's making it mighty fucking uncomfortable for you to remain human. If Kayla and I get killed and you become unwelcome in Pittsburgh, where would you turn?"

Something about what Jacob said niggled at the back of my brain. I set it aside to mull over along with all the other questions the creature's revelation had raised. *"My heart says that isn't the reason why my Mistress is doing this."*

A surge of anger flashed through Jacob, and the tires squealed as he took a corner too fast. *"Stop calling her that. She's never been your mistress, she never will be. She doesn't fucking own you, Kristair."*

"My apologies," I said, taken aback by Jacob's reaction. *"I didn't mean to offend you."*

Jacob pulled the Camaro over to the side of the road and slammed on the breaks. Kayla gasped and Steve swore as Jacob turned around and glared at me. *"Stop being so damned polite. Ever think that your damn heart could be wrong because it's fucking broken? You're hurt and you don't want to believe the worst of her. The truth is, Nerissa was a controlling bitch when I met her, and from what I gathered about your past with her, she was a controlling bitch then."*

Artemise studied the two of us with mild interest. "I hate to break up your argument, but it might be wiser if we get behind walls. This is, after all, shape shifter territory, and they do not look kindly upon those such as me or those who accompany them."

Jacob cursed violently and tore off the side of the road again. I sensed Kayla's eyes on me, but I ignored her gaze and stared out of the window. It was impossible to see much in the utter darkness. The headlights would illuminate brief bits of shadowed forest, and then they would be gone again.

"I'm probably going to regret this," Steve said, "but what do you mean by shape shifters?"

"Were creatures, wolves, bears, big cats," Artemise replied. "I'm sure you've heard the legends."

"I knew I should've kept my mouth shut."

Silence descended in the car once again, and I went back to my thoughts. I could not deny that Jacob was right in one respect. Discovering that it was Nerissa cut deeply, but I'd have liked to think that I wasn't in the habit of putting emotion over logic. There was far more going on than Nerissa having a moment of pique over me choosing a different fate than the one she had laid out for me.

There was a brooding heaviness stirring in the atmosphere, something that had been building for months. It set my teeth on edge. I had been so distracted with my investigation, and the more personal it became, the less in tune with my surroundings I'd become.

I shifted uneasily in my seat. Tony had told Jacob that a split was forming among the Ascended and that I had been the unwitting cause of it. Now that right there was most likely the cause for Nerissa's ire. If my actions had threatened her world…. But surely matters weren't that bad. The Ascended were linked. They wouldn't foster dissention among themselves.

That would be a terrifying thought indeed, with their power. Their stability came from their harmony and their agreement to the rules. I couldn't begin to imagine the harm that could be caused if they were at odds with each other. If that was the case, then we had a far bigger problem on our hands than a handful of vampires being slaughtered and our own personal problems.

Chapter 25

I DID not like where Kristair's brooding thoughts were taking him. They made me antsy and on edge, and not because it meant we were in a whole shitload of trouble. He was working himself up to something. By the time we returned to the cabin, he was completely lost in thought, and I was pretty sure he'd forgotten that I could hear every damn thing that went on in his head.

"So are we supposed to twiddle our thumbs until Ussier gets back?" Steve asked. "I want to know who this Nerissa is, 'cause you're all acting like she's the damn boogeyman or something. How come I've never heard of her before?"

"Soon, Mr. Teasia. It shouldn't take him long to dispose of the bodies and erase any evidence of our presence there. He's quick and thorough," Artemise replied. "There is no sense in having Kristair explain the situation we're in twice."

I remained quiet, my gaze intent on Kristair, who had drifted over to the window and was staring out into the night. I recognized the remoteness inside of him. I'd seen it a couple times before, and it never failed to make me uneasy, because I couldn't predict what Kristair would do next. Only that I probably wouldn't like it.

"How come the more pissed off I get, the calmer you get?" I growled in his mind.

I sensed his faint smile before he glanced over his shoulder at me. *"Call me perverse."*

"I do," I retorted out loud and went into the kitchen to grab something to drink. I'd really have killed for a beer right then, or something stronger.

Kristair had to be wrong. Tony would've said something if the situation had gotten to be that dire among the Ascended. I felt like I had an itch under my skin, crawling and tormenting me every time I thought about it. Dammit, where was he? Tony could have cleared up the whole thing in a heartbeat if the punk ass would just show his face.

We'd all separated to our own little corners of the room. Artemise sat on the couch in apparent meditation, his face smooth and calm. Steve scowled at the table, and Kayla stood with her arms crossed at another window. And me, I paced, resisting the urge to kick unoffending furniture out of the way.

I concentrated on what was going through Kristair's mind and pushed away my thoughts. Every time I let my thoughts drift, they returned to the doppelganger. The blood, there had been so much damn blood. I knew I'd smell the stink of it for a long time to come, feel its slick heat on my hands. And his eyes, god help me, those twisted, needy eyes.

I'd expected a fight from the creature when I'd untied it from the chair, but it hadn't. The creature had known, and it hadn't tried to stop me. It was like it was just grateful that I had killed him instead of Ussier or Kristair. It had died with my name on his lips.

Jerking my thoughts away, I realized I'd stopped pacing and was staring off. Scowling, I started again. The doppelganger didn't deserve any more of my thoughts, and it had died far cleaner than that family had.

Kristair turned and walked toward me, stopping me with his hands on my shoulders. He didn't say anything. I got the impression he didn't really know what to say. He'd never been the best at discussing what he was feeling.

"Yes?" I asked, striving to make my voice as mild as possible when what I longed to do was drag him back to our bedroom. I wanted to tie him to the bed, make him beg, make him scream with desire, make him forget anything else but the two of us and how it felt when we were fucking.

One expressive black brow rose, and a faint smile tugged on Kristair's lips as a surge of affection and exasperation came at me through our bond. *"What is it with you and sex and getting so very possessive at moments like these?"*

"You're pulling away from me." I seethed. *"You'd better not be thinking of doing anything stupid like sacrificing yourself to the Ascended gods or something like that, because I will turn you over my goddamned knee and spank you until you can't sit down anymore."*

Kristair blinked, such a startled expression crossing his face that it would've been damned adorable if the situation had been different. "I think you mean it," he murmured.

"You can bet your pretty ass I mean it," I growled out loud.

Kayla glanced our way, and Kristair's cheeks colored faintly. I didn't think I'd ever seen him blush before either, and it made me determined to get other blushes from him. *"Stop that,"* he demanded. *"Now is not the time or place for such things."*

I leaned closer and had the satisfaction of hearing his breath catch. *"Don't tempt me. I can think of any number of things I can do with you before Ussier arrives that won't interfere one damn bit with our waiting. And I don't care if the entire room knows what we're up to either."*

Kristair's hands tightened on my shoulders. *"I swear to you we will always be together. Do you trust me, Jacob?"*

"You know I do. Don't try to distract me with questions we both know the answer to. Because I also know you're not going to let everyone you know be slaughtered if you can find a way to stop it. Even if it gets you hurt in the process."

He smiled, and phantom fingers touched my cheek as he brushed my lips with a mental kiss. *"I'm not pulling away from you. I need to think, and I need to do that with logic, not emotion. Do you understand?"*

The door opened and Ussier walked in. "I guess I don't have too much of choice," I said.

"Have you checked on Lisabeth?" Artemise asked, rising up from the couch.

"There hasn't been any change." Ussier's face was grim. "Did you get back without any incident?"

"We didn't run into any trouble, though I will admit I'm becoming very uneasy about the whole affair," Artemise replied.

"You're not the only one." Steve stood up from the table and went to stand next to Kayla, glaring at Kristair. "Now that we're all here, how about some answers?"

"Of course," Kristair said. "But I would like to point out, Steve, you know more than Ussier and Artemise, here. If you put your intellect to the matter, I'm sure you will figure it out."

I raised my hand before Steve could retort. "Let's not start bickering now, Jesus." I cast my lover a glance. *"Behave."*

He grimaced and then shrugged. "I'll make this quick. As I said before, Nerissa was the woman who turned me into a vampire. She was also the one instrumental in keeping Jacob and I apart when I was missing for all those months."

Ussier's expression hardened. "Old man, we need to know what we're dealing with. I think it's time you tell us what happened when you disappeared."

"That is my intention." Kristair clasped his hands behind his back. *"Does that meet with your approval?"*

"If the Ascended really are behind all this bullshit, then they can't start crying foul over people finding out about them. They're the ones interfering in our lives, not the other way around."

"That was my thought as well." He looked at Ussier and Artemise sternly. "This cannot become general knowledge. For the moment, we have just Nerissa to be concerned about as far as I know. We don't want others like her getting involved, and I have no doubt they will if they think their secrets are threatened."

"I'm not looking to stir up more trouble, Ancient One," Ussier said, and Artemise nodded gravely.

"You have my word."

I watched Kristair intently, trying to get some hint of what he was planning. I knew he was. Fuck, I knew him too well not to know he was up to something, but I couldn't get one hint of it from his mind. Right now, he was concentrating too much on figuring out how much he could say to let them know what they were dealing with without giving them the knowledge he felt they shouldn't have.

"You guys aren't stupid," I cut in as Kristair glanced at me in surprise. "You know by now that ancient vampires don't die when they disappear. They change. Kristair once described it as a chrysalis or a kind of evolution."

"Thank you, Jacob." I flashed Kristair a tight grin as he gave me an admonishing look. "The Ancients who have evolved call themselves the Ascended. They don't have need of bodies anymore. They can move through time and space. They are extremely powerful, but for the most part benign. What one feels, they all feel, and that tends to keep them pacific. Strong emotion upsets their balance. They are more interested in study and contemplation than becoming involved in affairs."

"That has obviously changed," Ussier said.

"Very true, and that breaks one of their strictest tenets."

"I don't get it, though," I said. "They have a kind of group mind. I've touched on it with you, Kristair. I thought you said what one person knows, they all do. How could Nerissa be doing this without them finding out about it and stomping her down? Because if she's doing it with their blessing, I think we're fucked."

"We have proof they don't know everything, even if they'd like for us to think they do. I managed to trick them, remember? And Tony as well, when he helped me. If we could do it in our immaturity, Nerissa, with her vast experience, shouldn't have had a problem either. You don't always have to be a part of the whole; you are allowed to leave to study on your own if you wish, after all, the others are only a thought away."

"I'm not sure I entirely understand," Ussier said. "But I'll take your word for it. Is this what Artemise has to look forward to in a few centuries? Sounds like something he would love."

"Indeed," Artemise replied. "Though I'm certain Kristair is leaving a few details out."

"I am, but what I'm leaving out doesn't affect this situation. Besides, you should have the fun of figuring it out for yourself the way the rest of us did. You always did enjoy a good puzzle, Artemise."

"Okay, so Nerissa's got a hard-on for you," Ussier said. "Why? Why now? Some younglings and their creators never get along, but if she wanted you dead, you never would've made it as long as you have, so what's changed?"

"Jacob and I have differing theories on that."

"I'm just saying that I don't think it's that much of a stretch she'd turn fucking nutty on you," I said. "She likes things her way or no way. That creature practically called her by name and you still want to dismiss the idea that she could be the bad guy."

"No, I merely disagree with the reasons why she'd act in this way. I think it takes more than me saying 'no' to her for her to lose her mind. Because this has gone beyond just revenge. She's trying to play god. Creating the doppelganger was an act of madness. Something else has pushed her over the edge. I'm sure my defiance might've added to the stress, but it's not the only reason. One does not become an Ascended by having a fragile mind."

"I'm not frightened over the thought of trying to take on a higher being. Everybody has weaknesses, and I'm very good at exploiting them." Ussier grinned, his dimples flashing. "So, then, what's your theory for why she lost it? You seem damn reluctant to discuss it."

I glanced at Kristair sharply. Ussier was right, my lover was afraid. *"What else could possibly be wrong? I think we've pretty much already hit the worst-case scenario."*

"If my leaving caused a split amongst the Ascended, as Tony indicated, then we have a very big problem. We do not want them, with all their power, fighting amongst themselves. We do not want them emotional and taking it out on each other. I have no doubt the repercussions would be felt all over the world." Kristair paused, letting that all sink in to everyone around him. "If Nerissa believes that my actions threatened her world, then yes, I have no doubt at all she would try to retaliate against me."

"I knew I hated that bitch," Kayla said. "So if she wants you dead, why not just kill you? It would be easy for her."

My eyes widened as the pieces started to click together. "She doesn't want you dead, Kristair. She wants you to come back, doesn't she? She thinks that if you come back, then the reasons for the Ascended being all pissy with each other will be gone."

"That makes more sense to me than mere revenge. But she's broken her rules in the process, and I believe her own actions have added to her madness."

"But you're human now," Kayla said, looking bewildered. "How can you go back, even if you wanted to?"

"That's why you've been so afraid and resistant of trying to get our connection back, isn't it?" I asked Kristair. *"Because you knew it was possible. Like you always said, you can't go back to the way things were. Isn't that right?"*

Kristair didn't look at me, but I sensed the loving thought he sent me, felt the fear that had been plaguing him. Not just the worry over adjusting, but the worry that he would fail at being human, would use his abilities and have no choice but to go back.

"I am human because I chose to limit myself. But I still am an Ascended. I didn't make myself ignorant of everything that I'd learned. I couldn't bring myself to do that."

Kristair still wouldn't look at me, and then I realized he was afraid that I wouldn't understand, that I would think he was selfish, but I did understand. Kristair could have given up every supernatural ability he had without blinking an eye, but he couldn't give up knowledge he'd fought so hard to obtain any more than he could deliberately have hurt me. He just couldn't. And he blamed himself for not doing it and having the threat of failing hanging over his head.

"I don't blame you, love," I said softly. *"Why don't you give yourself a bit of a break?. After all, if you didn't remember any of this, then we'd really be in some deeper shit now."*

"So you still have the potential to go back among them. To be one with them," Artemise said.

"No," I cut in. Dammit, I knew it, I knew Kristair was up to something, and it had all been leading up to this. *"No,"* I repeated more firmly in his mind. "He's not."

A tense silence filled the room as everyone else looked between Kristair and me. "Jacob, we can't wait for Tony to decide to come back and give us some answers. I'm not talking about joining them again, merely trying to communicate with them. If I could contact the Ascended, I might be able to get some answers."

"Or you might get stuck there forever," I snapped, frightened because that idea had occurred to Kristair too.

"Do you have a better idea? If so, I'm more than willing to listen."

"I'm not even going to argue with you about it." Furious, I swept everyone in the room a cold glance and walked out. They were going to encourage him with this stupid plan, and I didn't have the stomach to listen to it. *"You're not doing it,"* I flung back at him.

"Jacob," Kayla called from the porch as I reached my car. "Where are you going?"

"For a ride."

"We're going with you." She bounded down the porch toward me, Steve right behind her.

"I'm not in the mood."

"Don't be an idiot. You can't go running off alone, and you need some time to think. I get it. I'll keep my mouth shut." She jerked open the passenger door as I started the engine. I scowled, and then Steve slid in the backseat and I was outnumbered.

"Don't argue, Jake, please," Steve said. " You need us."

My scowl deepened, but I resisted the urge to kick them back out. I could probably have counted on one hand the number of times Steve had said "please" to me.

I could sense Kristair in my mind, watching and silent. He didn't try to stop me, though, as I peeled out. I wasn't sure if I wanted him to or not. There was just too much going on inside of me. I needed to clear my head or I was going to lose it.

It didn't help that I still felt tainted by what had happened earlier. The image of that creature before he died was stuck in my head, but it didn't bother me nearly as much as the picture of that family or the sight of their dead bodies in the tub, piled up like discarded, broken toys.

I wanted it to end. Goddamn, I was so tired of all of this bullshit. We just wanted to be left in peace, was that too fucking much to ask for?

Kayla reached over and took my hand, and my jaw clenched, but she kept her promise and didn't say a word.

"So how fast can this baby go?" Steve asked, leaning forward.

I latched onto the change in conversation with relief. "A quarter mile in ten point four seconds, if I let her rip."

"Oh, sweet. How long did it take you to put her together? The last time I saw her, she was still in parts all over your garage."

"A couple of months. I wanted to take my time," I replied, and the pleasure of the memory pushed away all the bad shit. Kristair had been beside me the entire time, not understanding a damn thing about 355 cubic inch engines or a small block with Dart 215 cubic centimeter platinum series heads, but he'd listened to me ramble on about specs as if I had been giving a damned state address, his expression serious and his attitude attentive.

Damn, I loved him.

"I would've had to have kicked your ass if you'd gotten an automatic instead of a manual," Steve said as I smoothly shifted. "Damn, she's a beauty."

"You know, if you two talked to women they way you did about this car and with the same tone, you'd wind up in a lot less trouble," Kayla broke in.

"Baby, this car is custom made. There's a difference. Just listen to her."

I flashed Kayla a grin and took a corner fast. "Yeah, and she doesn't sass either."

Chapter 26

JACOB would feel better once he'd gotten some distance and had a chance to calm down. It didn't mean I had to like seeing him go storming off. It was better to let him go, I knew that much, and at least he wasn't alone. If anyone could help calm him down, it would be Kayla and Steve.

Ussier turned to me after the door slammed behind Steve. "How much would it take to contact these Ascended?"

"It's been a stressful evening. I'll need some time to meditate. The Ascended are very sensitive to moods, and they like their tranquility. If I attempt it now and am successful, then I might just set them off."

"How much time do you need?"

I thought about Jacob and our renewed connection. The last thing I wanted was to put a wall up between us. I needed him to be with me every step of the way, but Jacob really irritated the Ascended. If I had some time, I could get him to calm down enough to join with me. "Let's attempt it tomorrow evening. I'm sure you wish to check back in with your people in Pittsburgh, and you'll need to see to Lisabeth."

"What do you think her odds are of waking up are?" Ussier's eyes tightened, and it made me wonder just how deep his bond with Lisabeth went.

"Fairly high. Artemise thought she'd just been stung. Now that we know who set it, I'm sure the trap was meant for me. I would think she'd awaken by dawn, or the next night at the latest. Nerissa doesn't want me dead, at least not yet."

"She will recover completely, I'm sure of it," Artemise assured him.

"You'd better hope you're right," Ussier said, moving to the window and peering out into the dark. "Do you want me to go fetch Mr. Corvin before I leave?"

"No, I know exactly where he is and his state of mind. He hasn't gone far. If I leave him alone, he'll calm down quicker." Even as I said it, I wished Jacob were here now. "I suspect once he realizes that I'm by myself at the cabin he'll be here as fast as he can drive that insane car of his."

"No doubt about that." Ussier's quick flash of a grin turned serious. "I don't like any of you being out here in the back end of nowhere. Why don't you come back with us to Pittsburgh?"

I understood Ussier's uneasiness. The sense of an impending storm had only gotten stronger since we'd arrived back at the cabin. I was reminded of Gerard's visions, the ones that had prompted him to seek out Artemise. A war in the heavens and worlds being ripped apart. I wasn't one to pray, but this was something that could not be allowed to happen.

"It's dangerous in either location, but even if the weres do get whipped up into a frenzy over the unnaturalness in the air, they aren't hunting for us directly. We cannot say the same for the vampires back home."

"You've got a point there." Ussier stepped forward and clasped my hand. "I'll see you tomorrow evening, then. Try not to end the world in the meantime, okay, old man?"

"I'll keep that suggestion in mind."

The cabin grew very quiet and still after the two of them left. Jacob was parked on a ridge somewhere overlooking the town as he talked with Kayla and Steve. He would be safe. The three of them took care of each other. I tucked my awareness of him back into a little corner of my mind and went into the kitchen to prepare tea.

The ritual soothed and centered me. By the time I sat down at the kitchen table to let it steep, I had made my decision. There would be no better time to contact the Ascended than tonight. Events were reaching a critical point. It wouldn't take long for Nerissa to figure out that her creature had been killed or that Kayla could no longer be possessed. The fact that she seemingly hadn't noticed either yet drove home to me how distracted she must have been with the tensions among the Ascended.

And that didn't bode well either.

I lifted my mug and breathed in the gentle scent of the herbal tea. I had to at least try synchronizing my awareness with the Ascended again. And I didn't know if I was more afraid of failing or succeeding.

"Jacob." My lover's mind sharpened as I contacted him. I sensed him read me, his sudden spurt of worry and fear as he realized how remote I'd become. *"I need you."*

I couldn't do this without his full knowledge and consent. It wouldn't be right. Even if it would be far easier to slip away and take care of the problem before he realized what I was about.

"Do not do a damn thing until I get there," Jacob said, his mental voice implacable. *"Swear to me that you won't."*

"I do swear."

I took a sip of the golden tea, trying not to let his upset touch me. We would both need to be calm for this to work. I stared down at my hands, studying the fine network of lines on my knuckles. For centuries, I had killed with these hands, defending myself or my territory. I had never regretted the necessity; in truth, I'd been a warrior over half my life before I'd become a vampire. I understood battle and sacrifice, but Kayla and Jacob had introduced the idea of family into my life.

I had loved Jacob with these hands. I'd held Kayla when she cried. And now Jacob wanted me to raise children with him. As much as the thought had unsettled me at first, I now found it oddly intriguing.

But we wouldn't get our chance to get married or adopt if we didn't settle this once and for all.

And I was rather looking forward to getting on with the rest of my life with Jacob.

I heard Jacob's Camaro come roaring back, and moments later, he was striding through the door. "Dammit, I said I didn't want to argue about it."

"We're not going to argue, *mo chroí*." I straightened, meeting him stare for stare. "This is important and I need you with me." I looked past him at Kayla, then Steve. "I need all of you beside me."

Jacob stopped in front of my chair. "There has got to be another way; it's too risky. Dammit, Kristair, have you thought that this might be a trap? This is probably exactly what she wants."

"I don't think so. I think for the moment she's distracted and hasn't realized yet how badly her plans have gone awry. She doesn't want to trap me into becoming an Ascended again. Knowing Nerissa, she wants me to beg on my knees to go back."

"Kris, that really isn't convincing me to let you anywhere near that crazy bitch," Kayla said. "I cannot believe that I looked up to her my whole life."

"You both are too emotionally invested," Steve interrupted quietly, his gaze locked on mine as both Kayla and Jacob rounded on him. "You're not looking at this clearly." I didn't know who was more surprised by his comment, me or Jacob and Kayla. "Kristair, you know the Ascended better than any of us. Do you think it's actually possible to contact them?"

"I think we have to try. There's too much at stake to dawdle out of fear."

"Wait just a fucking minute. It's not fear, it's fucking common sense," Jacob snapped, glaring at both of us in turn. "And since when are you on his side, Steve?"

"I'm not saying I'm best buds with him, but we need to hear him out instead of immediately deciding not to listen."

Jacob's fists clenched as fury leapt inside of him. He took a couple of steps toward Steve. "What the hell is this? You've never liked Kristair and now you're trying to encourage him in this insanity."

I rose from my chair and caught Jacob's hand as Kayla's lips tightened. "Don't say something you'll regret. You know Steve better than that."

"Have I stepped into the middle of the fucking Twilight Zone, because if I have, somebody punch me," Jacob snarled. "I cannot believe you two are defending each other."

"All of you stop it, just stop it," Kayla broke in, clasping her elbows, hugging her arms to herself. "I don't know if I can handle you two agreeing with each other and Jacob ready to brawl with either one of you."

Jacob tensed, looking back at me. "Don't, please, I'm begging you, don't."

A pang went through my heart. More than anything, I wished I could give Jacob what he wanted. "I have to," I said gently. "You know that. If what we suspect is true, we have to stop it now."

"How, by joining them again?"

"No, by letting them know what Nerissa's been up to. Interfering with beings she's suppose to observe? Killing, creating doppelgangers? They have to know this."

"I'm not going to win this one, am I?"

I hated how defeated Jacob sounded, and I turned him to face me. *"Not this time, but if it makes you feel better, I want you with me. I want to keep the link open between us, but you'll have to calm down for me to do that. They aren't interested in having the both of us among them, and if you're with me, it'll make them pause. But you have to calm down. Do you understand?"*

"I can do that." Jacob's gaze sharpened. *"But I'm telling you this right now, Kristair. I know the secret of the Ascended, too, and I'm damn sure I have the will to use it. If you find yourself stuck back among them, trust me. I'll be joining you soon."*

"I do not doubt that for one moment." I touched his cheek.

"Father…." Steve slipped his arm around Kayla's shoulders as she spoke, and then she sighed. "Fine, just be careful, okay?"

"I want you all here with me," I said, looking at Kayla and Steve. "It'll help keep me grounded." I remembered the lure of the Ascended's song too well. How seductive it had been to be a part of the whole, sharing all that knowledge.

I finished my tea and went to sit down on the couch, struggling to find that equilibrium again amongst Jacob's worry and fury. He paced the room, muttering in his head as I sat down and closed my eyes, striving for that sense of calm and reaching out to envelope my lover in it when it finally came.

Jacob struggled briefly. It was not in his nature to surrender, but his need to be with me on this finally won over. I soothed him, taking my time until he was floating in a serenity similar to mine. I sensed him come closer until he stood in front of me, felt his eyes on my face. Then Kayla was there, too, her hand on my shoulder, and after a moment, Steve joined her.

This was my family, not the Ascended.

I reached out, stretching with my consciousness, feeling the strain on my mind. It was so dark and cold, the wall between me and them impossibly high. I stretched even more, throwing every ounce of my will into it until pain sizzled along my nerves.

I touched the swirling mass of minds and recoiled back from the dark emotions, jerking myself out of my meditation. Jacob crouched down next to me, his blue eyes dark with concern. "What is it?"

"Just give me a moment." I drew in a deep, shuddering breath. "There's so much anger and cold resolve. Tony was right, there is a divide among the Ascended, but it's gotten ugly since he's talked with you."

Kayla's hand tightened on my shoulder. "Maybe you shouldn't go back."

"I need to. If I can find Tony… at least I know it is possible to find them now." I looked at Jacob, took another deep breath at his nod, and closed my eyes again.

This time it was easier. The swirl of the Ascended's angry, discordant song swamped through me and threatened to trap me in its whirlpool. Jacob burrowed into my mind even more until I sensed the steady beat of his heart, until we became inseparable. It gave me the strength to step back and keep myself from being swept under.

The Ascended didn't even notice our presence. They were too worked up and belligerent toward each other. I moved through the edges, searching for Tony, hoping to stay unnoticed. This was worse than I had feared. The tensions were at a ripping point; all it would take was one ripple in the wrong place to set the explosion in motion.

I hoped my presence wouldn't be the trigger to set them off.

"I really don't like this," Jacob whispered in my mind. *"We might want to think of something else. There has to be another way of getting Tony's attention."*

"I think I have to agree with you." I started to pull back and had just managed to break free of the Ascended when someone else seized my mind.

"Kristair, what are you doing here?" Tony materialized, looking oddly haggard. "It's a bad idea. You have to go back; things aren't going well."

"Worse than even you know," I replied, straining even more to make myself visible to Jacob's friend, though I ended up looking like a wisp of a person next to him.

"You've got to go and you can't return. Somehow, they found out about what I did with Kayla, and hostilities are running really high. Even some of the people on my side think I've crossed the line and have joined Nerissa's camp."

"They think you shouldn't have interfered?"

"That's it exactly," Tony said. "And if they sense you here, it's only going to get worse, especially if you're seen with me."

"Nerissa is a hypocrite, Tony. She's the one behind the murders. She's the one who has been possessing Kayla." I sensed the shock ripple through Tony before he quickly tamped down the feeling. We both reached out to make sure the Ascended didn't notice the reaction. To our relief, they still seemed oblivious.

"Are you absolutely certain? This is serious, but I need proof."

"I don't have proof, and Nerissa has been crafty enough to keep her activities a secret from the rest of the Ascended."

"Then I don't know what I can do," Tony cut in, his expression troubled. "Nerissa has far more on her side than I do, and she has a stronger hold on them as well. Without proof, it'll be her word against mine, and I doubt they'd accept your testimony either."

"That's not the worst part."

Tony's eyes tightened. "Okay, hit me."

I frowned, thrown off by that odd statement. He couldn't mean literally, so it must have been a colloquialism, and then Jacob sighed in my head, confirming my suspicions. *"What am I going to do with you?"*

I ignored him and opened up my mind to Tony, sharing with him as the Ascended shared. It was somehow much easier for me without a body, and with Tony it was less of an invasion than it would've been with other Ascended. "Touch my thoughts, Tony. You'll see the truth of my words."

Tony slipped into my mind, he and Jacob exchanging quiet greetings. I let him see each memory, and as I did, Tony's dismay grew. I ended it with the confrontation between us and the doppelganger, and Jacob provided the images from his own encounters with the creature. The degradation of the creature was even more obvious seeing them back to back that way.

"That is against everything we believe in," Tony said harshly. "What is she thinking?"

"I don't know, but after seeing the situation you're facing, make sure you and your faction do not get the blame for this. That could also be her intention."

"Maybe. I'll have to think on what to do next. The situation is volatile here, and you need to go back. They may not care that you've chosen to live as a human, but they consider you an exile. They won't welcome you with open arms."

"I understand." I could feel my strength waning anyway. This exchange was taking a terrible mental toll on me.

"I'll try to sneak away and let you know if anything new develops," Tony promised.

"Don't take any undue risks."

Tony chuckled wryly. "Given the situation, I don't see if we have much choice. I'll be careful."

Then he was gone, somehow nudging us back to earth in the process. As Jacob and I hurtled back into our bodies, I felt exhaustion rolling over me in long, gray waves. I had the momentary impression of sitting on a couch with Jacob, Kayla, and Steve around me. My head felt swollen and fragile, and blessed darkness pulled me under.

Chapter 27

THE next day dawned dark and miserable, as if the sun were reluctant to show itself. I had just managed to get rid of Kayla and Steve for a couple hours so I could deal with my stubborn soon-to-be husband. Kristair hadn't been unconscious long last night, but it was clear he had no energy left. Not even enough to give me a proper protest when I'd bundled him into the bed.

At least one good thing had come from our visit to the Ascended. Kristair's burns and bruises had healed sometime while he was with them. There wasn't a mark left on him.

Kristair eyed me warily as I came back inside and locked the door behind me, his ever-present mug of tea clasped in his hands. "Where did you send them off to?"

"It doesn't matter. For the next two hours, you're mine, and I'm going to make every last second count." I had been looking forward to this, planning out the details in my mind since we'd left that horrible apartment last night.

Kristair took a sip of his tea, and I felt his mental query touch my mind. He frowned as I nudged it aside easily but didn't try again. "I'm getting the impression that you don't want to talk about last night."

I leaned against the back of the couch, cocking one hip on it and slowly eyed Kristair up and down. "I intend on doing something about last night, but it sure as hell isn't talking."

"Is sex your answer for everything?"

I snorted and gave him a wicked smile. "I've known you to resort to sex a few times yourself. But I don't plan on starting out with sex right away either. I'm looking forward to making you squirm first."

Kristair nudged against my mind again, swifter and harder this time, and I deflected that one just as easily. "That's cheating, love. Keep it up and you just might earn yourself another punishment on top of the one you've got coming."

Kristair gasped softly, his dark eyes going wide. "Jacob, this really isn't the…."

"Don't even give me that argument. Do you realize that you get so very prim and proper when I'm about to give you just what it is you're begging for inside?"

My lover shifted his weight, his expression smoothing as he took another sip of his tea. "I don't know what you're talking about."

"Liar," I grinned. "And for that, I think your pretty ass deserves a few extra whacks."

To my utter delight, his cheeks colored again. Not much, just a faint flush to his olive-golden skin, but oh, it set me on fire, and I knew my instincts were right. "Last night fucking sucked. This night might not be much better. In fact, it's probably going to be wretched until this whole mess is solved. We need to take time for ourselves whenever we can get it."

"And you think making me go through the indignity of being spanked will somehow fortify us against the bad things to come." Kristair shook his head. "That is a ludicrous bit of logic there."

"Ha, you can't fool me, Kristair. Even if I couldn't feel what was in your mind, I can see that your cock is hard from over here." This time the flush was more pronounced, and the tips of Kristair's ears turned red.

"Impudent brat." The thought rolled across his mind, but he kept his mouth shut.

"I don't think you've ever really indulged yourself, Kristair. See, I know you take comfort in giving me control. Even when it makes you squirm inside. Just like when you changed shape for me in the hotel room in Pittsburgh. It feeds something in you that you've never really explored. And for me, I love having that control over you. It's fucking sexy, fires me up inside. It doesn't make you look weak in my eyes. I know just how strong you are and that fact combined with your surrender…." I paused, letting him feel just how much it got to me. "I crave it."

Kristair set down his mug, studying my face. "It really does fulfill something inside you, doesn't it?"

"Not just me, Kristair. It's nothing I really wanted before, not until I met you. But then, there were quite a few things I hadn't wanted before you. Like marriage and all the stuff that comes after it." I smiled as Kristair's heart gave a little lurch of want. It seemed the idea of having a family had grown on him.

"I think I can understand that. You make me feel things that I've never felt before." He was nervous; he betrayed it with every shift of his feet, every time he toyed with his mug. "I'm not really all that good at letting go though, even if maybe I do want it."

"I'm very good at getting you to let go." I smiled, sensing his skittishness in my mind, but oh, he wanted this too. He might not say it out loud, he might not even admit it to himself, but he couldn't hide it from me. "Undress for me, Kristair."

He glanced toward our bedroom and back at me. "Right here?" I nodded. "What if they come back?"

"We'll hear their car pulling in and can make a dash for the bedroom." Kristair eyed the windows, where the curtains were only partially drawn. "We're a good mile from the nearest neighbor; anyone who wants to peek through the window into the living room can easily do the same thing in our bedroom."

Kristair bit back any more arguments and straightened, coming toward me as he shook his head slightly. I could sense how hard his heart was beating. "The things I do to indulge you."

"Believe me, I know." I winked at him and brushed a mental kiss over his lips. "But you're indulging yourself, too, you know. Be bad with me, Kristair. I promise, I only bite a little."

Kristair shook his head again and unbuttoned his shirt, tugging it off his shoulders. It was amazing how different he could look from one moment to the next. He had such a proper air about him at times, every inch the studious librarian. But he was my feral warrior, too, and now, with his tattoos revealed over his long, lean muscles, that was what I saw.

"Why do I let you talk me into the craziest escapades?" Kristair said, draping his shirt neatly over the arm of the loveseat.

"Because you love me and you trust me." I couldn't even pretend to feel guilty over it, not when I sensed the heated desire whipping through Kristair. "You don't really give yourself permission to do what comes naturally. I guess it's been too many centuries of trying to survive and you've buried all your inclinations deep inside. But you can let them out with me."

Kristair kicked out of his shoes and cast me a quick, unreadable glance. "I know I can."

I watched avidly as he finished undressing. There was something almost shy about Kristair as he did so. But as much as he kept his expression smooth, his eyes shuttered, he didn't try to hide one bit of the emotion swirling inside his thoughts, uncertainty and craving, love and anticipation.

Kristair came to stand before me utterly naked, his cock fully erect, and my breath quickened. Goddamn, he was gorgeous. My lover wasn't pretty; there were scars on his body, the tips of his ears were crooked, his eyes a little too deep-set, but to me, every one of those little flaws added up to fucking perfection.

I slid my fingertips down his lean side, sensed the whiplash reaction in him. Oh, how I'd missed that, the way we could sense each other's desire, our reactions to every touch. It just ramped up the intensity. I slid my hand around to his lower back and drew him closer to me. I wanted to take my time and devour him slowly, and heaven help me, there were so many places I wanted to touch at once.

Kristair plucked the front of my T-shirt. "How is it you're still dressed?"

"'Cause right now, I'm busy ogling you." I palmed his ass, smiling because I knew just how much jiggle I was going to get when I smacked it good.

"Jacob, you're not seriously thinking of spanking me, are you?" Kristair's voice was so grave I had to smile.

"We'd both be disappointed if I didn't." I circled my fingers around his wrists and straightened, drawing him around the couch.

Kristair followed, his expression troubled, his emotions swirling even faster. Anticipation warred with reluctance, but he wouldn't resist, at least not much more than a token. "You threatened me with a spanking if I did something stupid like sacrifice myself. I did nothing of the sort. I'm a grown man and a little old for punishments, don't you think?"

I sat down on the couch, looking up at my lover as he shifted from foot to foot. I would have bet he didn't even realize he was doing in. "I'm not spanking you to punish you, Kristair. I'm spanking you because it gets you all worked up inside. Remember the last time I did? You were fired up. I'm spanking you because I love the way your ass jiggles when I do and how it gets all red and hot to the touch. "

I flashed him a wicked smile and patted my thigh. "Come, lay across my lap, love. Let me do all those dirty things you want me to do."

I could almost taste the conflict within Kristair, it was so sharp. As much as he longed for it, he would have preferred I grab him and hold him down like last time instead of making him come to me, but I wasn't about to make it easier on him. It would lessen the experience for him in the end.

After another long hesitation, Kristair joined me on the couch and stretched out across my lap, his body tense. He trembled as I slid my hand soothingly down his back, his hard cock pressing into my thigh. Kristair had denied himself for so long that it was so difficult for him to just let go, even though I sensed he longed to do just that.

"Spread your legs a little wider," I ordered, rubbing my hand over his ass.

Kristair made an exasperated sound and did so, quivering again as I traced my finger along the shadowed cleft. "Are you going to get on with it, or just leave me like this until my daughter returns?"

I pressed my lips together hard to keep from snickering. "You know what your problem is, Kristair?"

"What?"

"You think too damn much."

Before he could come back with a retort for that, I brought my hand down on his upturned ass. Kristair jolted, his cock rocking against my thigh as he gasped. I soothed the sting with my palm, admiring the flush of pink against his skin. "*Mo chroí*, you are wicked."

I chuckled and spanked him again, letting instinct take over so he couldn't anticipate which cheek was going to get it next. He trembled, gasping with each smack, a little more of his reserve being knocked off of him with each one.

"Who's the more wicked, Kristair? Me for doing this and ogling your ass as I do, or you for enjoying it so damn much?" I teased.

He didn't answer me, but then he didn't have to, not when his hips were already lifting in anticipation of the next volley. Fuck, Kristair got me so worked up. And he knew it, too, which got him worked up in return, going around in such a heated loop I was surprised we didn't spontaneously combust.

The slap of palm against flesh seemed unduly loud, making my heart pound, and soon Kristair was circling his hips against my thigh, low, breathy moans escaping him. Excitement raced through me with every sweet jiggle of his ass as it flushed even redder.

My own cock throbbed uncomfortably in my jeans, and I longed to bury myself inside of him and feel the heat of his ass against my hips. But I didn't give in yet—it was too damned exciting to watch Kristair lose all sense of restraint.

"Jacob," he panted when I paused, uttering a little mewling sound as I slid my finger between his cheeks again. He shifted, trying to spread his legs a little wider without falling off the couch in the process.

"You want more, don't you?" I teased my finger over his perineum. "All ya have to do is ask. I'd give you more gladly."

Kristair groaned, wiggling his hips against me, hands clenching and unclenching. A hot wash of emotion flooded through him, and I almost came upon sensing it. He glanced back at me, a smile tugging on his lips as realization broke through his sensibilities. "You really are enjoying this." His dark eyes flashed wicked hot, and his smile turned sensuous. My heart stuttered from the force of it.

"Spank me, Jacob." His hips rocked against my thigh, and he didn't try to muffle or stop the moan that came from him. "Please, I want to feel your hand on me, making me burn hotter."

I groaned, bringing my hand down again, lust making me lightheaded. "And you say I'm wicked. You know what you do to me?"

"I think I have a fair idea." Kristair gasped, rocking his hips harder. "Fuck, Jacob."

My lover almost never cursed, only in extreme circumstances. I was the one with the potty mouth. But Kristair was truly worked up now. The tension was building in him to a breaking point, and I knew then that if I wanted to push him even more, I could get him to come from just having his ass walloped. So very tempting.

Kristair made a desperate sound, grinding against my thigh, and I chuckled, drawing a finger lightly over his balls. "Nope, not yet." I touched that spot in his mind, keeping his orgasm at bay. "Remember this game?"

Kristair's curses blistered the air, and he moved to push himself up off of my lap. I grabbed his wrists and pinned them to the small of his back, rubbing the hot red flesh of his ass. "How crazy can I make you, Kristair?" He moaned, a shudder wracking his body as I pushed a finger into him. "You want to come, don't you, getting yourself off by rubbing against my leg. Who knew you had such a dirty streak in you?"

"Jacob, let me up or let me come, or I swear you will pay."

"There you go, lying again. If you really wanted to be let go, you could fight me off easily." I slid my finger free of his tight heat and nudged his prostate with my thoughts instead. Kristair jolted, whimpering, renewing his struggles as I started spanking him again.

"Jacob… Jacob, please."

"Please what, my love?" Kristair was so damn close. I could barely draw in a breath, it was so damn sexy to watch. "How much do you want to let go? Would you beg for me?"

"Yes." Kristair hadn't even paused.

"Would you let me watch you get yourself off?" Kristair froze in shock, and I grinned, tipping his face toward me. "Yes, that's it, that's exactly what I want Kristair, I want to watch you pleasure yourself and beg me to let you come."

Chapter 28

JACOB couldn't be serious.

I looked back at him again and sensed his resolve even as I saw it written on his face. He was serious. "You want me to put on a titillating show for you?" I asked, and the brat had the audacity to grin.

"Why not? I seem to recall several occasions when you stood outside my window and watched me."

"That was different. You did that all on your own to try to lure me into your room." Jacob rubbed his hand on my ass, and he made it so hard to think when he did that. His touch emphasized the hot sting, and I could only imagine the sight I made. Another hard smack surprised me, and I gasped, heat flashing through me. My balls ached, and I couldn't stop myself from rubbing against his leg, much to Jacob's delight. Wicked, wicked man.

"You're doing it again. Stop that," Jacob said, his voice firm.

"Stop what?" I ceased trying to struggle and glanced over my shoulder at him. He was still fully clothed. It was unfair. I wanted to look upon him as much as he wanted to look at me.

"Thinking and fussing. Trust me, you look damn sexy lying across my legs with your red ass in the air. And I dare anybody to disagree with me."

Jacob's mental touch pressed against my spot, driving all thought from my mind. My body yearned for the release denied me, and all I could do was writhe, crying out with each accompanying hard slap until he let up.

"Jacob please...." But what did I want—for him to keep up his torments, or for him to release me? Some part of me cried out for more of Jacob's unique way of driving me crazy.

"When you used to watch me through the window, how did it make you feel?" Jacob asked, relentless in the pursuit of what he wanted. "You loved watching me, following me around, coming to my bedside while I slept. Well, today I get to be the voyeur, and you're going to be very, very naughty for me, aren't you Kristair?"

"Yes, yes...." As soon as the words left my mouth, Jacob released my hands, though he still maintained the mental block which kept me from coming. My heart pounded as I realized what I'd just agreed to. How my lover could get to me this much I still didn't understand, but his primal smile of satisfaction made me shudder.

It made me weak inside to realize how much he was looking forward to this little scene, and made me ever hotter to know that I wanted to do whatever he ordered me to do. Jacob squeezed my ass, and I hissed as it emphasized the stinging throb. I would be feeling the effects of his spanking for a good while.

"Kneel up on the cushions, Kristair," Jacob said, moving over to the other side of the couch when I did. Soon, under his direction, I found myself propped up against the other arm, my knees cocked up and spread wide. Jacob's eyes gleamed as he looked at me. He could see everything from my cock brushing against my stomach to my puckered hole and the bottom curves of my ass, which no doubt were still a bright red.

I'd never been put on display for another person, and that was exactly how I felt at the moment. However, it was hard to be very self-conscious about it when Jacob was studying me with avid interest, his hot gaze burning into my skin. I could sense how very much he was turned on by the display.

"So you want to watch me touch myself?" I said, trailing my fingertips down my throat.

"For starters." Jacob grinned, meeting my gaze. "I might change my mind and have you do something else later."

I shivered. I was sure he'd have something even more salacious for me to do when he did change his mind. I slid my hand lower, tracing the tattoo on my stomach, reading Jacob's thoughts and knowing where he wanted me to go next. My fingers pinched my nipples into hard little peaks, and I smiled as he wet his lips.

"You know, if you weren't sitting all the way over there, you could put your mouth on them," I teased. *"I could get you naked and we could cavort together."*

A very slow, very naughty grin crossed Jacob's lips. "Are you trying to tempt me, old man? Just be glad I don't want you out of my sight, or else I'd make you go get that vibrator to use on yourself while I watch."

Jacob inserted the image in my mind of me doing exactly that, and I moaned at how vivid it was. "You have quite an imagination."

"Oh yes, and you inspire me in all kinds of ways." Jacob's eyes slid down to my cock. "Stroke yourself. You're not nearly as worked up as I want you to be."

My breath caught, and my hand stilled on my stomach. My cock was aching so much already that I knew I'd come the moment I touched myself if Jacob would only release me. His eyes locked with mine, and I felt his mental touch as he manipulated my spot again.

My head fell back onto the couch, and I moaned roughly, my body sizzling with need. Not just to come. I wanted Jacob inside me, hard and urgent as he fucked me. "Jacob please… please."

"Touch yourself, Kristair. Touch that pretty cock of yours, the head is so slick, I can almost taste you when I look at it." His husky voice shivered over my skin.

Moaning, I wrapped trembling fingers around the hard length and gave it a tug. "Jacob."

"More, Kristair… you're not there yet." Ruthlessly, he nudged my spot, and my hips bucked up hard into my hand. "You're just teasing yourself. You think I can't feel what you're doing? Firmer, love, like you mean it, like you really plan on jacking yourself off on this couch."

I was past embarrassment, thoroughly held in thrall to Jacob's voice, his eyes hot on me. "Jacob... please," I panted, stroking my cock, thrusting up into my fist. It felt so damn good I thought I was going to fly apart, all this energy caught up inside of me. "Jacob, please, fuck me."

"Soon, my beautiful, proud man, soon. Fuck, I love ya, Kristair." I looked at my lover through slitted eyes, my breath stolen by the utterly rapt expression on his face. "You could drive a man fucking crazy."

He was one to talk. Jacob maintained his hold on me, keeping me on the edge, the tension in my body exquisite. "Release me, Jacob, please." I could have broken his mental hold on me easily, but I couldn't bring myself to take the control out of his hands. Not when it felt so right despite the aching of my cock.

"Not yet." Abruptly, he was leaning over me, his tongue dragging over the head of my cock. I shuddered, crying out, my fingers digging into the couch cushion as my other hand stilled on my cock. Jacob's slick, hot mouth sank lower, tongue lashing without mercy, and his fingers slid into me. He was as wild as I felt, sucking hard and making me crazier with need.

I dragged my hand up into his hair, fisting it, and tried to hold onto what shreds of control I had left. "Jacob... too much," I panted, saying his name over and over like a prayer.

His fingers rubbed against my spot and soon I was shouting, unable to form words as I begged him in my mind. Nothing else existed but Jacob and his insistent mouth and demanding hands. He owned me, body and soul. He always had, from the first moment I had seen him on the football field.

With a rough groan, Jacob pulled back, kneeling up on the couch. I reached for him, gritting my teeth. "Jacob, let me come." At that moment, I would've done anything he asked as long as he released me.

He shook his head sharply, yanking off his T-shirt. "Touch yourself, Kristair," he said, watching me with hard, intent eyes.

Helpless to do anything but obey, I began stroking myself again under his gaze, my mouth dry. I could sense the love and lust in him, the moment he decided to relent, though I knew he wasn't done with me yet. Jacob stood up, his eyes never leaving me as he stripped. I stared at his hard cock, and I would have sworn that if he fucked me then, as on edge as my body was, I would fall apart.

I wanted to get my hands on him, have his hands on me in return, feel his hard body against my own. Reading my mind, Jacob shook his head as he came toward me. *"You weren't thinking of touching without asking first, were you?"*

His cock was so close I could smell his arousal. All I had to do was turn my head, and I could take him into my mouth. All I had to do was ask. "Jacob." I tore my eyes away from the slick head of his cock dancing just before my lips and looked up at him. He might have been the one in control this afternoon, but at that moment, if we touched, we'd both be lost. "May I touch you?" I asked, my voice thick with need.

Jacob shook his head. "I like seeing you touch yourself too much. It's driving you crazy, isn't it? You want to come so damn bad."

A light sheen of sweat covered my body, and my hand slowed on my aching cock as Jacob's fingers slid around to the back of my head. I turned, my lips parting as Jacob's cock brushed my cheek. He pushed into my mouth, his taste hot and salty and exciting. With a groan, I reached for him, fingers curling around the base, cupping his balls. When he moved to bat my hands away I sank my mouth lower, sucking harder. *"Please, let me."*

"Fuck, Kristair, I can't resist your mouth." Jacob caressed my scalp, groaning as I hollowed my cheeks and began moving on his shaft. I slid my hand to his hip, then down his thigh, hungry to touch him as much as to taste him.

As my tongue lashed his cock and swirled on the head, I could acutely feel each aching throb of my own cock. Jacob's block didn't waver once, even as his own orgasm neared. *"Let me come with you."*

"Not yet. Soon, love, I promise. I want to watch you."

With that, he began to thrust, his fingertips stroking my scalp as I relaxed my throat and let him. We were so linked that I knew the moment the tension in his body reached that critical point, and when his release came I felt the euphoria of it even as Jacob also felt my own desperation. It dragged out his orgasm, filling my mouth with his salty, musky seed.

I clung to him, trembling, tongue stroking for every drop. Jacob slid his cock free of my mouth and caught my face between his hands. A desperate whimper lodged in my throat as he kissed me hard and bore me back down to the couch. I arched up against his hard body, my arms and legs winding around him. So close, so very, very close, and he still wouldn't release me.

"Jacob, release me, please," I begged in his mind as his mouth hungrily fed off my own. His hand slipped between our bodies and squeezed my cock. I cried out, shuddering, and felt my lover's cock stir once again against my ass, which still stung and burned. *"Jacob, please!"*

Jacob pulled back, panting, desire searing the both of us. His eyes blazed as he looked down at me, and I cried out as he pulled one of my hands from around him and brought it to my cock. "Get yourself off, beautiful," Jacob rasped, and as I began stroking, I felt him release the hold he had on my mind.

My fingers dug into his shoulder, and I couldn't make myself ease my grip as my orgasm ripped through me. Writhing on the couch, my gaze locked with Jacob's, I continued stroking, come splashing against both of our stomachs. It seemed to go on forever, rolling through me in long waves.

Jacob glanced down at my body, breaking eye contact, and I whimpered as I sensed the hot whiplash of lust in his mind. He wasn't done with me. Before I could register that thought and scramble away, he groaned and leaned down to drag his tongue across my stomach.

"Jacob," I gasped, my gaze riveted to him as licked and sucked every drop off of my skin. "Jacob, please... it's too much."

He ignored me, his rough tongue stroking over my cock, hot mouth teasing the head. I shuddered as he pushed his fingers into me, stretching me, and felt him smile against my skin. "You're so hot, Kristair, fuck… your body's so open for me. No resistance at all."

"Jacob… *mo chroí*… please…." I cried out as he pushed deeper, felt the hot, liquid surrender as he penetrated me. "Give me a moment." To catch my breath, to give my over-sensitized body a chance to calm down.

My lover knelt up, and I moaned as I saw his hard cock rising between his thighs and sensed his determination to fill the cabin with the sound of my pleas. "Jacob…."

"You know how fucking sexy your voice sounds when you say my name that way?" Jacob growled.

His hands came down on me, and I gasped as I found myself flipped over onto my stomach. He grasped my hips, pulling me up onto my hands and knees as I trembled wildly. "Jacob… Jacob, please, just give me a few minutes. I can't take it now."

"Sweet liar." Jacob kissed my back as his cock nudged between my cheeks and against my entrance. He smacked my ass, and I gasped, rocking forward as heat flared through my skin. Jacob's hands tightened on my hips. "Scream for me, love."

"Jacob!"

His hips snapped, filling me with one smooth plunge, and I cried out, head falling back. Every thrust nudged against my spot, tormenting my already overstimulated body. My cries got louder as Jacob encouraged them, and soon I was rocking back on his cock, clenching every time he sank deep into me.

Jacob's nails raked down my ribs, and hissing, I turned my head and bit him on his shoulder. We kissed, tongues battling, taunting and teasing, kissed until my lungs burned for air. Excitement, need, and love raced through us. I hadn't thought I could come again so soon after the intense orgasm, but there I was, on the edge again.

Jacob buried his face against my neck, his arm wrapped around my stomach. *"I love you, I love you so much."*

I slid my hand to the nape of his neck, held on as we came together. *"I love you, too, mo chroí, always and forever."*

Chapter 29

"CELEBRATING?" a woman said, cutting through our silent bonding as Kristair and I lay curled up on the couch, lost in the aftermath, entwined in each other's minds. "You've won nothing."

My heart just about stopped at the sound of a voice when I thought we were alone. Cursing, I sat up as Kristair's eyes went flat. Nerissa stood by the loveseat, her expression set, her brown eyes furious.

Holy fucking shit.

I'd seen her utter deadly threats she meant, and that didn't make my blood run cold as she did now. Even with my limited ability, I could sense the implacable will driving her, the absolute willingness to do whatever it took to achieve her ends, whether those ends were fucking insane or not.

Nerissa looked exactly the same as she had the last time she'd intruded on our privacy, a woman caught in the past, still wearing the kind of ancient Roman clothes she'd been wearing when she'd become an Ascended. Her honey-brown hair was still arranged in an elaborate knot, the same jewelry and attitude.

No, she wasn't the same. There was something different about her, but I couldn't quite figure it out.

"I was wondering when you'd show up again." Kristair sat up and reached for his pants as casually as if we were alone. If he felt any distress at Nerissa showing up at this time, none of it showed on his face. I could only hope that I showed half of his calm. "Your sense of timing is appalling."

"And here I thought I did rather well. I knew I wouldn't be able to get your attention when you two were rutting like animals."

Fury washed over me, and I jumped up, uncaring that I was buck-assed naked. That had been a private time, just for Kristair and me. The thought of anyone, especially her, peeking in on that and seeing Kristair so beautifully vulnerable made me want to throttle her. "What do you want, Nerissa? You pissed off now that your little bitch clone of Kristair has been destroyed?"

Her mouth thinned, and Kristair caught my arm. *"Get dressed, Jacob,"* he said in the deepest part of my mind where only I could hear.

Nerissa's eyes slid over my body, stopping at my crotch, and her lips twisted in a derisive smile. "I'm surprised you had the balls to do it yourself."

Kristair squeezed my arm as I opened my mouth to retort. Fuming, I bit my tongue and jerked on my jeans. Fucking bitch, I'd show her balls and hope she choked on them.

"What do you think you have done?" Nerissa snapped, turning her attention to Kristair. It struck me then what was different about her. Her voice was missing the choral sound that it had had the last time, the same sound that Tony's voice had. That had to be significant somehow. Maybe somehow she wasn't connected to the other Ascended anymore.

"I think I should be the one to ask you that." As angry as Kristair was at Nerissa, there was a deep sorrow in him as well, and that was what showed on his face as he looked at her. "Possessing Kayla, putting her in harm's way after you asked me to take care of your family. You tried to get me to murder her. What has gotten into you, Nerissa?"

I thought she was going to deny it, but she drew herself up arrogantly. "I did what I had to, to fix the mess you left behind when you denied what you were. Do you have any notion of the chaos you caused?"

"I was under the impression that my decision was unremarked upon by anyone but you. You know what I think?" Kristair said, tossing me my shirt. "I think you were the only one upset by my choice and the fact that the Ascended are whipped up into a frenzy is your fault."

Glaring at her, I tugged on the shirt, but I might as well have been invisible for all the attention those two were paying me. I turned my body to the side and slipped my cell phone out and quickly typed out a text message to Steve.

Bitch is here. Stay away.

I flipped it back closed and slipped the phone in my pocket. Fuck, this situation couldn't have been any worse. Nerissa had been limited somewhat when she was in Kayla's body, but now she could do anything she wanted, and we were be helpless. The way she'd manhandled us when she'd given us the Ascended's ultimatum all those months ago had been embarrassing.

"My fault?" Nerissa said, her voice rich with scorn. "You've been talking to Tony. That aberration never should've been allowed among us. A few of the Ascended, the weak-minded ones, have joined him. They now want to visit worlds, interact as you are, instead of just observing, learning. They want to change the rules that have been working for millennia."

"And what did you do? You sided against them, got others to join you. You pushed and prodded for them to yield because that's what you do. And when they didn't the Ascended got upset, splits formed, and you couldn't take that." I watched in fascination at the expressions that crossed Nerissa's face as Kristair's words struck home. "What I can't understand is what would push you to break your own rules."

"Breaking them? Be real, Kristair, she blew them the fuck wide open," I broke in, their polite verbal sparring driving me nuts. "What Tony and his friends might want to do is nothing compared to what she did do. They may want to break the letter of the law, but she destroyed its true meaning. She practically skull-fucked the rules."

Kristair winced. "As always, Jacob, you have a unique way of putting things, but you are right. Nerissa, you condemned me for not embracing my own change, and you would start a war among the Ascended to keep change from coming. Tony and the others could use your wisdom to guide them and now it's too late. They won't listen to you after what you've done."

Nerissa sneered, twisting her pretty features into an ugly mask. "Do you really think so? Why? Because that aberration convened a trial? Do you really think the other Ascended will take his word over mine? He doesn't belong among us. Do you think the others will be concerned with what happens to you? Do you know what they call you? The Exile."

"I can only assume you mean that as a slur, but it does happen to be true," Kristair said, sounding for all the world like they were having a discussion over fucking tea or something instead of a situation that could destroy the world.

"Stubborn, stubborn child."

It pissed me off to no end, the way she talked down to Kristair like that. It wasn't like he was a fucking baby. He'd been around for over two thousand years. It didn't matter if she was twice his age or not. In fact, there was a bigger age difference between Kristair and me, and he never talked to me like that. I didn't know why he took it from her. If someone treated me that way, I'd have knocked their fucking head off their shoulders, but Kristair didn't even seem to notice it.

It was almost like a movie playing out, but I got the feeling they could argue back and forth for a damned decade. They'd probably enjoy it, but I sure as hell wasn't in the mood to hear it.

"That's why you're here today," I cut in. "They're putting you on trial and you've got your panties in a twist. You only got yourself to blame. Why don't you run along before they realize you're gone and you're exposed for the hypocrite you are." I made a flipping motion with my hand. At that point I didn't fucking care if I set her off or not.

"None of you have proof. You're assuming it's me and that's what it's going to come down to. Your word against my word."

I sensed Kristair's sudden worry and glanced at him, but his expression was still smooth. *"What is it?"*

"She's very confident that the others will find her blameless. That tells me she's found some way to keep her activities hidden, even if they force her to open up her mind to them."

"Or maybe she's so damned arrogant she doesn't think they'd ever take that step. She's Nerissa, she's perfect, who could ever suspect her of something so fucking crazy?" Kristair didn't respond, his emotions rioting, and I touched his hand. *"I know you don't want to believe it."*

"My heart says that she is guilty, even if I don't want to believe it."

"I don't know what's happened to you, Nerissa. It's been centuries since you were my Mistress. You have to let go; you can't win every single fight."

"Mistress...." Nerissa's chuckle was ugly. "There was a time when I requested that you use my given name and you never would. Why the change now, Kristair?"

"I used that when I served you, Nerissa. I was still loyal to you even if we argued more often than not. But now? Killing, playing god." Kristair shook his head, his voice like steel. "I have no respect for you anymore."

Rage leapt into Nerissa's eyes, and I edged closer to Kristair, though I didn't know what I could possibly do to stop her if she went fucking berserk. My phone vibrated in my pocket, and I tensed. That had to be Steve. I hoped he had the goddamned sense to turn the car as far away from here as he could.

"Maybe I just need to teach you a little respect, Kristair," she said silkily. I might as well have been elsewhere for all she cared. It was Kristair she was focused on... it was Kristair who mattered.

All the little pieces clicked together. *"Keep pushing her, Kristair. Make her lose her cool."*

Shock jolted through my lover. *"Have you forgotten she's tried to have you killed and worse? I'm not risking her lashing out at you to get at me."*

"She barely fucking knows I'm here. All she cares about is you. I don't think she's as strong now as she could be. She's not linked to the Ascended, I would think she can only do so much without risking alerting them. If we push her, make her snap a bit—"

"How do you make someone snap a bit?" Kristair growled in my mind. *"I'm hearing a lot of unspoken ifs and maybes there. It's too risky."*

Nerissa's brown eyes sharpened, and she glided closer. "Ah, I almost forgot about the connection you two shared." She tsked, giving Kristair a reproving look. "I thought you meant to be only human, and here you are, dabbling in the preternatural. What are you two arguing about now?"

"Don't you threaten him," I snapped, drawing her attention to me. "I'm the one who reestablished our link. And I am fucking human."

She shot me a look of distaste. "Yes you are, and an irritating little man on top of it. I cannot even begin to fathom what Kristair sees in you."

I drew myself up and glared at her. "That's because you never bothered to get to know him at all." My stomach clenched as my cell phone vibrated again. Maybe warning them off hadn't been such a good idea. Kayla was more than capable of taking things into her own hands.

"I could break your mind open like an egg and leave you a drooling, babbling idiot for the rest of your life."

"Yeah, then why haven't you already?" I snapped back.

Kristair cocked his head, his curiosity roused along with his protective instincts. *"Perhaps you were right, Jacob. But if I'm going to push her I'd rather you not draw attention to yourself."*

"He has a good point, you haven't, and I don't think you will. If you had planned to harm either one of us you already would have. Exile or not, human or not, I'm still an Ascended in some ways. No, you won't lay hands on me. So why have you come, Nerissa?" Kristair asked.

"Oh, but there are many, many ways I can make you weep, Kristair."

Oh fuck. My blood turned to ice as Nerissa's gaze fell on me. "Now wait just a minute here," I said, tensing inside to keep from taking an instinctive step back. I'd be damned before I let her see that she scared the shit out of me. "You kill me, Nerissa, and I can guarantee you've lost any chance of ever making Kristair kneel to you."

"She can't kill you, *mo chroí*. If she raises her will against you, then she risks bringing the other Ascended's attention down on her. What's the price for killing, Nerissa? For trying to create life on your own?" Kristair asked, his voice a taunting, icy barb. "And she can't kill you with her bare hands without using her abilities. She can't fight the both of us. She's impotent."

There it was, the crack in her façade of calm. Nerissa's eyes glittered as her hands flexed. I took a step back as my cell phone vibrated a third time and slid my hand into my pocket, hoping she wouldn't notice the motion. *"I think you hit a nerve there, Kristair. She's been feeling helpless and she hates it."*

"Impotent? How dare you?" Nerissa's will lashed out toward me as I pulled out the phone, and my vision went dark as pressure squeezed my heart. I heard the cell phone clatter to the floor, and I fell to my knees.

And just as suddenly, the sensation was gone. I drew in a deep, shuddering breath as Kristair stepped in front of me. "Believe me when I tell you that I will do whatever it takes to protect him and Kayla."

"Oh god, Kristair, what have you done?" I said in horror as I realized he had been the one to stop whatever it was Nerissa had done.

"You broke your vow, Kristair," Nerissa hissed. "You used abilities you swore to give up."

"How will the other Ascended know, unless you tell them? And you can't without having to explain what you were doing here and the reasons why I broke that vow. You don't have the power of all the others behind you now. It's just you and me, and I can counter anything you throw at me."

Nerissa's eyes gleamed in triumph. Terror and despair tore at me as I struggled to my feet again. *"Kristair, don't leave me."*

"I'm not."

"Now that you've broken through your self-imposed block, what's going to stop you from doing the same again? Every time he is threatened you'll do it again. He makes your will weak, Kristair. You don't belong among us either."

"After what you've done, neither do you, Nerissa. You think you've won, but they'll be able to see right through you as they saw through me. It's over; let it go."

The sound of a car coming into the driveway had me lurching toward the door. No, no, no… god dammit. I was such a fucking idiot. Kristair's sudden alarm spurred me on. A car door slammed, and I heard Kayla's voice as she bolted up the steps. "Kris! Jake!"

"I'll take care of Nerissa. Stop her, Jacob!"

But it was too late. The door flew open, and Kayla's eyes blazed white as her face melted into a featureless mask when Nerissa took possession of her. Behind her, Steve got out of the car, scowling with a look of confusion in his eyes. "What the fuck is going on?"

Kayla spun around, her hand lifting, and Steve flew back against the Z28. The impact was brutal, and he slid to the ground in a boneless heap. I grabbed her arm, jerking her into the cabin. "What have you done?" I shoved her back into Kristair's arms and bolted toward Steve.

Chapter 30

NERISSA struggled as I wrapped my arms around her, and I tightened my grip, trying to be careful so I wouldn't bruise Kayla. Nerissa tried to stab at my mind, but the attempt was weaker than what I would have normally expected from her. "Let her go, Nerissa. It doesn't have to be like this. She's your family too," I hissed in her ear.

"I'll destroy her mind before I let her go, Kristair. You've brought this down on yourself."

Jacob had reached Steve and had knelt down next to him, checking his pulse. I kicked the door shut, hoping that not being able to see them would limit her abilities somewhat. I could only go on the premise that she didn't want me dead, at least not yet.

"Let her go or I swear that I'll bring the Ascended down on the both of us." I gave her a little shake, fury and terror making me hold onto her harder than I wanted to. "Your rampage is over with. Don't make the split between the Ascended worse. I don't want a war between them anymore than you do."

Nerissa raked her nails down the side of my face, drawing blood. "Never, Kristair."

"So be it."

I threw open my mind and clamped down on my emotions, stretching my mind out toward the Ascended. Nerissa gasped, jerking out of my arms, and spun around. "No!" Her eyes went incandescent, and I stepped forward, prepared to catch Kayla when Nerissa released her body, but it didn't happen.

My mind linked with Tony's and then onto the rest of the Ascended. Kayla's body jerked spasmodically. "Let me go!" Nerissa screamed. "What have you done to me?"

"Kristair? What's happening? Kristair! No!" Jacob's voice fell away with the room as the Ascended took the both of us, until he was only a distant spark.

"Is Steve safe?" I threw the thought back at him.

"He's unconscious, but he'll be okay, he's got a hard head," he whispered in my mind. *"What the hell happened? All three of you are gone."*

"I'm not sure yet. Get Steve settled and then join me."

"How the fuck am I supposed to do that?"

I tried to summon patience as I found myself in an all-too-familiar place. The ranks of the Ascended surrounded Nerissa, Kayla, and me. But this time, the mood was different as another trial convened. The split was evident in the way they arranged themselves. Nerissa's faction, much larger, was arrayed on one side, with Tony's faction on the other side. The sense of their unsettled mood was much more palpable this time, pounding down on me and completely drowning out Jacob's voice.

"What is the meaning of this?" Nerissa's faction said in one voice, outrage swelling the sound until the very air seemed to ring with the force of their anger.

"Proof of what I've been trying to tell you." Tony came to the forefront and gestured toward Kayla. "Nerissa has been taking control of her body and using it to kill other beings."

Nerissa struggled yet again to free herself, and I worried for the state of Kayla's mind, the damage she could be doing to her. "You trapped me," she hissed, surging toward Tony.

I caught her and drew her back to me again. "Release her, please," I said, appealing to Tony.

"Exile, you will not speak until you've been spoken to," Nerissa's faction said, bristling in outrage.

I clamped down on the rushing surge of anger at that. There were too many strong emotions swirling around as it was. Adding to it would only make the situation worse. Tony touched my thoughts in support, directing a thought toward me. *"Kayla is safe. I've buffered her mind and made it so that Nerissa cannot cause her physical harm, but I cannot let her go yet."*

"What have you done, Aberration?" Shock rippled through Nerissa's faction, muting some of their anger. I sensed them touch Nerissa's awareness trapped in Kayla's body. "Nerissa? Is this true?"

"You would take their words over mine?" she said, drawing herself up, as regal as any queen. It was as if my hands on her and Tony's trap meant nothing.

"When I laid the trap I hadn't realized it was for Nerissa. I was helping a friend," Tony said.

"Your human friends. Something that is forbidden," they said, righteous indignation in their choral voice.

"As you say, I am guilty, but if you judge me, you must judge Nerissa as well." He gestured toward her. "She also sought to interfere when she always preached that we observe and she sought to hide it from you by going about it indirectly."

More of the anger dissolved into confusion and dismay as Nerissa's faction was faced with some proof of her misdeeds. "We must have the whole truth before we proceed."

"Then let the Exile talk," Tony insisted. "If you want the truth, listen to his words and the words of his mate and then ask Nerissa what she's done. You'll know who's speaking the truth."

The choral voices hummed, shutting the rest of us out as they conversed. In that quieter moment, I sensed Jacob's presence in my mind, calling out to me. *"I'm here, mo chroí. I'm safe."*

"What about Kayla? Steve's awake and freaking the fuck out." Guilt tinged his mind. *"I'd texted him to let him know Nerissa was here so he could keep Kayla away. But she saw it instead and told him to*

come back. *He didn't know anything."* Misery sank deeper into his mind. *"I fucked up. It's my fault. I'm sorry."*

"No, Jacob. It is Nerissa's fault and she will answer for her crimes." I still couldn't believe it, and now that the moment of reckoning was here, I found myself to be conflicted. Nerissa needed to be stopped, but I didn't want her to be harmed. Despite everything, the ties between us were still strong.

Jacob didn't say anything at first, but I sensed his love and support, and that was enough. *"How did you want me to join you?"*

"Merge your mind with mine. Steve can keep an eye on your body so you should be safe. Just try to stay calm. We don't want to set them off."

"Okay. Give me a minute to explain things to Steve. What should I tell him? I still don't know what the fuck happened."

"Tony laid a trap in Kayla's mind. When Nerissa possessed her, she couldn't free herself. Now the Ascended have proof of at least that much of her crimes." I paused, glancing toward them. *"They haven't decided quite how to take it yet."*

"Damn, Kayla's lucky her brain isn't Swiss cheese by this point. Two traps going off in her head since last night.... Fucking mine field up in there."

"She'll be fine. They haven't done any damage to her and Tony promised me that Nerissa is not in a position to be able to hurt Kayla anymore."

"That's good to know. I'll be with you in a few minutes." Jacob caressed me with a loving thought and then was gone, the link weakening to the point where I had a very difficult time sensing him at all.

As I turned my attention back to the Ascended, Nerissa's faction emerged from their communication. "It will be as you say, Aberration. We will gather the Exile's mate and hear from everyone. Once we've discovered the truth, then we can determine the proper chastisement."

"We will make the determination together," Tony's faction said, and for a moment the mood became ugly again as the two sides locked together in an unspoken battle. Then the atmosphere relaxed, and I breathed a mental sigh of relief.

"We are agreed. Aberration, you know his mate well; bring him here."

I had to admire Tony's poise and strength of mind. This was the second time he had found himself in the middle of a group that was reluctant to accept him and again, despite the odds, he'd risen to a position of leadership among them. I hoped in this case it ended better for him.

Then Jacob and Steve were there, looking around with wide eyes. "Oh sweet fucking Jesus," Jacob whispered.

Steve swallowed hard and then noticed Kayla and came over to us, scowling as he took in her altered appearance. When he lifted his hand to touch her, Nerissa hissed at him, lunging forward and forcing me to tighten my grip on her. I shook my head at him, sympathizing with his fear for Kayla. "Soon, Steve, I promise."

"We said to bring the Exile's mate. Who is this other one?" The voices raised to a roar.

"He is Kayla's mate," Tony replied, both calm and firm as the mood turned ugly again. I had never imaged the Ascended could be so erratic, so far from where they used to be. "Kayla is the woman whom Nerissa possessed. He is tied to all of us as well." The argument raged back and forth. And I worried that Tony may have gone too far this time, that he'd gambled once too often.

Steve's jaw tightened, and he let his hand drop, though I could see how it cost him to back down. For the first time, I realized how much Steve truly did care for my daughter. Perhaps it was time I let her go.

Nerissa went still in my arms, and I looked down at the strange blank features of my daughter's face. Nerissa had been very quiet, offering nothing in her defense, and I didn't trust that. She was up to something. Like me, she would not give up now. She had one last desperate ploy in mind.

"Jacob, we need to be ready to counter Nerissa."

"How do you plan on doing that?" Unease rippled through him. *"I don't like it here, Kristair. We don't belong here. The shit is about to hit the proverbial fan."*

"No, we don't. But we need to have this resolved. The Ascended have to come to an agreement."

"I think that's even more impossible than keeping that bitch in check."

"Impossible or not, it must be done," I insisted. *"Keep yourself linked to me close, almost as if we were one, but leave you mind free enough to move your body about if need be. I'm going to do the same with her as subtly as I can. Then if she does try something, we'll be able to react quickly."*

"You sure you can dig into her head?"

I hesitated, reaching out the barest tendril of a thought to my former Mistress. *"We were bonded once. I have to try."* Nerissa had shielded herself from the other Ascended, presenting a calm, arrogant façade to them. But I knew her so well, and I soon found the minute chink in her defenses.

Behind the wall, her emotions raged out of control. There was so much chaos in her thoughts I could've shouted and she still wouldn't have heard me. When had this madness started? How had no one noticed?

Once again the Ascended became still and their attention turned toward us. The split between them was even more pronounced now, but at least they still had some measure of control. The storm around them had calmed somewhat.

"Exile, we will hear your words."

Nerissa yanked herself free from my grip. I tensed, ready to grab her again, but she didn't try to flee. Instead, she drew herself up again, and in her bearing I could almost see her clearly through the strange features of Kayla's face.

"As the accused, I demand the right to speak first."

"I have no issue with that," I said quickly, hoping to forestall another argument between the two different sides.

Silence reined, and then I sensed the Ascended's acceptance. "Proceed, Nerissa."

Jacob slipped over to my side and took my hand, reinforcing the connection between us. Steve stood with his eyes hard on Nerissa, his arms crossed. I had no doubt the moment Nerissa released Kayla that he'd be right next to her. I did not have to worry about my daughter.

"Did you possess this young woman, as the Aberration and Exile have accused?"

"I do not deny that," Nerissa said, letting everyone feel the strength of her conviction. "I did what was necessary to fix the damage Kristair and the Aberration created. Their actions have created a rift between us, a rift that must be mended."

"And you took it upon yourself to make this decision for us all?" Tony's faction said, new fury coloring their voices.

"I knew what had to be done to fix it, involving *you* would've brought on more argument. And thus I could not involve my own followers. The less who knew, the better chance my plan had of succeeding." Nerissa was so arrogantly sure of herself she could not see the effect her words had on her own allies, their confusion and they way they drew back. "I sacrificed my principles for the sake of us all."

I squeezed Jacob's hand at his swift flash of outrage. *"Do not rile them. Let her dig herself in deeper. Her mind is so clouded, she cannot see the damage she is doing to her own cause."* Jacob grumbled but subsided without a word.

"How would possessing this woman heal the rift?" Nerissa's faction chorused. "Your logic does not make any sense, Nerissa."

Nerissa's façade didn't flicker at all from the questions her own people hurled at her, but inside, uncertainty flickered and fueled her rage. "That is because you still cannot see the whole picture. Kristair caused the rift when he left us. Upon his return, we'll be one again." I squeezed Jacob's hand even harder. "To achieve that end, I vowed to take away the reasons why he left."

Nerissa made it sound so logical, so clinical. As galling as her arrogance might have been, her faction wasn't ready to condemn her yet. They murmured amongst themselves, and Jacob gave me a hard mental poke, striving to get me to say something, and still I waited. As much as possible, I wanted them to sort this out amongst themselves.

"And in doing so you extinguished seven beings, some of which who might've one day been among our ranks if you hadn't interfered with their fate," Tony's faction accused.

"They were weak. Easy. They never could've been one of us," Nerissa said, her voice rich with scorn. Once again, her faction stirred in unease at her words, but she didn't seem to notice this time. "Tony interfered in Kayla's fate as well. Why haven't you questioned him about that?"

"I admit to interacting with humans, but I only fixed what you changed. I set the trap, and now the rest of us can see your hypocrisy."

"She not only killed," I said, interjecting myself in to the tableau before they could ask him when he set that trap. "She also created a doppelganger of me, a creature that she controlled and sent out to harm. By using these tactics, she thought to keep you from finding out what she was doing. She thought she was keeping her hands clean. She cannot even understand the enormity of her crimes." I paused and looked directly at her. "She has no control left. She is mad."

A hush settled over the Ascended, and this time they drew back even more. Nerissa sensed it too. Her emotions skewed wildly as she realized that she was losing her influence over them. I slipped even deeper into her mind and held tighter onto Jacob. I still had no idea what Nerissa's backup plan was, she had buried it so deep, but I sensed I had only seconds to discover it.

If only the Ascended could sense Nerissa past the façade. Then there would be no argument. Even as the thought came to me, I felt her gathering her will. Sorrow for what I had to do almost made me hesitate, but I steeled myself.

"Forgive me, Nerissa," I whispered in her mind, and with all my strength, I tore down her wall as she screamed. Around us, the Ascended flickered in and out of reality, and we were tumbling through time.

Chapter 31

CURSES flooded my mind, but my throat was frozen, and I couldn't let any of them out. *"Kristair! What the fuck is happening?"* I could still sense my lover, and his mind was far calmer than my own. That alone kept me from completely losing my goddamn mind.

As abruptly as it started, it ended, and I found myself on a tiled floor, gasping for breath. I sat up, my head spinning, and looked around at the locker room at Pittsburgh. *"Jacob! Are you okay? Where are you?"*

I grabbed my skull as Kristair's voice crashed through it. *"Fuck, Kristair. Not so loud."* I scrambled to my knees and realized that I was alone. I couldn't see him or Nerissa anywhere. *"I'm in my old locker room. Where are you?"*

"The stadium. It's empty. We have to find Nerissa; she's somewhere close. We have to stop her."

I heard the door to the locker room open and I stared in confusion up at Coach Latimer as he came around the corner to my row and glared at me. I hadn't seen him since graduation, though I'd intended on stopping by to catch when practice started for him.

"Corvin!" Coach barked, his eyes narrowing even more in displeasure.

Old instinct had me scrambling to my feet. "Coach?"

"Do you think you're on vacation? At some fancy day spa where you get pampered? Get suited up and get out there with the others!"

Before I could stammer an explanation or ask what the fuck was going on, Coach was gone. *"Kristair. Please tell me what the hell is going on. I feel so fucking weird, like my skin is on backward."*

"That's because we don't belong here. I found a program for this night's game. It's September 2nd, 2006."

September 2nd... why did that tickle my memory?

"Because that's the night I first noticed you, when you made that amazing touchdown. That's the night I knew you were mine."

I sat down hard on the bench, my skin crawling, a shout lodging in my throat. For once I couldn't come up with a clever quip. *"Why? Why did she come here?"*

There was a long silence as Kristair's emotions rioted. *"I suspect to kill you. It's not sunset yet, and I had been late to the game. If you were dead before it started, I never would've known of you. Then when I became one of the Ascended I wouldn't have had that link luring me back to you. I wouldn't have left and the Ascended wouldn't have split."*

"And she wins."

I had been late for practice that day. Coach had reamed me out and almost pulled me from the game. I remembered that clearly because it was the last time I'd ever tried goofing off before a game. And the first game of the season. What an idiot I used to be. *"Is she here? Do you know? We all got separated; maybe she's in another time."*

"No, she's here. I can sense her." Kristair's mind was alive with the hunt. *"I should be able to find her."*

"I thought fucking with time was the ultimate no-no. Why haven't the Ascended stepped in and jumped the bitch?"

"She hasn't actually done anything yet. I don't think they believe she will go that far."

Before I could reply, the door banged open and another Jacob came running up to me, his head down, cursing under his breath. I leapt off the bench, my heart racing as my younger self stopped in front of me, his eyes widening as he saw my face. "What the fuck!" younger Jacob said.

"Son of a bitch." There was no time to think. My hand balled into a fist, and I punched my younger self as hard as I could, wincing in sympathy as he went down in a crumpled heap. I dragged him up by his shirt and slugged him again for good measure.

Oh fuck, my heart wouldn't stop racing. What the hell was I supposed to do now? *"Kristair, umm, I uh, just knocked myself out. That's not going to fuck with things is it? What should I do?"*

"It's a bit late to ask now. The deed is done." I waited anxiously while Kristair thought. *"Stash him somewhere and take his place."*

"What? How? Are you crazy? How's that not changing things?"

"We don't have much time. Nerissa is going to try to corner you when you're alone. If your other self is safe somewhere else, she'll have no reason to believe you're not him. If she attacks you, you'll have the upper hand. She'll be expecting her victim to be clueless and an easy target. Not fighting back."

The need to do something, anything, had me moving. I looked around for someplace I could hide myself, and my eyes fell on my locker. "Buddy, I'm so damn sorry, but it's to keep your ass alive." I dragged all my gear out of my locker, stuffed a sock in his mouth, and tied his hands with his jock strap. *"Oh man, this is so wrong. I think I hate myself."*

"What's happening?" Kristair demanded. *"I'm getting closer to Nerissa."*

"Don't worry about it. I'll explain later." Taking a deep breath, I stuffed the other Jacob into my locker. Oh god, this was fucking surreal. The next time I saw that bitch, I was going to whoop her ass, woman or not. I slammed the locker door shut and snapped the lock on. I couldn't believe I was doing this. This had to be the craziest, most insane situation I had been in yet.

"This is the worst idea I've ever heard of," I snarled as I stripped and started to yank on my old gear.

"Trust me, mo chroí.*"*

I finished getting dressed and tried to psych myself up to going out and joining my coach and the rest of my old teammates. How the hell was I going to pull it off? They'd figure me out in less than five minutes. And what if Nerissa started taking swipes at my old team just to get at me?

"Calm down, Jacob. They'll see what they expect to see. It hasn't been that many years. Your tattoos are covered up. Stop fussing so much and get out there before you change time even more. Right now only you have really been affected."

I bit back the urge to snarl even more at my lover and grabbed my helmet, rising from the bench as I heard the door open again. "I'm coming, Coach."

My heart flipped at the sound of a lock turning. *"Um, Kristair, I think she's here."* I heard the sound of someone coming down the aisle, and my hand drifted toward my gun under my clothes. *"What should I do?"* I couldn't shoot her—that was Kayla's body.

"Try to stall her, I'm almost there. I'd paused to investigate something odd."

"This isn't the time for curiosity! The door's locked, but it's cheap. You should be able to jimmy it or knock it down, okay? Just get your ass here." Metal scraped against metal from the weight room, and I grabbed my gun and eased around the corner. I needed to put myself between Nerissa and the other Jacob.

Stalling wouldn't work. Maybe if she hadn't looked so creepy with her blank features, I could hit on her or something, but that wouldn't be believable now. Then time ran out as Nerissa emerged from the weight room wielding a long weight bar.

Fuck pretending. I raised my gun and pointed it at her. "It's over, Nerissa."

Snarling, she swung at me, and I ducked out of the way, dodging around her as the bar clanged against a row of lockers. Son of a bitch, that didn't help at all. "Where is he?" she hissed, swinging at me again.

"You're never gonna find him." I ducked again, cursing my decision to bring the gun. I couldn't shoot her, and she knew it, but now I couldn't drop it either and wrestle her, or she'd go for the gun. I'd handicapped my own dumb ass.

I couldn't figure out why she didn't jump through time again now that this attempt had failed, or why the Ascended still weren't here. I dodged another blow, letting that one come closer as I tried to lure her farther away from my other self. I winced at the racket she was making, just waiting for Coach Latimer to come banging on the door to investigate.

"I'll crack your skull in," Nerissa rasped, this swing going directly toward my head with nowhere to dodge. "Then I'll find him and do the same to his skull. Your brains will decorate this room."

Cursing, I rolled out of way, scrambled to my feet, and ran. The doors to the locker room shuddered as something thudded against it. Another hard thud and they banged open. I spun around, raising my gun, and breathed in a sigh of relief as I saw Kristair. "'Bout time you got—"

A flash of metal out of the corner of my eye had me dodging awkwardly to the side. The glancing blow caught me on my shoulder, pain lacing through me, numbing my arm. The gun clattered to the floor. "Fucking a." I dove for it, slamming into a row of lockers as Nerissa swung the bar over her head again. I braced for the strike I'd have no chance in hell of stopping.

Kristair snarled, staff whirling as he intercepted Nerissa's swing. He shoved hard, pushing her back away from me, giving me the chance to find my feet again. "You okay?"

I rolled my shoulder, grimacing at the twinges. It would be sore, but I didn't think anything was broken. "I'll be fine."

Kristair and Nerissa continued to spar, moving so quickly I didn't dare try to intercept them. I glanced toward the door, which was listing off of one hinge. It was unnatural. Coach Latimer and the rest of the team were just down that hallway, getting ready for the game against Virginia, and no one had come to investigate. What the hell was going on?

I ran over to the door and shoved it back into the frame. The lock was busted wide open, not that it had done much to slow Kristair down anyway. I snapped the safety on the gun, shoved it in my pants, and dragged the weight bench over in front of the door. It screeched across the tiles, and still no one was coming to our rescue as I finished. I didn't know whether to be relieved or offended.

Kristair and Nerissa were still battling, only now she seemed to be tiring. Her weapon was heavier than his, and each swing was a little wilder than the last. Kristair twisted his staff, and the metal bar went flying to the ground. Breathing hard, his face set, Kristair shoved her against the lockers, pressing the staff against her shoulders, and pinned her there.

"Nerissa, stop this madness," he said harshly.

I reached out and touched him with a thought, wishing I could soothe him now. Underneath the implacable resolve was so much pain and fear. All because of this woman. I couldn't begin to really understand what he was going through. As much as could read him, share his thoughts, I'd never had to go through a betrayal like this. She had been mother, teacher, and friend. She'd completely changed his life, and he'd lived with her for five hundred years. He'd pledged to her that he'd care for her descendents, and the promise had meant so much to him that when one had showed up on his doorstep fifteen hundred years later, looking for shelter, he'd taken her in and adopted Kayla as his daughter.

Even when I had thought Tony had betrayed me, it hadn't run this deep.

Hadn't Kristair meant anything to her in return?

I wanted to help him, but I felt like an intruder. This was between Nerissa and Kristair. Perhaps it had been a long time coming, and as much as I loved him, all I really could do was offer mental support and try to keep any other intruders off their backs.

"You'll have to kill me, but you won't. You just don't want your precious Kayla to perish," she snarled, pushing against the staff to no avail. What had happened to her strength and quickness? She seemed to be equal to the both of us now.

"I don't want to lose either one of you," Kristair said, his face bleak. "I've mourned you once, Nerissa. Don't make me do it again."

I sensed Kristair's mind delve into Nerissa's, and because I was still linked closely with him, I followed. He had done it earlier, but I had been too distracted with the Ascended to notice her mindset then.

Her thoughts were a storm of clawing terror, mindless rage because the world that she thought she had intricate control over, a world she relied on for her mental wellbeing, was falling apart. She was driven to try to fix it, and she threw her considerable will behind that goal. She was so fixated on Kristair being both the cause and the cure that she could not see past him.

Nerissa needed to control everything. That was something Kristair could never see. It was why she had chosen to create him as a vampire, because she had wanted to bend him to her will. That she had never entirely succeeded had always eaten at her deep inside. It had bugged her so much that I didn't think she ever saw the respect or love Kristair had for her. What stupid senselessness.

"You mourned me?" Shock broke through the chaos.

"I kept my promise to you. What does that tell you?"

For a moment, I thought she'd relent, and then thoughts turned to stone. *"That changes nothing, Kristair. I will see you kneel before me before I back down."*

"Is that what you really want?" Then, to my surprise, Kristair stepped back, and the staff turned back into the rod. Nerissa straightened, staring at him in disbelief as Kristair sank to his knees.

"Kristair, no." Jealousy reared up at the sight of my proud lover humbling himself for her. Only I got to see him submit like that. Kristair only did that for me. I wanted to march over there and haul him up, and it shook me to my core.

I sought control with him too. Was I so different from her?

"Listen to me, Mistress. Our minds are joined, I cannot lie to you. At this moment, I cannot even hide anything from you. Will you listen?"

I tensed, and Nerissa did too. I stepped forward in case she decided to strike out. Kristair was so vulnerable. *"Stay back, mo chroí."*

"I will hear you." Suspicion colored her mind, and I watched helplessly as he took her hands in his. I struggled to control my own emotions, to keep them in check so as not to set her off further.

"My return won't solve the problems the Ascended have. Only you can do that. Just as only you can heal the rift in time you created. It's your thought and will that brought us here and only your thought and will can fix it."

"What does that have to do with the Ascended?" she snapped, drawing her hands back. "All I hear are demands from you, Kristair."

Kristair captured her hands again. He didn't seek to cage her; I'd seen him hold Kayla like this when he told her something she didn't want to hear. I knew his touch, strong and loving, and sensed how it calmed Nerissa without her even realizing it. There was a serene strength about Kristair that I had never fully appreciated.

Kristair's emotions surged with regret and sorrow for Nerissa, and I didn't understand it, after everything she'd done. Where was his anger? She deserved his hate.

"You're the one who caused the rift."

"Do not try to manipulate me," Nerissa said. *"I know you, child."* He held on tighter as she shook her head.

"You were angry when I left. You were furious that I managed to trick you, and you let it build up. Then, when some others decided that they wanted to go to other worlds and interact instead of just observe, you were terrified that they would follow me and you would lose them forever."

"They broke the rules."

"It's not about the rules, Nerissa. It never was." Kristair's voice was so gentle, yet underneath it, I sensed the steel in him. He would make Nerissa see the truth, whether she wanted to or not.

"Strong emotion makes the Ascended uneasy. You know how you all reacted to Jacob. But he was an outsider and it was an intrusion. You are a part of them and have been for a long time. Your anger infected the whole without any of you realizing it. When Tony's people wanted to take their explorations a step further, you whipped the rest into a frenzy with your words and your anger. And the more they defied you and got angry in return, the worse it became."

Nerissa shook her head wildly, hair whipping about her blank face, her emotions skewing about in a jumbled mess. "You lie! Stop twisting me about," she shouted.

I realized what Kristair was doing. Nerissa could hold her own against anger, she could fight forever against Kristair's obstinacy, but she had no defense when faced with him like this. I could understand. How many times had I backed down myself, lost an argument I wanted desperately to win because I knew he was only making that stand because he loved me?

Could I let go of my own anger and help him? All I really knew about Nerissa was that she had been my enemy long before she had turned against Kristair. She was the face behind the Ascended trying to keep us apart. But without her, I'd have had neither Kristair or Kayla. Maybe if I could just look at it like that.

Chapter 32

JACOB approached Nerissa and me, and I wished I could soothe his conflict, but I didn't dare split my attention more fully between them. Nerissa was on the verge of cracking, and I had no idea which way she'd go. I stood up and wrapped my arm around her waist, easing her down on a bench as I sat down beside her. "I'm not lying, Nerissa. You know that."

Jacob sat down on her other side, and I sensed the shock ripple through her as he touched her shoulder and let her see how troubled he was himself. "Let him finish," Jacob said.

I took advantage of her distraction and sank further into her mind, striving to calm the chaos so she could see clearly. Jacob went with me, his mind a soothing murmur, and united, we replayed the confrontation with the Ascended, forcing her to see their reactions to her words and deeds.

"Yield, Nerissa. For the sake of the world you love. Only you can fix this. What will happen to the Ascended if you change time? Do you really want to risk everything for the sake of hurting me?"

Nerissa had begun to waver, and then she stiffened. *"You deserve to be punished."*

"Why? Is what I did so wrong? Can't you understand the reasons?"

"Kristair was lonely for a very long time after you left," Jacob said, very softly.

"If he'd stayed with us, he never would've been lonely again," Nerissa raged, glaring at my lover. *"But he had to have you."*

"Nerissa," I said to draw her attention back to me. *"Do you need to know that we've been hurt, that we've been punished?"* Before she could reply, I delved into my memories and let her feel my anguish over knowing I'd hurt my daughter, how I'd almost killed her. I gave her my despair and sense of betrayal when I realized that she had been behind all the madness.

Jacob ached for me and reached past Nerissa to cup my cheek, caressing me with a thought. Nerissa tried to pull back her mind from the both of us, confusion and longing driving back some of her rage. I followed, refusing to release her. I was so close.

"Yield, Nerissa. This is against everything you believe in, and only you can make it right."

Nerissa stood up, and this time I let her go, though it was very difficult to do so. I wanted to go after her, make her see. Instead, I used that drive to push back my frustration and helplessness. I couldn't set her off at this point, and my instincts said it was time to back off and let her think. She had to do this of her own free will.

"You violated me."

Jacob stiffened next to me, and I laid a mental finger against his lips. "I did and I'm sorry that I had to do so. I never wanted to do that to you, but what you were doing was dangerous, not just to me. The Ascended needed to see what you were hiding." I rose, letting her feel my grief over that act. "And I'll carry my guilt with me the rest of my life."

Nerissa turned back toward us, a strange smile playing on her lips. "You will, won't you?" she laughed softly. "I think I like the sound of that, Kristair."

Once again, Jacob bristled, and this time I took his hand. *"Don't."*

"She's about to fuck you over and you're about to take it," he growled.

"Have faith in me."

Nerissa's gaze flashed to Jacob, and I was booted from her mind as her calm wall came back up again. "Fine, I'll return things the way they were."

I rose, took her hands, and raised them to my lips. "You'll submit to the will of the Ascended?"

"Always such a stickler for nuance." Nerissa patted my cheek. "If it will ease your mind, then yes." She pulled one hand free and reached out to Jacob. "Come, take my hand. We wouldn't want you to get lost, now would we?" she said with a kind of imperious malice.

Jacob rose, coming to my side, uncertainty and suspicion uppermost in his mind as his eyes narrowed on Nerissa. *"Kristair?"*

"All will be well. After all, Nerissa has us in her hands." I inclined my head ever so slightly in Nerissa's direction as my lover sputtered. "Take her hand, Jacob."

Jacob didn't say a word. He didn't have to for me to know just what he thought of that. He grabbed both of our hands, glaring hard at Nerissa. He was going to have words with me when this was all over with, of that I had no doubt.

Nerissa started to concentrate and then paused, giving me a direct look. "You haven't said thank you."

"How discourteous of me. Thank you, Mistress." I gave Jacob a quick mental poke, a silent plea as he seethed.

"Thank you," he muttered, between clenched teeth.

Nerissa smiled brilliantly. Behind the momentary crack in her façade, I sensed her pleasure and knew my instincts had been right. The locker room flashed around us, and then we were among the Ascended again. Much to my relief, the mood had changed considerably, and all of the Ascended were arrayed together, lined up to face us, their auras solemn.

"If you ever, and I fucking mean ever..." Steve said, moving quickly to our side.

"Yeah, I missed you too." Jacob yanked his hands free of us. *"Are you done playing games, Kristair?"* he said acidly in my thoughts.

"If the gamble works, are you still going to be mad at me?"

"I hate it when you know something I don't."

I stretched out my senses, touching the edge of the Ascended's awareness, striving to get some sense of where their loyalties lay, and I couldn't get anything, not even from Tony. I pulled back, striving for patience in the face of my uncertainty. I'd broken rules myself in the last twenty-four hours, and when this was over with, I wanted to be able to go back to the life I'd chosen.

"Nerissa, release the girl," the Ascended said, once again as one voice. That, at least, I could really be thankful for.

Steve stepped forward in the long pause and caught Kayla's body as she jerked. I wanted to be the one to catch her, but it was no longer my prerogative to be the first one to look after Kayla. She had chosen Steve. I took Jacob's hand again, willing patience as Kayla's face emerged and her eyes opened. I saw how tenderly Steve held her and finally accepted that my daughter had chosen well.

Nerissa appeared to the side, separate from both us and the Ascended. "Thank you," the Ascended murmured, and she nodded her head regally, a pleased smile flickering across her face. She truly was insane. I had kept saying it, and now I really did believe it to be true.

"What happened?" Kayla gasped, looking around wildly. "Where? What? Oh god, Father... Jake." She threw her arms around Steve and hugged him tight as he buried his hand in her hair and held her close, murmuring softly.

"You were right," Jacob said in disbelief. *"You were fucking right about it all. Everything you told Nerissa. You smug, over-brained son of a bitch. Now what are we going to do? They're all going to be up Nerissa's ass now that they're one big happy family again."*

"Would you like to know what I know?" I said, somehow managing to keep a smile from my lips.

"If you could bring yourself down to my level and enlighten me, yeah, I'd fucking like to know."

"The Ascended had already healed their rift and banded together before Nerissa returned."

The disbelief on Jacob's face would've been more satisfactory if I didn't still have lingering worries. Then Kayla stepped back and hurled herself into my arms before tugging Jacob to us and giving him a fierce hug too. "I'm so sorry. I should've listened and stayed away."

"Hey, don't go blaming yourself," Jacob said, squeezing his arms around her waist and picking her up. "I should've kept my mouth shut and never contacted you guys in the first place."

Steve joined our little circle, looking over his shoulder uneasily at the Ascended and Nerissa. "So what now?"

"Kristair was about to fill me in, but he's taking his sweet time about it." Jacob glared at me. "And I for one can't tell if she's still a threat or not. So will you please tell me how you know that the Ascended already kissed and made up and what that means to us if you have all the damn answers?"

"Wait a minute," Steve cut in. "How the hell did you know that? That happened after you all blinked out."

I glanced over at Nerissa, who was watching us, a strange, almost yearning expression on her face, which disappeared as soon as she noticed me looking. "I'll explain it all later. I suspect the Ascended want to get this over with and get rid of us as soon as possible."

"Nerissa, there is something you wish to say to us?" the Ascended asked.

"Yes." She turned, bowed low, and then straightened, confidence ringing in her voice. "I erred. I see that now. The only thing I have to offer in my defense is that I believe when the Exile was among us, still connected to his too-human lover, that their emotional state infected me. I was too close to him and unknowingly let him influence me."

"What?" Jacob stepped forward, and as much as he tried to clamp down on his seething fury, I sensed it, which meant the Ascended could too. I hauled him back next to me, trying to touch him on as many different levels as I could so soothe him.

"We'll get our chance to talk."

"Is that all you have to say?" the Ascended asked, the bulk of their attention on Nerissa. I'd have felt much more certain if I could have got an inkling of which way they would go. Even though the threat of imminent war was gone between them, there was so much at stake for me and Jacob personally, and I could not fully relax.

"It is. I repent the damage that I have done. In my arrogance, I reached beyond barriers that should have been left alone. It will not happen again. I submit to you, my brethren, and I accept whatever punishment you deem fit for my errors in judgment. However, I would like to point out that my surrender did bring about good for us all."

"Wow," Steve said under his breath. "That woman's got a lot of pride. She's not really giving an inch. Damn, you almost gotta hand it to her."

Kayla shot a glare at him, and I couldn't help but smile. "Humility does not run in her bloodline," I said. Steve met my eyes and smiled in return.

"It is true, your actions tore us apart, as you admitted to the Exile when you went back in time." There it was, the first flutter of unease on Nerissa's face, the first crack in her false calm. She hadn't been aware of their presence, and she should have been. "You violated our most sacred law when you attempted to change time, intending on ending Jacob Corvin's existence. That gross violation of what we believe in forced us to see what was happening, so in a sense, you could say you brought us together again."

Nerissa spun about to face me. *"You knew,"* she whispered in my mind. *"But you said...."*

"The Exile manipulated you as you attempted to manipulate him. And the both of you are trying to use us for your own ends," the Ascended continued.

"What you say is true," I said, unable to leave that without a response. "But I cannot do what you can. I cannot control Nerissa and keep her from causing more damage, only you can do that. It is not my place to judge or punish her for her crimes. I sought only to return her to you before she could cause further harm." I opened my mind to them, squelching my need for privacy. The only way they'd believe my sincerity was if I showed them I had nothing to hide.

I sensed them touch my mind, shifting through my thoughts and motivations. Jacob stiffened as they did the same to him. I sensed similar reactions from Kayla and Steve, but none of them offered a protest. Then the Ascended turned their attention back on Nerissa.

She stood proud and alone. She still couldn't see what was about to happen, and in that moment, I pitied her.

"You still attempt to hide from us, Nerissa. The Exile has told us what he seeks from us. To control you, so both the world and those he values are safe. He has opened his mind to us, as have his companions. They do not seek glory or praise, they simply wish to go home and be left in peace."

I breathed a sigh of relief and tightened my arm around Jacob's shoulders. *"Does that mean they're going to grant it?"* he asked.

"I hope so, mo chroí, *I hope so."*

"You have closed yourself off from us to a degree that you have unwittingly limited yourself and dulled your senses. Yet we can still read you because of the Exile's actions before you went back in time. You are not apologetic, Nerissa. Your humble guise does not fool us. You seek to hide among us until you can retaliate again and we cannot allow that to happen. You tried to alter time once and we sense that you wouldn't hesitate to try a similar tactic again. You are the true Aberration."

"Wait, what about Kristair's crimes? He was supposed to have given up his abilities so he could be human. Isn't that the reason why we allowed him to remain with his lover?"

"Even now you delude yourself. We did not allow him to be human. The Exile made that choice himself and, once made, it could not be unmade. He may have shown some minor abilities, but nothing compared to what he used to be able to do. Even contacting us before caused him pain. What little abilities he's shown have been unreliable and not even as strong as when he was a vampire. No, he did not renege on his vow to be human. He couldn't hold such power for centuries and have nothing at all when he gave them up for Jacob, but what little he did have he still kept locked up until he realized who he was dealing with. Whether or not he uses them from now on is of little concern to us as long as he vows never to try to merge his mind with us again."

"I do make that vow," I said. "Gladly."

"Remember when I said that I wanted to be there when you were wrong?" Jacob said, his mind exultant.

"I do."

"Hah! I was right and you were so wrong." Jacob grinned at me and kissed me hard on the mouth despite our audience, and Kayla stifled a laugh.

"Jacob."

"Don't, just let me gloat for a minute. I deserve it after the hell you've put me through this last hour. I told you the Ascended wouldn't care what you did."

One clearly had though, and I looked back at Nerissa as her eyes bore into me. It was over. I should have been rejoicing, but instead I felt weary. I just wanted to go home with Jacob, Kayla, and Steve. I just wanted to assure Ussier that his city and people were no longer in any danger from Nerissa.

"Then you're sending us back?" Steve asked.

"Not just yet. You must witness the judgment imposed upon Nerissa, the Exile, and Jacob."

"What?" Kayla gasped. "No, wait, they didn't do anything. You just said so yourself."

Shock rippled through Jacob, and I attempted to ease his fears through my own worries. What had we done? What had Jacob done? He was blameless in all of this.

"No!" Nerissa snarled. Energy swirled around her as she attempted to break free, and she screamed when it was thwarted. "You can't do this to me."

"You've given us no choice, Nerissa." I stepped forward as she screamed again, a glow surrounding her, and when it was gone, she laid there before them, a squirming infant.

"Oh damn," Jacob said under his breath. "They rebooted her."

I shot him a confused glance as Kayla stifled another giggle, this one with a slightly hysterical edge. "Exile." I stiffened, tearing my eyes away from the baby's chubby, kicking legs. She seemed somewhat older than a newborn, though I wasn't in much of a position to judge. It had been a long time since I'd seen any young child.

"She is helpless," I said, glaring at the Ascended. "Are you going to care for her? How long will she remain like this?"

"Don't you think your sense of outrage is a little misplaced, love?" Jacob said, though I could sense he was also taken aback by her sentence.

Tony emerged from the Ascended and reached down to pick up Nerissa. "She can no longer remain with us, Kristair. She is no longer Ascended. She chose to remove herself from our ranks as you did. We don't kill. By returning her to this state, we've removed her threat."

"And left her completely unable to take care of herself."

"That is now your job. Yours and Jacob's. The Ascended feel that the task should be given to you. They have deemed that Nerissa was right, you were the original cause of the problem, and Jacob had caused the first rip in time when he'd rendered his earlier self unconscious."

Tony handed Nerissa to me, and I held her up under her arms away from me, terror making my heart race. She was so tiny. What if I broke her? I glanced wildly over my shoulder at Jacob as he came up alongside me. He looked both incredulous and awed. "Kristair, I don't think we should argue with them, not after what they just did to her."

"Though it is my thought that it is because of you both that the rip in time is now fixed." Tony studied the both of us. "I also think that you are all that she has left. If there is anyone who can care for her, it is you two. She'll never be a completely normal child, just as you'll never be completely normal yourselves. Who better to raise her again? There are bonds there that you cannot deny."

I looked into Nerissa's eyes, at the world of lost confusion and fear in them, and knew I couldn't say no. "Jacob?"

"For god's sake, Kristair, she's not going to shatter." Jacob plucked Nerissa from my hands and tucked her in the crook of his arm. She looked oddly natural there, and an expression of amused resignation crossed his face as his thoughts whirled and scattered. And as he looked down at the baby, I sensed his surrender. "Ma is going to kill me. We haven't gotten married yet."

I glanced over at Kayla, who had her arms crossed, a stony expression on her face. "Kayla?" She had been affected by Nerissa's betrayal as much as I had, and I could not ignore her feelings on the matter.

The silence stretched out, and then Steve leaned down to whisper in her ear. "Oh fine, just don't expect me to be a doting big sister right away, got it?" Kayla came over and looked down at Nerissa, cuddled against Jacob's chest. "Just so you know, I'm keeping my eye on you."

Nerissa waved a fat little hand and broke out into a burbling laugh, her eyes brightening. "You go, Kayla. You've got her shaking in her booties," Jacob teased.

Chapter 33

IT WAS over with.

Tony brought us all back to the cabin to grab our things. After lengthy goodbyes, he returned Kayla and Steve to Baltimore, then Kristair, me, and the baby back home to Pittsburgh. He promised to check in on us from time to time; as much as the Ascended wanted to stay distant from all of us, they also wanted to keep an eye on Nerissa, and Tony was their obvious spokesperson.

It was good to know that I wouldn't have to lose all contact with him.

And I couldn't blame Kayla and Steve for bailing early. This new situation was going to take some time to get used to. Probably a couple years at least. I stood in the doorway of our living room, nursing a beer, and watched Kristair nap on the couch. The baby lay on his chest, and every time he snored, her head popped up, and she looked around before laying her head back down with a yawn.

It was unreal, and I wished I'd thought to buy a video camera when we were out shopping earlier.

Maybe we could come up with a new name for her, something that would distance us from who she'd been. For all intents and purposes, she was our daughter now. I smiled and took another sip of my beer as Kristair sleepily rubbed her back. He was crazy to think he'd be a bad father.

I went over and scooped the baby out of his arms, sending him a soothing thought as he stirred, half waking up. *"It's okay, love, finish your nap. Sunset will be here soon and you've got to explain to Ussier that he missed all the fun."*

Kristair needed his sleep. The first thing we had had to do after getting back was go shopping for everything we didn't have. He had worn himself out worrying about what we might have forgotten. "Rissa... what do you think about that? You like that name?" Rissa didn't respond. Her head had pillowed on my shoulder, and her thumb had crept its way back into her mouth. Tiny lashes shadowed her cheeks.

"What are we going to do with you?" I murmured, going out onto the porch and settling down with a sigh. I still had no idea how I was going to explain this situation to my Ma. It would be just another in a long line of interesting conversations I'd had with her since I'd met Kristair. But I couldn't see myself giving the baby up now either. My emotions surrounding the whole weird series of events were too complex to decipher.

"Rissa. Yeah, I think I like that." I tucked her into the crook of my arm and began to rock. She had Kayla's hair, the honey brown more golden now, and it curled in a springy fuzz on top of her head. She would have no memory of what she had been, what she had done. She had a clean slate.

The sound of the screen door and sense of Kristair's presence had me looking over at him. "What are you doing up? You need to sleep."

"I'll sleep enough tonight. The part of my life where I slept my days away is over with." Kristair sat down on the swing next to me and slipped an arm about my shoulders. "Are you sure you're okay with this? It's a lot to ask of you, *mo chroí.*" His fingers brushed my shoulder. "I just want you to be happy."

"I know that." I turned my head and brushed a kiss across his lips. "It'll take awhile to adjust, but I think in the long run we'll all be okay. I think the question is, what is Ussier going to say? Have you figured out how you're going to explain this whole thing to him?"

Kristair had left a message with the bloodsucker explaining that the situation had been resolved and to come alone to our house when he had the chance. I expected him the moment the sun disappeared. "I'm going to tell him the truth. We owe it to him, and he knows enough now that he might even be able to swallow it all."

"I've changed her name."

Kristair arched a brow and nodded. "That's probably a good idea. My people believed that there was a great deal of power in one's name."

"Is that why you always call me Jacob instead of Jake?"

"It is the name your mother and father gave you. It's a good, strong name." Kristair peered down at the baby and touched a finger to her cheek. "So what have you decided?"

"Rissa."

I sensed Kristair's pleasure as he curled closer in my mind. *"Good choice."*

We sat out there, enjoying the quiet, until Kristair rose to go inside and make dinner. I could get used to nights like these, sitting with my soon-to-be husband and daughter. Now Kristair couldn't give me any more ridiculous arguments about not being father material. Life was pretty fucking excellent.

Rissa seemed very content as we went about our evening. She sat in her high chair, kicking her legs and laughing every time one of us would look at her as we finished setting up her room with the bare necessities after dinner. The fear and anxiety I would have expected in her were not present.

"You know, I get why she reacts that way to you," I finally said to Kristair. "She's known you forever, so you'd at least be familiar. But she doesn't know me at all. You think the Ascended tampered with her emotions?"

"No, they had no need to. When they made her an infant, they erased her memories. She has the brain of an infant too."

"So what gives?" I glanced over at Rissa, and sure enough, she beamed and kicked, sending her seat to bouncing. I grinned as she waved her little hands and laughed. When I turned back to help Kristair piece the crib together, he was giving me an indulgent smile.

"There are two reasons why she reacts the way she does to you. One, every time you look at her, you smile, wave, and talk to her, so she's responding in kind." I never really thought of it that way. Then Kristair touched my mind, only it seemed a bit different this time until I realized I could sense Rissa too.

There weren't any real thoughts yet, more flitting images and sensations. I sensed contentment, recognition, and joy when she sensed my mental touch. She squealed, legs kicking faster, and beamed at me. And I realized there was love there too. She already loved the both of us, and it hit me hard.

She really was ours to raise.

"Rissa also senses how I feel about you. Between that and your smiles and the way you're not afraid to hold her and the way you interact with her, how could she not feel safe and loved here? I think all three of us are going to be just fine."

"Wow, I think it's going to take some time to adjust my thinking."

We worked for a bit longer in silence except for the sound of Rissa talking to herself. "I guess she really doesn't remember anything. We don't have to worry about waking up one day and having her trying to get back at us."

I realized I could read her as easily as I did Kristair. We'd know the instant anything changed with her, as we did with each other.

"No, she never will remember. It's probably kinder that way. The Ascended will never accept her again, just as they'll never accept me." Kristair smiled at me and brushed a mental kiss over my lips. "And I have no problems with that."

"Hey, wait a minute. Does that mean she's going to know everything we say to each other?" I lowered my voice and leaned in closer to him. "'Cause ya know how I like to get down and dirty with you in my head."

Kristair started laughing, and I gave him an offended look, which only made him laugh harder. "I'm serious." I swatted his ass and whispered low. "I don't want to corrupt her or freak her out, and I sure as hell don't want to start behaving myself."

Kristair laid a mental kiss on my lips that left me tingling and eager to drag him off to our bedroom. He smiled at me as I stood there dazed; then he picked up the next tool he needed. *Does that answer your question? We can block her from the more lurid side of your nature until she's old enough to try to peek past it. By then she won't want to know what a freak you are.*

A teasing smile played about his lips, though his eyes were oh-so-innocent as he glanced at me. He was really begging for it. *Guess this means no more spankings on the living room coach.*

"Don't bet on it, Kristair. I'm very good at taking advantage of opportune moments and creating them if need be."

A knock on the front door interrupted the discussion just as it was getting interesting. I glanced at the window and saw that the sky was dark. "I guess it's that time." I went over to Rissa, holding out my finger, and when she grasped it, a sudden wave of protectiveness went over me. "He's not going to try and hurt her, is he? Maybe I should wait in here with her while you talk with him."

"Ussier won't lay a finger on her," Kristair said. "He has to know what happened, and if he thinks we're hiding anything, he'll make it a point to find out on his own. I'd rather tell him and let him know at the same time that we consider her off limits."

Kristair eased Rissa out of her seat, still holding her as if she were fragile china. I knew how afraid he was of accidentally hurting her, and at the same time, I could sense how he masked that feeling from her. Good. He'd give her a complex and have her bursting into tears every time he picked her up if he didn't.

"Breathe, Kristair. Christ, you need to learn to chill the fuck out."

"And you need to learn to start watching your language."

I grimaced, realizing he had a point. My Ma would kill me if Rissa's first words were cuss words. I followed Kristair to the door, trying to anticipate what Ussier would say when he found out the entire story, but nothing prepared me for the vamp's reaction when he saw the baby in Kristair's arms.

Ussier stared at Rissa, his eyes widening as his hand came up to his forehead. "What is that? What is it?" he asked, pure exasperation in his voice. "I know it's not human. What is it, and can it destroy the city?"

Kristair's lips twitched, and he opened the door wider. "I'm afraid it's going to take some time to tell you the whole tale, but I assure you, your city is now safe. At least from anybody seeking to hurt me."

"I suppose that's all I can ask for, isn't it?"

I'd never seen Ussier like this, so off balance, and lord, it brought out the devil in me. "Feeling faint there, Ussier? Would you like me to fetch you a walker?" I was probably begging to have Ussier pull my ass out through my throat, but it was so rare that I got to fuck with the king bloodsucker of Pittsburgh.

"No, Mr. Corvin, I'm doing just fine, thank you. But I'm sure that if I were not dead already you two would help usher me to my demise."

"Be nice, Jacob."

"Oh fine, just ruin all my fun."

Kristair led Ussier to the living room and sat down in his favorite chair, holding Rissa gingerly. "This might take a bit of time to tell, and I'm afraid that what I have to say is only between us. Artemise and Lisabeth included, of course, since they know a bit. Is Lisabeth awake? Safe?"

"Yes, cranky but awake, and Tabitha will survive as well." Ussier sat down, still staring at Kristair and the baby as if he didn't quite know what to make of the situation. I couldn't say I blamed him. "You might want to give Lisabeth a wide berth for a little bit. She rarely holds grudges, but she doesn't forget things either. She has a very long memory and doesn't like to appear weak."

"Not that I planned on dropping in for tea, but I understand. She's not the only one who doesn't like to appear weak." I winked at Kristair and then grinned at Rissa as she kicked and waved, chirping a greeting at Ussier. At least, I hoped it was a greeting.

"Duly noted." Absently, Kristair gave Rissa his pinky, and she latched onto it, curling into him and sticking her thumb in her mouth as she eyed the vampire. Ussier listened as Kristair went through the whole story, from when he'd left us, to Nerissa possessing Kayla again, Tony's trap, the trial, and Nerissa's escape back in time. There was no expression on his face as Kristair explained how we'd talked Nerissa into returning and then told him of the Ascended's verdict and judgment and how we'd been tasked with raising her. "Tony has promised to look in on us when he can, but otherwise, we're on our own."

For a long time, Ussier remained silent, and I was beginning to wonder if I needed to get between him and Kristair and Rissa. Finally, Ussier shook his head, his expression still impassive. "All this time and we've been afraid of a baby? The whole city on red alert, people scared and jumping out of windows. In my final report it's going to say it was us against a dozen dragons, a six-headed demon, and three hundred ninjas. I had enough trouble explaining a doppelganger to Deke; he was sure the damn thing had to be bigger after all the trouble it caused."

I blinked, not quite sure how to take Ussier's exasperation. He didn't seem like he was ready to pounce, but then Kristair grinned. "If it makes you feel better to tell your people that, then I won't complain. I don't think most would believe the truth anyhow."

"There are all kinds of truth, Ancient One, and most people don't care about it. And I wouldn't worry about Alette. Even if she did find out, she'd leave the baby alone. She wouldn't ever harm a child, and she'd hunt down anyone else who tried. I guess she does have a few redeeming qualities."

"We will need paperwork for her, birth certificate, adoption papers and other such necessities. Would you arrange that for us as you did for Kayla?"

"Yeah, I'll talk with Deke. He'll get you everything you need."

I had never even thought of that. We'd have to have papers for courts, doctors, any number of other things. There was so much I hadn't thought of. What else were we missing? My brain spun as it went off in a dozen different directions. At least I knew that the documents we got from Ussier would hold up under scrutiny. I was sure he had plenty of practice.

"So does that mean our debt is paid off?" I asked him.

For the first time, those dangerous dimples of Ussier's flashed. "I'll get back to you on that."

"Figures."

"Yeah, our debt's done. Consider it a gift from the city to the new mother," Ussier said, looking directly at me.

"Asswipe." Damn, the fucker got me every time. One of these days I was going to one up him.

Ussier became serious. "In all sincerity, we owe you a great debt. If there is anything you need, the door is open." Then he paused. "Don't make it a habit."

Kristair inclined his head formally at him. "It is my goal to lay low for awhile. We've had an exciting two years. I'm getting a little old for all of this craziness." Then, in my head, for me alone, *"Besides, I know how much you want a normal life."*

"Kristair, life ceased to be normal the moment I met you. I think I've gotten used to it."

"I'm not sure, Ancient One. For some of us, trouble seems to seek us out, not the other way around."

"Well then, Jacob and I will just have to keep a close eye out for it." Kristair rose, glancing at the clock and then down at Rissa, who had fallen asleep in his arms, and a look of wonder crossed his face. "I think I'll go lay her down. If you'll excuse me, Ussier, as always, it's been a pleasure to see you again."

I watched him go, warming inside as I savored the fact he'd never be taken from me again. All of Kristair's fears about the Ascended claiming him were gone. He was mine forever, and I was going to cherish him. Then I looked at Ussier, surprised to find him studying me.

"I have to thank you, Ussier. You helped us out as much as we helped you. And as much as I might regret this at another time, if you need anything, you can ask." I paused, my brows furrowing. "It may sound crazy coming from me, considering what Kristair can do, but I just want to keep the both of them safe."

"I can understand that, Corvin. That's my job, too, to keep my family safe. And whether you like it or not, you knuckleheads are a part of my family. Don't get all mushy on me."

I tugged on my earlobe, grateful for once for Ussier's teasing. "Yeah, thanks, I was really afraid that we were about to have a moment there or something." I rose to escort him back to the door. "And if you do need something, try to schedule it offseason, okay?"

"Of course. Can't distract the ringer on my fantasy team."

I stared at Ussier, incredulous. "You have a fantasy team? Don't you have better things to do than watch my stats?"

"I've got to have some down time when I'm not saving your ass. Me, Deke, Hugh, and Taylor all have our own league. My youngling tried to draft you first. Her team is based on how cute the players' asses are. But I got you first, so I own your ass."

"Rest assured, Jacob. Your ass is all mine."

"Just wonderful. Go home, Ussier." I shook his hand, trying to convey everything I felt in that moment to a man that I was still afraid of, but who had won my respect. "I'm sure I'll see you around." Without another word, Ussier turned and left. I watched from my door as he got into his 4Runner and backed out of the driveway.

Then I turned my attention to my lover, who was waiting down the hallway for me.

Chapter 34

RISSA fussed sleepily as I got her ready for bed, but a soothing thought soon had her yawning. The crib wasn't ready yet, so I laid her down in her playpen and covered her with a light blanket. The room was an absolute mess. It would take us all week at least to get the house set up for a baby.

"What deep thoughts are you thinking?" Jacob asked softly, coming into the room and smiling down at Rissa. "I just can't keep up with your mind sometimes."

I slipped my hand into his. "I was thinking that things have not been quiet once since I met you. You know, I once went a whole decade once with nothing untoward happening, and then you came along."

I sensed Jacob's amusement as he lifted one brow. "Sounds damn boring if you ask me."

"Honestly, it was. I think I slept through half of it."

Jacob leaned down and rubbed the back of his knuckle against Rissa's cheek. I sensed his mix of emotions and shared them. We would just have to take it a little bit at a time. "I'm already separating the two of them, our daughter Rissa and that nutcase Nerissa. How weird is that?"

"Not at all. She is a different person now. Some personality traits I'm sure will remain the same, she'll be stubborn, demanding, and arrogant at times."

"So you're saying she'll fit right in with us."

I chuckled. "Exactly. But she won't be under the same pressures either. She won't be lonely. I doubt her mind will crack again, not with both of us there." I turned to face him. "You're able to separate the two because you're not the kind of a man to carry a grudge or to hold Rissa to blame for crimes that she cannot remember. She is lucky to have you."

"Come on." Jacob tugged on my hand, leading me out of the room. "It has been a very long day, and I'm dying to crawl into bed with you. After these last two weeks, I'm not moving until somebody wakes me."

I shut off the light and eased her door partially shut. Both of us would hear her stir in our thoughts long before she cried. I sensed Jacob kept the same light link with Rissa that I did.

"What are we going to do with her during the day?" Jacob asked as we entered our room. "I'm good until training camp starts, but that's not too far off."

"Nobody bothers me at the library. I'll carry her with me until we find someone suitable." Though I had been considering giving up my career as a librarian. It just wasn't the same without Kayla. And I liked to change careers every once in awhile, start something new. The recent excitement had me considering opening a private detective agency. But I was sure Jacob wasn't ready for me to take a step like that, so I had the idea on hold for now.

"You know, you never did explain how you knew the Ascended were with us," Jacob said, sitting down on the edge of the bed so he could take off his shoes. It still amazed me how he could leave his clothes each night in a little heap on the ground while I was compelled to put everything where it belonged, whether it was the hamper or the closet.

"They froze time, just as Nerissa had when she wanted to speak to us without Kayla overhearing. The moment you stuffed your other self into the locker, they intervened. You should've realized it yourself when no one came to investigate. Nerissa should've too."

"Not all of us are blessed to be nerds and have such overwhelming intellect." Jacob stripped down naked and carefully set his torc on the bed stand as he did every night.

"Well, I did have a little help coming to that conclusion," I admitted, pulling back the covers to our bed. "Remember how I said I'd stopped to investigate something? I noticed a security guard frozen in the middle of doing his sweep. The intervention had come just in time, really. I would've had to have knocked him out if he'd seen me. That would've delayed me even more."

Jacob shut off the light, and we climbed into bed. It still seemed incredible that it was all over with. No more nightmares, no more worries about my past catching up with me. I smiled as Jacob curled into me, his head on my shoulder, his leg over mine. Even in sleep, he was possessive.

I followed the progression of his thoughts as he went over the day again in his mind, sensed his concern again that there wasn't too much difference between him and Nerissa. I frowned, sinking into his thoughts. *"You two are vastly different."*

"Are we? We both want to control you."

I rolled over, pinning Jacob under me. "No, actually, you don't. This morning...." I couldn't actually believe it had just been this morning. "This morning when you wanted me to strip for you and to submit to you, I did it because I knew that if I couldn't you'd still love me, you'd still want me. You told me yourself that it was one of our ways of coping. You seeking control and me seeking submission, and you were right."

Jacob's brow was still furrowed, his eyes still troubled. "Yeah, but...."

I laid my finger over his lips. "No buts, *mo chroí,* the love of my heart. No buts. Nerissa never wanted an equal. By the time I came to her, she was already an Ancient. We were worlds apart. She cared for me, but she always saw me as a possession, nothing more. Even though she wanted it, she couldn't let herself bend that much. She was too set in her ways."

"You were an Ancient when I met you."

"Yes, but you demanded equality, and I have never been much interested in pets. I'd always wanted to love someone who could do that. I'd rather have a man step toe-to-toe with me than someone who'd let me do whatever I pleased without complaint. I fell in love with you because you were precisely that man."

Jacob softened, and he smiled up at me. "I love you, too, though I think we're straying from the subject."

I shook my head and nuzzled his throat. "No, we're not. It comes down to this, Jacob. You want what is best for me and us, and you'd be willing to give up your control if that's what it took to make me happy. Nerissa never would've been able to do that and that's what brought her down in the end. And that is why I surrender to you and no one else."

I smiled as I realized that my words had gotten through to him. "Well, when you put it that way," Jacob said, wrapping his arms around me and lifting his head up for a tender kiss. "I guess I'll just have to defer to you in this."

"There has to be a first time for everything."

"Don't get used to it. I'm sure the moment will pass." Jacob kissed me again, his mouth slanting as he sought deeper contact, and my heart skipped a beat as desire awoke in me.

"You sure she can't sense this?" Jacob asked. "Because it's still early and I'm nowhere damned near ready for sleep. Not with you naked and all up against me." He rolled the both of us over again so he was on top this time and grinned wickedly down at me.

"Just keep doing what you're doing and we'll be just fine." Jacob's eyes gleamed in the dim light, and I sensed the playfulness in him along with the desire. It was going to be a long night. My cock surged.

Jacob growled softly and rubbed his cheek along my jaw. I'd trimmed the shadow of a beard somewhat so that it was neater, but I left the bulk of it there. I sensed Jacob's pleasure at the raspy texture. All trace of weariness disappeared from his mind as he touched me.

"Where do you get your energy, Jacob?"

"The thought of fucking you senseless is enough to energize any man. But I'll go gentle tonight and won't make you beg too long."

My lover laughed softly as a shiver went through me. "How thoughtful of you."

"I know. Remember that." Jacob nudged my thighs apart, and I sighed with pleasure as he settled between them. "But I confess ulterior motives this time. I can't wear you out completely. After all, we've got a wedding to plan."

There was something in the way he said that that had me eying him warily. "Jacob, you promised me small, remember?"

"Of course. You worry too much, just put yourself in my hands, love."

Under the circumstances, what else could I do? I slid my knees up to cradle his hips as we traded kisses, the heat building up in slow, exquisite degrees. "Make it soon. I don't think I told you and I certainly didn't show it when you asked me. But I cannot wait to be married to you."

Jacob pressed his forehead against mine, and I sensed his surge of fierce love, embraced it as it washed over me. Emotions so intense that we ached with them, shared them as one.

"Are you going to take my name, Kristair? I know you've probably had Mercer forever, but I want us all to have my name."

I smiled and brushed my lips over his. "Kristair Corvin...."

Jacob's heart leapt at the sound of our names linked, and I slid my fingers into his hair. "That would be a real surname instead of a name I took from a land I barely remember. Yes, Jacob, I'll take your name."

"I have everything I ever wanted. And to think I didn't even know this was what I wanted until I met you. I thought it was all football and making a name for myself so everybody back home would have to swallow their words."

"You don't have everything you want quite yet." I grinned as Jacob's curiosity was pricked. *"But I think I can fix that."*

Jacob stared down at me, and I felt his mental poke as he tried to read my mind. "Okay, I give. What is it?"

I traced my tongue along the vein at his throat, and a shiver rippled through him, the scent of his blood mingling with his arousal, his anticipation, and the scent that was uniquely his. When I had still been a vampire, the blood would've dominated the rest, but now it was a heady mix.

"Jacob?"

"Yeah." His voice was an unsteady husky whisper, all need and want. I groaned, tracing my tongue over him again. It was like I could already taste him.

"Would you like me to bite you?"

Jacob shuddered this time, arching his neck, baring his throat to me. "How? You're not a vampire anymore. The Ascended said you can't do anything big time anymore, so you can't shape change." His breath quickened. "Oh fuck it, I don't care. Yeah, I'd love it if you bit me."

"We've used our minds to do all kinds of crazy, kinky things. Why not this too?" I closed my eyes, pressed my mouth to his throat, tasted the sweet salt of his skin. I felt the jolt run through him as I mentally sank fangs into him, felt the addictive rush of pleasure and pain. It made me as hungry as it ever had. The fierce rush and exchange of emotion, the bonding.

"Hot damn, Kristair. Do that again."

"Would you beg for me?" I teased. Then my breath caught as he growled and kissed me hard, pinning me under him.

"I'll show ya begging."

I laughed and arched against him sinuously. "You're going to have to work hard for it."

"It's more than worth it," Jacob promised. I smiled as his mouth met mine and sank into the moment so that it was just him and me in our own little world.

MARGUERITE LABBE has been accused of being eccentric and a shade neurotic, both of which she freely admits to, but her muse has OCD tendencies, so who can blame her? Her husband and son do an excellent job keeping her toeing the line, though. Together with her co-author Fae Sutherland, Marguerite has found a shared passion for beautiful men with smart mouths.

When she's not working hard on writing new material and editing completed work, she spends her time reading novels of all genres, enjoying role-playing games with her equally nutty friends, and trying to plot practical jokes against her son and husband. Her son is learning the tricks too quickly and likes to retaliate. You'd think she'd learn.

Visit Marguerite's web site at http://chasethedream.net/.

Don't miss the beginning of the Triquetra Trilogy
by MARGUERITE LABBE

Also from DREAMSPINNER PRESS

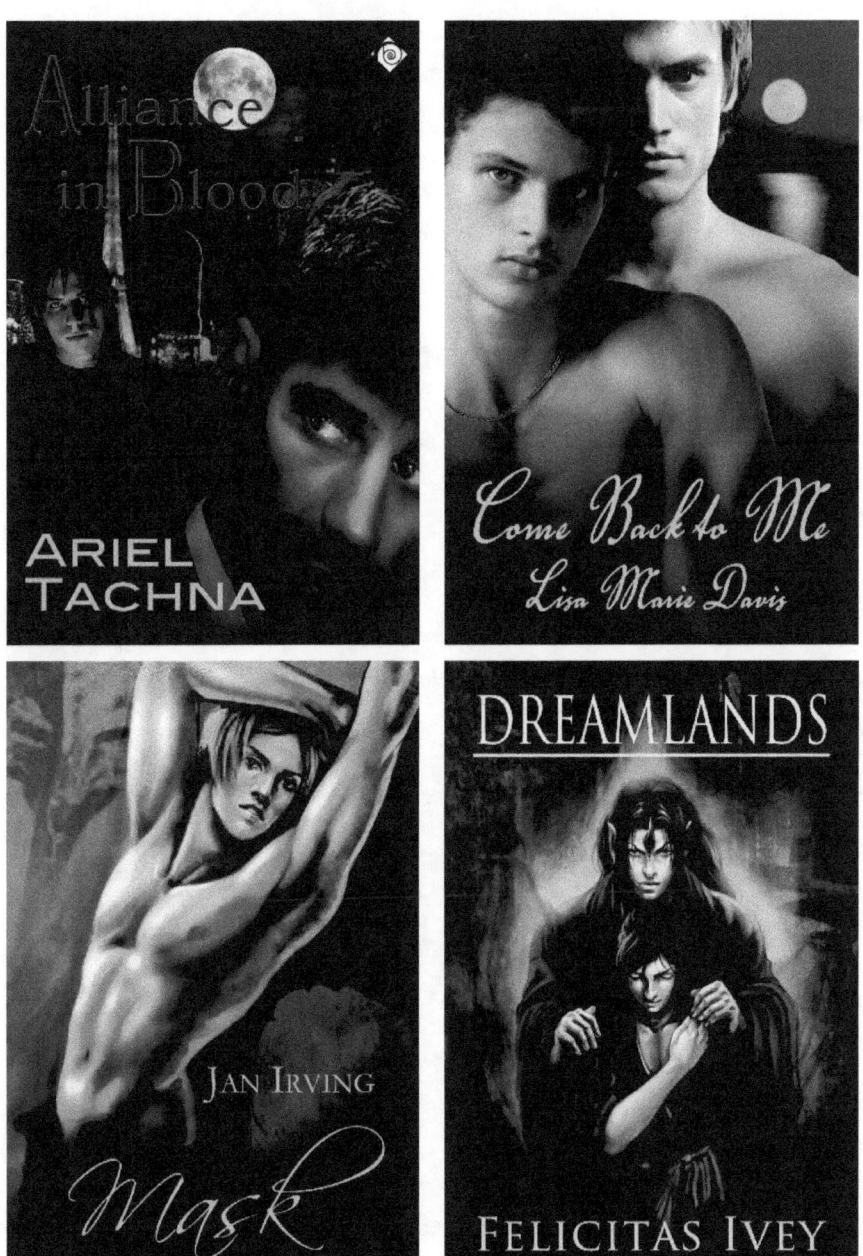

http://www.dreamspinnerpress.com

www.ingramcontent.com/pod-product-compliance
Lightning Source LLC
Chambersburg PA
CBHW070057030726
47506CB00002B/494